35444002830
PB KEL MY
Kelly, Diane, author
Against the paw
Logan Lake Library

"Fun [illegible] iet
Evan [illegible] ver

"Humor, romance, and surprising LOL moments. What more can you ask for?" —*Romance and Beyond*

"Fabulously fun and funny!" —*Book Babe*

"An engaging read that I could not put down. I look forward to the next adventure of Megan and Brigit!"
—*SOS Aloha* on *Paw Enforcement*

"Sparkling with surprises. Just like a tequila sunrise: you never know which way is up or out!"
—*Romance Junkies* on *Paw and Order*

ST. MARTIN'S PAPERBACKS TITLES BY DIANE KELLY

Paw Enforcement

Paw and Order

Upholding the Paw
(an e-original novella)

Laying Down the Paw

Against the Paw

THE TARA HOLLOWAY NOVELS

Death, Taxes, and a French Manicure

Death, Taxes, and a Skinny No-Whip Latte

Death, Taxes, and Extra-Hold Hairspray

Death, Taxes, and a Sequined Clutch
(an e-original novella)

Death, Taxes, and Peach Sangria

Death, Taxes, and Hot-Pink Leg Warmers

Death, Taxes, and Green Tea Ice Cream

Death, Taxes, and Mistletoe Mayhem
(an e-original novella)

Death, Taxes, and Silver Spurs

Death, Taxes, and Cheap Sunglasses

Death, Taxes, and a Chocolate Cannoli

AGAINST THE PAW

Diane Kelly

Thompson-Nicola Regional District
Library System
300 - 465 VICTORIA STREET
KAMLOOPS, B.C. V2C 2A9

St. Martin's Paperbacks

NOTE: If you purchased this book without a cover you should be aware that this book is stolen property. It was reported as "unsold and destroyed" to the publisher, and neither the author nor the publisher has received any payment for this "stripped book."

This is a work of fiction. All of the characters, organizations, and events portrayed in this novel are either products of the author's imagination or are used fictitiously.

AGAINST THE PAW

Copyright © 2016 by Diane Kelly.

All rights reserved.

For information address St. Martin's Press, 175 Fifth Avenue, New York, NY 10010.

ISBN: 978-1-250-09480-3

Our books may be purchased in bulk for promotional, educational, or business use. Please contact your local bookseller or the Macmillan Corporate and Premium Sales Department at 1-800-221-7945, ext. 5442, or by e-mail at MacmillanSpecialMarkets@macmillan.com.

Printed in the United States of America

St. Martin's Paperbacks edition / May 2016

St. Martin's Paperbacks are published by St. Martin's Press, 175 Fifth Avenue, New York, NY 10010.

10 9 8 7 6 5 4 3 2 1

3 5444 00283004 9

To K-9 handlers and their dogs.
Thanks for all you do to keep the rest of us safe!

ACKNOWLEDGMENTS

First off, many, many thanks to my brilliant editor, Holly Ingraham, for your smart and insightful suggestions. Working with you is always a pleasure!

Thanks to Sarah Melnyk, Paul Hochman, and the rest of the team at St. Martin's who worked to put this book into readers' hands. You're fantastic!

Thanks to Danielle Christopher and Jennifer Taylor for creating such fun book covers!

Thanks to my agent, Helen Breitwieser, for all of your work in furthering my writing career!

Thanks to Liz Bemis and the staff of Bemis Promotions for my great Web site and newsletters. You're the best!

Thanks to the "Bitches with Badges" for sharing your insights on law enforcement with me and fellow author D. D. Ayres!

And finally, thanks to my readers. I love connecting with you through the books, and I hope you'll enjoy this latest adventure with Megan and Brigit!

ONE
HEAD SHOT

Peeping Tom

She was looking the other way when his eyes locked on her long, dark hair. He imagined himself hot and naked and sweaty, tangled in those soft, silky tresses.

But she'll never be mine.

I know it.

And if she can't be mine, well, I'll do what I have to do . . .

Quickly and quietly, he steadied himself, sighted, and took aim. She tossed her hair and turned his way, a look of surprise flickering across her face. There was a blinding explosion of light as he contracted his finger and took the shot.

TWO
CHECKUP

Fort Worth Police Officer Megan Luz

"Up on the scale, Brigit." I led my black and tan shepherd-mix partner over to the large scale on the floor of the veterinary office and motioned for her to step onto the device.

Brigit placed a tentative paw with red-tipped nails onto the black rubber mat covering the metal surface. Satisfied it was safe, she climbed aboard. Once she was centered on the scale, I directed her to sit, pointing with my own red-tipped nail. I'd given us both mani-pedis the night before. While her manicure set contained different tools than mine, at least we could share the polish. Fortunately, we both looked good in Bodacious Rose.

She plunked herself down on her fluffy haunches and looked up at me and the vet tech expectantly, her mouth hanging slightly open as she lightly panted.

The tech consulted the scale's readout. "One hundred and three." She jotted a note in Brigit's paperwork and reached down to ruffle the dog's ear. "You're a big girl."

Brigit was indeed a big girl. Smart, too. She'd been a standout in our K-9 training class, besting all the others, putting them and their handlers to shame. I was proud to be paired with such an outstanding, if excessively hairy, partner.

Brigit and I had been together for just about a year now. Not to brag, but we made a kick-ass team. Despite our occasional head-butting, we complemented and completed each other. While my skills tended to be more mental, Brigit was a physical powerhouse, able to run like the wind, tackle a target, and leap tall buildings with a single bound. And while I could accumulate and process verbal and visual clues, she put her superior senses of hearing and smell to work, tracking fleeing suspects or searching for hidden ones, sniffing out drugs, alerting me to approaching dangers. Together, we were unstoppable.

Unfortunately, while Brigit's size and special skills made her the perfect partner on the beat, they made her a pain in the butt when it came to our personal lives. Not only did the dog eat kibble by the ton and shed fifty pounds of fur a day, she could be insistent and defiant. She behaved impeccably on the job, but after hours, she and I continued to vie for the alpha position in our two-member pack. She seemed as doggedly determined to claim the prominent position as I was. So far, it was a draw.

Despite being different species, Brigit and I had quite a few things in common. Both of us were mutts with mixed heritage, Brigit being a shepherd mix and me being an Irish/Mexican-American with a few drops of Cherokee blood tossed in, not uncommon here in Texas. Both of us could be very stubborn, but both of us were extremely loyal, too. We also tended to overlook each other's faults. She didn't mind my sporadic stutter, and I forgave her occasional bouts of flatulence.

The tech led us back to an examination room, closing the door behind us. "Has she been eating well? Having regular bowel movements?"

"I can vouch for both." As I'd mentioned, the dog consumed enormous quantities of kibble which, naturally, led her to litter the backyard of my rental house with turds the size of cow patties. I had to perform poo-poo patrol every couple of days lest the yard begin to smell like a feedlot. "She's healthy as a horse."

"Nearly as big as one, too," the tech noted. "I won't bother trying to get her up on the exam table. She'd probably break my back." The woman knelt down to take Brigit's temperature and look at her teeth, lifting the dog's black jowls for a closer peek at her chompers. "Her teeth look nice and clean."

As well they should. The dog was a master chewer. She'd eaten virtually every pair of shoes I owned before I wised up and began storing them in the top of my closet where she couldn't reach them. I bought her a never-ending supply of nylon bones to chew, as well as crunchy biscuits. I even brushed her teeth with a specially designed doggy toothbrush and beef-flavored paste. Heck, I took better care of the dog than myself. Here she was, getting her annual checkup right on time, while I was two months overdue for my women's exam. Not a big fan of the scoot and spread.

The tech finished her preliminary review, notated the file, and tossed Brigit a dog treat from a glass canister on the counter. "Catch, girl."

Brigit was on her hind legs in an instant, leaping to snatch the treat from the air with the grace and skill of a prima ballerina.

"Dr. Wickham will be in shortly." With that, the tech slipped through the back door and dropped the paperwork into a plastic bin mounted on the reverse side. The file slid to the bottom of the bin with a *thunk*.

I sat down on a green vinyl chair and held the dog's lead loosely in my hand, allowing her to snuffle her way around the room. She put her nose to the floor and took baby steps forward. *Snuffle-snuffle. Snuffle-snuffle.* She stopped at the corner of the examination table, paying particular attention to the base. *Snuffle-snuffle.* No doubt many a patient who'd preceded her had marked the spot. *Snuffle-snuffle.*

Her curiosity satisfied, she returned to me, virtually bending in half so that both her butt and face were aimed in my direction. She wagged her tail and gave me a soft *woof* that said, *Scratch my ass, would ya?*

"What have *you* done for *me* lately?" I asked.

She failed to respond, of course, but nonetheless I reached out and dug my short nails into the fur at the base of her tail, giving her butt a good and thorough scratch. *The things we humans do for our animals. Sheesh.* She raised her snout, her eyes closing halfway in pure canine bliss.

"You're spoiled rotten," I told her, as if she were at fault. Really, I had no one to blame but myself. When it came to my fuzzy-wuzzy partner, I could sometimes be a pushover.

A noise at the door alerted me that the vet had removed Brigit's file from the holder. A moment later, the door opened and the doctor, an attractive gray-haired man in his early fifties, stepped inside.

After we exchanged greetings, he glanced down at Brigit with admiration. "Hey, there, Sergeant Brigit." He bent down to her level and allowed her to sniff his hand. "Remember me from last year? I'm okay, right?"

Brigit's nose twitched a couple of times before she pulled her head back and raised a front paw. Dr. Wickham laughed and took her paw in his hand, giving it a shake.

The vet looked up at me. "According to the notes in the file, she's gained six pounds since her last visit."

She wasn't the only one. Sitting on my rear in a police cruiser all day didn't exactly burn a lot of calories.

"That extra weight isn't good for her joints and bones," the doctor continued. "You'll need to cut back on the food and treats."

On hearing the word "treat" Brigit wagged her tail, obviously thinking she was about to get another goodie when instead the doc had sentenced her to a diet.

"Will do." Looked like I'd have to be a little less generous with her favorite liver snaps.

He looked into the dog's ears and eyes, then gave her body a once-over. "Her coat looks healthy and shiny."

That pretty shine was precisely why I used Brigit's peach-scented flea shampoo on my own hair, too. But let's keep that between the two of us, shall we? My long, black locks were one of my best features so I did what I had to do to maintain them. My boyfriend Seth, a bomb squad officer with the Fort Worth Fire Department, enjoyed playing with my tresses. I, in turn, enjoyed the way Seth looked at me while he fingered my hair, as if he were burning for me and only I could put out the fire.

The vet proceeded to feel along Brigit's ribs and abdomen, spread her back legs to test her hips for dysplasia, then used a stethoscope to listen to her heart. "Strong ticker. Everything else looks fine, too."

Good to know. Although I hoped to make detective someday, Brigit and I would have several more years together before then.

The tech reappeared with three syringes for Brigit's shots. "Here you go, doc," she said, holding them out.

The vet took the syringes and motioned for me to join him on the floor. "She trusts you. See if you can hold her still while I give her these shots."

Wrapping my arms around Brigit to immobilize her, I murmured to distract her while the vet administered the inoculations. "Be a b-brave girl, Brigit. You can do it. Nothing to worry about."

As the doctor inserted a needle into the dog's hip she turned her head toward him and whimpered, but thankfully made no attempt to bite the man.

"Good girl!" the vet praised her when he finished, stroking her shoulder. He instructed me to continue holding her while he retrieved a long plastic stick with a narrow loop on the end. "Now for the fecal sample."

He circled around behind her, wrapped his hands under her abdomen, and lifted her to a standing position. "In we go."

He gently inserted the stick into Brigit's rear. Her eyes went wide and she emitted a *Ruh?* of shock before giving me a look that said she'd never, ever trust me again.

THREE
NO WAY TO TREAT A DOG

Sergeant Brigit

Pervert!

As soon as the vet removed the stick from her backside, Brigit plunked her hindquarters down firmly on the cold tile. If that sicko had any other plans for her rectum, he better just forget it.

She cast a glance at her partner. For the most part, she trusted Megan. But why her partner allowed this man to put Brigit through such an indignity the dog would never know. And she hadn't even given Brigit a liver treat afterward! If it wasn't for the fact that Megan let Brigit sleep in her bed with her at night as well as took her to the dog park on a regular basis, Brigit might consider putting in for a transfer.

FOUR
LOOKEE HERE

Peeping Tom

A row of well-established azaleas sat alongside the single-story stucco house. Given that it was now early May, the blooms had come and gone, leaving behind only thick, leafy bushes that did their best to block access to the window.

But he was determined.

At nearly eleven o'clock, the night was fully dark. With no outdoor lighting along the side of the house, he blended readily into the shadows. The few drivers who passed by on the street overlooked him lurking in the bushes. *Just as I'd hoped . . .*

He slowly forced his way between two bushes, the branches cracking as they gave way, the sound seeming as loud as fireworks in the otherwise quiet night. He hesitated a moment, his heart pounding like a war drum, but the sounds seemed to draw no attention. He inhaled a deep breath, taking in the cedar scent of the bark chips under his feet, and willed himself to relax.

He took another step forward, his face now only inches from the window. The miniblinds hung slightly askew, leaving a two-inch triangle of glass uncovered in the bottom right corner and providing him a clear view into the woman's bedroom. The bright overhead light in the room made it easy for him to see her moving about inside.

Gotta love those high-wattage energy-efficient bulbs.

Unfortunately, those bulbs also attracted moths, which fluttered around the window, occasionally thumping softly against the pane as they tried in vain to get closer to the light source. He waved a hand, temporarily dispersing the fluttering pests, and leaned in for a closer look.

The woman was tall and full-figured, with long, dark hair he'd loved to stroke and bury his face in. When she kicked off her stiletto heels, he knew he was only seconds away from his payoff. His anxious breaths came in quick succession, verging on hyperventilation. *Easy now,* he told himself. *Slow down and savor this.*

A moth ricocheted off his forehead as the woman tugged her clingy red dress up over her head and tossed it onto a nearby chair, revealing round curves and inch after luscious inch of bare flesh. She'd also revealed a plain beige bra and faded cotton panties, not at all like the black lace he'd visualized her wearing in his fantasies. He felt a twinge of disappointment, but got over it quickly. After all, he wasn't here to see lingerie. If that was all he wanted he could have simply pored over the Victoria's Secret catalog he kept in the top drawer of his night table.

As he waved the moths away again, the woman reached her hands behind her back to unhook her bra. His pulse throbbed as he put his face to the window, moths be damned.

She moved toward the front of the room as she wrangled with the clasp.

No.

No, no, NO!

Just as the hooks released, setting her breasts free, she

disappeared through the door of her bathroom and out of view.

He stomped a foot in the bark chips, releasing both his frustration and the woodsy scent of cedar. The bathroom windows faced the street. He couldn't risk attempting to spy on her from such a visible location. He could only hope she'd be bare when she returned to the bedroom.

But she wasn't.

When she emerged a half minute later, she wore a wrinkled, powder-blue nightshirt covered in cartoon sheep. If that wasn't unattractive enough, the robe bore a large coffee stain on the front and hung well past her knees. She plopped down on the edge of her bed and proceeded to trim her toenails with a pair of silver clippers, little half-moon pieces sailing through the air. *Yuck.*

So much for getting any gratification tonight. His balls felt as deflated as the ones Tom Brady had used in the 2015 Super Bowl.

He took a deep breath to calm himself. Unfortunately, along with the oxygen, he inhaled a small bug, one that was now lodged in his nostril, frantically flapping its tiny wings in an attempt to escape.

He wriggled his nose and exhaled sharply, but to no avail. The bug was stuck.

Uh-oh . . .

The sneeze came on like a runaway freight train, allowing him no time to back away from the window before it blasted from his nose. The best he could do was cover his face with his hands in an attempt to muffle the sound.

A-chuh!

The woman's head snapped to face the window. Thank goodness he'd worn running shoes because he was definitely going to need them.

FIVE
BUSHWHACKED

Megan

Tuesday morning, I dressed in my police uniform, buckled my belt, and left the bedroom Brigit and I shared to go in search of my K-9 partner. I found her in the living room. She lay sprawled on the couch next to my roommate, Frankie, a blue-haired, blue-eyed Amazon who stocked groceries by night and played roller derby for the Fort Worth Whoop Ass, also by night.

I greeted the two with a "good morning."

Frankie responded with a " 'mornin' " while Brigit responded with a tail wag.

Frankie and I had met a few short weeks ago when I'd taken a detour into the South Hemphill Heights neighborhood. She'd skated right in front of my moving cruiser, the bumper missing her by mere inches when I screeched to a stop. I'd pulled Frankie over—it was my first and only time to stop an eight-wheeled offender—and learned that only minutes before she'd been unceremoniously dumped by her boyfriend. Thus, her erratic, bordering on suicidal, behavior.

Lest she end up becoming roadkill, I gave her a ride home. Feeling empathy for her and realizing the bedroom her ex had used as his "man cave" now stood vacant, I'd suggested I take over his lease. Luckily for me, she agreed. I gave notice to the paunchy and pungent property manager at the seedy apartment complex where Brigit and I had been living, and moved our meager belongings into this relatively spacious bungalow.

The place was painted a light mauve with ivory trim, the front door a contrasting navy blue. A giant magnolia tree loomed over the front yard, preventing the grass from making any headway, but an ivy ground covering had creeped over from next door and did a fair job of hiding the dirt. A prefab one-car detached garage sat to the back and right of the house, added after the house was originally built. A six-foot wooden privacy fence enclosed the backyard, giving Brigit a safe place to play, chase squirrels, and do her dirty business.

Frankie and I had been roommates only a short time, but so far things had been going great. Brigit even got along with Zoe, Frankie's fluffy calico cat. Or perhaps "tolerated" was a more precise word. Zoe was like a pesky kid sister to Brigit. Even now, as Brigit wagged her tail upon seeing me, Zoe crept out from under the couch and swiped at my partner's moving tail with her paw.

Frankie had arrived home a half hour earlier after working the graveyard shift at the nearby Kroger store. Though it was breakfast time for most of us, the fact that Frankie would soon be hitting the hay made this early-morning meal dinner for her. Hence the partially eaten frozen pizza and bag of nacho cheese Doritos on the coffee table in front of her.

I stopped in front of the futon, noted the ring of Day-Glo orange powder encircling Brigit's fuzzy muzzle, and frowned at Frankie. "I told you Brigit can't have any more people food until she loses some weight."

Frankie didn't take her eyes off the television, where

she was watching a zombie show she'd recorded on the DVR. "I didn't give her any food."

I moved in front of the TV, forcing Frankie to look at me, and put my hands on my hips. "Are you lying to a cop?"

"No." A grin tugged at her lips. "I'm fibbing to my roommate."

"Who happens to be a cop."

She raised an unconcerned shoulder. "You're off duty."

I narrowed my eyes at her. "A cop is never really off duty."

It might sound trite, but it was true. Police work wasn't one of those jobs you could leave at the office, so to speak. The job followed the officers home, sometimes haunting them, other times consuming them. We cops suffered significantly higher-than-average divorce rates, a slightly higher-than-average suicide rate, and, according to several studies, shorter life expectancies than the average person. So why on earth would we do a job that asked so much of us and the people we loved?

I couldn't speak for all policemen and -women, but in my case it came down to a few simple things. One, the world could be a hard, cruel, and violent place, but it had the potential to be so much better. If I could help make it better, why wouldn't I? Two, I'd never been the type to aspire to a fancy house, expensive jewelry, or a flashy car. Rather, I enjoyed an intellectual challenge. Becoming a detective and solving crimes would give me that challenge I was looking for. Last, and definitely least, because I'd been a twirler in my high school band, I already knew how to handle a baton. Police work was one of the few, if not only, jobs in which baton-handling experience would come in handy.

Brigit nudged Frankie's hand, making a wordless request for more crunchy chips.

My roommate looked down at the dog. "Sorry, girl. Your mommy's cut you off." With that she grabbed the bag and noisily rolled down the top to close it.

Brigit cut a look my way, as if she knew I was the reason why the flow of carbs coated in fluorescent cheese powder had ceased.

I walked to the kitchen and poured a cup of the low-calorie dog food the veterinarian had recommended into Brigit's large aluminum feeding bowl. On hearing the clatter of kibble hitting metal, Brigit trotted into the kitchen. She looked down at the paltry serving in her bowl, gave the unfamiliar nuggets a sniff, and tossed me a look that said *Are you freakin' kidding me? Diet food?*

"You need to lose weight," I explained, as if the dog would understand me.

Evidently she didn't give a rat's ass about her fat ass. She put her paw on the edge of the bowl and flipped it over, spilling its contents all over the floor. She sat down, her expression now offering an insincere *Oops!*

I frowned down at her. "You know exactly what you're doing, don't you?"

I swept up the kernels and tried again, this time mixing the low-calorie food with her regular kibble. "How's that?"

She put her face in the bowl and began to eat.

"Good girl."

I fixed myself a bowl of healthy, whole grain cereal with soymilk. While working as a police officer involved the occasional foot chase, cops spent most of our time sitting in our cruisers, driving around. Not exactly good for the heart or body mass index. To avoid ending up with thick thighs or pancake butt, I tried to eat right and performed isometric exercises with my glutes while out on patrol.

I carried my breakfast to the kitchen table and took a seat.

Zoe, Frankie's furry calico cat, leaped up onto the table and tried to stick her head into my bowl.

"Scram," I told her, defending my cereal with a wave of a napkin.

Zoe took a couple of steps back and sat down on the table, lifting a leg and spreading her fuzzy toes to clean between them.

"Learn some manners," I told her.

The cat gave me a look even more arrogant and disdainful than the one Brigit had given me earlier. *When had these animals figured out that they were in charge?*

When I'd finished my breakfast and brushed my teeth, I returned to the living room and patted my leg. "C'mon, Brig. Time to get to work."

Brigit hopped down from the couch to follow me.

"See you later," I told Frankie as I opened the front door.

"If you happen to talk to Seth," she called from the couch, "tell him I'm ready to get back on the horse."

I stopped in the open doorway. "Really?"

I'd been pestering Frankie for days to go on a double date with me and Seth. I was tired of seeing her mope around, lonely and depressed, and there was no end of eligible young guys at the firehouse or the military base where Seth served his one-weekend-a-month army reserve duty.

"Yeah," she said. "Just make sure Seth gets me someone tall. I want a guy who can look me in the eye, not the mouth."

"Tall. Got it. Any other requests?"

She shrugged. "It wouldn't hurt if he was hot, too, as long as he's not a jerk."

"No jerks. That's fair."

Her lip curled up in a mischievous grin. "It wouldn't hurt if he was rich, either."

"It never does."

With that, I raised my hand in good-bye and led my partner out the front door. As we walked down the porch and over to my tiny metallic-blue Smart Car in the driveway, I sent a text to Seth. *Frankie's ready to date. Wants a guy who's hot but not a jerk.* I hoped I wasn't asking too much. After all, the hot gene and the jerk gene seemed to be linked. It probably went back to some attractive caveman who saw his reflection in a mud puddle and realized he looked damn good in that saber-toothed-tiger loincloth. *Me sexy. Oogah.*

I bleeped the locks open and let Brigit into the passenger seat. Circling back to my side, I climbed in, gently elbowing Brigit back to give me at least a partial view out of the side window. The enormous dog took up nearly the whole cab. "Sit back, girl."

She complied, settling back in the seat.

As I put the gearshift in reverse, a reply text arrived from Seth. *I'm on it.*

I drove to the Western-1 substation—W1 for short—where I'd been assigned since joining the Fort Worth Police Department a year and a half ago. The W1 division covered nine square miles. Bounded on the north by Interstate 30, on the east by Hemphill, on the south by Berry Street, and on the west by the shore of the Trinity River, W1 included Texas Christian University, Colonial Country Club, Forest Park, the Fort Worth Zoo, and several quaint and relatively quiet older neighborhoods. All in all, it wasn't a bad gig, especially for a cop like me who thrived on the mental feats posed by police work rather than the physical ones and was mostly just biding her time until she qualified to make detective.

There was only one bad thing about working in W1, and there he was now, exiting his truck and making his way into the station with his usual testosterone-driven swagger. Derek "the Big Dick" Mackey.

Blurgh.

While I prided myself on my brain, Derek's claim to fame was his brawn. He was built like a dump truck. Solid, immovable, and carrying a heavy load. But while dump trucks were generally filled with dirt or debris, Derek was full of himself. The guy was also known for his bravery, boldly going alone into situations where other officers would wait for backup.

To call Derek a thorn in my side would be an understatement, but in order to tell you what the guy really was I'd have to use at least five of the seven words the FCC wouldn't let anyone say on regular TV. Instead, how about I use creative license and say he's a *tasbard* and a *sasshole*?

Derek and I had been partners for several months when I'd first joined the force. During that time, he'd bombarded me with crude, sexist jokes and filled our cruiser with the scents of sweat, onions, and gas. Clearly, he'd been trying to break me. And break me he had. When we'd arrested a woman for driving under the influence and found a bag of meth in her car, he'd suggested I perform an on-the-spot body cavity search. The lewd remark was the last straw. I'd pulled out my Taser and replied to his comments via a high-voltage response that caused him to wet himself and very nearly got me fired. Derek's inappropriate comments could have put him out of work, too. Luckily for both of us, Derek and Police Chief Garelik were personal friends. The incident was kept off our records and I was allowed to keep my job on the condition I partner with Brigit, whose handler had resigned from the force to take a job in private security. While I hadn't been at all happy about being paired with a K-9 at first, now I couldn't imagine working with any other partner.

I parked, let Brigit out of my car, and clipped her lead onto her collar, leading her inside for the morning briefing. It would probably be over quickly. Things had been pretty routine in W1 the last few days. Routine was a good thing in my book. Over the recent months I'd dealt with a psychopath setting bombs around the city, a purse-snatcher/pickpocket who'd targeted tourists at the stock show and rodeo, and a brutal bastard who'd abused his girlfriend and their child, burglarized homes, and murdered a drug dealer. Who could blame me for wanting to take a break from all the crime and violence?

I took a space along the back wall of the briefing room next to one of the other female officers in W1. Summer had been with the force three years longer than me, had witnessed three more years of the havoc people could wreak on themselves and each other, yet somehow maintained a disposition as sunny as her curly blond hair. She must be an expert at compartmentalizing, a skill I had yet to fully develop.

"Hey, you two!" She sent a smile my way before crouching down to give Brigit a nice scratch under the chin. "How's Sergeant Brigit today, hmm?"

Brigit responded by licking Summer's face from chin to ear. *Slup!*

"Listen up!" came Captain Leone's voice from the front of the room, where he'd stepped up to the wooden podium. The captain, a fortyish guy with dark, spongy hair, ruled W1 less with an iron fist and more with his terrifying eyebrows. We officers feared that if we didn't obey his orders, his crazy, wiry brows would reach out and throttle us. "We've got several things to go over today before you head out on the streets."

Her cheek slick with dog drool, Summer stood back up next to me and we directed our attention to the captain.

"Number one," the captain said, scanning the room with a pointed look. "Check your spelling and numbers when entering traffic ticket information into your computers. The traffic court's been throwing out citations left and right."

He went on to say that one of the local attorneys who handled traffic tickets en masse had successfully argued dozens of cases where the data contained typos, claiming that if a cop couldn't accurately input a driver's license or license plate number, the officer might have also erred in putting in other data, such as the purported violation or alleged speed the driver was going. A rather lame argument, in my opinion, but since we officers rarely had time to appear in traffic court to defend our actions, the judge probably felt compelled to dismiss the cases. At least the offender still suffered, though his punishment came in the form of attorney fees rather than a bad mark on his driving record.

"Make regular rounds by the high schools during the morning and afternoon hours," Captain Leone continued. "Lunchtime, too. With the end of the school year nearing, students about to graduate might pull some crazy and stupid pranks. We don't want things to get out of hand."

While babysitting high school kids held little appeal to us officers, until the epidemic of senioritis died out in June it couldn't hurt for law enforcement to be more visible and to stay in the vicinity should things go awry.

"Last but definitely not least," Captain Leone said, "keep your eyes peeled for this SOB."

He held up a mug shot. It was difficult to tell much about the guy from my vantage point at the back of the room, but he appeared to be Caucasian with brown hair.

"Name's Ralph Hurley. He served three years in the state lockup for multiple counts of burglary, aggravated assault, battery, and criminal trespass."

He handed the picture printout to an officer sitting on the front row so it could be passed around. While the photo made its way around the room, the captain gave us the scoop. "Hurley broke into several homes in affluent areas of San Antonio at night. Despite being six feet four and two hundred and fifty pounds, he was able to sneak through windows without making a noise and surprise his victims. News reporters dubbed him the 'Silent Giant.'"

The captain went on to tell us that Hurley had threatened the residents, sometimes with a handgun, other times with a shotgun, forcing them to turn over their debit cards and provide the associated PINs with the proviso that if the PIN didn't work he'd return at some point in the future and make them very sorry they'd given him a false number.

"He'd hit their accounts right away," the captain explained, "and withdraw as much cash as he could before the victims could notify their banks to deactivate the stolen cards. In most cases he went after female victims who lived alone or whose husbands were not at home, which tells us that he cased their residences before breaking in."

An involuntary shudder went through me. Hurley's victims must have been terrified to face down a supersized man like him, especially when they were surprised alone in their homes and Hurley's intentions were unknown. And to realize that Hurley had been watching them while they went about their lives totally unaware? *So creepy.* Surely the victims would spend the rest of their lives looking over their shoulders, fearing any man who gave them a second glance.

"Hurley was recently paroled," the captain continued. "He'd been ordered to wear an ankle monitor to track his whereabouts, but he cut it off Sunday morning." Captain Leone went on to tell us that Hurley made a quick escape from the efficiency apartment he'd rented in San Antonio, which was a four-hour drive to the south of Fort Worth.

Given the limitations of an external apparatus like an ankle monitor, maybe it was time to insert a microchip in violent parolees so they could be tracked. Heck, Brigit had a chip in case she got lost or stolen. The mere thought of Brigit being in danger turned my insides to ice. Instinctively, I reached down to stroke her head. She looked up, her big brown eyes locking on mine as if she were trying to read my thoughts. When she gave my hand a comforting lick, I had to wonder if she could, in fact, read my mind. More likely, my emotions had caused me to release some type of fear pheromones and Brigit had picked up on the scent, a canine form of mind reading.

I raised a hand and Captain Leone lifted his chin in acknowledgment, inviting me to speak. "If he robbed and battered multiple victims," I asked, "why'd he only serve three years?"

"Plea bargain," he replied with a scowl. "Hurley always wore a ski mask and gloves when he broke into the homes and made the withdrawals at the bank. No one could positively identify him. He was also careful not to leave fingerprints."

In other words, all of the evidence against him had been circumstantial. The district attorney must have decided it was better to put Hurley behind bars, even if for a relatively short time, rather than risk a "not guilty" verdict at trial and having the man go free.

Without bothering to raise his hand, Derek asked, "He shoot any of the women?"

"None that could be confirmed," the captain replied. "He shoved one victim against a wall and pushed another down a flight of stairs. Broke her arm and collarbone. A woman was shot and killed in her home around the same time Hurley committed his other crimes, but law enforcement wasn't able to pin the murder on him. The bullet didn't match any of the weapons in his possession at the time of his arrest. San Antonio PD believes he ditched the gun."

Unfortunately, a significant number of murders went unsolved, the killers never brought to account for their crimes. The inability to apprehend and successfully prosecute violent criminals was the most frustrating aspect of law enforcement. Being a cop meant accepting that we could only do so much, that some scores would never be settled, that evil would occasionally prevail. We could only hope that, more times than not, the scales would tip in our favor and justice would be served.

Leone's grip on the podium tightened. "On Sunday night a woman in Alamo Heights was shot three times in her home. The bullets damaged some vital organs. One lodged in her skull. She's in intensive care, fighting for her life. Hurley's a person of interest in that shooting, too."

Summer took a quick look at Hurley's mug shot and handed it to me. My eyes moved over the photo. Hurley looked like your average Joe, with brown hair and brown eyes, no obvious distinguishing features. *Where's a gold-capped tooth or a Texas-shaped scar when you need one?*

A soft snort escaped me when I read the first three letters of his Isuzu Amigo's license plate listed at the bottom of the page. "DUH." Yeah, that pretty much summed up what he'd done. *What kind of idiot would risk his recently reacquired freedom by cutting off his ankle monitor?* When Hurley was captured, he'd definitely be heading back to the klink, maybe for life.

I passed the printout to the officer on my left and ran a quick search on my phone. *Ah. No wonder the make and model of his vehicle didn't sound familiar.* According to the information online, Isuzu had left the U.S. auto market in 2009 after years of financial woes. My search for images told me that the Amigo was a small SUV that came with either a hard or soft top. With the soft top down, the front seat remained covered by a short metal roof while the cargo bay and backseat were exposed to the air. The vehicle looked like it couldn't decide whether it wanted to be a pickup truck or a convertible and ended up as some kind of odd, genetically engineered hybrid.

I slid my phone back into my pocket and returned my attention to the captain.

"Hurley was spotted at a gas station in San Antonio around noon yesterday," he said.

Given his ordinary features and the multitude of brawny, barbecue-beef-fed men in Texas, Hurley didn't immediately catch anyone's attention. But while the clerk hadn't identified the man at his register as Hurley, he had taken notice of the telltale green Isuzu Amigo as it drove away from the pump. The attendant phoned police and reported that the escapee had turned toward the I-35 access ramps, which meant that Hurley could be anywhere from the southern border town of Laredo, Texas, to as far north as Duluth, Minnesota, assuming he'd stayed on the interstate. If he'd ventured onto other roads, or hopped onto a bus, train, or plane, he could be virtually anywhere by now.

Captain Leone began to wrap things up. "Hurley's older sister lives in W1. We think he might be headed our way."

Escapees often relied on family or friends to provide them with cash, food, and a place to crash. With his sister right here in town, it was possible, perhaps even likely, that Hurley was aiming for Fort Worth. Hell, for all we knew he could be here already.

"If Ralph Hurley dares to set foot in our division," the captain said, "I want him apprehended right away. Got it?"

Murmurs of assent followed. *Get the bad guy. We got it.*

Captain Leone ran his firm gaze across his troops for a final time before pointing at the door. "Go out there and make the world a safer place."

Our meeting/pep rally concluded, we shuffled in a big blue blob out the door, down the hallway, and outside, where we dispersed in the parking lot.

Summer vectored off with a smile and a parting wave. "Have a good one!"

"You, too."

While my coworkers headed to their standard patrol cars, Brigit and I headed to our specially equipped K-9 cruiser, which featured a metal mesh enclosure and carpeted platform where the backseat would normally be. Of course I'd made the space even more comfortable for my partner by adding an extra-large cushion and a half-dozen chew toys to keep her entertained.

Derek unrolled the window of his squad car as he drove past. "Get to work, bitches!" With an obnoxious laugh, he gunned his engine and burned rubber as he pulled out of the station. *Squeee!*

What a jerk.

Taking a quick glance around to make sure no one was watching, I scurried over to Derek's personal vehicle, a shiny black pickup truck, to exact a small measure of revenge. I whipped my lipstick from the pouch on my belt and drew a smiley face on the rubber truck nuts that hung from his trailer hitch. Whoever came up with the idea for those things had to be a disgusting perv.

Also a genius. Given the popularity of the novelty with macho truck owners, he was probably a gazillionaire, like those bearded boys from *Duck Dynasty.*

Brigit and I returned to our cruiser.

"Another day, another dog biscuit," I told my partner as she climbed into her enclosure. I joined her in the squad car, situated my police-issue laptop in its mount, and set out in the opposite direction Derek had gone. With any luck, our paths wouldn't cross again today.

SIX

FROM STREET TO STAR

Brigit

As her partner drove their cruiser around their beat, Brigit eyed the various toys scattered about her carpeted enclosure. A squeaky squirrel. A tennis ball. A knotted rope. A Frisbee. So many toys to choose from. And to think Brigit had once been a shelter dog, with nothing but her fleas to call her own.

Megan sure did spoil her. She'd even bought Brigit a comfy cushion to lie on in the cruiser. Brigit's last partner had been a nice enough guy, but Megan was more generous and much easier to manipulate. All Brigit had to do was whimper softly and bat her big brown eyes and Megan would buy the dog whatever she wanted. *What a pushover.*

Still, Brigit knew she was lucky to have been paired with such a softie. She returned the favor by being an attentive watchdog at their house, chasing off pesky skunks and possums, and alerting Megan to the arrival of the mailman.

Brigit picked up a nylon bone, settled down on her belly, and set to work. It wasn't enough to have a sharp mind, a K-9 officer needed sharp teeth. *The better to eat you with, my dear.*

SEVEN
PLAYING HIS TUNE

Tom

The postman might always ring twice, but no way would he return to the same house he'd visited the night before. Too risky. That stupid sneeze had nearly got him caught. *Damn moths.* He'd stop by the hardware store later and buy one of those bug zappers. That would teach them.

Fortunately, there were plenty more women to choose from.

As he drove through the neighborhood, the sounds of a piano met his ears, the notes filtering out an open window, a soft breeze carrying them to his ears. He had no idea if the song was Beethoven, Bach, or Rachmaninoff, but he knew the woman playing it could get *his* rocks off. She'd caught his eye before, standing in her doorway, greeting or saying good-bye to one of her students.

Oh, the things she could teach me . . .

He could only imagine what it might be like if she tickled his ivories. He'd bet the two of them could make beautiful music together.

Tonight, I'll be the maestro.

EIGHT
HIGH SCHOOL

Megan

It was a slow morning. I'd been assigned to work traffic detail on Berry Street, one of the department's most boring and hated tasks. I sat down a side street with my radar gun pointed out the window, clocking drivers on their way to work.

People seemed to be behaving today, leaving me time to ponder life's important questions, such as why do Japanese car manufacturers name their models after American cities? The Toyota Tacoma, for instance. There was one sitting at the red light ahead, waiting for it to turn green. Another example would be the Hyundai Santa Fe. Though of course the city of Tacoma was named after a Native American tribe and Santa Fe was a Spanish word, like Amigo. *What a culture clash, huh?* Now if the Kia Soul were instead spelled "Seoul," that would make sense. But who was I to second-guess the choices made by car manufacturers? I'd never taken a course in advertising or marketing.

I issued a grand total of three traffic citations that morning, ticketing only the worst lawbreakers and letting the lesser offenders go with a written warning and a boring lecture on the dangers of bad driving. Death. Dismemberment. Property damage. *Blah-blah-blah.*

"Drive safe, sir," I said as I stepped away from the man who'd earned ticket number three. "And have a nice day."

"A little late for that, isn't it?" he snapped.

Don't do the crime if you can't do the time, buddy.

When my stomach growled around one P.M., I gave up traffic duty and headed to Paschal High School. Captain Leone had asked us to keep an eye on the students, and the parking lot would make a convenient place to watch the goings-on while eating the lunch I'd packed. The presence of a police cruiser would also make any would-be prankster think twice about pulling a fast one today.

I pulled into the lot, found an empty spot at the end of the teachers' section, and parked, rolling down the windows to enjoy the spring air. Though it would be unbearably hot a month from now, today the weather was partly cloudy, the temperature comfortable.

I turned to look at my partner through the metal mesh that separated us. "Ready for lunch, Brig?"

Her ears pricked and her head cocked at the word "lunch." When I opened the back door to let her out, she hopped down immediately. No need to ask her twice.

I led her around the car and opened the passenger door so she could sit up front with me. Returning to my seat, I poured a cup of the diet kibble into a bowl for her. She turned up her nose at it again and flopped down on the seat, releasing a breathy sigh.

"At least try it," I coaxed. "This stuff cost fifty dollars a bag." A hefty price for something that wasn't even organic. I shook the bowl. "C'mon, girl. Just a bite or two?"

Alas, my pleas fell on deaf, furry ears.

"That's all you're getting," I told her, setting the bowl on the console. "Doctor's orders."

She turned her head away, canine body language for *I'm not listening.*

I unscrewed the top of my thermos, grabbed my fork, and dug into my pasta salad. Brigit turned her head back, watching intently as each bite went into my mouth, drool collecting on her jowls.

"This is *my* lunch," I told her, pointing at her bowl with my fork. "*That's* yours."

She continued to watch me, smacking her lips in anticipation. I did my best to ignore her, turning to look out my window and watch the upperclassmen, who were permitted to leave the campus for lunch. A few cast a glance at my cruiser as they came and went, but as far as I could tell none seemed to harbor any nefarious intentions. *Good.* I didn't want to be a party pooper, but I couldn't allow any pranks to go down on my watch.

As I neared the bottom of the thermos, Brigit emitted a soft whimper.

"No," I told her, willing myself to stay strong.

She whimpered again, this time a little louder and longer.

I frowned at her, though inside I felt myself beginning to waver. "What part of "no" do you not understand?"

She blinked her big brown eyes and my willpower crumbled. *Ugh.* I really needed to grow a backbone.

"All right, you crybaby. I guess a few noodles won't hurt."

I tossed the last three pieces of rotini pasta on top of the food in Brigit's bowl. No sense letting my poor partner starve to death. She promptly wolfed them down, but managed to avoid eating any of the diet food.

I packed up our food and turned to my partner. "Need a potty break?"

She stood and wagged her tail.

I let her out of the squad car, attached her leash, and

led her over to a small grassy strip that separated the teachers' parking lot from the student lot. She crouched down for a quick tinkle. When she stood again, she lifted her nose to the air, her nostrils twitching as she scented.

"What do you smell, girl?" All I could detect was the faint scent of sloppy joes and Tater Tots from the school cafeteria.

She tugged on her leash and I followed. Probably a squirrel had been out here earlier.

She stopped at a Volkswagen Golf in the teachers' lot and spent a few seconds sniffing intently around the edge of the door. *Snuffle-snuffle.* When she sat down next to the car, it took my brain a moment to realize she wasn't just sitting, she was issuing her passive alert.

She smells drugs in the car. Brigit had the best nose on the force, rarely giving a false alert. Someone would soon be getting busted. A teacher, no less! I might not be able to smell the drugs, but I could tell this situation reeked of scandal. Busting an educator who dared to bring drugs onto a school campus would surely earn me some brownie points with Captain Leone and Chief Garelik.

I made a mental note of the license plate number and returned to my cruiser, where I ran a quick search on my laptop. Time to find out who was putting the "high" in high school. Per the data on the DMV link, the VW belonged to a Joshua Schorndorf. A quick check of the criminal database indicated he had no record.

Yet.

Drug possession was bad enough, but bringing drugs onto a school campus upped the charges significantly. Joshua Schorndorf was about to find himself in some very deep doo-doo.

I pushed the button on my shoulder-mounted radio to

call for backup. "Assistance needed at Paschal High." Not only would I need another officer to keep an eye on Schorndorf while I searched his vehicle, but a regular cruiser would be needed to transport him to the station. With Brigit's space in the back, my K-9 cruiser had no place to put a suspect.

I crossed my fingers that Summer would be available, or maybe Officer Spalding or Hinojosa. No such luck. Instead, Derek's voice came across the airwaves. "Mackey on my way."

Crud. He was the last officer I wanted to see. Unfortunately, I had no choice in the matter.

"Let's go, girl." Brigit and I walked briskly to the front doors and made our way to the office. A blond student aide sat on a stool at the counter, her hand in her hair as she stared down at a textbook and a piece of lined paper covered in equations. Precal, if memory served me. While the girl erased an incorrect answer from the paper, a middle-aged staff member looked up from her desk behind the counter. "Can I help you, Officer?"

"I need to speak with Joshua Schorndorf."

"Is he a student?"

"I don't believe so. His car is parked in the teacher's lot out front."

"He's not on the regular staff," the woman said, standing. "I don't recognize the name. He's probably a substitute. Let me check the sign-in sheet." She stepped over to the counter and opened a three-ring binder, taking a look at the top page inside and putting a finger on a signature. "There he is. He's subbing for one of our PE teachers." She gestured to the blond girl, who was chewing on her pencil eraser as she stared at the incomprehensible mix of numbers and letters on the page. "Kaitlyn can show you to the gym."

On hearing her name, the girl looked up from her schoolwork. "Oh. Hi."

She set her pencil down and slid off the stool. When she came around the counter, she spotted Brigit for the first time. "Oh, cool, a dog! Can I pet her?"

"She'd like that." Brigit could be ferocious when need be, but when she wasn't actively pursuing or guarding a suspect she was as friendly as they come.

The girl bent over and gave Brigit several strokes down the neck. Brigit wagged her tail in appreciation.

Kaitlyn stood and led me and my partner out of the office. "The gym's this way," she said, gesturing to our right.

Brigit and I followed her down a long hall, my partner's toenails clicking on the tile as we passed lockers, restrooms, classrooms, and a science lab, before reaching the doors of the gym.

"This is it," Kaitlyn said.

"Thanks."

As Kaitlyn returned to the office, I pushed the door open and stepped into the gym. The smell of sweat, the squeak of sneakers on a freshly waxed floor, and the *thwunk-thwunk-thwunk* of basketballs hitting the court greeted me. A couple dozen boys milled about the space, practicing layups. On the bleachers across the room sat three more boys, suited up but not participating. A thirtyish man with shaggy, sandy hair lounged on the bleachers as well. He wore a pair of basic khakis and a button-down shirt, neither of which had seen an iron. No belt. Given that he was the only adult in the room, the man had to be Joshua Schorndorf. He stared down at the cell phone in his hand, engrossed in e-mail, Twitter, or YouTube, paying scant attention to the children he was being paid to supervise.

Brigit and I began to make our way around the busy court, both of us keeping an eye out for errant balls. The boys in this gym class weren't exactly varsity material. Most of their balls ended up falling short and rolling out of bounds. I used my foot to stop one and gently kicked it back onto the court.

"Hey, look!" one of the boys shouted. "A police dog!"

Schorndorf's head popped up, his wide eyes scanning the room before locking on me and Brigit. His surprised cry echoed through the space. "SHIT!" *Shit-shit.* He leaped from the bleachers and bolted for the door.

I pointed to the chubby, freckle-faced kid closest to me. "You're in charge!"

The kid's face broke into a grin. It was probably the only time he'd been picked first in gym class.

My partner and I were out the door only six seconds after the sub, but he'd already gained a substantial lead and was headed for the exterior doors. A man in a suit—probably the principal—came around a corner ahead of Schorndorf, stopping in his tracks when he saw the three of us thundering up the hall toward him. Quickly cluing in to what was going on, he stretched out his arms to block the way.

To avoid capture by the suit, the substitute hooked a left down a hallway. Brigit and I hooked a left, too, turning just in time to see him duck down another hallway. Realizing the school could be a virtual maze, that the guy could put students in danger, and that my partner's four legs could tear up these hallways much faster than my two, I reached down on the fly and unclipped Brigit's leash, giving her the order to take Schorndorf down.

She took off like a furry bullet, gaining on him as he aimed for the double doors at the end of the hall. *The double doors that lead to the cafeteria.*

He slammed into the doors, throwing them back against the wall with a resounding *bam!* Following the bang of the door was the roar of hundreds of students engaged in conversation, which was followed by a split second of radio silence as the students stopped their discussions to watch a crazed substitute run into the cafeteria, pursued by a police dog. A second later, the cafeteria exploded into an even louder roar. One student shouted, "Go, dog! Go!" and the others joined in. "Go, dog! Go! Go, dog! Go!"

By the time I reached the doors they'd swung closed again. I yanked them open and ran into the cafeteria to see Schorndorf zipping up and down the aisles between the long tables, Brigit loping after him. The lunch ladies in their white uniforms and hairnets stepped out from behind their serving counters and gathered with gaping mouths, one of them wielding an enormous metal serving spoon like a weapon, another with oven mitts holding a huge steamer tray filled with creamed corn.

Most cops favored their Tasers or pepper spray, but having been a twirler in the high school band, my baton was my nonlethal weapon of choice. I whipped it from my belt and flicked my wrist to extend it. *Snap!*

The kids leaped to their feet, some scrambling onto the tabletops to get a better view, all of them whipping out their cell phones and holding them up to record the chase. "Go, dog! Go!"

And *go* Brigit did.

With a leap that would make any long-jump champion proud, she hurled herself up and forward, onto Schorndorf's back, taking him down to the tile floor. *Whump!*

Finally, I caught up with them. "Good girl!" I praised Brigit before ordering her to release the man.

Pulling my cuffs from my belt, I knelt down next to Schorndorf, yanked his hands up behind him, and cuffed his wrists. *Thank goodness this has been resolved with only minor incident.*

As I stood, a chicken nugget sailed past me and nailed Schorndorf in the ass, leaving a greasy smear on the back of his pants. The nugget was merely the opening salvo. In seconds, the students unleashed a barrage of chicken nuggets, Tater Tots, and French fries, enough to virtually bury the man. A celery stalk pinged Schorndorf on the forehead. *At least one of these kids packed a healthy lunch.*

The chant of "Go, dog! Go!" was replaced by "Seniors rule! Seniors rule!"

When an onion ring bounced off my left boob, I stepped aside, getting myself out of the line of fire.

"Seniors rule! Seniors rule!"

Schorndorf curled up in the fetal position and shrieked, "Stop, you little assholes!"

A pint of chocolate milk sailed through the air, nailing the man in the shoulder and sending up a spray of brown liquid. *Sploosh!*

The chant grew louder, many of the teens accentuating their cries with fists thrown in the air. "Seniors rule! Seniors rule!"

While Brigit took advantage of the mayhem to scrabble around Schorndorf and gorge on the edible projectiles, I turned to the students and raised a hand, keeping my baton down at my side. "That's enough! Sit down!" My voice was barely audible over the din in the room. Too bad I hadn't had the foresight to bring my bullhorn inside with me.

While the bombardment lessened slightly, it didn't stop. The seniors did, in fact, rule.

"Enough! Stop!" I yelled again.

By this time, the kids had become bored with throwing things at Schorndorf and were now tossing tidbits directly to Brigit. She snapped morsels of hot dog and pepperoni pizza from the air. *Snap! Snap!* A French fry. *Snap!* The tail end of a bean burrito. *Snap!*

I turned to Brigit and ordered her to return to my side. "Now!" I added when she ignored me, making no move to obey. *Sheesh.* She was as bad as the seniors. But if she didn't stop now she'd end up with an upset tummy. Was there something I could give her for that? *Pup*to *Bitch*mol, perhaps?

I made one more attempt to quell the mayhem. "Everyone sit down!"

Alas, not a single butt in the lunchroom found its seat.

The lunch lady cast a glance my way. "I can handle these monsters." She overturned a five-gallon bucket labeled VEGETABLE SHORTENING and stepped up onto her makeshift plastic pulpit. Brandishing her huge metal spoon, she hollered, "Next kid who throws something is going to be very sorry!"

Immediately, the students stopped chanting and lobbing their food and took their seats. *Who needs dragnet when you've got a hairnet?*

The principal ran up to me, his foot sliding on a trio of greasy Tater Tots. I grabbed his arm to keep him from falling back on his butt.

When he'd regained his balance, he looked from Schorndorf to me. "What on earth is happening here?"

I gestured to Brigit, who was gobbling down a hamburger bun someone had thrown like a Frisbee. "My dog alerted on Mr. Schorndorf's car in the parking lot. He's subbing for a gym teacher today. When I came inside to speak with him, he took off running."

The principal looked down at the grease-stained and chocolate-milk-soaked man on the floor, glanced over at the students, and shook his head. "I better get to the gym and check on his class."

"Good idea."

Derek strolled up, shaking his head. "This is what happens when you send a girl to do a man's job."

It took everything in me not to whap Derek with my baton. Instead, I took a deep breath, closed my baton, and returned it to my belt. "How much did you see?"

"Everything." He waved his cell phone in my face. "And so will the chief. I sent him the video."

If I didn't have sufficient reason to despise Derek before, I certainly did now.

While the custodians came around to clean up the mess and the teachers on lunch duty chastised the students, I yanked Schorndorf to his feet and Brigit and I escorted him out to the parking lot.

I stopped as I reached the teachers' lot. *Groan. So much for preventing senior pranks.* Every car in the lot—including my cruiser—was covered in shaving cream and colorful Silly String. The only car that had been spared was Derek's squad car, which sat at the curb, lights flashing.

"This is all on you, Luz," Derek said with a snort. "It was like this when I got here."

Fan-damn-tastic.

Schorndorf had yet to say a word or meet my eye, though he scowled down at Brigit as she licked what appeared to be banana pudding from the leg of his pants. So much for her diet. Her calorie intake today was off the charts.

My cell phone rang, the caller ID indicating it was Chief Garelik calling. I cringed, bracing myself as I answered the call. "Good afternoon, Chief."

"Good God Almighty, Officer Luz!" he cried. "You started a food fight in the cafeteria?"

"Food fight" wasn't exactly the right word. What happened was more like some type of culinary blitzkrieg.

But no point in correcting him. "I didn't start it," I replied through clenched teeth. "The students did. And if Officer Mackey had been performing his duties rather than recording the events on his phone, things would not have gotten so out of hand."

I cut my eyes to Derek. I had both the chief and Mackey there, and they knew it.

"Get back to work," the chief said.

"I never stopped working, sir."

The *click* of the chief hanging up was the only reply.

Derek kept watch over Schorndorf while I returned Brigit to her enclosure and searched the VW. Sure enough, Schorndorf had a dime bag of marijuana under the driver's seat. I held up the bag. "Bingo. Brigit's nose always knows."

Derek opened the back door of his cruiser and motioned for the substitute teacher to take a seat inside, all the while reciting his Miranda rights as casually as if he were ordering a draft beer at a local bar. Once the man was secured, he held out his hand. "Gimme."

I handed him the dime bag so he could turn it in at the station for processing. Without another word, he slid into his seat, started his car, and drove off.

I returned to my cruiser, climbed in, and activated the windshield wipers, doing the best I could to clear the shaving cream and Silly String from the glass. With any luck, the rest of it would blow off as I drove.

As I pulled out of the school parking lot, my radio crackled with a call from dispatch. "Need an officer to speak with a resident of Berkeley Place. She thinks someone was in her bushes last night."

Derek's voice came back on the airwaves. "If I'd been in her bushes, she'd have known it." He followed his crude comment with his signature guffaw. *Haw-haw-haw!*

The last thing a worried woman needed was a macho shithead like Derek Mackey showing up on her doorstep. Besides, he was tied up taking Schorndorf to the station. I grabbed my mic from the dashboard. "Officers Luz and Brigit responding."

We headed up the road into the Berkeley Place neighborhood. It was an upscale area, with most houses in the half-million-dollar range, a high price by Texas standards where housing came relatively cheap. Part of the Mexican government's Peters Colony back in the mid-1800s, the area had later been turned over to gringos as part of a land grant. W. Lee "Pappy" O'Daniel had lived in a farmhouse in the area before becoming governor of Texas. Deed restrictions from a century ago prohibited wooden homes, so stucco and brick became the materials of choice for those building residences in the area. Given their age, the vast majority of the houses had been gutted and updated multiple times over the decades. Some even came with separate guesthouses in the backyards. *This is living.*

My cruiser rolled to a stop at the address the dispatcher had provided. Like most of the homes in Berkeley Place, this house was a mix of stucco and brick, with a manicured yard that had been professionally landscaped and maintained. I emerged from my patrol car and freed my partner, who promptly relieved herself in the grass by the curb.

As I approached the front door, a woman opened it. She looked to be in her early thirties and wore a pair of bejeweled sandals and a gauzy, feminine dress. Her long, dark hair hung to nearly elbow level, approximately the same length as my own, though mine was currently pulled up into a professional-looking bun.

The woman stepped onto the porch. "Thanks for coming, Officer. I'm Kirstin Rumford."

I introduced myself and shook her hand, then tilted my head to indicate Brigit. "My partner, Sergeant Brigit."

When Brigit raised her paw, Kirstin smiled and bent down to shake it. "Nice to meet you, Brigit."

"I understand you might have had an intruder?"

The woman's expression grew sheepish. "Maybe I'm just being paranoid, but last night I thought I heard someone sneeze outside my window. When I came outside this morning to leave for work I noticed the azalea bushes on the side of my house were broken." She motioned for me to follow her around to the side of the house and stopped in front of a large window.

While Brigit sniffed around at the base of the foliage, I took a look at the bushes. A few branches on two of the bushes directly under the window were broken, the pieces that had been fully severed having fallen into the bush or all the way to the ground. Other broken limbs dangled.

"It definitely looks like the bushes have been damaged." I bent down and looked at the bark chips covering the surface of the flower bed. They, too, appeared to have been disturbed. Because the layer of bark chips was so thick, no soil was exposed. If anyone had been in the bushes, the chips had prevented them from leaving footprints.

Kirstin's face drew and she crossed her arms over herself in an instinctive reaction of self-protection. "I phoned the neighborhood watch last night. One of the men drove over right away, but he didn't see anyone around."

She'd been smart to notify the neighborhood watch. We police couldn't be everywhere and, as hard as we tried to familiarize ourselves with our beats, residents often knew better than law enforcement when something or someone was out of place in a particular area.

Brigit came up next to me and put her head to the ground, sniffing what appeared to be some type of small animal scat.

I looked up at the woman. "There's some small poop here. Do you get raccoons?"

"Sometimes," she said. "But I've never heard of them climbing bushes."

Neither had I. Trees, sure. But bushes, no. Of course if two male raccoons had gotten into a tussle out here anything was possible.

I lifted my chin to indicate the window. "What room is inside there?"

"My bedroom," the woman said. "That's why this got me so worried. I mean, to think that a man might have been out here peeping at me . . ." Though her words trailed off, she completed her sentence with a shudder, taking me back to my own shudder in this morning's meeting when the captain had been telling us about Ralph Hurley.

I leaned over the broken bushes to examine the screen. It appeared to be tightly in place. "It doesn't look like the screen has been tampered with." The closed miniblinds, however, hung slightly askew, the bottom edge not quite reaching the sill on the right side. *Would a person be able to see in through the small space?*

I stepped back and took a look around, walking up and down the side of the house, my eyes scanning the ground, bushes, and up the outer walls to the eaves. While I'd seen a light fixture on the woman's porch and up-lights mounted along the front of the house, there didn't appear to be any lighting along this side. In the dark of night, it would be easy for someone to hide himself in the shadows. Still, I needed to consider all of the possibilities. As I looked around, I noticed that the azalea bushes near the rear of the house had been trimmed more than the others. "The bushes have been cut back more here. Why is that?"

"A roofer was out here last month to fix a leak," she said. "A guy from Zinniker and Sons. That's where he put up his ladder. When he left I noticed it had broken some branches on the bushes so I had my gardeners trim them."

I glanced back down the row to the bushes under her bedroom window. "Could it be possible that the roofer also damaged the bushes under your window but that you didn't notice until now?"

She mulled the proposition over for a moment. "I suppose it's possible, but if he'd damaged those bushes, too, I think I would've noticed it last month."

Her explanation made sense. The bushes had probably been damaged more recently. "Do you l-live alone, ma'am?"

"Yes," she replied. "My husband used to live here, too, but we separated a year ago. We're in the process of getting a divorce."

A woman home alone, Hurley's typical victim. He'd had ample time to drive from San Antonio to Fort Worth yesterday afternoon, but he wouldn't yet have had time to case this woman's house, would he? Then again, he could have simply followed her home from somewhere and looked for clues that she lived by herself. The lack of other cars in the garage or driveway would be a giveaway, as would lights on in only one room of the house at a time. Of course Hurley might have had nothing at all to do with the broken bushes. It was anyone's guess at this point.

"Has your divorce been amicable?" I asked.

Kristin cocked her head, her brow furrowing. "What do you mean?"

"Would your husband have any reason to be out here? Maybe spying on you and a date out of jealousy? Or coming to take some item of property you two might be squabbling over?"

I'd seen all kinds of bad behavior during my relatively short time on the force. Jealous exes who vandalized their former boyfriend's or girlfriend's cars. Men who rooted for rival sports teams trying to tear each other apart in the parking lot of a sports bar. An angry neighbor who'd taken a baseball bat to a set of noisy wind chimes. Nothing would surprise me now.

"No," Kirstin said. "I can't imagine my husband doing anything like that. Besides, I haven't changed the locks and he still has a key. There'd be no need for him to break in."

"Have you seen anyone unusual hanging around the street? Somebody odd come to the door? Anyone following you?" *Maybe an oversized escaped parolee in an Isuzu Amigo?*

Her eyes went wide. "You think someone might have been following me?"

I raised a palm to calm her. "Just trying to examine all potential angles."

She chewed her lip. "I haven't noticed anyone following me, but I haven't really been looking. Nobody strange has come to the door that I recall. I work long hours and only come out front to check the mail so I don't see much of what's going on in the neighborhood."

"The police department received an alert for a convict from San Antonio with a history of breaking into homes and forcing the residents to give him their cash and debit cards. He tends to target female victims who live alone. It couldn't hurt for you to keep an eye out for a large, brown-haired man in an Isuzu Amigo."

Her eyes went wide again. “Has he been spotted here?”

“No, but he has contacts in the area so he might head this way.” Then again, he might be headed to Cozumel with plans to sun himself on a beach. His stolen dollars would go much further there.

I turned to face the road and looked up and down the street. A pair of squirrels chased each other around and up the trunk of a tree across the way, capturing Brigit’s eyes as well as mine. Fortunately, she was on her best behavior and made no move to chase them. A blue jay alighted on a fence post, her head jerking this way and that as she surveyed her surroundings. Next door, a black-and-white soccer ball sat forgotten beside the driveway.

Hmm . . .

I pointed to the ball. “Think some kids might have k-kicked their ball into your bushes?”

Kirstin eyed the ball and visibly relaxed, her tight shoulders loosening. “That would explain things, wouldn’t it?” She exhaled a long breath of relief. “I feel silly now for calling the police.”

“No need to feel silly,” I assured her. “Better safe than sorry.”

We stepped back around to the front of her house.

“Just in case it wasn’t kids,” I added, “you might want to take some extra precautionary measures. Straighten your miniblinds and make sure they completely cover your window. Maybe add some lighting down the side of your house.”

Brigit flopped onto her back on the lawn and wriggled around, scratching her back on the grass.

The woman smiled at my partner’s antics. “I suppose I could get a watchdog, too.”

“Couldn’t hurt.” Dogs were an effective warning system, though, like their electronic counterparts, they were prone to giving false alarms, especially if a skunk was in the vicinity.

I gave Kirstin my business card and told her to be sure to call again if she saw anything suspicious. With that, Brigit and I bade the woman good-bye and set back out on patrol.

NINE
JUNGLE LOVE

Brigit

Brigit enjoyed working in the W1 division. Forest Park and the TCU campus had large grass expanses where she could stretch her legs. The Trinity River provided a place for her to take a nice swim, though her partner never seemed too happy when Brigit bounded into the water and returned to her side to shake herself dry. But what Brigit liked best about working the district was the zoo.

The zoo provided an intriguing range of animal sounds and smells she'd never experienced anywhere else. Zebras. Rhinos. Lions. Of course if Brigit realized that a mere cat had been deemed king of the jungle she would have wholeheartedly protested, no matter how big the cat was. Dogs, of course, were the far superior species, paws down.

As they cruised past the zoo with the windows open, Brigit lifted her nose to the air. She smelled the popcorn they sold at stands throughout the grounds. She smelled the sweat of the workers as they hauled food and supplies around the habitats. And she smelled sex hormones. A bull elephant in the zoo was in musth, producing sixty times his normal level of testosterone. He reeked of lust.

Of course this wasn't the first time today that she'd scented sex hormones. She'd smelled their faint scent lingering in the bushes at the house they'd just visited. Those hormones had not been from an elephant, though. Nope, those hormones had been from a human male. She should know. Her first owner was a twenty-something dipstick who was always on the prowl for women. He didn't have much going for him, though, and was rarely successful. He might have had better luck if he'd brushed his teeth more than once a week.

When they'd passed the zoo, Brigit flopped down onto her cushion. After sniffing out the drugs in that car and taking down the man in the school, this dog had earned a catnap. But while her brain wanted to rest, her tummy had other plans. It gurgled and seized, no longer happy about the smorgasbord of chicken nuggets, hot dog bits, and French fries she'd gobbled down in the school cafeteria.

Hork.

Megan turned around in the front seat. "You okay, Brig?"

Brigit stood up and stretched out her neck when her stomach seized again. *Hork.*

"I'm pulling over!" Megan cried, making a quick turn onto the road that led into Forest Park. "Hang on!"

Hork! Hork!

Megan jumped out of her seat and yanked the door to Brigit's enclosure open. "C'mon, girl!" she cried, motioning for Brigit to hop down to the asphalt. "Now!"

But there wasn't time for Brigit to get out of the car before her stomach gave one final, powerful squeeze. *Hooooork!*

"Ewww!" Megan cried.

Brigit didn't know what her partner was so upset about. As for herself, she felt much better now that her stomach was lighter. She grabbed her Frisbee in her teeth and looked up at Megan, wagging her tail. *How about a game of catch in the park?*

TEN
JUST IN CASE

Tom

Wednesday night he was out again. He had to be extra careful. The woman he'd targeted tonight was married. The last thing Tom needed was an angry husband coming after him.

He drove slowly up the street, turning off his headlights as he approached. He rolled to a quiet stop across the street under a live oak tree with sprawling, leafy branches that blocked the light from the street lamp. The flickering light in the bay window at the front of the house told him someone was in the room watching television. He lifted his binoculars to his eyes and aimed them at the window, which was covered only with sheers to take advantage of the natural light in daytime.

There was her husband, sitting on the couch in a pair of rumpled pajamas, a bottle of imported beer in his hand. His gaze was fixed on the television. Tom shifted his binoculars slightly to take a look at the screen. Sure enough, the guy was watching a dirty flick on Cinemax. On the screen, a young, busty woman in a tight red dress and rhinestone-covered stilettos grabbed the necktie of the businessman standing in front of her and pulled his face down to hers. As they kissed, the man ran a hand down her arm, stopping to cup her ass.

Titillating, sure. But not nearly as titillating as watching a real woman in a secret, unscripted scene she had no idea she was starring in.

Tom wondered if the wife knew what her husband was up to. Probably not. Women were easy to fool. More than likely the guy claimed he was staying up to watch sports highlights. Then again, sex was a sport of sorts. It took two opponents, each of whom was trying to score.

He lowered the binoculars and returned them to the glove compartment. With her husband distracted in the living room, the woman would likely be alone in her bedroom now. *Perfect timing.*

ELEVEN
BLUE PLATE SPECIAL

Megan

Starting on Wednesday, my beat schedule changed to the 4 P.M. to 1 A.M. shift. Working the swing shift stank. There wasn't enough time to get much done before going to work, and it was difficult to stay awake past my usual bedtime. But a girl's gotta do what a girl's gotta do, even if she needs an extra-large coffee to keep her alert enough to do it.

Just after nine o'clock, dispatch came on the radio. "Officers needed in Frisco Heights. Victim reports a home invasion. Shots fired. Suspect appears to have left the scene."

The Frisco Heights neighborhood sat just north of Texas Christian University, home of the fighting horned frogs. The neighborhood was in the throes of gentrification and redevelopment, many of the smaller, older homes being torn down to make way for larger models that came with modern conveniences, custom features, and hefty price tags. Some of the smaller single-family homes in the southern part of the neighborhood bordering the university were being torn down and replaced by apartment complexes and condominiums.

Before I could grab my mic, Officer Spalding took the call. "Officer Spalding responding."

Dispatch gave him the address, which was on Sandage Avenue.

Brigit and I were only a few blocks away. I grabbed my radio from the dash. "Officers Luz and Brigit providing backup."

Flipping on my lights, I admonished Brigit to "Hold on!" and sped to the scene, keeping an eye out for cars or pedestrians that appeared to be making a hasty getaway. Nothing unusual caught my eye.

Spalding's cruiser was already parked at the curb as I turned onto Sandage. Spalding was in his early thirties, black and stocky, with the kind of muscles that said he spent most of his free time at the gym. He rushed up the front porch of the stately one-story home, gun at the ready in case the suspect wasn't as gone as the victim believed him to be. Fueled by adrenaline, I leaped from my car, readied my gun, and joined Spalding on the porch, each of us taking a spot on alternate sides of the ornate double doors.

He raised a fist and pounded on the door. "Fort Worth Police!"

A moment later, a person appeared behind the door, the diamond-shaped glass panes in the door creating a kaleidoscope effect. The door swung open to reveal a fiftyish blond woman in a pink nightgown. A white elastic headband kept her hair off her face, which bore a coating of white cold cream. She hurled herself in my direction. "Thank God you're here!"

I barely had time to lower my gun before she grabbed me in a bear hug so tight it's a wonder my rib cage didn't implode.

"He shot up my wall!" she cried in my ear at ten million decibels. "I thought he was going to kill me!"

When she burst into an all-out sob on my shoulder, I wrapped my left hand around her back and gave her a few pats. "It's going to be okay, ma'am. You're safe n-now."

The woman released me, leaving my shoulder wet and gooey with cold cream, tears, and mucus. *Job hazard.* I pulled a small package of tissues from my pocket and handed one to the woman.

She took the tissue, dabbing at her eyes. "I just can't believe it! I was in my bathroom taking off my makeup and a huge man in a ski mask walked right up behind me!"

"Are you hurt?" I asked.

She shook her head. "Just . . ." A fresh sob divided her words. "Scared."

Spalding came closer. "Did he rob you?"

The woman turned her gaze on my coworker. "He made me give him my debit card and PIN number." She gasped for air between sobs, her voice evolving into an all-out wail. "He said he was going to the bank and if the PIN number didn't work he'd come back and kill me!"

Spalding and I exchanged glances. *This situation fit Ralph Hurley's MO to a T.*

The woman closed her eyes and shook her head, fighting to gain control of her emotions. When she'd calmed a little, she opened her eyes. "He snuck right into my house," she said, her lip quivering and voice quavering. "I hadn't set my alarm yet. It has a motion sensor so I don't turn it on until I'm going to bed."

Her behavior was typical, and likely explained why Hurley had struck in the late evening rather than in the wee hours of the night when home security systems would be armed.

The woman sniffled again. "On my way to get my purse I went for the panic button on my alarm system in the kitchen. He shot up the wall before I could get to it." She burst into a fresh sob. "I thought he was going to shoot me next!"

I'd faced some scary situations on my job, including an armed gang who'd turned multiple guns on me at once, but at least I'd had a Kevlar vest, my own set of weapons, and extensive training. The defenseless woman must have been completely terrified. My heart went out to her.

"Did he touch anything in your house?" I asked, hoping the crime scene team might be able to lift a fingerprint and positively identify the robber.

"He grabbed my jar of face cream out of my hand and threw it to the floor. He touched the front doorknob when he left, too. But he was wearing gloves. Black ones."

Darn! With the suspect wearing gloves, the odds of getting a print were slim.

Spalding looked up and down the street. "Did you see the vehicle the man was driving?"

"No," the woman said. "As soon as he ran out the front door I locked it and went straight for my phone."

Spalding squeezed his shoulder-mounted radio mic. "This is Officer Spalding. Suspect in the Frisco Heights home invasion demanded the victim's debit card and PIN. It could be Ralph Hurley. Keep an eye on all banks and ATM locations in the vicinity. Victim did not see the suspect's car, but he could be in an Isuzu Amigo."

I hiked a thumb at my cruiser, where Brigit stood in the back, fogging up the window with her warm, moist breath. "I'll get Brigit on the trail."

While Spalding remained behind to question the woman, I rushed over to my car and released Brigit, who wagged her tail, eager to perform. Gotta love her work ethic, especially when she didn't even get minimum wage. It was probably just as well. If she did get a paycheck, she'd probably spend it all on shoes, like many females. But unlike other females, she'd eat the shoes rather than wear them.

I directed my partner to the front door and ordered her to trail. While Brigit wasn't trained like a bloodhound to search for a particular person, she was trained to follow after the source of a disturbance. Her body tensed in concentration as she snuffled around the porch. *Snuffle, snuffle, snuffle.* She found the scent, trotted down the steps, and set off.

"We'll be in touch!" I called over my shoulder as I took off after her.

She made her way down the walk and into the street. While I kept a flashlight locked on her and kept an eye out for oncoming cars, she hooked a right onto West Cantey Street, continued past Merida Avenue, and slowed as she approached Lubbock. She veered into the middle of the street, then took a right down Lubbock Avenue. A hundred feet down she stopped and snuffled around in front of a house, coming back twice to the same spot. *Snuffle-snuffle.* On her third go-round, she stopped at the spot, sat down on her haunches, and looked up at me, wordlessly telling me that this was where the trail ended.

"Good job, partner!" I scratched that sweet spot behind her ear to show my appreciation and gave her a single liver treat, hoping she wouldn't notice the pay cut. A good track usually earned her two treats, at least.

The intruder must have climbed into his car here. I glanced around. It was no wonder the thug chose to park in this spot. The surrounding houses were relatively dark, and a large tree blocked light from above, casting the road in shadow. It would be easy to overlook a car parked here.

I shined my flashlight on the house, looking for the number. When I found it, I jotted down the address in my notepad and radioed Spalding. "The trail ran cold on Lubbock."

His voice came back a moment later. "Detective Bustamente and crime scene are on their way to Sandage Avenue. Keep things secure at Lubbock Avenue until the techs get there."

"Will do."

I moved back, out of the street, and ordered Brigit to sit by my side in the yard. Standing still so as not to disturb the scene, I shined my flashlight around on the ground, looking to see if the suspect might have left evidence behind. In their haste to escape, criminals sometimes left a clue or two. A footprint with an identifiable sole pattern. A cigarette butt with their fingerprints or DNA on it. Heck, more than one criminal had even unknowingly dropped their wallets. That blunder made things easy for the cops and prosecutors.

Unfortunately, the only thing I saw was a fresh oil stain on the asphalt. Maybe we'd get lucky and Hurley's engine would quit on him, strand him high on a freeway overpass where he'd have no way to escape unless he wanted to go out like Butch Cassidy and the Sundance Kid.

Twenty minutes later, a crime scene tech arrived in a van and secured the area. Having worked with Detective Hector Bustamente before, I dialed his cell.

He answered with a chuckle. "I knew it was only a matter of time before you'd call, Officer Luz."

The detective knew I aspired to follow in his footsteps one day, and had been gracious enough to let me shadow him in earlier investigations. It was nice to have a mentor.

"Can I come take a look inside the house?"

"Be my guest," he said. "Just leave the dog in your car and be sure to put on a pair of booties before you come in."

Brigit and I retraced our steps to the Sandage Avenue house. I loaded her back into her enclosure in the cruiser, and proceeded to the front porch, where an evidence tech handed me a pair of blue paper booties.

"Don't touch anything," he warned. "Eyes only."

"I'll be careful," I promised. This wasn't my first rodeo.

I found the detective in the kitchen. Having spent so much time at the dog park with Brigit, I'd become familiar with the different types of dogs, their looks and temperaments, and subconsciously begun to equate humans with dog breeds. Detective Bustamente was the human equivalent of a basset hound, with droopy eyes and stumpy legs and a portly build. He had thick lips, like Megan Ryan after the plastic surgery disaster, though his were naturally pouty. He wore a green knit golf shirt with the collar curling up on one side and a pair of khaki pants that were three inches too short, revealing the white socks he'd paired with his black loafers. But while the guy couldn't be less impressive appearancewise, he couldn't be more intelligent brainwise. What he lacked in fashion sense he more than made up for in crime-solving savvy. We'd worked the rodeo purse-snatcher case together, even pretended to be a married couple as part of the investigation. The guy could really think on his feet, a skill I hoped to develop.

Bustamente stared through a jagged, watermelon-sized hole that had been blasted through the Sheetrock adjacent to the alarm panel. If the homeowner was interested in adding a pass-through bar to her living room, the hole would be a good start. Severed wires curled inside the open space, while shards of drywall, white Sheetrock powder, and a spent shotgun shell lay on the Italian tile floor below.

I stepped up beside him. "What're you thinking, Detective?"

He turned from the hole to me. "I'm thinking it's a good time to pay a visit to Ralph Hurley's sister. You up for it?"

Join in the investigation? Heck, yeah! "Yes, sir!"

My cruiser's clock showed 10:02 as I followed Bustamente's plain sedan into the parking lot of an older, no-frills apartment complex on east Seminary Drive. We took spaces side by side near the back of the lot. Though I feared bringing Brigit with me lest Ralph Hurley answer the door with guns blazing, I feared more that he'd drive into the lot, spot my cruiser, and open fire on the car while my partner was trapped inside, helpless. At least with her by my side I had a chance of defending her.

The detective and I glanced around the lot, looking for an Isuzu Amigo. Though neither of us spotted Hurley's car, my eyes landed on a shiny grease spot in a parking space partially obscured by a cockeyed garbage Dumpster.

"Fresh oil," I said, pointing. "There was an oil spot on Lubbock Avenue, too. Right at the place where Brigit lost the scent."

Bustamente grunted. "Looks like Hurley's car may have sprung a leak."

We made our way down the sidewalk, stopping when we found unit 103. Though the porch light was dark, soft light filtered through the slits in the vertical blinds, and the sound of the local news playing on TV came through the door. *Could Hurley be sitting inside, watching to see if there was any news of his crime yet?* Part of me hoped he was, that we'd catch the fugitive quickly and without incident. Another part of me hoped I'd never run into the guy. I'd seen what his shotgun could do to drywall and two-by-fours. It could do far worse to flesh and bone.

While Bustamente rapped lightly on the door so as not to disturb nearby residents who might be sleeping, I readied my gun. Forcing myself to breathe, I listened as intently as possible, trying to make out noise from inside the apartment against a backdrop of traffic noise from Seminary Drive and the *ba-dum ba-dum* of my throbbing heartbeat.

Ba-dum. Ba-dum. Ba-dum. Click.

Holy crap! Was that a shotgun being cocked? *BA-DUM-BA-DUM!* As the door swung inward I realized the sound had been the dead bolt sliding free. *Thank God.*

The door opened a few inches, as much as the safety chain would allow, and a woman's face looked out and down at us. *Whoa.* Hurley wasn't the only giant in his family. His sister stood at least five eleven. With brown hair and eyes and otherwise ordinary features, she looked like her brother, too.

On seeing my uniform, she released a slow sigh. "Figured I'd be getting a visit sooner or later."

With that, she slid the safety chain free and opened the door. She appeared to be in her late thirties and wore knit shorts and a long tee. Improvised sleepwear, I surmised, judging from the jiggling action under her shirt as she moved, indicating she'd retired her bra for the night.

My eyes quickly surveyed the room behind her as the detective introduced himself. All I saw was a tired-looking sofa, a cheap dinette set, a small TV, and a potted peace lily with three white blooms. There was no sign of anyone else in the room, nor any bedding on the couch or floor indicating someone was crashing here.

"Sorry to bother you so late," the detective said. "You're Ralph Hurley's sister, correct?"

She snorted. "Unfortunately. I'd much rather be known as Chris Hemsworth's secret lover."

If she were *known* as Hemsworth's lover it wouldn't be a *secret,* but I didn't bother pointing out her contradiction.

Bustamente cocked his head, eyeing the woman intently. "You seem to know why we're here."

"Yeah. You're looking for my good-for-nothing brother." She rolled her eyes and shook her head. "Ralph's been nothing but a pain in the neck since the day he was born."

"Is he here?" Bustamente asked. "Has he been staying with you?"

She scoffed. "Ralph wouldn't dare show his face around here or I'd kick his butt. He borrowed two grand from me years ago and hasn't paid back a cent. If that wasn't bad enough, last time I saw him he stole fifty bucks from my purse. Besides, harboring a fugitive is a felony, right? I'm not about to put myself on the line for him."

She sounded sincere, but could it all be an act?

Bustamente gestured with his hand. "Mind if we come in and look around?"

The woman would be within her rights to refuse to let us in. A grease spot in the parking lot wouldn't constitute sufficient probable cause for suspecting her of hiding Hurley. But if she gave us permission to come inside and perform a search, probable cause wasn't necessary.

When the woman hesitated, I glanced down at Brigit. She stood at my side, her body rigid as she awaited instruction. But she wasn't scenting the air, and she wasn't sniffing the carpet. Nothing in her demeanor told me she recognized any of the smells here. Maybe Hurley's sister was telling the truth and her no-good brother had never been here.

"There's nothing to see in my apartment but a bunch of dirty laundry and dust bunnies." She shrugged and stepped back. "But suit yourself."

I ordered Brigit to stay close by my side as we followed the detective into the apartment. I stood near the door with Brigit as he opened the coat closet and glanced inside. He checked the bedroom, even dropping to a knee to look under the bed. He stepped into the bath and pulled back the shower curtain, but no Ralph was to be found. Though the kitchen cabinets seemed much too small to hide the Silent Giant, Bustamente opened each and every one. "You never know," he told me. "I once found a meth-head curled up inside a garbage can."

Figuring I might as well help out, I opened the refrigerator. Nothing there but a half-empty bottle of inexpensive white wine, the usual assortment of condiments, a block of cheddar cheese, and several takeout containers. Who could blame her? I knew from experience that it wasn't easy cooking for one. At least once I'd been partnered with Brigit I'd had her to share my meals with.

When Brigit stepped forward to sniff at a white box with red Chinese lettering on the side I pulled her back. The last thing I needed was my partner performing a Technicolor Szechuan yawn in the back of my cruiser. I'd cleaned up enough puke recently.

Turning his attention back to Hurley's sister, the detective asked, "Have you heard from him?"

She hesitated again. "Look, he called me yesterday and asked if he could shack up here for a few days. I told him in no uncertain terms that he wasn't welcome and that was it. He hung up on me. I have no idea where he was calling from or where he might have gone."

Bustamente handed the woman his business card. "If he calls or comes by, will you try to find out where he's staying and let me know?"

She took the card and stared down at it, releasing a long breath before looking back up at the detective. "Honestly? I don't know. I mean, the guy's a waste of human flesh but he's still my little brother. And he's never seriously injured anyone. I mean, not . . ." She looked up, as if seeking the right word on her ceiling. "Not *permanently*."

While we appreciated her honesty, we'd have appreciated her cooperation even more. Even so, I could understand her reluctance to rat on her brother. Turning in a family member, knowing he'd go back to prison, would be difficult.

"I hate to tell you this," Bustamente said, "but your brother is a person of interest in a shooting death in San Antonio three years ago. Another woman was shot in the head in her home Sunday night, just a few hours after your brother cut off his ankle monitor. She's clinging to life in intensive care, but things aren't looking good. San Antonio PD thinks your brother could be involved."

Hurley's sister shook her head, her face morphing from shock, to horror, to denial. "No. No! Ralph wouldn't kill anyone. I'm sure of it!" The high pitch of her voice belied her words, and denial quickly turned to anger. "I'd like you to leave. *Now*."

The detective nodded, nonplussed. As long as he'd been with Fort Worth PD, he'd heard it all before. "Take care now, Miss Hurley."

Brigit and I followed the detective out the door.

Back at our cars, Bustamente cast a glance my way. "Cruise by here every few hours during your shifts. Baby brother might decide to pay his big sis a visit."

I reached down to pat Brigit's head. "You can count on us, Detective."

TWELVE
WORKING LIKE A DOG

Brigit

She was disappointed Megan hadn't let her sink her teeth into that container of sweet-and-sour chicken. It would've made a nice late night snack. At least Megan had given her lots of pats and strokes and scratches tonight, letting Brigit know she appreciated the hard work the dog had put in.

She hopped back into her enclosure and lay down on the cushion. Megan started their car and drove around for a few minutes, the white noise and vibration from the motor lulling the dog to sleep. Just as Brigit had nearly dozed off, a squawky voice came over the radio and she pricked up her ears to listen for words she recognized. Megan picked up her microphone and said something in response. Although she was disappointed that nobody said the words "walk," "park," or "treat," Brigit knew from experience that when her partner spoke into the microphone it meant they'd be making a stop somewhere.

A few minutes later, Brigit swayed with the car as it turned into a parking lot and rolled to a stop. Instinctively, Brigit's nose began to twitch. *Is that sausage? And bacon?* She stood and lifted her snout into the air. *Yes! Yes, it is!*

Things had definitely taken a turn for the better.

Thompson Nicola Regional District Library System

THIRTEEN
HARDCOVER PORN

Tom

The house he'd visited two nights earlier had been surrounded by pesky azalea bushes. Fortunately, this house had no bushes along the side to impede him, just a soft surface of thick grass. Even more fortunately, the couple's bedroom had two full-length windows he could peep through. Because the windows faced both north and toward the back of the house, they'd covered them only with a set of sheers on the inside. Clearly they hadn't expected anyone to be tiptoeing around their yard spying on them.

The early May night was cool and the windows had been left open a few inches to let in the light breeze. A bedside lamp shined inside, bright enough to provide him a nice, easy view into the room, but not so bright as to attract the swarm of moths and bugs he'd had to contend with last time.

In an abundance of caution, he pulled a pair of disposable lightweight cotton gloves from his pocket and slid them onto his hands. While he didn't plan to touch anything, he saw no sense in taking a risk that he'd inadvertently leave a print behind. No one could ever know he'd been here. If he were discovered, he'd lose everything.

He stepped lightly and carefully over to the window, flattening himself alongside it. Slowly he arched his neck to take a look.

There she is.

The woman sat on top of the covers, leaning back against the pillows reading a book. Tolstoy's *Anna Karenina.* Her long dark hair was pulled up in a loose, sexy pile on top of her head, several locks escaping to hang down next to her face. She wore a silky white spaghetti-strap nightie that came only to mid-thigh, leaving him thinking of what lay between those long legs stretched out in front of her.

She looked good. *Better than good.* You'd never know she'd given birth to a baby only a few months ago. She must do Pilates. Or maybe she jogged on that treadmill in the corner.

He'd enjoy watching her now, but he didn't dare indulge himself yet. He was too new to this to take chances, too nervous. Once he'd perfected the art of voyeurism, however, he hoped to take things to that next level. For now, though, he would observe the woman, burn her image into his mind, and take the memory home with him to enjoy her over and over and over again . . .

As she turned the page of her book, one of her shoulder straps slid down her arm, the fabric gaping to reveal the curve of the side of her breast. To his delight, she made no move to return the strap to her shoulder. He imagined himself nibbling along her neck, making his way down to that bare shoulder, sliding the other strap down . . .

Sssss.

The quiet was broken by a loud hiss that seemed to be coming from the ground. *Shit! Could it be a snake?*

Before his lust-addled brain could make sense of the sound, the automatic lawn sprinklers kicked on full force, a stream of cold spray hitting him directly in the crotch. A cry of surprise sprang from him—"Aah!"—followed by another cry of surprise from the woman inside the house. "Aaaaah!"

She leaped from her bed, shrieking for her husband. "Chris! Chris! Oh, my God! There's someone outside!"

Not anymore there isn't.

His legs pumped like pistons as he sprinted across several yards and into the street, hoping anyone who spotted him would assume he was merely out for a run. He lost his footing going around the corner and fell to one knee on the rough, unforgiving pavement. *Damn, that hurt!* But he couldn't let a banged-up kneecap slow him down. He was back on his feet in an instant, racing to the car.

He had to get the hell out of here.

Now!

FOURTEEN
A BUSY NIGHT

Megan

At 10:45 P.M., only minutes after parting ways with Detective Bustamente, I sat in the wood-paneled dining room of the Ol' South Pancake House, taking a report on a dine-and-dash. This was proving to be a busy shift. Fine with me. It beat those slow shifts that seemed to go on and on and on until my mind and muscles turned to mush.

The suspect had ordered a couple of fried eggs and a stack of silver-dollar pancakes, but left without leaving any dollars of his own to pay for the meal. Brigit sat on the floor by my side, smacking her lips as the smells of pan-fried breakfast meats permeated the air. The sixty-ish, gray-haired waitress who'd been stiffed was kind enough to treat my partner to a couple of sausage links while I made notes, though I'd cut the dog off when the waitress offered a third link. "That's enough, Briggie." The woman had also given me a fresh mug of piping hot coffee, God bless 'er.

I took a sip of the drink, set it on the tabletop, and held my pen poised over my pad. "How t-tall was the guy?"

She raised a flattened hand only an inch or so above her head. "About yea big."

That would put him at only five six or so, on the short side for a man, a peewee perpetrator. "Hair color?"

"None."

I looked up from my pad. "None?"

"He was bald as a newborn baby."

"Gotcha." I jotted a note on my pad. *Bald.* "What about his build?"

"Round. He weighed two-fifty if he weighed an ounce."

Bald, short, and round? Sounded to me like she was describing Humpty Dumpty. Of course if he were Mr. Dumpty, the fact that he'd eaten eggs would make him a cannibal.

When the waitress had given me all the information she could, I thanked her for the coffee and the meaty treats she'd supplied to Brigit. Though the odds of finding the culprit were, unlike the culprit himself, slim, I assured her I'd keep an eye out for the suspect. "If I catch him, I'll see to it that he pays you a big tip."

She gave me a smile, stood, and picked up her steaming carafe of coffee. "And if he ever shows his face in here again, I'll see to it that he gets a lapful of scalding hot decaf."

Street justice. Can't say I'd blame her. "Be sure to make it look like an accident."

"Oops." She raised her pot in salute and gave me a wink.

Knowing that Seth was wrapping up his shift at the firehouse, I texted him. *Meet me at Ol' South?* I hadn't yet taken my meal break and now seemed as good a time as any.

He replied immediately. *On my way.*

I placed an order for both of us. While the waitress went about her duties, I typed up a report. All the caffeine I'd ingested had left me feeling both wired and inspired. I decided to prepare my report in the form of a poem.

The diner he ate, then oh how he dashed.
Ignoring his bill and leaving no cash.
Lacking scruples and hair, he's round and short,
Immortalized here in my rhyming report.

Not bad for someone who'd once earned a C in high school English class. Of course the lackluster grade was due to the zero my teacher gave me for refusing to give an oral book report in front of the class. With my intermittent stutter and teenage self-consciousness, staying in my seat seemed the right thing to do. Luckily, my stutter had improved with time, though it still snuck up on me on occasion. The speech impediment no longer controlled me, however. The older I got, the more I realized that everyone had some sort of personal cross to bear, whether it be a stutter or a hairy mole or excessive foot odor. Besides, being a cop, I saw some pretty awful stuff. An occasional stutter was a small matter compared to abject poverty, an abusive boyfriend, or a meth addiction.

Ten minutes later, Seth and his explosives-sniffing dog, Blast, entered the restaurant. Both were blond-haired with square jaws and strong shoulders. Unlike his dog, Seth had a FORT WORTH FIRE DEPARTMENT T-shirt stretched taut across his muscular chest, a sexy chin dimple, and gorgeous green eyes. Those green eyes locked on me as he headed my way, setting my nerve endings to tingling and sending my body temperature up a notch or two, the coffee no longer the only thing that was steaming.

Seth and I had been dating for several months and, while things seemed to be on track now, we'd gotten off to a somewhat rocky start. He'd been abandoned by his mother as a child, lost his loving grandmother not long after, and was raised by a cold and distant grandfather. The experience had given Seth attachment issues, and he didn't trust easily. Eager to escape the unhappy home, Seth dropped out of high school and joined the army only to suffer the loss of friends and fellow troops in his explosive ordnance disposal unit. Needless to say, he carried a deluxe set of emotional baggage. A few months ago, when I'd attempted to peek into the baggage, he'd zipped things shut and slapped a lock on it. In other words, he'd backed away from our relationship. Hard as it was, I'd let him go. If you love something, set it free, right? Especially if that period of freedom allows you to enjoy a guilt-free fling with a mounted sheriff's deputy.

After a few weeks apart, Seth had come back with his tail between his legs. Heck, he'd even admitted he needed me. It was a huge step, both for him and for us.

We'd patched our relationship with some metaphorical duct tape and, slowly but surely, Seth was beginning to trust me, to open up and let me get close. I didn't force things, letting him take his time. Clearly the guy suffered PTSD from his time in Afghanistan and, after all, I was only in my mid-twenties. No need to rush the relationship. Besides, I was an independent, ambitious woman. I enjoyed some romance now and then, but my career was important to me, too. I was bound and determined to make detective as soon as I had enough years under my belt to apply. *Keeping my eyes on the prize.* Of course, my eyes didn't mind being kept on Seth, too. He sure was easy on them.

Our food arrived just as Seth ordered Blast to lie down next to Brigit and dropped into the seat across from me. He looked down at the plate, then up at the waitress. "Thanks. This looks delicious."

"So do you, hon." She gave him a wink.

As she returned to the kitchen, I eyed Seth across the table. "Don't worry. If she tries to take a bite out of you I'll club her with my baton."

Seth cut me a grin as he reached for the syrup. "Glad to know I'm safe."

Safe? Hardly. If I had my druthers, I'd rip Seth's jeans and T-shirt off, cover him in maple syrup, and—

"More coffee?" Another waitress appeared with a steaming pot of brew. Funny how women tend to materialize when there's an attractive fireman around.

"No, thanks," I said. Any more caffeine and my body would begin to levitate.

To the woman's disappointment, Seth also declined, instead tossing Blast a bite of his sausage patty. After the dog snatched the morsel from the air, Seth returned his attention to me, a grin playing about his lips. "Your video has over a hundred thousand hits on YouTube."

Damn. "You saw it?"

"*Everyone* saw it."

I looked up at the ceiling and groaned. Unfortunately, "K-9 Cafeteria Takedown" wasn't my Internet debut. Brigit and I were also featured in a clip in which she jumped up to lick tuna salad from my hair. Needless to say, our partnership had chalked up more than its share of memorable moments. It probably wouldn't be long before Ellen DeGeneres called to invite us to be guests on her show. It also probably wouldn't be long before the media and Captain Leone got wind of what really happened at the high school. I'd purposely left out a few details in my report, stating only that "the suspect was apprehended by K-9 Brigit in the school cafeteria."

Seth sipped his orange juice. "I'm on duty from noon Friday to noon Saturday, but I was thinking we could go down to the Brazos River on Sunday, maybe rent a canoe and spend a day on the water."

As much as I'd love a day of relaxation on the river, it would have to wait for another time.

"Seth, Sunday is Mother's Day." Given his family history, I hated to mention it. But my mom and dad were expecting me to spend time with them and my four siblings. As fun as a canoe trip sounded, my mother would disown me if I didn't show up.

"Oh." Seth turned to look out the window, avoiding my gaze. "I forgot about that."

Seth had never known his father and had told me precious little about his mother. All I knew was that she lived out of town somewhere and that he hadn't seen her in a long time.

"You could come with me," I suggested tentatively. He had yet to meet my parents. It would be a big step in our relationship. "We're taking my mom out for dinner."

Seth turned back to me, his eyes blank, his expression passive. Looked like he'd shut down once again. Hence my surprise when he softly said, "Okay."

"Okay? Really?"

He nodded and our eyes held for a moment over the table, communicating things we were afraid to put into words. *We're getting serious, aren't we?* And *My God, I never thought my stomach could hold this many pancakes!*

"In the interest of full disclosure," I replied, "my family can be loud and boisterous and annoying."

He gave me a small smile. "I've handled IEDs and four-alarm fires. I think I can handle a few irritating relatives."

I reached across the table and gave his hand a squeeze. He captured my hand and raised it to his mouth, licking a stray drop of syrup from my knuckle. "Yum."

Yum, indeed.

When I'd eaten all I wanted, I set my plate on the floor

so Seth's dog could consume what remained. "Have at it, boy." A bad habit on my part, treating the dogs like garbage disposals. That's how Brigit got into the predicament she was in.

A white-haired man in a booth nearby looked down at Blast licking the plate. His lip curled back in disgust, but he seemed to know better than to complain to me, what with the gun on my hip.

Seth paid our bill, leaving a generous tip for the waitress to make up for Humpty Dumpty stiffing her. We exited the restaurant with our dogs strolling along beside us. Seth walked me over to my cruiser, waiting while I loaded Brigit inside.

Once she was secured, he stepped closer, his green eyes sparkling with mischief. "Can I kiss you, Officer Luz? Or would you like to cuff me first?"

I glanced over at the restaurant, then at the cars making their way past on University Drive. The parking lot was well lit, the two of us clearly visible. As much as I'd like to, it would be best not to engage in any such personal activities while in uniform. I sighed and gestured at the passing traffic. "We'd better not."

Seth groaned, then turned hopeful eyes on me. "Will you make it up to me next time I see you?"

"And then some."

"That's what I like to hear."

With that, he returned to his car, a seventies-era blue Chevy Nova with orange flames painted down the side and license plates that read KABOOM. Apropos for a bomb expert, huh?

I climbed back into my squad car and had driven half a mile down the street when yet another call came in from dispatch.

"We've got a prowler report in Berkeley Place. Who can respond?"

Another incident in Berkeley Place? Perhaps those broken azalea limbs hadn't been due to kids playing soccer, after all. Or maybe Ralph Hurley was going for a twofer tonight, hitting another unsuspecting victim. Berkeley Place sat directly to the northeast of Frisco Heights, where he'd hit earlier.

Pulse racing, I grabbed my mic and claimed the call. "Officers Luz and Brigit responding. What's the address?"

The victim lived on Glenco Terrace. As soon as dispatch gave the house number, Brigit and I were on our way. Given the late hour, I didn't activate my siren and risk waking up the entire neighborhood, though I did turn on my flashing lights and put the pedal to the metal, driving as fast as I dared.

In the wee hours on a weekday, road traffic was light and we arrived at the house in record time. I pulled past a bronze-colored Ford Expedition SUV parked at the curb. The back bumper bore dealer license plates, as well as a sticker that depicted the American flag and said THESE COLORS DON'T RUN. The rear window sported a decal with the black and gold U.S. Army star. Attached to the driver's side door was a reflective magnetic sign that read NEIGHBORHOOD WATCH with the image of a large, angry-looking eye beneath the lettering.

The house was a classic two-story Tudor style, painted a light gray with white trim. A detached garage sat behind the house at the end of the driveway, protected by an iron gate. In the front doorway of the house stood a woman in a robe, one hand clutching the top closed at her neck, the other clenching the fabric at her chest in a death grip. An average-sized man in pajamas stood on the walkway that led from the porch to the street, waving me down. Next to him stood a hulky, bulky man sporting lightweight black nylon workout pants and a black tee over well-developed pecs that, by my best estimate, equated to 46B. His T-shirt bore the same neighborhood watch logo as the car sign, the angry eye seeming to lock on my cruiser. Both of the men and the woman appeared to be in their mid- to late thirties.

I turned off my lights, rolled down the windows for Brigit, and climbed out of the car. Brigit put her face to the mesh, her nose raised and wriggling as she scented the air.

The two men stepped forward. The one in pajamas began to speak but the large man cut him off. "Good. You're finally here."

Finally? When someone's scared and on edge, mere seconds can feel like minutes, so I chose to ignore the implicit criticism about my response time (which, by the way, was excellent).

The man gestured at the street. "I've already been up and down the block on foot twice looking for the guy. There's no sign of him."

The search would explain the small beads of moisture on his forehead and why his shirt appeared damp. *Sweat.* Up close like this I could smell his perspiration. He wore his brown hair in a short, military-style cut. He also wore an improvised tool belt equipped with a Maglite, pepper spray, and a holstered gun. The guy looked like a modern-day John Wayne and seemed to think Berkeley Place was the new Wild West.

I looked from the big man in the neighborhood watch shirt to the other. "Are you the homeowner?"

The guy in the pajamas nodded. "Yes, I am."

"What's your name, sir?"

"Christopher Lowry."

I pulled out my pad and made a note of the man's name, asking him to spell it. "You had a prowler?"

Again the bigger man answered before the other had

a chance to speak. "Someone was in the yard, just outside their bedroom window."

I looked to Christopher Lowry for confirmation.

"That's correct," he said.

Mister Muscles crossed his beefy arms over his chest. "If the automatic sprinklers hadn't come on, the thug would have forced his way into the house."

Maybe. Maybe not. Depended on what the suspect was after.

"What's your name, sir?" I asked him.

"Garrett Hawke. I'm president of the Berkeley Place Neighborhood Watch."

He said it with such self-importance I had to fight the urge to say "la-di-da." I jotted his name down, too, using all lower-case letters, my own secret code for a person who was difficult to deal with.

Hawke tucked his thumbs into his tool belt. "This is the second prowler report we've had this week."

"I'm aware of that," I said. "I responded to the first c-call, too."

"Any progress?"

"Not yet." I'd interviewed Kirstin Rumford, assessed the physical evidence, and made a report. Standard procedure. "There wasn't much to go on."

He grunted. "Might've been if you'd dusted for prints."

The department had a limited number of crime scene techs, and it had seemed unnecessary to call one out when nobody had been hurt, no property had been stolen or permanently damaged, and there'd been no clear evidence a crime had even been committed. But I wasn't going to waste my time explaining my thought processes. I'd learned from experience that trying to explain sometimes led to further argument. Nonetheless, I sent a pointed look up at him. "Please remember we're on the same side, Mr. Hawke. I appreciate what you do for your neighborhood, and I'd appreciate you letting me do my job, too."

He lifted a palm, as if inviting me to take over, and stepped back, moving with a barely perceptible limp. *Wonder what the story is there.*

I returned my attention to Lowry. "Tell me exactly what happened here."

He gestured back toward his wife. "My wife was in the bedroom when she heard someone make a noise at the window."

I looked up at his wife and motioned to her. "Ma'am?"

Lowry's wife came down from the porch to meet us on the walk. Her eyes were worried, her mouth tight, her shoulders drawn as if she were trying to shrink into herself. Obviously, she felt terrified and vulnerable and exposed. I offered what I hoped was an empathetic and reassuring nod.

As she stopped before me, it struck me that she was similar in appearance to Kirstin Rumford. Both were Caucasian, with long, dark hair. If there was a peeping Tom in this neighborhood, he clearly had a type. Then again, for all I knew it could have been Ralph Hurley at the Lowrys' bedroom window, hoping to gain entry and force the couple to hand over their debit cards. Hurley normally targeted women who were home alone, but perhaps he hadn't realized Mr. Lowry was in the house or thought he'd be able to take on the couple. He'd had good success so far. Maybe he was becoming bolder. Or maybe he was becoming more desperate. *Blurgh.* Desperation was never good. It could make criminals do stupider, more dangerous, more violent things. *Permanent* things.

I readied my pen again. "May I get your name?"

"Alyssa Lowry," she said, her voice meek.

As I wrote the name down, I asked, "Can you tell me what happened, Mrs. Lowry?"

"I was in bed reading. Since it's a nice night, we'd opened the windows an inch or two to get some fresh air. I heard the sound of the automatic sprinklers kicking on and right after that someone cried out by the bedroom window. The sprinklers must have surprised him."

"Him?" I repeated. "Are you sure it was a man?"

She raised a shoulder. "I guess I can't say for certain, but my impression from the sound was that it was a man."

"Could it have been a child? Maybe a teenager?" After all, children, especially teens, didn't always respect boundaries and looked for shortcuts. A kid from the neighborhood could have been sneaking through yards and hopping fences and been unexpectedly caught in the spray.

"I suppose it's possible," she replied, though she didn't sound convinced. "If the kid was old enough that his voice had already changed."

"Can you show me the window?"

"Sure."

She walked gingerly across the damp yard in her slippers, leading me around the side of the house, stopping short of the back fence. The house was L-shaped, wider here than it was farther back. She pointed to two windows set four feet apart. The windows faced the backyard, though they were not inside the fence. The glass was covered by white sheers on the inside. A bedside lamp offered soft lighting, not enough to illuminate the entire room but enough to make the bed, and anyone who might be sitting on it, easy to see. A thick book lay on the dark, rumpled bedspread. Tolstoy, if I wasn't mistaken.

"Which window did the sound come from?" I asked Mrs. Lowry.

"I don't know," she said. "I just heard the cry and bolted out of the bedroom."

I pointed to a window on the second floor, directly over their bedroom. "Whose room is up there?"

"Our son's," Alyssa said.

"How old is he?"

"Eight months."

Too young to have a friend out here who might be pulling a practical joke, or to be sneaking out of the house himself. "Anyone else live here?"

Alyssa shook her head. "No. Just the three of us."

All I saw was thick Saint Augustine grass, wet from the sprinklers. "Any chance it could have been an animal that cried out? Maybe the sprinklers surprised a raccoon or possum or stray cat out here."

Mrs. Lowry's face looked doubtful. "I've never heard an animal make a sound like the one I heard."

"And you're sure it wasn't the baby?"

I wasn't trying to discount anything she said, but was only trying to get the facts straight and eliminate other possibilities. After all, the police department received a high percentage of reports that proved to be nothing. Cars reported stolen that were in use by another family member. Late-night prowlers that turned out to be a possum digging through a garbage can. Fireworks or backfiring cars reported as gunshots.

"I'm sure the noise wasn't our son," she said. "The baby monitor was on my night table on the other side of the bed. It was quiet."

"I'd just checked on him," Christopher added. "He was sound asleep."

I pulled my flashlight from my belt and shined it around the area. Hawke did the same and began to step forward.

Reflexively, my arm shot out in front of him, preventing him from going farther. "Stay back or you could contaminate the crime scene."

I crouched down for a better look, but saw no footprints, no handprints, no evidence whatsoever left behind. Of course the thick grass wouldn't retain a footprint, so the lack of clues didn't necessarily mean no one had been here. "I'm not s-seeing anything."

Hawke, who'd dropped to a knee next to me, concurred. "Me, neither."

Where human eyes fell short, Brigit's nose could once again compensate. It paid to have a partner with a specialized skill set. "I'll get my partner back here, see if she can follow the trail."

If a someone had been lurking about back here, Brigit would let us know.

FIFTEEN
THE NOSE KNOWS

Brigit

He's been here, too.

Inside the cruiser, Brigit lifted her nose to the open window and flared her nostrils, scenting the same man she'd smelled two days ago at the other house. Whoever he was, he sure seemed to get around.

When she noticed her partner returning to the car, she wagged her tail, hoping Megan would let her out to explore, to put her skills to use. Brigit wasn't some fluffy lapdog whose only purpose was to look pretty. Brigit had been born with an innate sense of purpose, a drive to keep watch and protect and track. Also an instinct to herd sheep, though she hadn't been able to put that skill to use yet. The only sheep she'd ever come across were at the stock show, and the woolly beasts had already been rounded up and stuck in a pen. At that point, Brigit had been more interested in eating them than herding them.

Megan stepped over to the cruiser and opened the back door. "C'mon, girl. You're up."

Yippee! Brigit hopped down from her enclosure and looked up at her partner, awaiting instruction. She hoped she'd be ordered to chase someone. She loved playing chase.

Megan led her around the side of the house, then issued the order for Brigit to find the source of disruption on the ground and track the perpetrator. Brigit was more than happy to oblige. Tracking was a game to her, a fun challenge, one that sometimes led to a pursuit but always ended with Megan rewarding her with liver treats. Megan had been oddly stingy with them the last three days, ever since they'd visited the sicko who'd put the stick in Brigit's butt. At least Megan had let her have some sausage at the diner tonight.

The man's scent was strong here by the window. He'd been standing here not long ago. The dog knew that with one hundred percent certainty. He seemed to roam around houses in the dark, leaving his scent behind, like an unneutered tomcat marking his territory and looking for love or a fight.

Brigit put her nose to the ground and turned to head out after him. She wanted another liver treat and she'd do whatever it took to earn one. *I'll lead Megan to this guy if it's the last thing I do.*

SIXTEEN
DAMPENED SPIRITS

Tom

Damn sprinklers!

Tonight had not gone as planned. Not at all.

There would definitely be fallout.

He only hoped things would blow over quickly.

SEVENTEEN
INTO THE NIGHT

Megan

Brigit snuffled around the base of the windows, moving over and lifting her head to sniff alongside the one on the left. As intently as my partner was scenting, it was clear she was on to something.

"This must have been the window where the prowler was," I said.

Alyssa's grip on her robe tightened even more.

Brigit put her face back to the ground and headed out, moving with purpose across the yard. Working with a K-9 was like having a secret, furry high-tech weapon. I felt like a female Iron Man. Or maybe it was more like being a magician, but instead of a magic wand I had a magic dog who could track down clues no human cop could detect. Either way, I was proud to be part of a K-9 team, even if it meant always having fur on my uniform and being responsible for bagging Brigit's poop.

"I'll come back, let you know what we've found," I told the Lowrys as I headed after my partner.

Brigit trotted along and I followed behind, rounding to the front of the house and continuing across the Lowrys' front yard into the one next door.

While the couple returned to their home, Hawke

lumbered along after me, an uninvited sidekick. Guys like him could be problematic. Wannabe heroes who took their citizen patrol duties too seriously. The last thing the world needed was another overzealous asshole like George Zimmerman hurting or killing an innocent person. Still, so long as he didn't get in my way, Garrett Hawke was within his rights to traipse along after me and my partner. Besides, these watch groups could sometimes be instrumental in solving or preventing crimes. It would be best if Hawke and I stayed on each other's good sides.

I glanced back at him as we went. I thought I'd seen a slight limp when he'd stepped back before, but now it was certain. His traipse had a little tick, his right leg looking stiff as he stepped.

"Keep back," I warned him. "Brigit needs space to keep on the trail." It was a white lie. Brigit's nose had an impressive track record, and she never let humans distract her. But frankly I didn't want the guy in *my* personal space.

My partner continued around the corner of the street, making her way into the road and turning left two streets down onto Hawthorne Avenue. She stopped to snuffle a piece of white, crumpled trash in the street—*a bakery bag?*—continuing on a moment later to the curb three houses from the intersection. She snuffled the curb, lifted her head in the air, and looked off down the road before sitting down on her haunches, and turning her head up to face me. She looked a little disappointed. Probably she'd been hoping for a chase. Brigit loved a good chase.

Despite my admonition to keep back, Hawke stepped up next to me. "Dammit!" he barked. "She's lost the trail."

I gave Brigit an appreciative scratch behind the ears, thanking her for her good work before turning my attention to Hawke. "She didn't lose the trail. This is where it ends. Whoever was at the window must have gotten into a car here."

Just like it was no surprise that Hurley had parked under the tree on Lubbock Avenue, it was no surprise this prowler had chosen this spot to leave his car. The house he'd parked in front of had a FOR SALE sign on the lawn and stood vacant. All of the lights were off and several newspapers lay strewn about the driveway, a clear indication that nobody was living here at the moment.

Of course it was also possible that whoever had been in the Lowrys' yard had an accomplice who had parked here, waiting for the suspect. Maybe the person who'd been at the window was, in fact, a teenager. Maybe he'd snuck out of his house, hopped some fences, and been picked up by a friend or girlfriend here. Heck, I'd snuck out of my parents' house a time or two when I was a teenager. Or maybe Hurley had indeed attempted to strike again, but been thwarted by the Lowrys' automatic sprinklers. *Had Hurley's Isuzu Amigo been parked here only moments before?*

I glanced around but saw no oil stain. *If only the mailboxes could talk.* The windows of the houses nearby were also dark, the inhabitants likely already in bed. The meager light emitted by the porch lights didn't extend to this stretch of the street. Given that there'd been no injuries, it seemed unnecessary to roust the residents from their beds to question them. Nonetheless, it couldn't hurt for me to come back tomorrow and see if any of the residents had noticed anything, spotted any unusual cars parked here.

I clipped Brigit's leash onto her collar and she stood, tail wagging as if to say *What now, boss?*

"C'mon, girl." Brigit and I turned to go back to the Lowrys' house, Hawke still tagging along. Brigit once again paused to sniff the crumpled white thing on the ground.

I shined my flashlight on it. "What is that?"

"Trash," Hawke said. "A used napkin or tissue."

I bent down to take a closer look. No, it wasn't a tissue, and it wasn't a napkin. It wasn't a bakery bag as I'd previously thought, either. Whatever it was, it was made of a lightweight fabric. While it had a stitched seam along part of it, another part looked unfinished. *Weird.*

I snagged a twig from a nearby yard, pulled an evidence bag from my pocket, and used the twig to pick up the scrap and put it in the bag.

Hawke's nose twitched in disgust. "Why are you taking that used tissue?"

It wasn't a tissue, but I didn't bother correcting him. "It could be a clue." Then again, it could merely be a piece of trash as he'd suggested. Still, the fact that Brigit had stopped to sniff the thing both times we'd come upon it told me she thought it might be important. Of course Brigit also thought that squirrels and other dogs' butts were important, so her judgment couldn't always be trusted.

Hawke motioned to the bag. "Can you get DNA from a tissue?"

"Sure," I said. "Mucus is a good source of DNA." Hence the standard collection of mucus via a mouth swab.

"How do you even know that belongs to the guy?" Hawke said. "Maybe someone just dropped it here."

"And maybe they didn't."

First the guy complains that I hadn't dusted Kirstin Rumford's house for prints, and now he questions my ability to evaluate evidence. *Ugh. Give me a break.*

I returned to the house and rapped on the door.

Mr. Lowry opened it a moment later, his wife standing behind him with her sleeping baby cradled in her arms.

Before I could speak, Hawke said, "The trail ran cold on Hawthorne."

"I'll get a crime scene tech out here." Probably a futile effort, but I felt the need to do something more. The thought of Ralph Hurley victimizing women, especially in W1 and on my watch, made my blood boil. It also made me fear for the safety of the citizens I'd sworn to serve and protect. "I don't want to unnecessarily alarm you all," I told the three, "but a man entered a home tonight in Frisco Heights and demanded the victim's debit card and cash." He'd also taken her sense of security and her faith in mankind, but those critical intangibles never made it into the reports. "Given the proximity of your neighborhood, it's possible the two crimes are related. We believe the suspect in the robbery might be a parolee who cut off his ankle monitor."

"Did he—" Alyssa cried before putting her hand over her mouth as if afraid to ask the question, afraid to know just how much danger she might have been in only minutes before.

Although she didn't finish, it was clear where she'd been going. "No," I said. "He didn't physically harm her in any way."

"Thank goodness," she said on an exhale, her shoulders relaxing.

"He did fire a warning shot with his gun, though."

The shoulders tensed again.

Hawke cocked his head. "I think I heard about this guy on the news yesterday. He's from San Antone, right? Drives a green Amigo?"

"That's the one," I said.

"So he's here in town?" he asked.

"It's possible," I said. "We'd appreciate your watch group keeping a lookout and letting us know immediately if you spot his car." I provided Hawke with Hurley's license plate number. "He's armed and dangerous. Be sure to tell your volunteers not to approach him."

"I'll tell 'em," Hawke said. "But I can't make any promises about what I might do if I see the bastard."

"Please, Mr. Hawke," I said, "leave law enforcement to the police, okay?"

He responded with a noncommittal shrug.

I turned back to the Lowrys. "I'd also like to ask you two a few more questions." I glanced up at Hawke, giving him a meaningful look. *"Privately."*

Hawke raised his palms high as if surrendering. "Message received." He returned his focus to the Lowrys. "Let me know if there's anything else I can do."

"We will," Mrs. Lowry said. "Thanks so much, Garrett. Knowing you're around makes me feel so much safer."

Chris Lowry's gaze went from his wife to Hawke's back as the large man retreated across the yard. Lowry's narrowed eyes and clenched jaw told me that Hawke made him feel emasculated, like he'd let his wife and child down when it came to fulfilling his role as their protector. He hadn't, of course. Calling the police and the watch group were the best things he could have done. Chasing down the person who'd been in his yard could have proved dangerous, even fatal. What good would he be to his family if he'd been hurt or killed?

"Come on in," Mrs. Lowry said, stepping back to allow me and Brigit inside.

I stepped into a hallway that seemed to be a shrine of sorts given the multitude of framed baby portraits hanging on the wall. Who could blame the proud parents, though? The kid was a cutie, all curly dark hair and dimples and toothless grins. He made the Gerber baby look like a troll.

A moment later, I was seated on a love seat with Brigit lying at my feet, shedding on a Persian rug that probably cost more than I earned in a month. The Lowrys were huddled on one end of their couch, Chris's arm draped reassuringly over his wife's shoulders, their baby dreaming comfortably, nuzzled against his mother.

I pulled out my notepad. "Have you seen anyone unusual in the area lately? Maybe had a suspicious solicitor come to the door? Noticed anyone watching you or your house?"

They both shook their heads.

"What about someone who's done work at your house?" I wanted to get information, but not lead them too much, so I tried to be subtle. "Have you hired a painter recently? Maybe a plumber or yard care service?"

The Lowrys exchanged a meaningful glance before Mrs. Lowry spoke. "Our usual exterminator was on vacation last week and the service sent a replacement. The guy who came out gave me the creeps. He took three times as long as the regular tech and he asked a lot of nosy questions when he came to the door to collect the check."

"Nosy questions?" I repeated. "Such as . . . ?"

"He asked whether I'd taken the day off from work. When I told him no, that I worked from home, he wanted to know what kind of business I'm in."

I suppose my expression told her I was wondering the same thing.

"I teach voice and piano lessons." She gestured to the white baby grand piano situated at the far end of the room. "I used to teach music at Shulkey Elementary but

I quit at the end of last school year so I could stay home with the baby." She glanced at her husband again. "The exterminator saw our son's photos hanging on the wall and asked how old he was, what his name was, whether he was crawling yet."

None of the questions he'd asked were necessarily unusual in and of themselves, and it was possible that Alyssa Lowry's maternal instincts were simply in overdrive, but I also knew that seemingly benign questions could sometimes be a fishing expedition. Had the exterminator been trying to determine when Mrs. Lowry might be home by herself? Maybe. But if that were the case, and he was trying to catch Mrs. Lowry alone at a time when her husband wouldn't be home, why would he have waited until late in the evening to return to the house? After all, there was a much greater chance her husband would be home at night than in the daytime.

I'd need to mull these questions over. In the meantime, it would be helpful if I could identify the exterminator. "Any chance you know the guy's name?"

"It might be on the paperwork." Mrs. Lowry stood from the couch. "I think I've still got our copy in the kitchen."

She rushed off to the kitchen and returned a moment later with a carbon copy of a form from Cowtown Critter Control. I was familiar with the service. Their signature yellow vans had round bug eyes on top that resembled oversized mirrored disco balls. You didn't want to come up on one of their vans from the other direction on a sunny day or your retinas would be fried by the multiple reflections.

Mrs. Lowry had signed the form at the bottom to indicate that the service had been performed to her satisfaction. Although the tech had also signed the form, his penmanship was deplorable, his name impossible to read. Best I could tell it read "Qiamond Ovabo." Not likely. Luckily, the form came with the tech's name preprinted higher up on the page. Leonard Drake. *Seriously, dude. Work on that penmanship. Practice makes perfect.*

I jotted the name on my pad. "What did the guy look like?"

Her eyes squinted as she thought back. "He was an older guy. White. Thinning hair that he combed straight back." She waved splayed fingers in front of her face. "Looked like he'd spent too much time in the sun."

I made note of her description. "Any chance you've had any roofing work done recently?" Might as well see if the Lowrys had any connection to Zinniker and Sons, the roofing company that had done work at Kirstin Rumford's house. If the Lowrys also mentioned having a roofer out lately, I just might have a concrete lead.

"No," she said.

"Have you seen a roofing truck in the area? Maybe one of your neighbors getting some repairs done?"

"Not that I recall." She glanced over at her husband. "Have you, Chris?"

He, too, responded in the negative. *So much for that potential lead.*

I tried to sound as casual as possible when I asked the next question. "What can you two tell me about Garrett Hawke?"

"Garrett?" Alyssa looked taken aback, her brows drawing inward to form deep parallel lines. "What do you mean?"

I raised a shoulder with feigned nonchalance. "How long have you known him? Has he been president of the watch group for long?"

As the guy himself had mentioned, he'd responded quickly to their call but found no one in the area. He'd been moist, too. Maybe that hadn't been sweat dampening his shirt and brow. Maybe it had been water from the Lowrys' sprinkler system. Or maybe the guy had just rubbed me the wrong way and I was having trouble letting it go.

Alyssa sat up straighter. "Garrett and his wife moved into the neighborhood a couple of years ago with their three kids. He's the one who organized the neighborhood watch. He can come on a little strong sometimes, but he means well. He's caught kids egging houses and once he even caught a guy trying to break into a car. Garrett restrained him until the police came."

More to mull over. "Men like him can be a big help to both the police and their communities," I said, *as long as things don't get out of hand.* "I noticed Mr. Hawke seemed to have some trouble with his leg. Either of you know anything about that?" My gaze moved between Chris and his wife.

Alyssa responded first. "I heard he was injured when he was serving with the army in the Middle East. Shot in the leg, if I remember right."

I cringed involuntarily at the thought. "Ouch."

Chris cocked his head as he looked at his wife. "Someone told me he'd stepped on a land mine."

The fact that Hawke was a veteran made me warm to him and, regardless of which version of events was correct, it appeared he'd been injured while on duty. Anyone who'd served his or her country couldn't be all bad, right? Seth had served in Afghanistan. In fact, he continued to serve in the reserves. It was one of the things I admired about him. Of course I also had to admit that I found the eagle tattoo that spanned Seth's back and shoulders incredibly sexy. *U-S-A!*

I turned to Chris. "Are you involved in the watch group?"

"Not really," he conceded. "I've made contributions to help cover the cost of supplies and been to a meeting or two, but my career isn't conducive to volunteering. I'm in medical sales. I work long hours and travel a lot."

"So you're gone quite a bit?"

"Yes," he said. "In fact I just returned from a trip to Tucson today."

Hmm. A woman with an absentee husband fit the description of Hurley's typical victim. But Alyssa's husband was home tonight. And would Ralph Hurley be reckless enough to go back out on the streets so soon after presumably robbing another victim? Surely he had to know that the police in the area were keeping a close eye out for him and his car.

I suggested some safety measures for them to take and stood to go.

As the Lowrys led the way to the door, Brigit seized the opportunity to plunk her rear down on the expensive rug and drag her butt across it as we followed behind them. I couldn't very well call her out, but I jerked on her leash and gave her a look that said *Cut that out!* She gave me a look back that said *My butt itches. Sue me.*

As Chris opened the front door to let me and Brigit out, a male crime scene tech came up the walk. The Lowrys repeated their story for him and showed him the window.

I pulled the evidence bag from my pocket and held it out to the tech. "I deployed my dog and found this in the street when she was tracking the suspect. I'm not sure if it belonged to him or if someone else dropped it, but I picked it up just in case."

The tech, who'd donned a pair of protective gloves, carefully removed the crumpled white fabric from the bag. He gave it a swift shake to uncrumple it and held it up to take a look.

Now that it was no longer balled up, it became clear that the fabric was a lightweight glove of some sort. While the stitching around the fingers, thumb, and sides was solid, the edge at the wrist was left unfinished, which seemed odd. The gauzy material wouldn't be waterproof, so it couldn't be a glove used for protection from moisture or hazardous liquids. Perhaps it was some type of glove liner, maybe something used in sports or snow skiing, or inside a more heavy-duty work glove. Or maybe it was intended for use by someone who was sensitive to latex and needed a protective layer. Maybe Hurley had been wearing it underneath the black gloves his earlier victim said he'd been wearing when he broke into her house and shot up her wall.

"What kind of glove is that?" I asked the tech. "Or do you think it's just some type of liner?"

"Could be," he said, returning the glove to the bag. "If I can't figure it out myself, I'll check with the other techs, ask around."

With the situation now in hand, I bade everyone goodbye, giving both the Lowrys and the tech my business card.

The tech tucked the card into his breast pocket. "I'll let you know what I find out."

"Thanks."

Brigit and I returned to our patrol car. I drove down the street and turned, making my way back to the spot where Brigit had lost the scent. There, I pulled to a stop and unrolled the windows, letting the night air invade the cruiser.

"Who are you?" I said into the night, addressing the unknown person who'd been at the Lowrys' bedroom window and later disappeared from this spot. “And where did you go?”

Alas, the night provided no answer, just the a soft breeze and the rhythmic *chirp-chirp-chirp* of crickets.

EIGHTEEN

NO WAY TO TREAT A DOG

Brigit

Megan had stopped their cruiser at the spot where the scent of the fleeing man had disappeared. Though Megan spoke, her words were soft and slow. Brigit had learned that when her partner talked that way she was talking not to Brigit but to herself. What a weird thing to do. You'd never catch a dog having a conversation with itself, though Brigit wasn't above tossing a tennis ball in the air to play catch on her own.

She stood at the mesh enclosure and let out a soft whine. The ear scratch had been nice, but a liver treat would be much better. Might as well give Megan a reminder that she'd forgotten to give her partner the treat she'd earned.

But Brigit's whine earned her no treat. In fact, Megan turned around in her seat and commanded Brigit to "hush!"

Screw that.

Brigit quieted and waited until Megan had turned to face forward and driven a dozen feet down the road. Then the dog put her mouth to the mesh directly behind Megan's head and issued the loudest, sharpest, shrillest yip she could muster.

YIP!

Megan started in her seat, inadvertently jerking the wheel and narrowly missing a brick mailbox. "Brigit!"

If Brigit were capable of laughing, she would have. *Payback's a bitch.*

NINETEEN
DREAMGIRL

Tom

He crept into the place, just as he'd crept out of it an hour before. Not that the tiptoeing was necessary. Hell, as deep as that woman slept he could've ridden a Harley through the place and not risked waking her. Those three spoonsful of liquid sleep aid he'd slipped into her second glass of wine earlier had been genius. She hadn't even noticed the taste.

Now she was passed out on the bed, dead to the world, the television playing a sitcom rerun. Nevertheless, he tried to be as quiet as possible. No sense taking chances. If she realized he'd been out, she'd want to know where and why. *It's none of her damn business.*

He flopped down onto the couch, covering himself with a blanket. Though he was the only one under the covering, he was hardly alone. He'd brought Alyssa Lowry home with him, dark hair and all.

Knowing it could be a while before he'd be able to spy on another woman, he figured he'd better make the most of the short memory he'd made tonight. He closed his eyes, letting his imagination take over.

There she is, her firm thighs exposed, her long hair

begging to be loosed, Tolstoy in the hands I long to be touched by. Oh, yeah. Alyssa Lowry can dog-ear my pages anytime . . .

TWENTY
MEET AND GREET

Megan

Thursday afternoon, as I pulled into the station, the crime scene tech called.

"Any luck?" I asked.

"None," he said. "The only recent prints on the Lowrys' window screen belonged to Chris Lowry. Apparently the prowler had made no attempt to remove the screen or, if he had, he'd worn gloves, maybe the glove you found."

"Did you figure out what kind of glove it was?"

"Nothing definitive on that end, either, but I think you might have been right when you said it could be a liner. I found some online that looked similar."

He went on to tell me that people who worked in the medical field, clean rooms, industrial settings, or refrigerated spaces often wore gloves or glove liners under a heavier rubber or leather glove. The liners wicked away moisture and made the gloves more comfortable. People who handled certain types of fragile objects also wore gloves and glove liners.

I mulled things over for a moment. "What do you make of the fact that the seam around the wrist was unfinished? Does that mean the glove or glove liner was meant to be disposable?" After all, gloves or liners intended for more than one-time use would likely be finished all around, wouldn't they?

"Yes," he agreed. "In fact, we crime scene techs and the people who work in the evidence room use disposable gloves like this for handling certain types of evidence. X-rays, for instance. We have to make sure they're free of lint and other things that might damage the film. Most brands of disposable plastic gloves are treated with powder so we can't use those."

Unfortunately, none of this information really helped me narrow down the list of potential suspects, even assuming the glove had been dropped by the prowler, which might or might not be the case. I had little to go on. But I did have a couple of things I wanted to look into.

Those things were Leonard Drake and Garrett Hawke.

Something about Hawke didn't sit quite right with me. I hoped I wasn't letting my pride get the best of me. He'd been mildly insulting, but mostly he'd just been direct. Even so, he'd seemed to be attempting to steer me away from the glove I'd picked up in the street. Had that been intentional?

On our way in the station door, Brigit and I met Summer coming out. She crouched down to put a hand under Brigit's snout and lifted it for a noisy smooch.

Brigit returned the sentiment, giving Summer a lick on the cheek. Unlike Lucy, who cried out for iodine and disinfectant when Snoopy kissed her, Summer simply used the back of her hand to dry her cheek.

"You two working swing tonight?" she asked, standing.

"Yeah," I replied. "I hate the swing shift. Screws up all of my biorhythms."

Summer cringed in empathy. "Sucks to be you."

It dawned on me then that my fellow W1 officers

might have some intel on Hawke. Maybe they could help me decide whether I was barking up the wrong tree by considering him a potential suspect in the prowler cases. "You ever meet the president of the Berkeley Place Neighborhood Watch?"

"Big guy?" Summer asked, arcing a brow. "Kinda full of himself?"

Yep, she's met him. "That's him. His name's Garrett Hawke. He responded to a prowler call last night. Got there before me and looked around but didn't see anyone."

"Typical," she said.

True, but . . . "You ever get a bad vibe from the guy?"

"No," she said, "but I've only spoken with him once or twice when I was working nights."

Looked like I was probably off base.

Summer hiked a thumb to the bulletin board in the lobby, where a full-color photo of Ralph Hurley was tacked. "Hurley was spotted in Grand Prairie this afternoon. Someone called it in, but by the time their department could respond he was gone."

Grand Prairie sat east of Fort Worth. Was Hurley on his way out of town? Or was he merely meandering about the area, looking for his next victim?

"Did he rob someone else?" I asked.

"Not that I know of," she said. "The person who reported it said he was buying a pair of running shoes at the outlets."

Hmm. Perhaps he was equipping himself in case he had to make a getaway on foot. Or maybe he had aspirations of running a marathon. Or maybe he just liked comfortable shoes. Heck, criminal or not, who could blame him for wanting comfy footwear? After a shift standing in the street directing traffic, my feet always hurt like heck. And who didn't like the good bargains the outlets offered? Shopping there would make his stolen cash go further.

With a final "See ya'," Summer headed out to her car and Brigit and I headed down the hall to the officers' administrative room. Given that we street cops took our laptops with us when we were out on patrol, our squad cars served as a type of mobile office. Occasionally, however, we needed a real desk to print reports, prepare paperwork, or meet with a witness. The shared administrative space served that purpose.

There were only a couple of officers in the room. Both were male and both were typing on their laptops. I snagged a desk near the front of the room and sat down to do some research.

The first thing I did was run a criminal background check on Leonard Drake, the creepy exterminator Alyssa Lowry had mentioned. I found one listing for a Leonard Roy Drake, age fifty-one. Last fall, he'd pleaded no contest to a misdemeanor criminal trespass charge he'd racked up after a student reported him wandering the halls of a freshman girls' dormitory at TCU, knocking on doors. He'd served no jail time, but paid a $500 penalty.

To make sure he was the same Leonard Drake who worked for Cowtown Critter Control, I pulled up his photo. Sure enough, the guy had craggy, sun-weathered skin and thinning hair combed back over his head, exactly as Alyssa Lowry had described him.

Could Drake be the prowler? It was possible. Maybe he'd been at the window to peep at Alyssa. And he might have been wandering the halls of that dorm, hoping to catch a glimpse of a scantily clad coed through an open door.

Or worse . . .

Ugh. I so didn't want to go *there.* The mere thought was scary and sickening and upsetting.

Drake's current address showed him living in east Fort Worth, not far from the crappy apartment complex I'd lived in before moving in with Frankie, but miles from Berkeley Place. Nevertheless, if he had several exterminator clients in Berkeley Place, he might be familiar with the area. I made a mental note to follow up with Kirstin Rumford, see if she might also be a client of the extermination service.

Having gone as far as I could with Drake for the moment, I switched my focus to Garrett Hawke. Alyssa Lowry had mentioned that Hawke had been instrumental in a few arrests, and I was curious about how things had played out, whether the reports that had been filed might give me more insight on the guy.

I'd just typed his name into the search box when—*rap, rap, rap*—Captain Leone tapped a knuckle on the glass wall that separated the admin room from the hall.

"Luz!" he called, his voice muffled through the glass. "Get your butt over here!"

I stood and stepped over to the wall.

He slapped a piece of paper up against the glass. *Smack!*

I look at the document. It was the report I'd filed on the dine-and-dash at the pancake house.

With his free hand, he pointed to the report. "What the hell is this?"

"It's iambic pentameter, sir." Well, all but the last line. I'd flubbed and put an extra syllable there. But I suppose that's precisely the type of thing allowed by poetic license, right?

One of the captain's crazy brows arched, as if preparing to break through the glass and come for me. I took an instinctive step back. If Captain Leone didn't like that report, he certainly wouldn't enjoy the automobile accident reports I'd written last week. My ode to the

Oldsmobile. My sonnet for the Sonata. My limerick about the Lincoln.

The captain just shook his head and said, "Check in with Detective Bustamente."

"Yes, sir."

I exited the room and walked farther down the hall to the detective offices. Bustamente had seniority and thus had a corner office, complete with a view of the station's parking lot and a half-dead Indian Hawthorn bush. *Ah, the perks of public service.*

I found the detective engaged in a battle with his desk phone, the long cord having wound itself into a series of impossible knots, giving him an approximate and unworkable four-inch range. I rapped on the door frame. "Any luck on Lubbock Avenue? Anybody see Hurley's car parked there?"

"Nope," he replied. "Nobody saw anything."

"Darn."

"Darn, indeed." He waved me in.

As I stepped into his office, my eyes landed on enlarged photographs spread across his desk. The photos depicted a fiftyish woman matted with blood from what appeared to be a bullet wound in the side of her head. My knees turned to noodles and I had to put out a hand to stop myself from wilting to the floor. My voice squeaked through my tight throat. "Is that the woman from San Antonio? The one who's in intensive care?"

"Yes, it is. San Antonio PD had copies overnighted to me. Sorry business, isn't it?"

The sorriest. My heart clenched in my chest. What a horrible tragedy for the woman and her grief-stricken family. I swallowed the lump of emotion in my throat. "Have they found any evidence definitively linking the shooting to Hurley?"

"Not yet. The woman's bedroom window was unlocked

and the screen was missing. There was no sign of forced entry, no defensive wounds, and no signs of a sexual assault. Her debit card is missing and a large cash withdrawal was made from her bank account shortly after the gunshot was reported by a jogger on the next block. The ATM camera footage showed a large guy in a ski mask and gloves. The same goes for the woman on Lubbock Avenue who was robbed. Whoever hit her debit card also wore a ski mask and gloves when he made the withdrawal. It's gotta be Hurley." He turned weary yet determined eyes on me. "We need to find this guy, Officer Luz. ASAP."

No pressure, huh? My heart climbed into my throat now. "Captain Leone said you wanted to see me?" I managed to squeak out.

"Yeah," the detective replied. "Give me just a second here. This darn thing's driving me nuts." He stood, unclipped the phone cord, and raised the end of the cord into the air, letting the receiver dangle and spin until the knots undid themselves. He clipped the cord back into the phone and flopped into his chair, turning his gaze on me. "I heard you responded to a couple of prowler calls in Berkeley Place this week. The president of their watch group called today."

Why am I not surprised? "What did he say?"

"The usual," the detective said. "The police department's not putting enough resources into catching whoever's been sneaking around their neighborhood."

Enough resources? I was going above and beyond, putting in unpaid overtime on behalf of the people of W1, and I didn't appreciate getting crap in return. I felt my temper begin to rise. "I got to the victim's house in record time last night. I rounded up a potential piece of evidence—a glove—and I had a tech dust the window for prints. The only ones he could lift belonged to the homeowner." I pointed at the wall, in the general direction of the administrative room. "I came in early today to research a couple of leads, and as soon as I finish I plan to head back over to Berkeley Place. Brigit tracked the prowler a couple streets over until the scent disappeared. I'm going to check in with the residents to see if anyone noticed a car parked there last night."

Bustamente dipped his head in acknowledgment. "I read your reports. You did your job, Officer Luz. Hell, you did my job, too. Nobody here thinks you've fallen short. But this Garrett Hawke's getting everyone in Berkeley Place riled up. We need to nip this thing in the bud if we can. I'm going to attend their neighborhood watch meeting tonight, and I want you to come, too."

I wasn't much in the mood to be insulted and challenged by Garrett Hawke again, but if there was anything I could do to protect the residents of W1 I'd do it. After all, I'd taken an oath to protect and serve, and there was no exception for situations involving difficult people. Besides, I was terrified for the women under my watch. If something happened to one of them, I knew I'd be forever second-guessing myself, wondering if I'd overlooked something, fallen short somehow.

"I'll be there," I said.

Bustamente gave me the time and place. "Got any ideas on leads we should look into? Assuming it wasn't Hurley, that is."

"The Lowrys' exterminator," I replied, "and Garrett Hawke."

"Hawke?" His brows rose in question. "Why him?"

"The guy looked a little damp last night. It could have been sweat—"

"Or it could have been the Lowrys' sprinklers," he said, his brows returning to their normal position.

"Right."

Bustamente cocked his head. "I'm assuming you've already done some snooping?"

"I have. But I'd like to do some more if it's okay with you." He knew I had aspirations to become a detective one day. He also knew I was willing to do any grunt work he wanted to pawn off on me. He looked at it as lightening his load and I looked it as training and mentorship. It was a win-win situation. Win-win-win if you included the residents of W1 in the mix. They were getting services above my pay grade.

"You have my blessing," the detective said. "Plus my undying gratitude." He gestured meaningfully to the towering stack of files on the end of his desk. "Let me know what you find out."

"Will do." I returned to my desk and completed my search.

Per the information provided in the responding officers' reports, none of which were nearly as eloquent as mine, Garrett Hawke had apprehended teenagers committing acts of vandalism on two occasions. On a third occasion, he had discovered a man in his early twenties using a tool to try to force the locks open on a Cadillac Escalade parked in a driveway. He'd restrained the suspect, going so far as to shackle his hands with a pair of zip ties until the police arrived. I supposed I shouldn't have been surprised that Hawke had zip ties on him. After all, he'd carried pepper spray and a gun on his belt last night. Still, securing the suspect's hands behind his back was going a bit overboard, wasn't it? Surely Hawke must have manhandled the guy to get him secured like that. That type of behavior was risky, to both Hawke and the suspect, and could easily escalate.

Ideally, a neighborhood watch should function like hall monitors in junior high, not like vigilantes or subcontractors for law enforcement. They should observe and report, not apprehend and restrain. Hawke could easily get out of hand. He seemed to want to be a hero. But there was a fine line between heroism and recklessness. I also had to wonder if he'd contacted the department with the intent to throw us off his scent, too.

Armed with information, I returned to Detective Bustamente's office.

He looked up from his desk. "Find anything on those leads?"

"Possibly." I told him about Drake's trespassing charge. "What do you think?"

"I think the prowler is someone else," he replied. "Different MO. Drake wasn't hiding in the dorm. He was in plain sight. But that doesn't mean we can rule him out. Let's you and me pay him a visit after the meeting."

"It's a plan." I returned to the desk to sign off my laptop and set out for patrol.

I swung by Hurley's sister's apartment complex. There was no sign of Hurley's car. I let Brigit out to sniff around, watching to see if she showed any signs of recognizing familiar scents. She spent a good amount of time checking out a fire hydrant and trash bag someone had left on their porch, but other than that she showed no particular interest.

A man with a little boy passed by as we headed back to the car. "Look, Daddy!" the boy cried when he spotted Brigit. "It's Scooby-Doo!"

I supposed that made me Velma or Daphne. *Hmm. Which would I rather be?* Velma had the brains I aspired to, but Daphne was hotter. I supposed I liked to consider myself a combination of the two. Reasonably attractive but with better-than-average smarts.

When I smiled at the little boy, he waved to me. "Bye, Shaggy!"

Shaggy? Sheesh. Way to feed my ego, kiddo.

Though I spoke with several residents in the vicinity of the house where Brigit had led me last night, none had noticed a car parked there. Not surprising, given the late hour and the fact that most people tended to keep their eyes glued to their television sets or computer screens once they were home. Even if someone had looked out a window, it probably would have been too dark to identify a car parked in the shadows. If nothing else, at least I'd done my due diligence.

At a quarter till seven, I pulled into the parking lot at Forest Park. Though the watch group normally met at one of the members' homes, Hawke had sent an e-mail to the residents of the neighborhood's five-hundred-plus homes and a large turnout was expected. Hence the move to the park.

The lot was beginning to fill with the vehicles of nervous residents. A mother with three young children climbed out of a minivan. Parked next to them was a Saturn Vue SUV fitted with one of those removable vinyl rear window decals. The decal depicted a cartoon mouse with a camera sitting atop a slab of Swiss cheese. SAY CHEESE! was written in large, bright yellow print over the mouse, with PORTRAITS AND SPECIAL EVENT PHOTOS/VIDEOS written in a smaller font underneath. A dark blue Mercedes was in the next spot. I pulled my cruiser into an open space on the other side of the Mercedes, let Brigit out of the back, and attached a leash to her collar.

At the far end of the parking lot sat a news van with Trish LeGrande, a field reporter from Dallas, standing behind it. Trish sported a set of perky, oversized breasts and fluffy hair the color of circus peanuts. As usual, she was dressed in her trademark pink, today wearing a tight silk dress that revealed a lot of leg and a lot of cleavage. Though she looked like a bimbo, she was too clever to be branded with the term. The woman could sensationalize the news like no one else, manipulating quotes to fit her needs, leading interviewees to say what she wanted them to say, coaxing them to reveal more than they intended.

I was surprised she'd come all the way from Dallas for this meeting. After all, it wasn't entirely clear any crimes had even been committed in Berkeley Place. For all we knew, the person who'd cried out at Alyssa Lowry's window might have been nothing more than a high-school kid jumping fences and walking through yards to take a shortcut. Really, how much valid information could be gleaned from one yelp? Then again, it could very well have been Hurley. Maybe he'd planned to nab the Lowrys' debit cards, but had been thwarted somehow. Maybe he'd spotted a neighborhood watch vehicle on patrol and decided not to risk it. And we still couldn't be sure that there hadn't been someone in the bushes at Kirstin Rumford's house.

It was frustrating not to know exactly what, and *who,* we were dealing with. Were all of these crimes attributable to Ralph Hurley? Were we dealing with two different perpetrators here? Maybe three? The possibilities seemed endless.

Brigit and I followed a fortyish couple and their two red-haired teenaged daughters as they made their way over to the open space where the meeting was to be held. Hawke had pulled his Expedition onto the grass, his neighborhood watch signs displayed on both the driver and passenger doors. As noted on the sign placed at the curb, parking on the grass was not permitted, but Hawke evidently thought his position as president of the neighborhood watch gave him some kind of diplomatic immunity. Still, I wouldn't get the large crowd rankled up by issuing their leader a citation. No sense giving them the impression that the police department wasn't on their side in this. Better if we worked together.

A hundred or more people were already there, some sitting in folding lawn chairs, others on blankets, more sitting directly on the grass. A few stood around the back edge of the group. Still more were wandering up, presumably walking over from the streets close to the park.

Garrett Hawke stood at the front, dressed in black all the way from his army boots up to his dark sunglasses. He was speaking with a tiny woman wearing heels, gray dress pants, and a lavender blazer. Her blond hair flipped up in playful layers about her head, giving her the look of a little yellow canary. She appeared to be in her late thirties or early forties. A quilted tote bag in a lively print was slung over her shoulder. A group including a dozen men and three women, presumably members of the patrol group, stood in a line behind them, a display of force.

There was no sign yet of Detective Bustamente. My eyes scanned the crowd, searching for Kirstin Rumford. My gaze fell on several women with long, dark hair before finding the right one. *There she is.*

I circled around the back of the crowd, making my way up the side to where Kirstin sat on a beach towel. She was dressed in spandex, her hair pulled up in a ponytail. The light sheen of sweat on her face told me she'd likely jogged over.

"Hi, Ms. Rumford," I greeted her, crouching down to her level.

She sat up straight. "I heard there was a peeping Tom looking in someone's windows last night. Did you catch the guy? Do you think it was the same man who was in my bushes? Do you think it's that escaped convict from down south?"

I don't know what to think. "We're working on some leads," I told her.

She slouched back. "I hope you find him soon. None of the women in our neighborhood will get a decent night's sleep until he's behind bars."

"Understandable," I agreed, though if people realized all the bad stuff that happened in the city every night no one would ever get a second of shut-eye. "You mentioned that you had roofers at your house recently. Can you tell me whether you've had other workman at your place? Maybe a painter or yard service or exterminator?"

"No." Her brow furrowed. "Why?"

I wasn't sure whether to tell her about Leonard Drake. It was unclear how solid a lead he was, and if these people thought an arrest was imminent, they'd be disappointed and upset if it didn't happen. Still, I needed to collect some facts. "Someone who works at a house can get to know the layout and the residents and their routines," I explained.

More than one unscrupulous repairman had sneakily unlocked windows at the homes where they worked, enabling them to return later to rob the families while they were out. A man who'd done some work at the home owned by Elizabeth Smart's parents was the one who'd kidnapped the Utah teen and held her hostage for months before she was thankfully found alive.

Kirstin pulled her bare knees up to her chest and wrapped her arms tightly around them. "Do you think it could have been the roofers I hired?"

"We can't rule out anything at this point," I told her, "but for what it's worth the other victim wasn't familiar with Zinniker and Sons Roofing."

She let out a shaky breath.

I realized that even if Kirstin hadn't hired an exterminator, one of her close neighbors might have. I hated to tip my hand, but I also needed to see if the exterminator might be a priority lead. "Have you seen anyone from Cowtown Critter Control in your area?"

She looked down at her shoes, as if thinking, before looking back up at me. "They're the ones with the bug eyes on top of their trucks, right?"

"That's them."

"I've seen them around a time or two"—she slowly shook her head—"but I can't say I've seen them recently."

"What about a green Isuzu Amigo with a soft top?"

Her eyes narrowed and she tilted her head, her body language indicating she wasn't familiar with the car.

"It's like a convertible SUV," I explained.

She shook her head. "I don't remember seeing anything like that."

"All right. Thanks for the information. If anything pans out, I'll be in touch."

"Thanks."

As I stood, I spotted Detective Bustamente pulling his unmarked car onto the grass next to Hawke's SUV. "C'mon, girl," I said, rousting Brigit from her prone position on the ground. She and I made our way over to meet the detective as he exited his vehicle.

"Holy cow," he said. "This is quite a group."

By now, the crowd had doubled. My best estimate told me that there were two hundred or so people crowded on the lawn.

I told Bustamente what Kirstin Rumford had said, that she'd seen Cowtown Critter Control in her neighborhood a time or two, but didn't have a recollection of seeing them recently.

"Uh-huh," he said, nodding as he appeared to be mentally filing away the information. He glanced around. "So where's this Hawke fella? *El presidente?*"

"That's him," I said, gesturing to the front of the crowd. "The one dressed in black."

Hawke paraded around in his tight T-shirt and tool belt, showing off his pecs and biceps as he greeted the latest arrivals with handshakes and shoulder pats. He was wearing a pair of dark sunglasses as if he were a movie star, but at least he wasn't wearing his gun tonight. The current city code prohibited the carrying of firearms in a city park area not designated for gun activity. Of course there was a push by gun owners to overturn that ordinance, which they deemed excessively restrictive. After all, one never knew when a rampaging horde of rabid squirrels might decide to launch an all-out attack on picnickers.

Bustamente took one look at Hawke and emitted a groan. "He looks like a man who wants to take charge."

"What you see," I told the detective, "is what you get."

TWENTY-ONE
A WALK IN THE PARK

Brigit

Woo-hoo! Brigit loved going to the park. Megan normally let her run free and play a little. No such luck tonight. Megan had attached her leash and ordered her to stay close. Still, it beat being cooped up in the back of the cruiser. Maybe they'd find a dead body here again, like they did a few weeks ago. Maybe it would have been dead even longer and Brigit could roll around on it. *Wouldn't that be great?*

As Megan led her from the back of the crowd to the front, she twitched her nose, scenting. She picked up all kinds of smells. The acrid stench of spray from a feral cat who'd marked a tree in the wooded area nearby. The greasy smell of a burger and French fries someone in the crowd had picked up for dinner. *Maybe they'd share.* Pureed green beans that had processed through an infant and were, at this very moment, being emptied into a diaper.

Her nose also picked up the smells of familiar people. The scent of the two women who lived in the houses they'd visited recently, as well as the man that lived with one of the women. That big guy up front who had followed her when they'd trailed.

A breeze kicked up, carrying with it the scent of another human, one Brigit had yet to meet, but whom she could recognize by smell with one hundred percent certainty. It was the man who'd been outside the windows at the houses Megan had taken her to, the one she'd trailed the night before. She hadn't been able to lead Megan to him last night because the trail had ended in the street. But Brigit could take her partner to him now. Maybe she'd even get that liver treat Megan owed her.

Brigit tugged on the leash, trying to lead Megan over to the man. But Megan ordered Brigit to stop pulling and to heel. Looked like Megan had changed her mind and was no longer interested in the man.

Brigit sighed. *So much for that liver treat.*

TWENTY-TWO
IT'S MY PARTY

Tom

Everyone was gathered here because of *him*. The thought made him want to laugh. In fact, this gathering gave him an easy opportunity to watch Kirstin Rumford and Alyssa Lowry up close, without a pane of glass or screen between them. With his dark sunglasses on, nobody would be able to tell where his eyes were looking.

Kirstin had her hair pulled up in a ponytail tonight. He would've preferred it down. But at least she was dressed in a skimpy tank top and a pair of shorts that barely covered her butt and left him lots of leg to take in, inch after luscious inch . . .

Alyssa, on the other hand, had worn a big, loose jumpsuit that left everything to the imagination. She might as well be wearing overalls or a burka. No problem, though. He knew what was under that fabric and he had plenty of imagination. He could mentally undress her.

But wait. Who is that woman with the long dark hair pushing the Rabinowitz baby in the stroller?

He hadn't seen her before. But he'd sure as hell take a good look now.

It's my party and I'll spy if I want to . . .

TWENTY-THREE
CLONES

Megan

Bustamente, Brigit, and I made our way to the front, where I introduced the detective to Garrett Hawke.

"We appreciate you coming out," Hawke said. "Our people are sure to have some questions for you."

I was glad the detective was here to answer them. I didn't mind standing up here in front of a crowd, but I didn't like speaking in front of them. I couldn't trust my stutter to stay at bay. Though the speech impediment didn't get in the way of me doing my job, if someone misinterpreted my shutter as an anxious stammer, it could undermine my appearance of authority.

The small blonde in the lavender blazer stepped closer to us, her heels drilling down into the soft grass and dirt. Definitely not the best shoes for walking in the park. As she stepped up, I realized just how tiny she was. She stood five feet one at best in the heels, and would be only four feet ten without them. A tiny little Tinkerbell sans the lime-green strapless minidress.

She stuck out her hand to Bustamente. "I'm Nora Conklin. Secretary for the watch."

The detective had been introduced by Garrett Hawke

earlier and didn't bother mentioning his name again. "Pleasure," he said.

After they'd exchanged a handshake, Nora turned to me and extended her hand.

"Officer Megan Luz," I said. I shook her hand, then cocked my head to indicate the partner on my side. "This is m-my partner, Brigit."

Nora put her hands on her knees and bent over to speak to Brigit. "Aren't you a cutie?"

Brigit wagged her tail and gave a soft *woof* in agreement.

Nora stood and reached into the breast pocket of her blazer, pulling out two business cards. With a gleaming smile, she handed one to the detective, the other to me. "I'm in real estate. Conklin and Associates. I'm sure you've heard of us?"

I hadn't, and I suspected Detective Bustamente hadn't, either. Nonetheless, we offered assurances.

"Sure."

"Of course."

I looked down at the card in my hand. It featured a pastel blue cartoon door on a pale yellow background, along with the slogan CONKLIN & ASSOCIATES REALTORS. TAKING PEOPLE HOME SINCE 2004. Provocative, maybe, but clever. The business card also featured a nice head shot of Nora wearing a blue blouse and a broad smile. Under the head shot, in minuscule print, was © SAY CHEESE! INC. Looked like she'd utilized her neighbor's photography services. Maybe he offered a discount to fellow members of the watch.

"If you know anyone who's looking to buy a house," Nora said, "send them my way. I might be small, but I mean business!" She wagged her brows for emphasis and offered a lilting laugh.

Trish LeGrande and her cameraman stepped up to us. Though Trish and I had crossed paths before, she showed no signs of recognition when her eyes met mine. She turned to address Hawke, first giving him a once-over, clearly impressed by what she saw. "I hear you're in charge of the neighborhood watch. Got a second for a quick interview?"

He removed his dark sunglasses, tucked them into his shirt pocket, and offered her a broad smile. "I've got all the time you need."

Ugh. Brigit might have been the one to throw up a few days ago, but I was the one tempted to toss my cookies now.

Trish turned to stand next to Hawke and motioned for her cameraman to start rolling.

"I'm here in Fort Worth," she said, "with Garrett Hawke, president of the Berkeley Place Neighborhood Watch. Stay tuned for an exclusive interview you'll see only on our station."

Exclusive interview? Looked like Trish had manipulated things to her advantage again. But I had to wonder who'd called her station with the tip, and how they'd convinced her it was a story worth telling. While all of the outlets had covered the robbery in Frisco Heights, other local media hadn't deemed a couple of prowling incidents newsworthy. If I had to hazard a guess, I'd say it was Hawke himself who'd contacted the station. The guy seemed to enjoy being the center of attention.

Trish continued her lead-in. "Residents of Berkeley Place were terrorized this week when an unknown suspect prowled the neighborhood, presumably watching women through their bedroom windows. Mr. Hawke, what can you tell me about the incidents?"

"In both cases," he said, "the victims were unaware that they were being watched. The first victim discovered broken limbs on bushes outside her window the following morning. The second heard the suspect shout when her automatic sprinklers turned on and surprised him."

Trish looked up at him, batting her eyes. "I'm sure the women of Berkeley Place appreciate having someone like you in charge of protecting them."

"I'm happy to serve," Hawke replied with a nod.

The exchange was so overdone it was nauseating. I looked away, lest my expression betray my emotions. It was then my eyes spotted a paunchy, silver-haired man sitting in the front row. His arm might be draped across the shoulders of his wife sitting next to him, but his gaze was locked on Trish's ample chest. *Dirty old man.* My hand went instinctively to the handle of my baton. I'd like to give the guy a nice *whap*, tell him to put his eyes back in his head.

"Is there anything else you'd like to tell our viewers?" Trish asked Hawke.

Hawke expanded like a pufferfish, sticking his chest out and flexing his biceps for the camera. "I can tell you that the watch will not rest until we apprehend the person responsible." He looked directly into the camera. "If that person happens to be watching this newscast right now, be forewarned. The watch is coming for you."

Talk about melodrama. I fought the urge to roll my eyes. But no sense making anyone think I wasn't taking the case seriously. I was. I just thought that Garrett Hawke might be overreacting, making a mountain out of a couple of molehills.

Then again, an ounce of prevention is worth a pound of cure. Who knows? There was nothing certain in law enforcement. Criminals could be unpredictable. If there truly was a peeping Tom in Berkeley Place, we had no way of knowing whether the suspect was merely a voyeur who'd remain satisfied ogling women through their windows, or whether he might become disenchanted with merely spying on women and go on to something worse. I hoped he'd stick with ogling. And, of course, there was always the chance that the broken bushes at Kirstin Rumford's house and the cry outside the Lowrys' bedroom window were unrelated, or that my theory about teenagers cutting through yards was correct. At this point, all we had were a bunch of theories and virtually no concrete clues.

Nora Conklin slipped between Hawke and Trish and flashed her gleaming smile at the camera. "I'm Nora Conklin, secretary for the Berkeley Place Neighborhood Watch and owner of Conklin and Associates Realtors. Now is the perfect time to buy or sell a home in Fort Worth. Just give me a call!" She rattled off her phone number for the camera.

Trish looked down at the tiny Tinkerbell and frowned, obviously not appreciating Nora's attempt to use the newscast for free promotion. I had no doubt Nora and her impromptu commercial would end up on the cutting-room floor.

When Trish turned to Detective Bustamente, he motioned to the camera. "Would you like a statement from Fort Worth PD?"

Trish looked the detective up and down, her expression telling us just how she felt. Bustamente lacked the star quality Trish liked to feature in her broadcasts. "No, thanks," she replied. "I've got what I need." As she turned away, she spotted Brigit sitting beside me and gestured to her cameraman. "Get a shot of the dog."

The man lowered his camera to Brigit's level. As if realizing she was being taped, she hammed it up for the camera, wagging her tail and offering a playful growl and a bark. *Grrr-woof!*

When the cameraman turned his viewfinder back on

her, Trish said, "Stay tuned to hear more about the Berkeley Place Peeper as details develop."

Berkeley Place Peeper? I wasn't sure the name fit. For one, though the suspect might have been engaging in voyeurism, it wasn't entirely clear the prowler had been at the windows to watch the women, or whether his motives might have been robbery or something even more sinister and violent. It was possible the prowler had been Hurley, casing his next victim. I understood the reporter was going for memorable sound bites, but putting a label on the culprit could mislead the public. Of course there wasn't anything I could do about it. It's not like I had any concrete evidence about the prowler's motives.

The brief interview complete, Hawke glanced at his black sports watch and said, "Let's roll."

Nora took a step forward and clapped her hands loudly three times to get the crowd's attention before cupping her hands around her mouth. "Attention!" she snapped, sounding like a military drill sergeant. "Time to get started."

The murmurs died down instantly. Nora might be little, but she had a big presence. She stepped aside, giving Hawke the floor. Or should I say "the grass"?

"As you know," Hawke bellowed to the crowd as he paced to his left, "two women who live in Berkeley Place were violated this week."

Though "violated" wasn't necessarily inaccurate, it seemed a strong word choice and could be misinterpreted by the crowd as something more than mere peeping. At the same time, this was Hawke's show. I supposed he could use poetic license when it came to word choices. And, while peeping alone might not be much of a crime, it wasn't clear whether a mere look-see was all the suspect was going after. The situation had the potential to escalate. I could only hope we'd catch the creep before it did.

My eyes scanned the audience, taking in the women, wondering if one of them might be the next victim. A sick feeling filled my gut at the thought.

Hawke paced in the other direction. "Some creep has been watching women through their bedroom windows. It's possible these incidents were committed by the same man who robbed a home in Frisco Heights earlier this week and shot a hole in the victim's wall. We need to make sure the residents of Berkeley Place are safe, and we will. I'm as committed to this as I was to a successful mission when my paratrooper unit was deployed to Iraq."

His comment earned generous applause, as well as whistles and whoops of appreciation.

"To that end," Hawke continued, "I've invited Detective Bustamente from the Fort Worth Police Department to speak to you about their investigation."

With that, he stepped to the side and raised a hand, inviting the detective to address the crowd. Next to me, the detective took a step forward. Several people looked him up and down. None looked as impressed as they had when Garrett Hawke had stood before them.

"Ladies and gentlemen," Bustamente began, "we want to assure you that Fort Worth PD is taking these crimes seriously and will do what we can to catch the person or persons responsible. We had our crime scene specialists analyze fingerprints that were obtained at the scene. Unfortunately, the only ones that were found belonged to the residents. In the meantime, I suggest that all of you turn on your outside lights at night, double-check that all of your doors and windows are securely locked before going to bed, and keep your entry alarms set at all times." With that, he stepped back into place beside me.

The man with the two red-haired daughters stood. "That's it?" he called out, disdain and disbelief in his voice. "Turn on our lights and lock our doors? I don't want some pervert setting his sights on my girls!"

The girls shrank back on the grass, embarrassed that their father was making such a scene, too young to realize how lucky they were to have a father who was looking out for them. Not every child was so lucky.

Bustamente raised a hand to calm the crowd, which had exploded in angry muttering. "We plan to beef up patrols in the area. An additional officer has been assigned to night duty and will focus on your neighborhood."

Hawke took his place in front of the crowd again. "The neighborhood watch is also 'beefing up patrols,'" he said, borrowing the detective's words. "Starting tonight, we'll have *three* extra volunteers assigned to each night shift." He held up three fingers for emphasis and sent a cutting glance over at me and Bustamente.

A gray-haired woman stood from her lawn chair and called out to Bustamente. "What about the sex offenders who live around here? Are you planning on bringing any of them in for questioning?"

"If evidence leads us to suspect a registered sex offender has committed a crime," Bustamente replied, "we will certainly look into it."

"But *only* if you get further evidence?" the woman asked. "You don't plan to question any of them now?"

Bustamente explained that voyeurism, the act of spying on someone for a lewd purpose, was considered disorderly conduct under Texas Penal Code Section 42.01. "It's classified as a Class C misdemeanor, punishable by a fine of up to five hundred dollars but no jail time. It's not an offense for which a convicted person has to register as a sex offender."

"Well, it sure as hell should be!" hollered the angry dad.

The crowd broke out in buzz of outrage. Part of me couldn't blame them. A mere fine seemed insufficient to punish a creep who ogled naked women without their consent or knowledge. But another part of me thought they were shooting the messenger.

"You'll get no argument from me on that one," Bustamente said loudly, raising his hands to quell the murmuring. "We realize it can be extremely upsetting to think someone might be watching you. But remember, law enforcement is on your side here. We'll do the best we can with the resources we have available."

He couldn't promise these people the moon when we didn't have the moon to offer. The force had limited budgets and manpower, and had to allocate them primarily to high-priority crimes. We couldn't conjure up more officers from thin air.

Hawke crossed his arms over his chest. "There's nothing to prevent us from looking into the sex offenders ourselves, is there?"

"I can't stop you," Bustamente conceded, "not at this point anyway. But I'll warn you. These guys are quick to file harassment and trespassing charges. I'd rather you let the police handle this matter, but if you're going to ignore that advice, tread very lightly."

Hawke grunted. Clearly he had every intention of ignoring the detective's advice to leave the investigation to the police and absolutely no intention of treading lightly. He'd probably lace up his army boots and stomp all over the place. Of course part of me couldn't blame him. It wasn't in my nature to sit by and do nothing when I saw a danger or injustice, either.

"Help us help you," Bustamente said, wrapping up his spiel to the crowd. "If you see anything suspicious, call nine-one-one immediately to report it. But be careful.

Don't try to apprehend anyone on your own. We don't want anyone getting hurt. Okay?"

Hawke reminded residents to call the watch, too, if they saw anything suspicious. "We can be there in seconds. The police might take longer." He cast a meaningful glance my way.

Ugh. Way to undermine the people who are trying to help.

Nora stepped up next to Hawke. "Everyone be careful out there!" She clapped her hands a final time to signal that the meeting had been wrapped up. After giving the crowd a good-bye wave, she reached down into her tote bag, withdrew a stack of stapled documents, and held them out to Hawke. "Here are the new patrol schedules and updated rosters."

Bustamente angled his head to indicate the woman. "Let's get ourselves a copy."

We stepped over.

"Got copies you can spare?" the detective asked.

"Sure do. I made extras." The woman riffled through the documents, which were now in Hawke's hands. She handed two documents to Bustamente, and a second set of the same two documents to me.

My eyes took in the top pages. The first was entitled NEIGHBORHOOD WATCH SCHEDULE and contained a calendar. While there was only one last name listed per shift on the dates preceding today, starting with tonight there were eight last names listed for each day, four of which were assigned to the earlier 9 P.M.—1 A.M. shift, the other four of which were assigned to the 1 A.M.—5A.M. shift. Each member's cell phone number was listed next to his or her name.

The second document was entitled BERKELEY PLACE ROSTER. It was a lengthy document with names and contact information organized both alphabetically and by street. Under each address, the name of the homeowner and all residents of the house were listed, along with e-mail addresses and phone numbers. Someone had gone to a lot of work to pull this information together. I had to give these people credit for being so organized and neighborly. Heck, I hadn't exchanged more than a word or two with my new neighbors, let alone names and contact information. The only thing I knew was that the rat terrier who lived to our left was named Speedy. I'd heard the neighbors call his name a few times when he'd been out in the backyard.

The silver-headed ogler in the front row had folded his chair and set out across the grass. I gestured to him. "Do you know that man's name?"

"Sure do," Nora said. "That's Victor Paludo. He's one of our most reliable volunteers. Why?"

Why? Because he gave off a pervy vibe, that's why. But I couldn't very well accuse him with no other evidence than the fact that his gaze had been locked on Trish's chest during her entire report. Heck, for all I knew he was nearsighted and hadn't even realized where he'd been looking. "He looked familiar is all."

"Got one of those faces, I suppose," she said, unconcerned. "Anyway, it was nice meeting you, Officer Luz. Bye, now." With that, Nora turned and traipsed back across the grass in her heels, making her way over to a brown-haired man who stood in the shade of the trees. He looked to be around my height. Five feet five wasn't short for a woman, but was definitely on the smaller side for a guy. Still, with his shorter stature, he seemed perfectly sized for Nora. The two made a cute couple, like little dollhouse people.

Another woman stepped up then, one who was taller than average and had long, black hair. She put a hand on

Hawke's shoulder. "The kids asked if we can order pizza. Is that okay with you?"

"Go ahead," Hawke said, "but tell the kids I expect to find their rooms clean when I get home."

"All right." The woman slid her hand down Hawke's back and gave him a circular rub. "See you back at the house, hon."

As she stepped away, he called, "Get me some garlic knots!"

I might not have made detective yet, but I could put these obvious clues together and determine that the woman was Hawke's wife. It was the only clue I'd managed to decipher in this investigation so far.

Bustamente and I turned and headed back to our cars.

Once we were out of earshot, Bustamente glanced back at Hawke. "There's something off about that guy."

I agreed that there was something *off* about him. He was *off*-putting. A show-*off*. Maybe even a bit of a jerk-*off*.

As I was pondering the detective's comment, Derek Mackey stormed up, his face nearly as red as his flaming hair. "Why wasn't I told about this meeting?"

He was probably angry he'd missed out on a chance to play hotshot in front of the crowd. Mackey had played both football and baseball in his high school days, and still lived for glory. Sometimes I think he'd become a cop more for the accolades and attention than because he had any real desire to serve the community or make the world a better, safer place.

Bustamente looked up at Derek. "There was no need to call you," the detective said dully. "Officer Luz and I had it covered."

Derek wasn't just unpopular with his fellow street officers, he was disliked by those up the chain as well. At least as far up the chain as the assistant chief. The police chief, on the other hand, considered Derek his golden boy. The two were also hunting buddies, joined at the grip.

Derek looked from the detective to me. "Next time there's something big going on, you need to let all of the officers in W1 know. I'd hate to have to tell the chief about your lousy communication."

I didn't appreciate his insinuation that Bustamente and I had purposely kept our coworkers in the dark, or his implied threat to tattle to the chief. I was doing my job the best I could and so was Detective Bustamente. The detective and Captain Leone had put sufficient resources into what at this point was technically only a trespassing/peeping Tom case. If things escalated, more would certainly be done. But for now, we all had followed both common sense and established protocols.

I decided to try some reverse psychology with Derek. "Wouldn't a big guy like you rather be out on the streets busting skulls than picnicking in the park with a bunch of nervous nellies?"

He narrowed his eyes at me as if trying to assess whether I was being sincere or was full of crap. I was both. Sincerely full of crap.

Bustamente turned his back on Derek and asked, "Ready to pay Leonard Drake a visit?"

"Sure am," I replied.

Was it too much to ask that Drake would confess to ogling the women right off the bat, that we could announce the crime had been solved, and that Garrett Hawke and I would never cross paths again?

Evidently it was, indeed, too much to ask.

Three times we rang the bell at Drake's apartment. Three times we followed up with a lengthy knock. Three times the only response we got was from a lazy beagle inside. He pushed back the curtain at the bottom of the window and issued a halfhearted bark. *Wooh.* Deciding that he'd fulfilled his watchdog duties, he left the window, presumably to go lie on the couch.

Bustamente heaved a sigh. "Looks like we'll have to check back later."

We'd driven separate cars to Drake's place, so we parted ways in the parking lot.

Bustamente raised his hand in parting as he plopped into the driver's seat of his unmarked cruiser. "Have a safe patrol, Officer Luz."

"Will do."

Once again I cruised by Hurley's sister's apartment, and once again I saw nothing to give me pause. Had Hurley stashed his car somewhere out of sight nearby? Was he hiding out at his sister's place? Time would tell. Eventually, Hurley's luck had to run out again. I only hoped luck would stay on the side of his potential victims.

It was nearing nine o'clock and twilight settled in as Brigit and I drove back to the Berkeley Place neighborhood. I rolled down the windows on the squad car, partially to enjoy the cool evening air, but even more so to listen for telltale sounds of a prowler. Footsteps. Feet scrabbling on fence boards. Dogs growling or barking.

I drove slowly and deliberately up and down the streets, occasionally shining my spotlight into the dark areas between houses, determined to show the residents that we were being true to our promise to amp up patrols. The streets seemed better lit than usual, the residents having heeded our advice to turn on their outside lights. If there was anything criminals didn't like, it was lights shining on them, exposing them, giving them fewer places to hide.

A police cruiser came up the street from the opposite direction. Before I could see who was driving it, I raised my fingers off my steering wheel in my standard friendly greeting. In return I was greeted by a blast of high beams.

Despite being temporarily blinded, I could identify the nasty cackle my fellow officer emitted from his open window as he drove past.

Derek Mackey.

Ugh.

He and Garrett Hawke were cut from the same cloth. Arrogant. Unreasonable. Uncompromising. Still, they worked to protect others. I had to give them that, even if I thought their reasons were less about concern for others and more about basking in hero worship.

I continued on, hooking a right onto Patton Court, which backed up to the Burlington Northern and Santa Fe railroad tracks. Though the night was now too dark for me to see it, I could hear the sounds of a slow-moving freight train as it rolled along toward the main rail yard on Vickery. *Clack-clack-CLACK-clack.* Thankfully, the conductor didn't lay on the horn. Brigit didn't like the sound and would send up a wail of her own when she heard one.

As I circled around at the end of the court, something dawned on me. *Hawke's wife.* She resembled the two peeping victims. Caucasian. Tall. Long, dark hair. I'd surmised when I'd first met Alyssa Lowry that the peeping Tom had a type—assuming, of course, that there even was a peeping Tom. If there was, looked like Tom and Garrett Hawke had something in common.

But could they have more in common?

Could they be one and the same?

I pulled to a stop, put the gearshift in park, and turned on the inside light. I reached over to the passenger seat and retrieved the calendar the tiny woman had given me. Though the calendar indicated it had been revised today, May 7, it showed the schedule for the entire month, including the preceding days when only one person had been assigned to each watch shift.

On Monday the fourth, the night before Kirstin Rumford had summoned the police, a man named Victor Paludo had been scheduled for the 9 P.M. to 1 A.M. shift. Garrett Hawke had worked the 1 A.M. to 5 A.M. shift. Of course we had no way of knowing precisely when during the night the peeping Tom had been in Kirstin Rumford's bushes, if, in fact, he'd been in them at all. Last night, both Paludo and Hawke had been assigned to the earlier shift, the shift during which someone had been at Alyssa Lowry's window. Still, those two particular men had been on duty both nights.

Was it coincidence? Or was it *evidence*?

TWENTY-FOUR
LEFT UNTREATED

Brigit

Pathetic.

The word might be too complex for Brigit to comprehend, but she understood the concept. It described the beagle at the apartment they'd visited earlier. Some watchdog he'd been, issuing that soft, lazy bark. Heck, that sound wouldn't scare a newborn kitten, let alone a police dog and two full-grown humans. *What a wimp.*

She wasn't sure why Megan had stopped the cruiser, but the lack of motion often meant they were about to get out of the car and go to work. Brigit lived for those times. She loved to sniff and trail and chase. Besides, she wanted a liver treat, doggone it! Megan hadn't given her an edible reward in what seemed like forever. Praise was nice. A butt scratch was even better. But nothing beat a liver treat. Brigit knew she was more likely to receive a treat if Megan asked her to perform a task.

Brigit stood in the back of the car and eyed Megan, looking for signs that her canine skills would be needed. Megan stared at a piece of paper, making no move to reach for the door handle.

Rats.

Brigit flopped down on her belly, rested her chin on her paws, and heaved a loud sigh.

TWENTY-FIVE
LUST AT FIRST SIGHT

Tom

He lay in bed Thursday night after the neighborhood watch meeting, daydreaming about the Rabinowitzes' au pair.

Au what a *pair* she had . . .

He couldn't have her. Not yet anyway. With both the police department and the neighborhood watch increasing patrols he couldn't risk venturing to her window.

Looked like he'd have to find another way to fulfill his needs for the next few days.

TWENTY-SIX
PEEPHOLE

Megan

After realizing that both Garrett Hawke and Victor Paludo had been on watch duty the nights of the prowler/peeper incidents, I'd run criminal background checks on both of them. Both men were clean, at least in the sense that they'd never been arrested for a serious crime. Hawke had an arrest from his much younger days for public intoxication, though the charges had not been pursued by the district attorney, who had much bigger fish to fry. If I had to hazard a guess, I'd say Hawke had probably been out drinking with buddies and gotten a little rowdy. It happens. Heck, in Texas an arrest for public intoxication was virtually a rite of passage for young men. Most times we tossed the offenders in the drunk tank, let them dry out overnight, and released them in the mornings, their hangovers constituting their punishment.

At half past six Friday evening, Brigit and I met Detective Bustamente in the parking lot of Leonard Drake's apartment building.

The detective pointed to a toffee-brown Jetta parked nearby. "That's his vehicle."

So Drake was home. Presumably.

The Jetta sported a purple bumper sticker with white lettering that spelled MY DAUGHTER AND MY MONEY GO TO TCU. He also had a sticker of the horned frog mascot on his back window. He appeared to be a proud papa. The only question was, *Is he also a peeping Tom?*

It was one of life's ironies. Sometimes even the worst criminals had a good side. I'd learned that early on in my law enforcement career. A gangbanger who'd shot up a member of a rival gang might be a devoted son or brother. A woman with a dozen shoplifting offenses might rescue stray, starving cats. A teenager caught with crystal meth could be the lead tenor in his church choir. The penal code, in a sense, imposed a set of societal morals, but everyone had their own personal code that guided their behavior. Some people imposed a more restrictive moral code on themselves. Others bent the official rules, following only those they agreed with.

What code does Leonard Drake live by?

With some luck, we'd soon find out.

We headed toward the apartment.

"Any word on the shooting case in San Antonio?" I asked, the images of the woman still vivid in my mind.

"None."

I was almost too afraid to ask the next question. "How is she doing?"

He released a long, weary breath. "No improvement. But no decline, either."

Though I sometimes prepared myself for the worst so that I wouldn't be as shocked when it happened, a big part of me wanted to look on the bright side here, to acknowledge that she was hanging on and that could mean she'd survive.

The detective and I reached Drake's door. After he knocked, both of us instinctively turned sideways to make ourselves a smaller target and to be poised to run.

For all we knew, the guy could be some type of wack-job who intended to open fire through the door. The beagle reached the door first, treating us to another soft, lazy *wooh* from the other side. Brigit didn't bother snuffling the threshold. She didn't seem interested in the dog.

A moment later, a male voice came from inside. "Who is it?"

Bustamente and I exchanged glances. The door had a peephole and it was still fully light outside. Surely the guy knew exactly who was on his doorstep. I found it ironic that here we were, wanting to speak to this man and determine whether he'd been peeping in on women, and now he was peeping out at us.

"Fort Worth Police Department," the detective said. "We need your help, Mr. Drake."

"With what?" the man called through the door.

Bustamente cut a glance my way. "It would be easier to speak if you'd open the door, sir."

Several silent seconds passed in which Drake was probably debating whether he wanted to open the door. Eventually he acquiesced, opening the door just far enough to poke his head through. "What do you need help with?"

In case Drake said something that gave us probable cause to arrest him, it would have been better for me and the detective if the man stepped outside where we could conveniently handcuff him. Perhaps Drake knew that from his earlier arrest and didn't want to make things easy on us. Still, he would be within his rights to refuse to talk to us at all. Sometimes it was better not to push your luck and to take what you could get.

Bustamente got right to the crux of the matter. "A customer of Cowtown Critter Control had a prowler outside their house this week. We're wondering if you know anything about that."

Drake's eyes narrowed and his body became rigid. "Like what? What could I know about it?"

Bustamente shrugged. "You were all around the house spraying for bugs. We hoped maybe you saw something."

The detective's technique was clever. Rather than making Drake think he was a suspect, he was leading the man to believe we were only interested in him as a potential witness.

Drake's posture relaxed and he opened the door a little more. His beagle ventured out onto the porch and raised his nose to sniff at Brigit's chin. She ignored him, instead focusing her attention on Drake, her nostrils flaring as she took in his scent. Did she recognize it from the bushes at the Rumford and Lowry homes? If only she could tell me. Too bad she didn't speak English. Or that I didn't speak canine.

Drake cocked his head. "Which house was it?"

"The Lowry home," Bustamente replied.

"Lowry?" Drake repeated. "That name doesn't ring a bell."

Bustamente checked his notes and rattled off the address. "It's in Berkeley Place."

"Berkeley Place isn't in my usual zone."

"I understand," the detective said. "The homeowners said you're not their regular tech. You were filling in for someone?"

"That's right. One of the other guys was out on vacation and the rest of us divvied up his calls this week." His mouth turned up in a smile. "Collected some sweet overtime."

Overtime pay. Hmm . . . I remembered Mrs. Lowry saying that Drake had taken much longer than their usual tech. I'd assumed it had been so he could case the place. But if he were paid by the hour, had he slowed down on purpose simply to get a bigger paycheck?

Bustamente continued. "Mrs. Lowry said she spoke to you. She mentioned she was a music teacher, gave piano lessons in her home."

Drake shook his head. "Still doesn't ring a bell. I make small talk with all the customers. You know, to make them more comfortable."

His small talk had done anything *but* make Alyssa Lowry more comfortable. Still, the guy inhaled a lot of chemical fumes all day long. Maybe the toxins had killed a few too many of his brain cells.

"What did the house look like?" Drake asked.

"Two-story Tudor," the detective said.

Drake looked up as if trying to visualize the house. "I think I remember that one. Bad fire ant problem, right?"

Bustamente cut a questioning look my way.

"I'm not sure what their issue was," I said. Perhaps I should've asked. It hadn't seemed like a relevant fact at the time.

"If it's the house I'm thinking of," Drake replied, "I didn't notice anything odd there. 'Course I was only looking for ants."

"Understood." Bustamente bobbed his head slowly a few times, a habit that meant he was buying himself some time as he decided how to proceed. "Mr. Drake, I'm aware that you had a criminal trespassing charge a while back."

Drake's eyes flashed with anger and alarm and he stood up straight. "My attorney settled that with the prosecutor."

"What happened?"

Drake was quiet a moment, his face pensive. My guess was that he was wondering whether he should call his attorney before speaking about the case.

Bustamente raised a palm. "That matter is a done deal. There's no double jeopardy. You can't be tried again. I'm just wondering what you were doing in an all-girls' dorm without permission."

"My nineteen-year-old daughter lives in that dorm," Drake spat. "I'm spending every penny I have, working all the overtime I can get, and eating peanut butter sandwiches for dinner every night to send her to that expensive school, and she's just playing around and having fun and getting a bunch of Cs and Ds. Her mother—my ex—won't do jack shit about it, and when I tried to talk to my daughter about it on the phone she hung up on me. Ignored me every time I tried to call or text her after that. I had no choice but to try to track her down and tell her she had to get her act together or I'd cut her off."

"But why not check in at the front desk?" Bustamente asked. "Go through the proper channels at the dorm?"

Drake snorted. "If my daughter knew I was there she would've refused to come down. It would've been a waste of my time."

He'd come up with the story quickly. It was surely the same one he'd given his defense attorney. It made sense, though it still didn't excuse him going into an all-girls dorm without permission. But I could see how an overworked father could be angry enough under those circumstances to ignore the visitation rules.

Evidently Bustamente felt the same way. He thanked Mr. Drake for his time, even wished him a good weekend. Drake didn't return the sentiment, but at least he didn't slam the door in our faces when he closed it.

As we returned to our cars, I asked, "Are you going to cross him off the list of potential suspects?"

"Not quite yet," Bustamente said, "though my gut tells me he's not our guy."

"My gut's saying the same thing."

I looked down at Brigit. "What's your gut saying, girl?"

TWENTY-SEVEN
GROWLS

Brigit

What's my gut telling me? It was telling her that it was empty and that Megan had better give her a liver treat soon or Brigit was going to make herself a royal pain in the rear until she got what she wanted. She knew how to do it, too. Claw at the mesh in the car. Bark incessantly. Whine in that shrill way that made humans cringe. Snuffle at Megan's pocket to give her dumb partner the unmistakable hint that she was way overdue for a treat. Seriously, how could Brigit be expected to work under these deplorable conditions? Weren't there canine labor laws?

Fortunately, Megan was good at reading clues. All it took was a growl from Bright's belly, another from her throat, and a snuffle at her partner's pocket for Megan to give in.

"Okay, girl," Megan said, reaching into her pocket, "but just one treat. You're supposed to be on a diet."

When her partner pulled out a liver treat, Brigit wagged her tail to say *It's about time!*

Megan tossed the treat her way and Brigit snapped it out of the air with a *chomp.*

TWENTY-EIGHT
STARRY, STARRY NIGHT

Tom

He sat in front of his laptop, watching a porn movie called *Shear Pleasure* that featured a trio of dark-haired hairstylists who gave their male customers some good *trim*.

Unfortunately, the movie wasn't working for him at all. The young women on-screen, though pretty and stacked, couldn't act for shit. The sounds they made were so contrived and insincere. *Ooooh. Aaaah. Uhhhh.* It was like they were playing *Wheel of Fortune* with only vowels.

He exited the movie and closed his laptop.

How long would he have to wait before he could venture out again?

TWENTY-NINE
BAD LANDINGS AND BUSTED KNEECAPS

Megan

Early Saturday afternoon, I once again caught Frankie feeding junk food to Brigit. This time it was Fritos.

"She's got to lose weight!" I said, snatching the bag away. "Those extra pounds are bad for her joints."

Frankie frowned up at me from the couch. "I feel cruel sitting here snacking and not giving her any. She keeps looking at me with those big brown eyes and it's impossible to say no."

I sighed, handed the bag back to my roommate, and flopped down on the couch. "I know what you mean. She sure knows how to sucker people."

"What if I take her out for some exercise?" Frankie suggested. "I could skate and she could run along with me. That would burn a bunch of calories."

It was the perfect solution. Though I sometimes took Brigit jogging with me, she always wanted to go faster and farther than I was able. But on roller skates, Frankie would be able to go as fast and far as Brigit wanted. Luckily, Brigit knew to stay beside the person leading her, so at least I didn't have to worry about her crossing in front of Frankie and getting her paws run over or tripping my roommate.

"That would be great, Frankie," I said. "I'll grab her leash."

Frankie rounded up her skates from her bedroom while I clipped the lead on Brigit. A minute later, they were ready to go. I walked out to the driveway to see them off.

"Be back in a few!" Frankie called, setting off down the street.

Brigit bolted along beside her, clearly enjoying the high speed.

While they were gone, I figured I'd mow our small lawn. The front was mostly ivy, but the back had some grass, at least in the spots where Brigit had yet to dig holes. Frankie's boyfriend had taken their lawn mower when he'd moved out, and we'd been making do with a weed whacker. But I'd figured it was time to get some real equipment so I'd ordered a mechanical lawn mower online. It was an old-fashioned model that required no gasoline and thus wouldn't pollute the environment. It would be cheaper to operate, too, and much less noisy.

I went to the garage and used a flathead screwdriver to cut through the tape on the box. Luckily, the mower required minimal assembly. Four bolts later and the thing was ready for its maiden voyage.

I opened the gate and set off across the backyard, the mower giving off a *whip-whip-whip* sound as it sent cut grass into the air. *Not bad.*

I made my way back and forth across the yard, occasionally having to clear clumps of grass from the blades. As I performed the task, my mind mulled over important topics. How police and detective work could be both incredibly rewarding and absolutely frustrating. How it would be a great idea if the Berkeley Place Neighborhood

Watch hosted a women's self-defense course. How cutting the grass was like shaving Mother Earth's legs.

"Where'd you get that mower?" Frankie called from the back door when she and Brigit returned a half hour later. "Nineteen fifty?"

I ignored her jab and the chuckle that followed it. "How'd it go?"

"Great!" she said. "Until she stopped to sniff a fire hydrant and I tripped over a curb."

"Ouch."

She waved a dismissive hand. "That's what knee pads are for."

Brigit pushed past Frankie and trotted out into the yard. She proceeded to gulp down the entire contents of her water bowl and flopped down in the shade, happily exhausted.

"Thanks for taking her," I told Frankie.

"Thank *you* for getting me a date tonight."

Seth had found a friend for Frankie and the two of us planned to double-date that evening. I hoped Frankie and Zach would hit it off. Frankie deserved to have a nice guy in her life.

At eight that night, Seth picked me and Frankie up in his Nova, leaving Blast behind at our house to keep Brigit and Zoe company. We left the *Animal Planet* channel on for their entertainment. Every time the chimp on the screen chittered, Blast cocked his head, his ears pricked, trying to make sense of the unfamiliar sound. So cute.

"Zach's going to meet us at the VFW," Seth said as he leaned the front bench seat of his Nova forward so Frankie could slide into the back.

"The VFW?" She paused at the door, frowning. "Isn't that for old farts who want to relive their glory days over beer and shuffleboard?"

I'd had the same thought. I'd just had the sense not to say it out loud.

Seth took the slight in stride. "Sometimes. But other times, like tonight, they bring in a band. It can be a lot of fun."

"If you say so," she replied, skepticism lacing her words. She gathered up her skirt and slipped into the back.

We made small talk as we drove over to the VFW hall on White Settlement Road, not far from the military reserve base. Seth's army buddy Zach was waiting in the lot when we arrived. He was tall, as requested, standing at least six feet two. He had a trim but muscular build. He wore black boots, jeans, and a long-sleeved gray shirt rolled up to the elbows. Like Seth, his hair was cut in a short, military style. But where Seth's hair was blond, Zach's was dark brown.

Frankie stuck her head over the seat, virtually salivating, the same thing the dogs did when we pulled into a fast-food hamburger joint. "Is that him?"

"Yep," Seth replied.

"Daaang," Frankie drawled, grinning. "I should've had you set us up sooner."

While Seth climbed out of the driver's side, Zach stepped forward to help me and Frankie out of the car. His good manners earned him another ten points in my book.

Seth put a hand on my lower back and introduced us. "Zach, this is Megan."

"Great to m-meet you," I said, taking his hand.

"Same here." Zach turned to Frankie, cocking his head to eye her blue hair. "You must be Frankie."

She gave him a smile and shook his hand as well.

As two more cars pulled into the rapidly filling lot, Seth took my hand. "We better get inside so we can get a good table."

Frankie and Zach followed us into the building. On a low stage up front, the band was setting up, its lead singer stepping to the microphone for a mic check. His voice boomed through the speakers. "Testing one, two, three."

We weaved our way through the crowd and snagged one of the few remaining tables near the back corner.

"First round's on me," Seth told Zach before turning to Frankie and me. "What sounds good?"

"Fuzzy navel," I said, taking a seat on the backside of the table.

Frankie dropped into the seat to my right. "Make it two."

While the guys went to get our drinks, we looked around the place. It was a typical bare-bones multipurpose room with a scuffed parquet floor and pine paneled walls, the kind of unpretentious place that made you feel relaxed and comfortable. Along the wall near the entrance stood a couple of vintage arcade games, Pac-Man and Galaga. Three dartboards hung on the wall a few feet farther down. All three were in use. Set back a few feet were a Ping-Pong table, an air hockey table, and two pool tables.

Though it resembled a typical rec room found at any community center, the flags and photos on the wall pegged it as a gathering place for members of the military. There were photos of servicemen and -women in uniform taken over many decades and in many places, ranging in time from as far back as the 1930s, and ranging in geography from Afghanistan to Zaire. Some were serious photos of units in uniform saluting the camera. Others were candid, quirky snapshots, including one of a female soldier hanging upside down from the long gun of a tank and another of three male soldiers playing in an inflatable kiddie pool in the middle of the desert. In one photo, a soldier was throwing a Frisbee for his military dog. I surmised that, like police work, serving in the military could be dull at times. Troops, including K-9 troops, had to find their fun where they could.

A flyer tacked to a bulletin board announced a memorial service for a military pilot from Fort Worth who'd recently lost his life when his plane crashed while attempting an airdrop of ammunition to Syrian rebels. *So sad.* I turned to see Seth staring at the flyer, a faraway look in his eyes as he disappeared inside himself. No doubt the pilot's death reminded him of other deaths, some of which he'd witnessed. I reached over and took his hand in mine. While he didn't look my way, he pulled my hand upward in an unconscious gesture, holding it briefly to his chest as if it could help to soothe the heartache. I hoped that, in some small way, it could.

The band spent a few seconds warming up on their instruments and launched into their first song, a cover of the Aerosmith classic "Sweet Emotion." The overhead lights dimmed, while the colored lights aimed at the stage illuminated.

After a trip to the bar, Seth returned with a fuzzy navel in each hand, Zach carrying a pitcher of beer and two mugs. Once they'd poured their beers, Seth raised his glass in a silent toast. We all four tapped our glasses together, though the sound was inaudible over the music.

We sat and sipped our drinks for a few songs before the band segued into "Mony Mony," which drew everyone from their seats and onto the dance floor. We remained there for a dozen more songs, including Lynyrd Skynyrd's "Sweet Home Alabama" and Bon Jovi's "Livin' on a Prayer". When the band excused themselves for a ten-minute break, we returned to our table.

Zach turned to Frankie. "So, what do you do?"

"For a living?" she replied. "I stock groceries at night. For fun? I play roller derby."

"Stocking groceries, huh?" Zach took a sip of his beer.

"So what's the long-term plan? You going to school, too? Or planning to go for a management position?"

Frankie laughed and gestured to her hair. "Do I look like management material to you?"

"I suppose not," he said, smiling back at her. "But surely you've got some end game in mind."

Her eyes darkened and she looked down at the table for a moment. When she looked back up, her face was pensive and her voice feeble. "I guess I haven't really figured out what I want to be when I grow up. Sometimes I feel like I'm just spinning my wheels."

Frankie might not be the most accomplished of women, or the most ambitious, but she had many good qualities going for her and I hated to see her feel hurt or insulted, even if it was unintentional. Besides, the conversation had become awkward, and good roommates had each other's backs. "Spinning your wheels?" I repeated. "Good derby pun, Frankie."

Zach and Seth chuckled. Frankie's face relaxed and she cut me a grateful look.

Seth eyed Frankie. "As tall and tough as you are, you should join the fire department. We could use a woman around to cook and clean up after us."

The quirk of his mouth told us he was joking, yet we females weren't about to let his comment go unaddressed. Frankie balled up her cocktail napkin and threw it at Seth, pegging him in the forehead.

I narrowed my eyes at him. "If I had my baton on me right now, I'd give you a nice whap."

He arced a hopeful brow. "Promise?"

Frankie took a sip of her drink and returned her attention to Zach. "Were you in the army with Seth?"

"We were active duty at the same time," Zach said, "but Seth was in ordnance and I was a paratrooper so we never crossed paths. We met doing reserve duty."

Zach had been a paratrooper? I wondered if he knew Garrett Hawke. Chances were probably slim. After all, the army was huge, with nearly half a million active-duty personnel. Yet how many of those lived in Fort Worth? A much smaller number. And of those, how many were paratroopers? A much smaller number still. It was possible, right?

I leaned forward, resting my elbows on the table. "Any chance you know a retired paratrooper named Garrett Hawke?"

"The name sounds familiar," Zach said. "What's he look like?"

"Tall," I said. "Ripped. Brown hair. He walks with a limp."

"A limp?" Zach said. "I think I know the guy you're talking about. He was part of Charlie Company out of Fort Hood, same as me, but he got out a few years earlier. I played pool with him here once."

"He's a member of the VFW?"

"This guy wasn't," Zach said. "He came with a friend. He didn't qualify to join."

"Why not?"

Zach took a sip of his beer. "He got hurt during training. Made a bad landing, permanently jacked up his knee, and received a medical discharge. He never went overseas."

Surely Zach was talking about someone else. After all, at Thursday's neighborhood watch meeting, Garrett Hawke had specifically stated that he'd served in Iraq, hadn't he? Sure he had. The crowd had applauded him for his service. Besides, it probably wasn't unusual for a paratrooper to end up with a permanent leg injury. After all, they came in for landings at fairly high rates of speed. And my description of Hawke as tall, ripped, and brown-haired could probably apply to a lot of guys in the military. Soldiers tended to be physical men, like Seth and Zach, who were in good shape and prided themselves on their strength.

Frankie stirred her drink with the short red straw. "What do you do for a living now that you're out of the army?" she asked Zach.

He leaned back in his chair. "I work in shipping at the Miller Beer plant south of town. Got ten men under me. I give skydiving lessons on occasion, too."

Frankie eyed him with an expression of unfettered attraction and awe. "What makes a person jump out of a plane? You must be a little crazy."

I'd wondered the same thing when I'd first learned that Seth had volunteered to dismantle and defuse bombs and IEDs.

Zach smiled and lifted a noncommittal shoulder. "I don't know. I guess I'm just the type of guy who likes a thrill." He stuck out his elbow and nudged her. "What makes you play roller derby?"

"I don't know," Frankie said, mimicking his words with a grin. "I guess I'm just the type of *girl* who likes a thrill."

"Feel like having your sexy ass kicked in a game of pool?"

"Only if you do."

"You're on."

The two of them stood and left the table.

Once they'd gone, Seth turned to me, reaching out to toy with one of my long locks.

"Did you ever meet Garrett Hawke?" I asked. "The guy with the limp?"

"No," he said. "Why? Who is he?"

"He's the president of the Berkeley Place Neighborhood Watch."

"The guy you mentioned? The one who threatened to take matters into his own hands?"

"Yeah."

Seth cracked his knuckles. "Need me to take care of him?"

"Thanks for the offer. But he's really not that bad." Not to mention that the problem might actually be *me,* feeling overly sensitive about the minor bruise he'd inflicted on my ego. "Besides, I can handle Hawke on my own."

"All right. You can fight your own battles. I get it." He tugged teasingly on my hair. "But I know there's at least one thing you need me for."

A hot blush rushed to my face. "Shut your mouth."

Seth laughed softly when he noticed the color in my cheeks. "Summer's almost here."

"That's true."

His green-eyed gaze roamed over my face, lingering on my lips before returning to my eyes. "Let's go camping or something. Just you and me."

Of course I knew that "just you and me" would include our dogs, as well. It went without saying. Seth planning to spend Mother's Day with me and my family was a significant step forward, but a vacation would be an even bigger step for me and Seth. Spending all of that time alone together could make or break a relationship. But it was a step I was ready to take. As much as I enjoyed having a roommate for the companionship and bill-splitting, it made it more difficult for Seth and me to have privacy. Call me old-fashioned, but I wasn't the type of woman who could enjoy intimacy knowing her roommate was in the house and might overhear. "I'll put in for vacation. Let's compare our calendars tomorrow."

Seth offered me a look so hot it could melt the ice in my drink. "The sooner," he said, "the better."

THIRTY
JUVENILE DOGLINQUENTS

Brigit

Megan had left her at home with Blast and Zoe . . . *unsupervised.*

Time to party, doggy style!

Given that Megan had been less than generous with her food and treats lately, Brigit decided to take matters into her own hands . . . or paws. Besides, no party was complete without snacks, right?

Brigit trotted into the kitchen and sniffed around the cabinets, exploring her options. One cabinet contained only canned and bottled food. Nothing a dog would want to snack on. The next cabinet, the one under the sink, contained cleaning supplies, the smells of bleach and disinfectant causing a slight burn in her nostrils. She moved on to the third cabinet.

Bingo was his name-o.

The cabinet contained a package of Oreos, the rest of the bag of Doritos Frankie had shared with her earlier in the week, and a box of cheddar-cheese-flavored crackers.

Here we go.

Brigit pawed at the cabinet door. When moving her

paw in one direction didn't work, she tried moving it the other way. *Aha!* The cabinet door opened slightly for a moment, but closed again a moment later. She swiped at the cabinet again, this time shoving her nose into the opening before it could swing shut again.

She nudged the door open, moved forward so that her body blocked it, and looked back at Blast who stood in the doorway, watching. She sank her teeth into the box of cheese crackers and pulled it out of the cabinet. As she turned to go back into the living room, her wagging tail smacked the cabinet door and it closed with a *whap.*

The two took their treat onto the couch to enjoy, tearing at the box with their teeth and claws until the crackers spilled out. Zoe ventured over and sniffed at the crackers pouring out of the box, but turned up her nose at them. *Cats. So finicky.*

Brigit and Blast polished off the box of crackers in two minutes flat. Remembering that she'd been chastised before for eating people food without permission, Brigit decided it would be best to eliminate the evidence, so she ate the cardboard box, too.

Not bad. Not bad at all.

THIRTY-ONE
PHONE BONE

Tom

He might not be able to peep for a while yet, but maybe some phone sex would suffice for the time being. He'd never resorted to calling one of these chat lines before, but desperate times called for desperate measures.

There was a prerecorded message informing him that the call would cost him $3.95 per minute. Steep, but given all his pent-up frustration he figured he wouldn't have much staying power and could reach satisfaction in twenty dollars or less. It seemed a small price to pay.

When the recording ended, a woman answered, her voice breathy and low. "Hi, there," she purred like a sex kitten. "With whom do I have the pleasure of speaking?"

He was disappointed not only by her perfect grammar, which reminded him of Mrs. Snyder, his frumpy high school English teacher, a cock block if ever there was one, but also by the incessant murmuring in the background. *Ugh.* This phone sex thing was no different than those other telemarketing places, was it? At least phone sex hadn't been outsourced. This woman spoke unaccented English so he'd be able to understand her. Then again, the thought of an Indian woman with long dark hair kind of got him going. He felt a twitch of interest inside his boxers.

"I'm . . . Tom," he said. After all the comments at the neighborhood watch meeting about the "peeping Tom," it was the first name that came to mind.

"Well, hello, Tom," the woman said. "You sound like you're ready to have some fun."

"I sure am," he replied.

"How would you like to start, Tom?" the woman asked.

He'd been hoping she'd be the one to kick things off. "Uh . . . you're the expert," he replied.

"Okay," the woman said. "What kind of women do you find attractive, Tom?"

"Tall ones," he said. He'd always liked the thought of long legs wrapped around him. "Women with long, dark hair."

While another woman moaned in the background, the woman on the other end of his line issued a seductive giggle. "Tall with long, dark hair? Oh, Tom, it's like you can see me through the phone."

He doubted the woman actually looked like his fantasy lover. But given that she was all he had for the time being, he was willing to play along.

She began to issue instructions to him, ways to prepare himself for what she assured him would be the experience of a lifetime.

"Could you hold just a second, Tim?" she asked.

"It's Tom," he reminded her. Mrs. Snyder had never been able to remember his name, either.

"Tom. Right. Sorry."

There was a grating sound as she apparently put her hand over the mouthpiece to muffle the conversation taking place at her end. Tom heard a man's voice say, "When you're done with this call, take your lunch break."

Whatever twitch he'd felt was long gone. This phone-sex job was just that to the woman on the other end. A *job.* A paycheck. His pleasure wasn't truly important to her.

She came back on the line. "Where were we?"

You were about to go nuke a frozen dinner in the office microwave. "You were telling me to rub my hand over my chest."

"Oh, right," she replied.

He wondered if she had a script and was looking for her place.

She continued to tell him what to do, speaking her lines with a practiced purr that was too perfect to be real. She could probably recite the script in her sleep. As for himself, he could still recite the first few lines of Marc Antony's speech from Shakespeare's *Julius Caesar.* Mrs. Snyder had made all of her students memorize it and recite it in front of the class. "Friends, Romans, countrymen, lend me your ears." But ears weren't exactly the body part he'd like to be focusing on at the moment.

A couple more minutes into the call and he realized this just wasn't working for him. It was no better than that stupid porn movie he'd watched on his laptop. Nothing could compare to a real woman, and he wasn't willing to settle. But as long as he was going to be charged, he figured he might as well have some fun. "I've got an idea," he said. "How about you come to my house and suck on my toes while I polish my guns and read Tolstoy?"

She paused for just a moment, then made an attempt to improvise. "You're into Tolstoy, are you? Will you be my lord of the cock ring?"

"*Lord of the Rings* is Tolkien, not Tolstoy," he snapped, immediately feeling guilty afterward. This woman might have confused her literature, but at least she was trying. And at least he now knew for certain that it was not

Mrs. Snyder on the other end of the line. She would've known the difference.

"I'm doing my best!" the woman snapped back, the purr gone, replaced by a deeper, forceful voice. "Give me a fucking break."

The low-pitched voice had him wondering now if the woman at the other end of the phone even was a woman. She sounded like a drag queen now. Not that he had anything against drag queens, given his own proclivity to sexual taboos. But a drag queen would not be his choice of bed partner.

Tom sighed. "This isn't working for me."

"You know what, buddy?" said the voice, clearly a male speaking now. "It's not working for me, either."

THIRTY-TWO
FAMILIARITY

Megan

Zach and Frankie drove separately back to the house in his car. When we returned home, the two of them remained on the porch while Seth came in to round up Blast.

I bent over in the living room and cupped Brigit's chin in my hands. "Did you miss me, girl? I missed you. Yes, I did!"

She replied with a tail wag and a cheese-scented pant. *Hmm.* I glanced over at Seth. "Does Blast's breath smell like cheddar?"

Seth arced an incredulous brow. "You want me to smell my dog's breath? *On purpose?*"

He had a point. I looked around for a cracker box. While there was no food packaging in sight, the couch pillows were strewn about the floor, the rug lay askew, and telltale tufts of loose fur and orange crumbs appeared around the room. A glance through the open door of my bedroom showed that the covers of my bed, which I'd made this morning, were rumpled, as if someone—*a couple of rambunctious dogs, perhaps?*—had engaged in a playful tussle atop them. It didn't take a detective to discern what had happened here.

I gestured at the rug and pillows. "Looks like Brigit and Blast had a wild party." I looked down at my K-9 partner and pointed a stern finger at her. "Busted. You're grounded for two weeks."

She gave me a tail wag that said the punishment was well worth the fun she'd had. Being the forgiving sort, I gave Brigit a pat on the head and turned to give Seth a warm good-night kiss on the lips.

The door opened and Frankie came in, putting an end to our embrace.

"See ya'," Seth said as he passed her on his way out.

After the door closed behind him Frankie leaned back against it, her eyes gleaming, a soft smile on her lips.

"If you're going to swoon," I teased as I gathered up the couch pillows, "give me some warning so I can toss these under you to break your fall."

Fortunately, she opted for flopping onto the futon instead. "I really like Zach," she said. "I owe you one, Megan."

"Clean up the poop in the backyard all next week and we'll call it even."

Her nose scrunched in disgust. "It's bad enough I have to clean Zoe's litter box. Besides," she said teasingly, "I took you in off the streets. Have you forgotten that already?"

Frankie had given me and Brigit a place to live when we'd had trouble finding a pet-friendly place in my price range. She owed me nothing. "You win. We'll call it even."

With that, Brigit and I headed out back so she could take a final tinkle before going to bed for the night.

My cell phone rang on my bedside table at eight Sunday morning, rousing me from sleep. I lifted my arm from around Brigit, whom I'd ended up spooning during the night, and picked up the phone. She let out a groan and put her paw over her eyes, clearly not ready to face the day after the wild party she'd thrown last night.

My blurry eyes looked at the phone screen. The readout indicated it was Detective Bustamente. I jabbed the button to accept the call. "Hello, Detective," I said, my voice still hoarse with sleep.

"Sorry to wake you," he said, "but I figured you'd want to hear this breaking news. Hurley put in an appearance at a used-car dealership in Burleson last night."

The town of Burleson sat just a few miles south of Fort Worth, one of the many smaller jurisdictions that made up the suburbs.

I sat up in the bed. "Sounds like he's starting to mix things up."

"A little," the detective replied. "He pulled a gun on the owner, and demanded both his debit card and the keys to a white pickup that was for sale in the lot."

He went on to tell me that, as usual, Hurley had worn a ski mask and gloves, and left no prints behind. He had set off in the truck, promptly made a withdrawal at a branch bank ATM, and disappeared before the city police or the Johnson County Sheriff's Department could get on his trail. Thankfully, nobody had been shot. It was a slight variation on Hurley's usual MO, which in the past had involved a home invasion, but perhaps the dealership had looked like an easy target. And evidently, he'd decided he needed some new wheels.

"What about his Isuzu?" I asked.

"It was found on the side of the road a half mile away with no oil in it. The engine must've seized up on him. He'd replaced his original license plates with stolen ones, but the VIN number matched his registration."

Though Hurley had left no concrete evidence behind at the other crime scenes, the fact that his car was found so close to the dealership was solid evidence that Hurley was the culprit in this particular crime. The guy should have spent a few measly bucks of the stolen money on a can of oil. *Dumbass.*

I put the detective on speakerphone and opened my notes app. "What's the license plate on the truck?"

As Bustamente provided the combination of letters and numbers, I typed them into my phone for later reference. Of course they might or might not be helpful. Chances were Hurley would change the license plates again. "Got it. What kind of truck was it?"

"Ford F-150."

The make and model was a popular one in Texas, both for personal purposes and for businesses that involved heavy equipment or hauling, such as landscaping or agriculture-related companies. There had to be hundreds of them on the roads in and around Fort Worth. Hurley had made a smart decision in choosing that vehicle. Too bad he hadn't chosen something more unusual and attention-grabbing, like a lemon-yellow Mustang.

Garrett Hawke might be a minor thorn in our sides, but I had no doubt he could quickly disseminate the information about the pickup to the residents in his area. If Hurley was the one who'd been prowling around Berkeley Place, I wanted the residents to know to look out for a white pickup now and to call in any sightings. Heck, maybe Hawke and his watch group would even help us catch Hurley. "Have you notified Garrett Hawke?" I asked.

Detective Bustamente chuckled. "I've saved those honors for you, Officer Luz."

"Gee, thanks."

When we ended our call, I rounded up the schedule Nora Conklin had given me for the Berkeley Place Neighborhood Watch, scanned the schedule for Hawke's phone number, and dialed it.

He answered on the first ring. "Hawke here."

"Good morning, Mr. Hawke," I said. "This is Officer Megan Luz. I'm calling to let you know—"

"Did you catch the prowler? Has there been an arrest?"

My frustration flared at the interruption, but I tamped it down by closing my eyes and counting to five. "Not yet. But there's been a development." I told him about the car theft and asked that he notify his neighbors and ask the volunteers on patrol to keep a watchful eye.

"We will," he said. "I appreciate the call, Officer Luz. And I apologize if I've stepped on some toes during all of this. I've been told more than once that I can come on too strong. I'm working on it." A good-natured chuckle followed his words.

"I appreciate that. You have a good day."

It took a big man to apologize. *Hmm.* Had I been wrong to suspect that Hawke could be a peeping Tom? Was he nothing more than a concerned citizen trying to keep his family and neighborhood safe? I couldn't be sure. The only thing I was certain about was that a cup of coffee would taste darn good about then.

Late that afternoon, Seth and I climbed into his Nova to head to my parents' house for the family Mother's Day celebration.

He glanced my way before turning his attention back to the street in front of us. "What have you told your family about me?"

"When we first started dating, I told them what a hero you were, that you'd served in the army and worked on the bomb squad. When you dumped me, I told them you were an asshole."

He laughed mirthlessly and looked out his window. "I suppose I deserved that."

"Don't worry. They know you came to your senses and begged me to take you back. That you groveled shamelessly."

He looked my way, chuckling for real this time. "I kinda did, didn't it?"

I gave him a pointed look. "I wouldn't be here if you hadn't."

We passed the zoo sign, which featured two rhinos, their horns sticking up from their snouts.

"I heard that one of the jaguars just had kittens or puppies or whatever you call baby jaguars," Seth said.

"Cubs," I replied.

"Cubs? Really?"

"Mm-hm. If the adults of the cat species roar, like lions or tigers or jaguars, then their babies are called cubs. If the adults purr, like housecats or cougars, then their babies are called kittens. At least that's what they told us at zoo camp when I was seven."

"How do you still remember that?"

I shrugged. My mind tended to stockpile information, most of it relatively useless. I'd been one of those children who lived in their heads. Now I supposed I was an adult who lived primarily in her head, hence my desire to become a detective, a cerebral job if ever there was one. "The camp focused on charismatic megafauna." Okay, now I was just using big words to show off.

"Charismatic *what*?"

"Megafauna. It means the large animals that humans find interesting or cute, and rally around. Like lions and tigers and giraffes and elephants." Nobody ever rallied around a blobfish, after all. The fish, which resembled the lovable yet pathetic cartoon character Ziggy, was considered one of the world's ugliest animals.

"Megafauna, huh? There you go again. Blowing my mind with another brainy factoid." Seth took his hands off the steering wheel, splayed them around his head, and imitated the sound of an explosion. *Kaboom.*

My parents' house was a single-story wood-frame model in Arlington Heights, a neighborhood that sat just southwest of downtown. The house had three small bedrooms, two tiny and outdated baths, faded yellow paint, and peeling trim. My parents were anything but pretentious. Raising five children on a working-class income, they hadn't had the time or money to be.

I was the oldest of the brood, followed by three brothers and, finally, another sister. Gabby and Joey, the two youngest, were still in high school and lived at home. My other two brothers, Daniel and Conner, had come home from college for the weekend.

Seth followed me to the cockeyed front door, which had stuck for as long as I could remember. I put my shoulder to the surface and forced it open.

Seth took a moment to inspect the door frame. "I could fix this."

"That would put you back in the 'hero' category."

My father tended to let things go around the house. He worked on the line at the General Motors plant and the last thing he wanted to do when he got home was more physical labor. Who could blame him? Still, it would be nice to be able to visit my family without risking a shoulder dislocation.

We entered the house, as usual walking into utter chaos. After all, chaos required the least energy to maintain. It was a basic physical law.

Gabby, Joey, and Daniel were flopped on the couch, a cluster of arms and legs and pillows, among which lazed my mother's three indistinguishable tabby cats. My siblings were essentially younger versions of me, a culture clash of our Irish and Mexican heritage, dark hair tinged with varying amounts of auburn highlights, a smattering of light freckles sprinkled across their faces. The television played a mindless action movie, something with Tom Cruise in it.

"Hey," I said by way of greeting.

Gabby looked up from the couch and, on seeing Seth, emitted a sound that was half gasp, half squeal, her cheeks turning pink. *Instant crush.*

I pointed at each of my siblings in turn. "Gabby, Joey, and Daniel."

"Hi!" Gabby gushed, waving her hand. "It's great to finally meet you, Seth!"

My brothers were less demonstrative, greeting us with grunts of acknowledgment delivered without taking their eyes from the TV. Such manners, huh?

Seth followed me to the kitchen where we found my remaining brother, Connor, sitting at the kitchen table working on his laptop. Despite the late afternoon hour, he still looked hungover. Odd, given that he was only twenty and thus not able to drink legally.

I put a finger under his chin and raised his face. "Your eyes look beershot."

"Don't you mean *blood*shot?"

"No, I don't. Did you go out d-drinking last night?"

He raised his palms. "I plead the fifth, copper."

No doubt he'd been out partying with his high school buddies last night, one of whom had been held back and already celebrated his twenty-first birthday.

I circled behind him to look at his computer screen. "What are you working on?"

"A paper for my history class. It's on the Industrial Revolution."

"Want me to take a look at it when you're done?"

Other than the Fs I'd received for refusing to do oral reports in high school, I'd made good grades in English. All that reading I'd done as a child had provided me with an extensive vocabulary and excellent grammar. I'd earned As in English in college, and high marks on papers I'd written in my other subjects.

My mother fluttered into the room, her sundress swirling around her, her feet bare, a single sandal in her hand. "Ask Daniel for help," she told Connor. "He's good at that stuff."

My gut clenched as my Irish ire rose. Daniel might be the one majoring in engineering, but he didn't have a monopoly on intelligence in our family. Seth eyed me, his eyes narrowing slightly, before stepping forward, extending a hand to my mother. "Hello. I'm Seth."

"Great to meet you!" She transferred the sandal to her other hand so she could give him a shake. "Megan says you're a firefighter? And a member of the bomb squad?"

"That's right."

Mom bent over to peek under the table, looking for the match to the sandal in her hand. "Not there. Y'all excuse me for a second." She greeted me with a drive-by hug as she scurried into the living room to see if the shoe was under the couch.

Judging from the whine of the water pipes, Dad was still in the shower. Typical. Our reservation was in ten minutes, but my family could never get anywhere on time.

"Let's see about the door." I led Seth out to the garage, where we retrieved my father's toolbox.

Seth carried the box back to the porch, set it down, and examined the door frame. When he found no problem there, he opened the door and took a look at the hard ware.

"The hinges are loose," he said. "That's why it's hanging wonky."

He rummaged through the toolbox until he found the right screwdriver. While I stood on the porch and admired the way his biceps and shoulders flexed as he worked, he tightened each of the screws. When he finished, he stepped back and closed the door. "Give it a try."

I reached out and turned the handle. The door swung open easily. All those years of fighting the damn thing and all it needed was a few turns of a screwdriver. *Sheesh.*

Seth returned the tools to the box and stood to find me waiting for him with a grateful kiss.

"I like that you're handy."

"I like that you're smart." He gave me a kiss of his own, then leaned back against one of the porch supports. "Your family doesn't know it, do they?"

"Not really." It seemed that no matter what I accomplished, no matter how much I knew, my parents retained the opinion they'd formed of me back when I was in elementary school and struggling with my stutter. It was bad enough that the other children had assumed my stutter meant I was stupid, but having my own parents overlook my intellect wasn't just insulting but hurtful. Still, what's a kid going to do? Even when she's not a kid anymore?

Good thing Seth saw me as the person I was today. The capable and smart cop, who could examine evidence, put clues together, and bring the bad guys to justice and some awesome moves to a dance floor.

A half hour later, my father had finished his shower, my mother had found her missing sandal, and all eight of us were sitting at a long table in my mother's favorite Italian restaurant.

Mom took a sip of her wine and looked across the table at Seth. "Did you see your mother earlier today?"

Next to me, Seth stiffened. "No. My mother lives out of town."

"Where?" my mother asked.

"Out west."

The vague answer made me wonder whether he even knew where his mother was living and when he'd last had contact with her. When my mother opened her mouth for another question I knew Seth wouldn't want to answer, I grabbed my gift bag from the floor and shoved it across the table. "Here, Mom."

She took the bag and gave me a smile in return. "Thanks, Megan." She yanked out the tissue paper and pulled out the gift, a wooden organizer designed to be hung on a wall. It had hooks for key rings and two separate bins for mail. She cast me a look. "You trying to tell me something?"

"Yes. Get organized." I gestured to the bag. "There's more."

She reached in to find a decorative container of scented bath salts. "Jasmine! My favorite."

She might not know me as well as she thought, but I certainly knew her.

My siblings proceeded to give my mother their gifts, which included costume jewelry, candy, a pair of slippers, and a vanilla candle. My mother was a sucker for those "as seen on TV" gadgets, so my father had bought her something called a Veggetti that would shred zucchini, carrots, and other vegetables into long, spaghetti-like strips. As if that would make Joey and Gabby eat vegetables.

"Thanks, everyone!" The gifts might be crappy, but her appreciation was sincere. Mom might not be the most organized or observant woman, but she was easy to please. I had to give her that.

We enjoyed our meal, as well as tiramisu for dessert. After exchanging good-bye hugs in the parking lot, Seth and I returned to his car.

He didn't say much as he pulled away from the curb, and he was quiet as we drove toward my house. Was he wondering what it would have been like to have had siblings? To be part of an imperfect yet loving family? Or was he struggling with his feelings toward his own mother?

He turned into the parking lot of the grocery store where Frankie worked. A special tent was set up for shoppers to make quick and easy holiday purchases. "I'll be right back." He climbed out of his car and disappeared inside the tent. He returned a moment later with a bouquet of pink roses.

He headed north on University Drive, heading away from Travis Avenue, where I lived. I wondered where he was going, but the tight expression on his face told me not to ask, that I'd find out soon enough.

He continued on until we reached Greenwood Cemetery. He drove slowly down the car path and rolled to a stop at the side of the lane. He sat still for a moment as if collecting himself before reaching for the flowers. When he spoke, his voice was soft and sad. "Come with me?"

"Of course." I climbed out of the car, following Seth past several gravestones until he came to one marked with a simple, flat headstone on the ground. The stone read RUTHIE RUTLEDGE, and provided the dates of her birth and death. It took me only a moment to realize this was the grave of his grandmother, the woman who'd raised him, who'd been much more of a mother to him than his biological mother had ever been.

Seth bent down, holding the flowers, and closed his eyes for a moment, as if having a private, telepathic conversation with his grandmother. A few seconds later, his eyes opened again and he gently laid the flowers on her grave.

Tears blurred my vision. I was touched, in so many ways. Touched that Seth had remembered to honor his long-dead grandmother today. Touched that he'd expressed some vulnerability. But especially touched that he'd included me in this tribute. He might have attachment issues, but he was clearly beginning to overcome them, to let me in, to trust me.

As he stood, a warm breeze blew past, feeling like the soft caress of an unseen hand.

THIRTY-THREE
DOGGIE BAG

Brigit

Her ears perked up when she heard Seth's car pull to a stop out front. She hopped down from the futon where she lay alongside Zoe and trotted to the door. As Megan approached, she brought the scents of leftover spaghetti marinara with her.

Brigit wagged her tail as Megan and Seth came inside. To her disappointment, Megan went straight to the fridge with the carryout container. What was wrong with that woman? They didn't call it a *doggie bag* for nothing, you know!

THIRTY-FOUR
TWILIGHT TRYST

Tom

"We're out of toilet paper," he said.

"Really?" Her face registered surprise. "I thought I'd bought some last week."

She had. Earlier, while she'd been puttering around out back, he'd taken the unopened twelve-roll package from their bathroom and put it in the trunk of his car. Toilet paper was the one thing they couldn't do without, the one thing he could think of that could get him out of the house for a bit.

"I'll run to the store." He grabbed his keys and headed out before she could think of anything else for him to pick up. He had no intention of going to the grocery store. *Hell, no.*

Seven-thirty was the time he'd spotted the Rabinowitzes' new au pair taking the baby out for a walk on Friday. He could only hope that the woman was a creature of habit, that she'd be out with the baby again tonight.

He pulled out of the garage and headed down the street, turning and making his way to Huntington Lane.

There she is.

She must have started early tonight, because she was already heading back up the Rabinowitzes' driveway. She wore shorts that barely cleared the bottom curve of her butt cheek and exposed a long stretch of smooth, creamy thigh. Thank goodness the tiny shorts were in style right now. That body was not built for Bermudas.

He cruised slowly by. He hadn't paid much attention to the Rabinowitz home before, but now he took a closer look.

The home, a two-story model made of gray brick, sat on nearly half an acre. A wide porch and expansive balcony spanned the front of the house. While the sides of the backyard were enclosed with a six-foot wooden privacy fence, along the front of the house the fence was a shorter, four-foot wrought-iron style. Through the bars, he caught a glimpse of a detached structure in the backyard. The yard had no pool, so it couldn't be a pool house. The house had a three-car garage on the other side with plenty of room for lawn equipment, so it wasn't likely a storage building. Besides, the arched windows and red door told him it was a guesthouse.

The only question now was whether the au pair lived in the main house with the Rabinowitz family, or whether she lived in the guesthouse in the backyard.

I'll just have to find out . . .

THIRTY-FIVE
ON THE OFFENSIVE

Megan

Call me crazy, but I'd actually volunteered to work the night shift this week, trading spots with Summer, who was more than happy to take my day schedule and avoid the inevitable disruptions that working nights caused to a person's sleeping and eating patterns.

I felt invested in the Berkeley Place case, and hoped that I might be able to put some clues together this week that would help me identify the peeping Tom. Better yet, maybe I'd catch him in the act and drag his sorry ass off to jail, easy peasy.

Alas, things were rarely so easy.

Or so peasy.

I'd stayed up as late as I could Sunday night, trying to force myself to sleep in Monday morning so that I'd be well rested for my night shift. Despite working out with a Jillian Michaels *Kickbox FastFix* DVD to keep my blood flowing, I'd only made it until one-thirty before my eyes had refused to stay open any longer. I woke at nine this morning, unable to go back to sleep.

I made breakfast, took Brigit for a long walk, even brought out Zoe's fishing pole toy to play with the cat. As Zoe swatted at the catnip-stuffed goldfish at the end of the stretchy line, I wondered, *Could Hawke have been right? Could a registered sex offender be responsible for the peeping incidents in Berkeley Place?*

I retrieved my laptop and logged onto the sex offender database, typing in the zip code for Berkeley Place and the surrounding area to narrow things down. Steeling myself, I began to cull through the list. My studies in criminal justice at Sam Houston State University and my police training told me that each sexual predator tended to favor a certain type of victim. The Berkeley Place peeper tended to prefer grown women in their twenties and thirties, so I focused my efforts on cases in which the victims were adult females.

A half hour later, I'd narrowed my list down to three potential suspects.

The first was a man named Jerry Jeff Gilbreath, alias JJ Gilbreath, who was in his late forties now. Eleven years prior, he'd been convicted of a nighttime home invasion and attempted sexual assault in the nearby town of Colleyville, another upscale area. Fortunately for the victim, her husband arrived home to find her with her clothing torn as she attempted to fend Gilbreath off with a kitchen mop. The woman's husband beat Gilbreath within an inch of his life. Fingerprints obtained from Gilbreath linked him to a similar crime committed two weeks earlier. Luckily, the previous victim had been able to grab a phone and dial 911, which scared Gilbreath off before he'd gotten what he came for. He'd served ten years, had been released last year, and now lived in an apartment on Jennings Avenue, not far from Berkeley Place.

The second possible perpetrator was a man in his early thirties named Nathan Wilmer. He'd been convicted five years ago of three date rapes in which he'd drugged the women by slipping a sedative into their drinks. He'd met all three women via an online dating site. I had to do some digging to find the names of the victims, and more digging to determine what the women looked like. Sure enough, each of the women's driver's license photos showed a brunette. Two had long hair, while the third had hair that wasn't long, per se, but did reach down to her shoulders. All three victims had been in their late twenties or early thirties, around the same age as Kirstin Rumford and Alyssa Lowry. According to the arrest report, officers had found high-powered binoculars in his apartment, along with a telescope aimed from his bedroom window into that of a young woman in the adjacent building.

Not surprisingly, Wilmer lived in another apartment complex on Jennings, not far from Gilbreath's. Sex offenders tended to cluster in areas where landlords couldn't be too picky about who they rented to.

The last potential suspect wasn't listed on the sex offender database. As Bustamente had informed the group at the meeting in Forest Park, voyeurism wasn't an offense for which a convict had to register. This particular man, Blake Looney, had been a loss prevention supervisor at a Nordstrom store in a local shopping mall. According to the report, the store manager had walked into Looney's office and discovered the man with his eye to the carpet, spying on women through a hole he had drilled in the floor of his office, which sat directly above the ladies' dressing rooms. Looney lived in a house on McCart, only a couple blocks south of the Berkeley Place border.

I searched for additional men with voyeurism convictions but, not surprisingly, found very few. In most cases, when a person was discovered watching someone else, the event could be explained away as an accidental observance rather than an intentional act. Unless a third person witnessed the suspect intentionally spying on the victim, there was usually insufficient evidence to warrant prosecution. Looney's case was unusual.

I phoned Detective Bustamente and told him what I'd found. "What do you think?"

"I think you're a hardworking young woman," he said, "with lots of ambition. I also think I don't have time to visit these creeps. Besides the Hurley investigation, I'm working three homicides, two armed robberies with injuries, and a carjacking."

In other words, he couldn't justify spending time chasing these leads given that there'd been no attempt by the suspect either time to enter the victims' homes and no injuries or significant property damage. I understood that priorities had to be made and that minor offenses would have to fall by the wayside. I just hoped the Berkeley Place Peeper would stick with peeping and not take things any further.

Given that I was wide awake, I rounded up Brigit and headed to work at eight o'clock, an hour before my shift officially began. Detective Bustamente might not have time to visit the men on my list, but that didn't mean I couldn't drive by their places and perform some surveillance.

I loaded my K-9 partner into the cruiser and we drove through the gathering dusk to the apartment complex on Jennings. I ran a quick search of the DMV records on my laptop to see what kind of car Gilbreath drove. The records indicated he owned a gray Jeep Renegade and provided the plate number. I looked over at his unit. Sure enough, there sat the Jeep, right in front of his apartment.

I parked and let Brigit out of the back of the squad car. Given that Gilbreath had a history of violence, I experienced more than a little trepidation, my heart pumping as if I'd just jogged a few minutes on the treadmill. In case Gilbreath happened to come outside while I was snooping around the parking lot, I readied my baton, pulling it from my belt and extending it with a flick of my wrist. *Snap!* As I made my way to his apartment, I performed a simple flat spin with the baton, working off some of my nervous energy. The baton gave off a *swish-swish-swish* sound as it completed its rotations, the sound soothing my nerves. Some people calm themselves with liquor, others with cigarettes. My relaxant of choice just happened to be my baton. The fact that it could perform double duty as a defensive weapon was the icing on the cake.

I made my way first to Gilbreath's car, peeking in the windows to see if there was anything incriminating in sight. All I saw was a greasy burger wrapper on the floorboard and a cardboard coffee cup in the cup holder. I'm not sure what I expected. Surely he wouldn't be stupid enough to leave a list of his intended victims and their addresses in plain sight.

I looked over at Gilbreath's front door. The blinds on the windows that flanked it were closed, but light filtered through the slats, indicating he was inside. Slowly, quietly, I crept to his front door, stopping outside to listen. The telltale *click-click-click* of a game show spinner came through the door, followed by Pat Sajak's voice calling out "Six hundred" and a women's voice crying, "N!" The exchange was followed by a voice from inside the apartment muttering, "Dumb bitch. You shoulda guessed T."

A misogynist. Oh, so charming.

I hadn't gleaned anything from this visit, but at least I knew Gilbreath was at home and not up to his old, horrible tricks . . . *at least for now.*

Brigit and I returned to the cruiser and made our way down a block and a half to Nathan Wilmer's apartment complex. As I circled through the lot, looking for apartment 246, my eyes spotted two men coming out of a second-floor apartment. One had a television in his arms, while the other wrangled a treadmill. The first kicked the door closed behind him. Metal numbers nailed to the outside of the door told me they'd just exited Wilmer's unit.

I glanced at the driver's license photo of Wilmer I'd printed out. The picture showed a man with chubby pink cheeks and white-blond hair. Both of the men now coming down the stairs were heavyset, with shaved heads and dark goatees.

I climbed out of my cruiser and raised a hand. "Excuse me, guys. You were just in Nathan Wilmer's apartment?"

"What about it?" said the one carrying the TV. "We got a legal right."

"Yeah," agreed the other.

I stepped closer. "What do you mean?"

Mr. Television explained. "We work for the property manager. The tenant's two months late on rent. We came to take his nonexempt property."

"Yeah," said the other, again.

The first set the TV on the asphalt, reached into his back pocket, and pulled out a document folded in thirds. He handed me the paper. "Here. See for yourself."

I unfolded the paperwork to find a copy of Wilmer's lease, which included a clause stating the landlord could, and would, seize nonexempt property to satisfy unpaid rent. Looked like they were within their rights. Assuming, of course, they actually worked for the landlord and weren't pulling a fast one. Frankly, I didn't give a crap. Wilmer was a scumbag and if someone stole his television and treadmill, well, that was simply karma exacting a small measure of payback.

Attached to the lease was an eviction notice dated with today's date. The notice gave Wilmer three days to vacate.

I looked up at the closed door. "Is he home?"

"No. No sign of him."

Of course Wilmer might have decided to hide in his closet when these two beefcakes knocked at his door.

As I debated whether to go up and see for myself, the men stowed the television and treadmill in the back of a small truck. The first reached out a hand for the paperwork I was still holding. I handed it back to him. As I watched, he trotted back up the steps and tacked the eviction notice to the door. Unencumbered now, he took the stairs two at a time coming down, returned to the truck, and motored off without another word to me.

My eyes scanned the parking lot, looking for the blue Mazda3 registered in Wilmer's name. There was no sign of it.

Brigit watched from the back window of the cruiser as I went upstairs and knocked on Wilmer's door. There was no answer. Reaching to the pouch on my tool belt, I pulled out my cell phone and snapped a pic of the eviction notice.

Texas law required a registered sex offender to notify local authorities at least seven days prior to an intended move, and required the offender to register with the authorities at his new address within seven days after the move. Failure to comply was a felony. Surely Wilmer knew this eviction was coming. I wondered if he'd notified the chief of police as required. If not, he'd broken the law, even if he hadn't yet figured out where he was going after his landlord tossed him out.

I slid back into my squad car, phoned the chief's office, and was transferred to the phone of the administrative employee who maintained the registry. Unfortunately, she'd gone home for the day and all I got was her voice mail. I left a message. "This is Officer Megan Luz. I need to speak with you regarding a registered sex offender named Nathan Wilmer. Please give me a call back ASAP." I followed up the message with my cell phone number.

My work here done, I backed out of the parking spot and aimed for Blake Looney's house on McCart. Unfortunately, he wasn't home, either.

Having done as much as I could for the moment, I drove past Hurley's sister's apartment, looking for a white Ford F-150 pickup. Though I found one in the lot, the license-plate number was not the one Bustamente had given me, and the truck's plate matched a registration for a man who lived at the complex.

I headed to Berkeley Place, cruising slowly through the dark night, my eyes peeled for any unusual activity. If the BP Peeper was out tonight, Brigit and I would get him. "Won't we, girl?"

No sooner had the words left my mouth than my eyes spotted a shadowy figure slip between a couple of oleander bushes in the yard of a gray brick home a little farther down the road. *Holy guacamole! Could it be Hurley? Or the peeper?*

I sped forward, screeched to a stop, and activated my car-mounted spotlight, shining it into the bushes. While the foliage shrouded parts of the person, a pair of blue tennis shoes, a lock of sandy hair, and a pair of eyes blinking against the bright glare were visible.

My pulse reaching near stroke levels, I grabbed the mic and activated my public address system. "Come out of that bush with your hands up!"

As the person stepped out of the bushes, I climbed out of my car, whipped my baton from my belt, and flicked it open with a *snap!* As I stepped forward, the door to the house opened. The mortified face of the sandy-haired boy from the park looked from me to the front door, where an Asian man stood.

The boy looked back my way, putting up a hand to block the intense light, and cried, "Sorry!" His preapology delivered, he took off running.

"What's going on?" yelled the man from the porch.

There was no time for me to explain. I had a kid to catch. "I'll be back!" I called as I rushed back to the cruiser. As fast as I could, I let Brigit out of her enclosure and the two of us took off in the direction the boy had run.

There he was, sprinting under a streetlight a block ahead. *Damn, he moves fast!* He must be on the track team.

"Stop!" I hollered after him. "Or I'll deploy my dog!"

The kid ignored me, putting more distance between us. No way was I ever going to catch him. Thank goodness my partner was much faster on her four feet.

I gave Brigit the order to take him down. Nails scrabbling on the asphalt, she took off like a furry bullet train.

The boy must have heard her paws thundering toward him, because he looked back, yelped, and ran into a yard, out of my line of vision. By the time I got to the spot where he'd turned, all I found was Brigit leaping up onto a six-foot privacy fence, unable to get over it. I tried the gate, but it was locked. Shining my flashlight over the fence, I swept it over the backyard, looking for the boy. An ankle and a blue tennis shoe disappeared over the back fence. The kid must have climbed onto the utility box and dived over it headfirst. Would serve him right if he ended up with a concussion.

The house was near the end of the block. With any luck, maybe we could catch him one street over.

I ran, ordering Brigit to follow me. Circling the block, we came around on the other side. I swept my flashlight around, but saw no trace of the boy. *Could he still be in the backyard?*

When Brigit sprinted toward a fence and began leaping up and down on it, I got my answer. He was still in the yard. Fortunately, this gate was unlocked. I whipped it open and Brigit and I dashed through. It took less than three seconds for her to corner the boy behind a shiny barbecue grill on the back patio.

He threw his hands in the air, once again crying, "Sorry! I'm so sorry!"

Oh, he'd be sorry all right. "Turn around and put your hands on the wall!"

He did as he was told, and a few seconds later I had him handcuffed with his back to the bricks. His eyes were wide with panic, his face flushed, his chest heaving from the exertion of running and vaulting over fences.

"What's your name?" I demanded.

"Dalton!"

"Dalton what?"

"Livingston!"

"You want to explain yourself?" I asked the kid.

"I was leaving a note!" he cried, panting. "And flowers!"

"For who?"

"Ashley Pham," he said between gulps of breath.

"Is she your girlfriend?"

He shook his head so hard it threatened to come off his neck.

"Calm down," I said. "Take some deep breaths."

He wheezed in and out several times, but seemed to be settling down.

When he was breathing more normally, I asked, "What did the note say?"

He looked down as if embarrassed. "It just said I thought she was the prettiest girl at school and that she has a beautiful voice and that someday I hoped she and I could be together."

"So you two know each other from school?"

"I know her," he said. "I'm not sure if she knows me. I mean, we had choir together last year, but . . ."

He let his words drift off, though I could fill in the blank. *But he had no idea whether she had ever noticed him, was even aware of his existence.*

"I thought if I did something romantic," he continued, "it might make her more interested."

"I'm going to have to go back to the house, verify that you l-left a note and flowers."

"Do I have to go back, too?"

If there were no note and flowers, he'd have some more explaining to do. Besides, I couldn't very well leave him here. "Yes. You do."

The panic returned, his face contorting in mortification. "But then she'll know it was me!"

"Didn't you sign the note?"

"No! I just signed it from a secret admirer."

Sheesh. This situation was a bit sticky, and I wasn't just talking about the sweat on my back. I was angry at this kid for running from me, but teens tended to overreact. Maybe I could let it slide. *Who am I to stand in the way of this would-be Romeo?*

"If you promise you'll never run from a cop again," I told him, "I'll check things out without identifying you."

"I promise!" he cried.

I led the boy out of the backyard and around the corner, cuffing him to the back door handle of my cruiser. I ordered Brigit to keep watch over him and allowed him to duck out of sight while I returned to the Pham home. Ashley's father stood on the porch, his wife next to him now, a bouquet of pink roses and an opened card in her hand.

"Did you catch the boy?" Mr. Pham demanded.

"I did. But he'd like to remain anonymous. He has feelings for your daughter and left the flowers and note in the hopes of wooing her."

"Woo schmoo!" he snapped. "I don't need horny boys running around my yard, sniffing around my daughter. Take him to jail."

His wife held up the card. "He sounds sweet to me. He says Ashley's voice is like an angel's."

Mr. Pham rolled his eyes. "That old cliché?"

Mrs. Pham rolled her eyes right back. "You never were a romantic. I'm taking this up to Ashley. Let her have some fun. She'll be old and married before she knows it." With that, the woman turned and headed back into the house.

I eyed Mr. Pham. "So, we done here?"

He exhaled a long huff. "Yes. We're done." He slammed the door behind him as he went inside.

As I unlocked the boy's cuffs, he gave Brigit a once-over. "Is that the dog that was in the Paschal High School cafeteria a few days ago?"

My dog was apparently more memorable than me. "Yes, it is."

"She was nominated for prom queen. I voted for her."

"Let me know if she wins," I told the kid. "I'll swing by the school and pick up her tiara."

He rubbed his wrists and stepped away from the car. "Am I free to go now?"

"Yes. But with that peeper on the loose you'd be wise not to be out after dark. There's also an escaped convict in the area. Things could get dangerous if you stumble onto either of them. Go straight home."

"I will," he promised.

I pointed a finger at him. "If I catch you out at night again I won't go so easy on you."

"Thanks for not taking me in."

"You're welcome," I said, unable to fight a smile. "Good luck with the girl."

THIRTY-SIX
NIGHT SHIFT

Brigit

Brigit had enjoyed chasing the boy. Chases were fun! She only wished she could've made it over the fence and pounced on him.

As Megan drove, clouds gathered in the sky and obscured the moon. The night grew darker and darker. Cooler, too. Megan unrolled the windows so Brigit could stand at the mesh and enjoy the fresh night air.

Brigit loved working nights. The sounds were different at night. The smells were different, too. There were more creatures about. Possums. Raccoons. Skunks. She even caught a whiff of Derek Mackey wafting on the breeze, his unique blend of sweat, burgers with plenty of onion, and jock itch ointment.

As Megan turned down a street, Brigit twitched her nose, scenting. She recognized this place. They'd been here just a few nights ago. This was where Brigit had trailed a man from the window of a house until his scent faded out a street or two over.

With any luck, she'd get to trail again tonight.

THIRTY-SEVEN
PARTY POOPER

Tom

It was Wednesday, the thirteenth of May. Thirteen was normally an unlucky number, but he'd decided to push his luck tonight. He simply couldn't wait any longer. His imagination had run dry and he needed some fresh inspiration.

He had no doubt the Rabinowitzes' new au pair could give him plenty of inspiration . . .

He chose an especially dark spot on Windsor Place to park, and set out for Huntington Lane on foot, ducking into the shadows when a minivan trolled slowly past. In less than a minute, he stood in front of the house.

Though the Rabinowitzes had heeded warnings to turn on their lights, the perimeter of their large lot remained in shadow, making it easy for him to circle around the edge of the yard. Pausing in the shadows, he slid the ski mask over his face.

The gate on the four-foot iron fence was latched but not locked. Carefully, he put on another pair of disposable gloves, just like the ones he'd worn last time. It had worried him when he'd taken his pants out of the dryer and found only one of the gloves in the pocket. He'd taken them off at his car door and stuffed them into his pocket, forgetting about them until he'd washed and dried his pants. Probably the glove had fallen out in the laundry hamper and gotten mixed in with the whites or been thrown away. But he didn't want to raise suspicions by asking about it.

He put a finger under the latch, lifting it, slowly and gently swinging the gate open. Luck was with him. The hinges made no noise.

Inside the backyard now, he closed the gate just enough so that it would appear to be shut but was not actually fully latched. He didn't want the latch slowing him down if he had to make a quick escape like last time. *Damn the Lowrys' automatic sprinklers!*

He glanced up at the back of the main house. All of the windows were dark, the inhabitants presumably fast asleep. He turned and looked ahead now. The windows of the guesthouse were dark, too. *The au pair must be getting her beauty sleep.*

He moved swiftly and silently to the front wall of the small structure, stopping for a moment to let his eyes adjust to the darker space. He approached the window and peered inside, his view unobstructed by the café curtains which, by design, left a portion of the window uncovered. The light from the back porch of the main house came through the side window, providing just enough illumination for him to see a kitchenette with a toaster oven and microwave on the counter and a dorm-sized refrigerator situated next to the lower cabinets. A single barstool stood at the counter, providing a place for the au pair to sit for her meals. The kitchenette opened onto a small living area furnished with a love seat, coffee table, and small television set.

He stepped around the side of the structure where he'd have less chance of being seen from the main house. Flanking the guest cottage was a narrow flower bed filled with pink petunias and what, judging from the barnyard smell, had to be fresh composted cow manure. *Ugh.* Not exactly a turn-on. But he'd risked too much to let a little poop ruin this party.

There were three small windows down the left side of the guesthouse, all of them sitting halfway up the wall. Careful to remain on the grass, he leaned in to peek into the first window. Like the windows along the front, this one featured café curtains and looked into the kitchen and living room.

He continued to the second window. This one was fully covered by a curtain. *Damn!*

He crept quietly down to the third window. While a curtain hung in this window, too, it had been pushed aside by a gray cat who lay on top of the dresser inside, providing him with a clear view into the bedroom. The cat continued to sleep, unaware of his presence. *Good pussy.*

Inside the bedroom, a night-light shone, providing enough illumination for him to see the au pair lying on her back on a twin bed. The covers lay in a tousled heap at her feet, as if she'd kicked them back in her sleep. She wore a sleeveless pink nightshirt and matching shorts. The shirt had ridden up, exposing her flat belly. Another inch higher and the bottom curve of her breast would have been exposed.

He stepped closer for a better look, in his excitement forgetting about the compost. As his foot sank into the soft matter, he remembered. Oh, well. Too late now. Besides, he could wipe his shoes clean or throw them out if need be. It was a small price to pay for an up close and personal look at the gorgeous young woman sprawled on the bed before him.

He put his face closer to the screen. A white oscillating fan stood on a desk, slowly sweeping back and forth, sending air across the young woman's exposed body. He willed the fan to blow harder, to send her top up over her head, giving him a full view of her chest. Alas, the fan could not be willed to short-circuit.

Oh, how I wish I could reach out and touch her . . .

But he couldn't.

He'd have to settle for the next best thing.

Tonight, he'd come equipped with a state-of-the-art low-light video camera small enough to fit into the pouch at his waist. While his memory wasn't bad, permanent footage would be much better.

He pulled the camera from the pouch, removed the black plastic lens cap, and set the cap on the windowsill. He'd been too nervous before to photograph the women, afraid he might be caught with evidence, but since he'd gotten away so far he'd grown a bit bolder. More importantly, though, his needs had grown. He could no longer be satisfied with his memory and imagination. He wanted real images of real women.

He bent down, folded out the camera's flip-out screen, and aimed the camera through the window. *Dammit!* The window screen, though not much of an impediment to the human eye, was putting a grid over the image and causing it to pixelate. He fooled with the buttons on the camera, trying different settings, but every time he got the same lousy result.

Good thing he'd brought some tools with him, just in case. He pulled a Swiss army knife from his pouch, opened it, and carefully put the tip of the blade to the screen to cut it back. He'd managed to slice through an inch or two and had his eyes focused on the blade when the cat woke, saw him at the window. With a fierce and feral *RRRRROWWW!,* the beast leaped onto his hind legs and batted his paws at the glass as if trying to break through. *BAP-BAP-BAP!*

Holy shit! Tom jerked back, throwing himself off balance and falling to his ass on the grass.

Woo-woo-woo-woo! The house alarm kicked in, the force of the cat's paws on the window enough to activate the window sensors.

Tom scrambled to his feet and took four steps toward the gate before he remembered the lens cover he'd left on the windowsill. *Shit!* He scrambled back and frantically swiped it from the sill. In his haste he moved too fast and ended up knocking the cap to the ground. Reaching down for it, he banged his head on the wall so hard he saw stars. *Fuck!* The last thing he needed was to knock himself out and be lying here unconscious when the police arrived.

He put a gloved hand to the wall to steady himself. When the stars cleared, he saw the edge of the cap peeking out from under his shoe. He pulled his foot back and grabbed it, turning and taking off for the gate as fast as he could run.

He only hoped it was fast enough.

THIRTY-EIGHT
BANG-BANG

Megan

After releasing the boy, I drove by Hurley's sister's place again. Still no sign of the white pickup he'd stolen.

I went to Blake Looney's house and Nathan Wilmer's apartments next, but had no luck. Nobody answered when I knocked on their doors. There were no lights on in their places that I could tell. The only sign of life at Wilmer's apartment was that the eviction notice had been removed. Had he made good on his past-due rent and been allowed to stay? Had he already taken off for parts unknown? Or had the notice simply been blown off by the wind?

As I slid back into the driver's seat of my cruiser, the dispatcher's voice came over the radio. "We have an attempted breaking and entering in Berkeley Place. Who can respond?"

I grabbed my mic. "Officer Luz and Brigit—"

"Mackey to the rescue!" came Derek's voice over the radio.

Damn him! I'd responded first!

I listened for the address. It was only five blocks from my current location.

"Hang on tight!" I warned Brigit as I turned on my lights and floored my gas pedal.

In seconds, we pulled up in front of the house. Derek careened in from the opposite direction, the two of us nearly having a head-on collision at the mailbox. More headlights were coming up the street. I'd bet that the approaching car was Hawke's Expedition.

I leaped from my car. Derek leaped from his at the same time. We ran to the front door, elbowing each other aside as each of us attempted to be the first to reach the porch. I might have more determination, but the Big Dick had longer legs. He beat me by two steps. *Jackass.*

Derek pounded on the door. *Bam-bam-bam!* "Fort Worth Police!"

A moment later the door opened to reveal a couple in their early thirties. The woman had worry lines on her forehead and a bawling infant in one arm, her other arm draped over the shoulders of a tall, dark-haired woman who appeared to be a decade younger. The younger woman was crying, dabbing her blue eyes with the sleeve of the fluffy white robe she wore. The robe hung at a haphazard angle and her feet were bare.

Derek hooked his thumbs into his belt and rocked back on his heels. "Y'all reported an attempted B and E?"

Before the people could respond, Garrett Hawke stormed up the walk behind us. "Everyone okay here?"

Derek turned to Hawke and looked him up and down, taking in Hawke's well-developed muscles, as well as his tool belt, fully equipped tonight with a handgun. "Who are *you*?"

Had Derek arrived earlier to the meeting at the park, he would've met Hawke already. But since he showed up as the meeting disbanded, he hadn't had the opportunity.

"I'm Garrett Hawke," the man said. "President of the neighborhood watch."

Hawke, too, hooked his thumbs in his belt. Was it just my imagination, or did he flex his biceps, too? I took a closer look. *Yep. Definitely flexed.*

Derek issued a derisive snort and turned back to the frightened people huddled in the doorway. "What happened here?"

"The house alarm went off a few minutes ago," the man said. "The first thing I did was check to make sure everyone in the house was okay. Then I called our au pair." He gestured to the young woman. "She lives in the guesthouse out back."

The young woman sniffled and pushed her long hair back from her face. "Someone was at my window," she said in a voice tinged with an accent I couldn't readily identify. "My cat howled and woke me and I saw a moving shadow outside my window and then the alarm started ringing."

The woman with the baby released the au pair and stepped back, putting her now-free hand to the back of the baby's head and swaying side to side to calm him. Or her. Hard to tell when the baby was bald and dressed in unisex pastel green. Could go either way.

"What's your name?" I asked the au pair.

She sniffled again before answering. "Korinna Papadakis."

Greek. The mystery of her accent was solved.

"And yours?" I asked, looking to the couple.

"Joel and Rachel Rabinowitz," Hawke supplied before they could respond. Despite having received no invitation to enter the home, he pushed his way past me and Derek and stepped through the open door and into the foyer. "Don't y'all worry. Everything's going to be okay."

When he raised a hand to pat Korinna's shoulder, she

recoiled. No wonder. She was already on edge. She didn't need a man she hardly knew touching her after having a stranger at her window.

I reached into the left breast pocket of my uniform and pulled out a small package of tissues. I always kept a pack in one of my pockets, as well as a few Tootsie Rolls in another. You run into a lot of upset people as a cop. The tissues came in handy for drying tears, while the candy could appease a frightened child, at least momentarily. I offered the tissues to Korinna.

"Thanks," she said, taking them from my hand.

Though Korinna's build was thinner than that of Kirstin Rumford or Alyssa Lowry, like the two earlier peeping victims Korinna was tall with long, dark hair. While I'd wondered before if Hurley could be behind these prowler cases in Berkeley Place, that the women might have been intended victims, my gut told me that he wasn't our guy. Hurley was after cash and debit cards. Whoever had been at the women's windows seemed to be looking for a sexual thrill. Even so, my brain told me that the physical similarities between the peeping victims could be purely coincidental, and not to rule Hurley out just yet.

"Other than the shadow," Derek asked Korinna, "did you get a look at the intruder?"

She shook her head, her lip quivering. "No. I jumped out of bed and ran to my bathroom and locked myself in. I didn't come out until I heard my cell phone ringing."

Hawke interjected now. "Could you tell anything about him from the shadow? His size or what he was wearing?"

"No," Korinna said. "Not really."

Hawke continued. "So you can't say what hair color—"

"Step back!" Derek barked at Hawke. "You need to let law enforcement handle this."

The two engaged in a heated staring match for several seconds, like two gorillas who'd come face-to-face in a jungle.

As the men stared each other down, I turned my attention to Mr. and Mrs. Rabinowitz. Thankfully, the baby had calmed and his or her wails were now only a minor blubbering. "Did either of you see the prowler?"

"No," Mrs. Rabinowitz answered. "We didn't even know what had set off the alarm until we spoke to Korinna and she said she'd seen someone at her window. Joel grabbed a flashlight and went to check things out while I went to get the baby."

Poor thing. It had probably been sleeping soundly when the loud noise went off. Talk about a rude awakening.

"I've got a K-9," I told them. "If you'll take me to the window, she can track the prowler." Neither Derek nor Hawke could compete with that. Before we stepped away, I turned to Korinna. "I'll have some more questions for you when I get back. Okay?"

She nodded.

Joel stepped outside. I followed him with Derek and Hawke coming right behind us.

I went to my cruiser and released Brigit. "C'mon, girl. You're up."

Joel led us around the side of the house and approached the gate.

"Wait!" I called. "Don't touch it. The prowler might have left fingerprints on it." I pulled my baton from my belt and flicked my wrist to extend it. *Snap!* I reached over the top of the fence and used the baton to lift the gate latch. The gate swung open and the five of us stepped through.

Joel walked down the grassy stretch alongside the guesthouse. As we went along, my nose detected the earthy scent of compost. I looked for the source, noting a small curved flower bed along the side of the house.

Joel passed the first two windows, stopping at the third. "This is the one."

Derek and I shined our flashlights on the window. Sure enough, the screen had been sliced. It was a clean cut, probably from a knife or box cutter. My thoughts went back to the poor young woman with the gunshot wound, to Detective Bustamente's comment that the screen had been removed from her bedroom window. Could that case have anything to do with this one? Was this more than a mere peeping case? Had Hurley tried to break in here? Or could this be a totally unrelated crime, an attempted sexual assault or murder? My thoughts tossed about in my mind as if my brain were juggling them.

Before I could stop him, Hawke stepped into the flower bed and leaned in to look at the screen, resting a hand on the metal frame.

"Get back!" I spat. "Now!" *Seriously, does this guy have compost for brains?* "I warned you last time not to contaminate the crime scene."

Hawke raised his palms, the flashlight now aimed at his head, giving his face an eerie glow. " 'Scuse me for trying to help."

Veteran or not, I'd had enough of this guy and his ego and his need for control and attention. "When we want your help, Mr. Hawke, we'll ask for it."

Backing me up for once, Derek cut Hawke a pointed look and hiked a thumb over his shoulder. "Wait over there."

Too bad it took a common enemy for Derek and me to get along.

As I bent down next to Brigit, prepared to order her to track, my eye spotted something in the dirt. I shined my flashlight on it. It was flat and black and made of plastic. One edge was a smooth semicircle, while the other was jagged in an irregular pattern. Whatever it was appeared to be only part of something round that had cracked. *But what?* "Any idea what that is?"

Joel and Derek leaned in for a look.

"It's probably part of a sprinkler head," Joel said. "My lawn service is constantly running them over and chewing them up with the mower."

His explanation made sense, and he was probably right. But just in case he wasn't the crime scene techs should collect it and check it for prints.

I gave Brigit the order to track. As we set off, I called back over my shoulder. "Call crime scene. Get Detective Bustamente out here, too."

"I know the drill," Derek snapped. "I'm the one who trained you, remember?"

How could I forget? The few months I'd been partnered with that jerk had been the worst of my life.

Snuffle-snuffle-snuffle. Brigit took the lead, trailing the scent. When she reached the gate, which had a spring and had swung closed on its own, I used my baton once again to open the latch. My partner put her nose back to the ground and continued. I trotted along after her, reduced now to her sidekick.

Brigit made her way down the block, hooked a left on Warner Road, then turned right onto Windsor Place. She stopped in an especially dark stretch of the road and lifted her nose in the air. She slowly stepped forward, head high, before turning her head and taking a couple of steps in the other direction. Eventually she gave up and sat down, looking up at me.

"This is where he got into his car, huh?" I bent down and put one hand on each side of her furry neck, treating her to a nice, two-handed scratch. "Good girl, Brigit. Good girl."

She *woofed* as I stood.

"Quiet," I ordered. It was late at night and her bark risked waking the residents.

She *woofed* louder as she stood and looked up at me. *Woof-woof! Woof-woof-woof!*

"Quiet!" I hissed again.

She stepped over and shoved her nose into the pocket where I normally kept her liver treats. I hadn't brought any with me tonight and she was none too happy about that. She let me know just how she felt by flopping down on the ground and looking up at me with an expression of pure and utter disgust.

THIRTY-NINE
RESIGNATION

Brigit

If Brigit had had opposable thumbs she would have typed up a letter of resignation. Working for belly rubs and butt scratches was for amateurs. She deserved better. She deserved a liver treat, dammit!

Surely there was some type of canine labor law that required compensation to be delivered in edible form. Maybe she'd round up the other K-9s, form a union, issue a list of demands. That would show these humans who was boss.

If Megan wasn't going to give her any liver treats, then she'd go on strike, refuse to work. She flopped down on her belly like a furry anvil and refused to move.

Kiss my fluffy butt.

FORTY

SELF-LOVE LEADS TO SELF-LOATHING

Tom

He reached into his pocket for the lens cap, felt the jagged edge, and realized he had only a broken part of it. Panic gripped his chest.

Where is the other half?

Is it still in the flower bed or did I drop it somewhere?

FORTY-ONE
CONDUCT UNBECOMING

Megan

Brigit wouldn't budge. When coaxing her didn't work, I went full-on alpha, barking orders as loud as I dared this late at night and physically attempting to lift her to a stand.

She wasn't having it.

When I saw her eye my pocket once again, I realized what the problem was. Brigit was angry that I hadn't given her a liver treat lately. Who could blame her? She loved the things and she worked hard to earn them.

I bent down and ran a hand over her back, looking her in the eye. "If you're a good girl and come with me now, we'll stop at the store for a whole box of treats. How's that sound?"

As if she understood, she wagged her tail and got to her feet.

"Good girl." I gave her a peck on the snout.

She and I headed back to the Rabinowitz home. As many cars as were at their house now, you'd think they were having a party. In addition to the two police cruisers, Bustamente's plain sedan, and Hawke's Expedition, there were three other cars, all sporting the neighborhood watch signs. The first was a Mercedes E250 in a shade of blue so dark it appeared nearly black. The second was a burgundy Chrysler 300. The last was a white Honda Odyssey minivan.

Bustamente, Hawke, and Joel Rabinowitz stood on the porch speaking with three other men, presumably the other members of the watch who were currently on duty. One of them was Victor Paludo, the creep who'd been staring at reporter Trish LeGrande's breasts at the meeting at the park. There was no sign of Derek. He was probably still at the guesthouse protecting the crime scene.

I clipped Brigit's leash onto her collar and led her up to the porch. As we walked, I noticed she put her nose to the ground and began to snuffle again. Probably some creature of the night had been out here.

As Brigit and I approached, Bustamente turned from the men to me. "Any luck?"

"Same as last time." I stepped onto the porch. "The suspect must have gotten into a car."

The three men with Hawke and Joel Rabinowitz seemed to represent a cross-section of Berkeley Place. The first was the silver-haired Paludo, who looked to be around seventy-five. He wore a loose tee and a pair of stretch-waist nylon running pants, though the potbelly told me he wore them for comfort rather than exercise. The instant I stopped in front of him, his focus shifted down from my face to my chest. The pervy vibe he'd given me at the meeting in the park was back with a vengeance, and this time it was personal. I crossed my arms over my chest, hoping he'd take the hint. His eyes moved back to my face, though they continued to flicker downward.

"Nice to meet you, Officer Luz," he said, casting a glance down at Brigit. "Beautiful dog you've got there."

"Thanks. She's smart, too. Top of her training class." It was more than I could say for myself. Though I'd excelled at the written tests, I performed average on the physicals tests, and barely eked by on the shooting test.

Brigit sniffed intently at his pants.

"She must smell Bitsy," the man said. "That's our Chihuahua. She's a handful."

I wasn't sure whether he meant a literal or figurative handful, but either could probably apply.

The second man was fiftyish and dressed in a golf shirt and khaki shorts. His brown hair bore a few subtle streaks of gray. "Rick Westmoreland," he said, taking my hand.

I gave him a firm handshake and a nod.

The last was a brown-haired man in his mid-forties who stood no taller than me. He looked vaguely familiar. It took me only a moment to realize he was the one who'd been with the Realtor at the watch meeting at the park. "You're Nora Conklin's husband, right?"

"That's how I'm known around here." The man smiled, but it seemed halfhearted. Perhaps he'd spent too much time living in the shadow of his tiny yet larger-than-life wife.

Brigit stepped up to the man, sniffing him intently. A moment later, she sat down in front of him and stared straight ahead, giving her passive alert. *Uh-oh.*

I took a step closer. "Sir, is there something in your pockets that shouldn't be there?"

His face tightened in unease. "What do you mean?"

"I'm talking about drugs. My dog seems to have alerted on you."

"Oh!" Conklin chuckled, his face relaxing. "No drugs, but I did bring a snack." He reached into his pants pocket and pulled out a small foil package of peanuts. The package had been opened, half of the contents eaten, the top of the bag folded over so the remaining nuts wouldn't fall out. He pulled out all of his remaining pockets, too, showing me that all they contained other than the peanuts were his wallet and keys.

"My apologies." I glared down at my furry partner. "My dog's been on a diet and she's none too happy about it."

"No problem," he said, pushing his pockets back into place.

My gaze ran over the men. "Did any of you notice any cars parked on Windsor Place just east of Warner Road?"

"If there was a car parked there," Paludo said, "it didn't catch my eye."

Maybe it would have if the car had sported breasts.

"I don't remember seeing a car, either," said Conklin.

Westmoreland simply raised his palms and his shoulders.

The sound of a vehicle pulling up to the curb behind me drew my eye. It was a crime scene van, driven by a boxy female tech with thick black hair. We'd crossed paths before. She was no-nonsense, thorough, and efficient.

"Excuse me," I said to the men, leaving them in the detective's hands for now.

I led Brigit down the front walk to the van.

The woman hopped down from the truck, her plastic toolbox in her hand. "Where'm I goin'?" she asked, wasting no time.

"Around back," I said. "I'll show you."

Bustamente came down from the porch. When Hawke and the other men made to follow us, he raised a hand. "Sorry, guys. Police only."

Hawke turned back to the men. "It's just as well. We should get back out on patrol in case this creep is still around."

The tech followed me and the detective around to the

guesthouse, where the Big Dick stood waiting several feet back on the grass.

I stopped and pointed to the damaged screen. "The prowler did that."

She pulled out her flashlight, turned it on, and took a look.

She ran the beam of light over the compost. "Looks like someone with very large feet stomped around under this window."

Hawke. "The president of the watch group stepped in there before we could stop him."

She grunted. "If there were other footprints in this soil, he mucked 'em up."

Damn him! "Wait." I pulled my flashlight out again and shined it on a flat, half-moon spot near the outer edge of the flower bed. "Is that a different footprint?"

The tech squatted down. "Looks like a partial print. The toe. It's much smaller, though. Definitely from a different shoe. Doesn't look like it belongs to a grown man unless he's a small one. Could it have been the nanny? Or the wife?"

"I don't think either one of them have come out here since the alarm went off," I said.

The tech stood. "I'll check on that. It's also possible that one of them left the print earlier, maybe when they were watering the flowers. Or the print could belong to a kid."

Could the peeping Tom be merely a curious adolescent? I supposed it was possible. Pubescent boys had raging hormones. They also had poor impulse control thanks to the lack of full connection between their frontal lobes and the rest of their brains. Their frontal lobes also lacked a sufficient coating of myelin or "white matter," the fatty material that helped the different parts of the brain communicate. I'd learned this in my juvenile justice class. Basically, it explained why tweens and teens do so many risky, dangerous, and outright dumb-ass things, like drag racing and experimenting with drugs and having a friend pierce their ear with only an ice cube and an unsterilized safety pin. Talk about an infection waiting to happen.

I motioned to the broken piece of black plastic. "The homeowner said he thinks that's part of a damaged sprinkler head, but I figured it couldn't hurt for you to take a closer look."

Using a pair of long metal tongs, she fished the piece out of the dirt and dropped it into a plastic evidence bag.

Derek held out a hand to the tech. "Got your crime scene tape? I'll mark off the area."

The woman pulled a roll of yellow tape from her pocket and handed it to him.

While the two taped off a perimeter, Bustamente took me aside. "What kind of feeling did you get from Paludo?"

"An icky one."

"Me, too. I noticed he seemed awfully interested in a couple of things . . ." He gestured to my chest but kept his eyes on my face.

"My shiny badge and name tag?" I provided.

Bustamente snorted. "Yeah."

"I noticed that, too. You think he could be the peeper?"

"I think we'd be wise to keep an eye on him."

Ugh. Rather than narrowing down the list of suspects, the investigation only seemed to provide new ones. There was Jerry Jeff Gilbreath, of course, and Ralph Hurley, the man who'd cut off his ankle monitor in San Antonio, fled, and been purportedly spotted in north Texas. Though Hurley's history indicated he was after money rather than sexual gratification, it was possible he'd been the one at the windows, attempting to gain access in order to steal the inhabitants' debit cards. Garrett Hawke was still near the top of my list, too. Though his standard MO differed, Nathan Wilmer had not yet been eliminated. Despite the fact that I'd stopped by his house two more times, I had yet to speak with Blake Looney, the loss prevention officer who'd spied on women in the dressing rooms at Nordstrom. And now Victor Paludo could be added to the list of potential suspects.

Seriously, is the world full of lawbreakers and perverts or what?

As much as I'd like to stick around and see what the detective and tech might find, Derek had clearly staked his claim here, trying to horn in on the case, probably hoping to garner some of the glory when the case was solved.

Brigit and I strode back to the front of the house. Although the minivan, the Chrysler, and the Mercedes were gone, Hawke's Expedition remained. He sat in the front seat looking down at a tablet that lit up his face.

Several questions popped haphazardly into my mind, like mental popcorn.

Hawke's touching Korinna had been an overly familiar gesture, a violation of her personal space. *Did it mean anything?*

Hawke was on duty every time the BP Peeper struck. *Did that mean something?*

Zach had mentioned that the former paratrooper he'd met had been injured in training and never served overseas. *Was the man he met Garrett Hawke? Had Hawke ever served in Iraq?*

The only one of these questions that I could get a definitive answer to at the moment was the last one. I led Brigit over to Hawke's car, noted that he'd pulled up a page of communications equipment on his tablet, and rapped on his window.

He didn't seem startled, so he must've seen me coming in his peripheral vision. He pressed the button to roll the window down. "Did y'all find any clues back there?"

"Just your footprints so far," I said. "Got anything you'd like to confess?"

He barked a laugh, as if the idea of him being the peeper were absurd, but quickly quieted when he saw the intent look on my face.

I leaned in closer. "You mentioned at the meeting at Forest Park that your unit served in Iraq. Tell me more about that."

Alarm flickered over his face, though he acted nonchalant, lifting a shoulder. "What would you like to know?"

I, too, feigned nonchalance, lifting my own shoulder. "What did you like best about serving there?"

"What did I like best about serving in the army?" he said. "I guess it was the camaraderie. It certainly wasn't the food or—"

"I didn't ask what you liked best about serving in the army. I asked what you liked best about serving *in Iraq*."

He hesitated a moment, his jaw flexing as he obviously debated how to respond. He chose, wisely, to respond with the truth, probably knowing the police had ways of verifying information. "I never made it to Iraq."

"You said at the meeting that your paratrooper unit had been deployed to Iraq."

"It was," he said.

"But you weren't with the rest of them?"

The jaw flexed again. "No."

"Why not?"

He lost his cool. "Because I shattered my fucking leg at Fort Hood, that's why!" He attempted to deflect my questions by turning things on me. "Is this the way Fort

Worth Police treats veterans? By putting them through an inquisition?"

I decided to be blunt. It was probably the only approach that would work with this guy. "It seems like you were trying to mislead the people at the meeting."

He took his hands off his tablet and raised them in innocence. "I never claimed to have been in Iraq. If they misunderstood, that's their problem."

I gave him a pointed look. "Are we on the same side, Mr. Hawke? Because if we are, I'd appreciate you shooting straight with me."

He cast me an irritated look, glanced away for a moment, and turned back, his face strained. He scrubbed a hand over it. "People like to know that someone's looking out for them. They need a hero."

What he said was true. But it was only half of the story, wasn't it? "And some people need to *be* that hero, don't they?"

He snorted softly, mirthlessly. He stared out his windshield, sitting quietly for a moment. "I suppose so," he said finally. After another short silence, he turned to me. "Look. I joined the army thinking I'd get to make a difference. But I was just a dumb-ass kid back then and I did some stupid things and got myself injured. The day the army gave me my medical discharge papers was the worst day of my life. Do you have any idea what it's like to feel that you're no good to anybody anymore?"

I related to his need for purpose, his desire to help others. Heck, I felt the same way. That's why I'd become a police officer.

He let out a long breath. "I suppose serving in the watch makes me feel like I'm doing something, making amends for screwing up before. I know I can go a little overboard at times, but I'm not one of those people who can stand back and do nothing when I see a job that needs to be done. Especially if that job is protecting my family and neighbors."

Hawke and I had much more in common than I'd realized. "Thanks, Garrett. I appreciate you being honest with me."

"You didn't give me much choice, now, did you?" Though he scoffed indignantly, the small smile he gave me seemed sincere.

I gestured to his tablet. "Whatcha got there?"

"I'm shopping for radios for the watch crew. If everyone has radios we'll be able to get in touch with each other faster than we can using our cell phones."

"Good idea." I stepped back from his car. "Take care now."

Bustamente came around the corner of the house and motioned for me to follow him. Brigit and I went with him to the front door of the house. He knocked lightly. Joel Rabinowitz answered a few seconds later.

"Got some questions for y'all," Bustamente said.

Joel stepped back to allow us to enter. There was no sign of his wife. She'd probably taken the baby back to bed upstairs.

"Korinna's in the kitchen," he said, gesturing to his right.

The au pair was seated at the kitchen table, a mug of steaming fruit-flavored tea sitting in front of her. She looked a little less shell-shocked now, but still worried.

Bustamente dropped into a chair across from her, and I took the one next to him, giving Brigit the order to lie at my feet. She sniffed around under the table, searching for errant crumbs, but found none. The Rabinowitz home was spotless.

Though Bustamente would take the lead in questioning the victim, I pulled my pad of paper and pen from my pocket to take notes.

The detective introduced himself to Korinna. He tilted his head to indicate me. "Officer Luz will be assisting me in this investigation."

When she looked my way, I gave the young woman a nod and a sympathetic smile. She nodded in return.

The detective folded his hands on the table. "Can you tell me whether you've seen anyone suspicious around?"

"Like a stranger, you mean?" Korinna asked.

"Maybe," he said. "Or maybe someone you know who might have taken an unusual interest in you. A clerk at a store where you shop. Someone from church or the park."

"Maybe an acquaintance or neighbor?" I added. *Victor Paludo, for instance.*

She shook her head. "I can't think of anyone."

Bustamente nodded. "Have you noticed a green Isuzu Amigo with a soft top? It's a type of convertible SUV."

She shook her head again. "I don't think so."

"What about a white Ford F-150 pickup truck?"

Her shoulders lifted. "I do not pay much attention to cars."

The Hurley connection was probably a long shot, anyway. Hurley was after money, not sexual thrills as this intruder seemed to be. Besides, Hurley would be more likely to target the residents of the main home, who'd have more money, right? Then again, maybe he'd figure the guesthouse would be an easier target.

Bustamente continued his questioning. "What about men doing work on the house or in the neighborhood? An exterminator or painter? Anything like that?"

"No, not that I remember." Her eyes darkened and she chewed at her lip. "The only one I can think of . . ." Her voice trailed off.

"Who is it, Korinna?" the detective asked.

She slumped in her seat. "It might be my ex-boyfriend."

"Your ex? What's his name?"

"Jamie Gowan."

I asked her to spell the name for me and jotted it on my pad. I looked back up at her. "What makes you think it might be him?"

She hesitated a moment, chewing her lip, as if afraid to answer. "He slapped me a few times while we were dating. That is why I broke up with him."

I felt my body go rigid in anger, the woman in me instinctively itching to take hold of my baton and go in search of the jerk, treat him to some street justice. The cop in me knew that would be a very bad idea, especially if I wanted to hang on to my badge and make detective one day.

"How long ago did you break up?" the detective asked.

"Two months," she said. "That is when I took this job and moved here."

"Two months," Bustamente repeated as he made a note on his own pad. "Where did you live before?"

"In Houston," she said. "I worked for a nice family there but I was afraid to stay so close to Jamie. He kept calling me and coming by the house when he knew the husband and wife would not be home. I was afraid that I was putting the family in danger so I asked the placement service to find me a new job in another city."

"Does Jamie still call you?"

"No. I bought a new phone when I moved here. He doesn't know the number."

"Does he know where you moved to?"

"I don't think so," she said. "I told the family that I worked for that I was moving to Fort Worth, but they would not have told him."

"Did you post anything on social media? Facebook, maybe? Instagram? Even a picture can sometimes give away clues."

"No," she replied. "I took down my Facebook page before I left Houston. I do not use any other social media."

"What about a friend? Could one of them have posted something on their pages?"

"I don't have many friends in America. Only a few other au pairs and a friend from high school who works in California. They do not post very often."

"What about the placement office? Could he have obtained your new address from someone there?"

"I would not think so," she said. "They are supposed to only take messages and pass them on to us. They are not supposed to give out our phone numbers or addresses."

Even so, it was possible her ex had weaseled the information out of someone who worked at the placement office. People could be gullible and easily persuaded, especially if they thought the situation was urgent.

She gave us Gowan's address and told us that he worked as a bartender at a Mexican restaurant in the northern suburbs. "I don't remember his phone number," she said. "I deleted it from my contacts list."

I jumped in again. "Did you report the abuse?"

She shook her head. "No. It didn't leave any marks. He told me it would be my word against his and that the police would not believe a foreigner."

Ugh. Abusers could be so manipulative. "You realize that's not true, right?"

Tears welled up in her eyes. "I do now."

I reached across the table and gave her hand a squeeze. "I'm glad the alarm went off, Korinna. Before anything bad happened to you."

She swallowed hard, as if forcing down a lump of emotion. "Me, too."

As I stood to go, Rachel Rabinowitz appeared in the kitchen doorway. "I've got the spare bedroom made up for you, Korinna."

The young woman stood, too. "Thanks."

"We'll be back in touch," Bustamente told the two of them, "as soon as we know something."

Brigit had fallen asleep on the floor, so I nudged her butt with my toe to wake her. "Time to go, girl."

She lumbered to her feet and we followed Rachel to the door.

"Take care," the detective said. "Keep a close eye on things."

"Believe me," she replied, keeping her voice low, "we will."

Bustamente and I parted ways at the curb. "Have a good night, Officer Luz."

"You, too, Detective."

As I returned to my cruiser, ideas exploded like popcorn in my mind once again. Was this incident committed by the same man who'd spied on the other women, or could Korinna's ex be the one who'd been outside the guesthouse tonight? Did Ralph Hurley have anything to do with this? What about Victor Paludo? Hawke had seemed sincere earlier, but did that mean he was no longer a suspect?

And perhaps the most important question of all was *When will we get some damn answers?!?*

FORTY-TWO
MIDNIGHT SNACK

Brigit

Brigit would have liked to have some of the peanuts that man had in his pocket earlier, but he hadn't offered her any. Of course the peanuts weren't the reason why she'd alerted on him. She recognized his scent and thought Megan might want to know. Of course she recognized the scents of the other men, too. The big one and the older one. They didn't seem quite as important, though.

As promised, Megan stopped at the grocery store and took Brigit inside with her to buy a box of liver treats. They stopped down another aisle where Megan spoke briefly with Frankie, who was stocking shelves. Brigit nudged Frankie's hand, knowing their roomie was always good for a scratch. Frankie did not disappoint, treating Brigit to a ten-fingered neck massage.

Back at the cruiser, Megan opened the box and fed Brigit five treats, which she wolfed down in rapid succession, hardly bothering to chew. *Yum!*

FORTY-THREE
NIGHT SHIFT

Tom

Another dose of the sleeping aid in her second glass of wine was all it took to knock her out. Good thing she was such a lightweight. Her arms lay limp on the bedspread, her mouth hung open like a dead trout's, and her head lay at an odd angle on the pillow. She'd probably wake with a crick in her neck, but he made no move to adjust her head to a more comfortable position. Her head could fall off and roll away for all he cared.

Dressed in dark green, he slipped out the door. He'd decided to try a new strategy tonight. Normally, he chose quiet nights to sneak around, assuming there would be less chance of being noticed. But on a Saturday night, when there was much more activity on the streets and many more sounds on the airwaves, maybe he'd actually be less conspicuous, less likely to be heard at a window or to raise the suspicions of passersby.

His strategy worked. He kept his head down as he walked, making long strides. None of the cars that passed slowed for the driver to take a closer look. A group of adolescent girls who'd likely snuck out of a slumber party paid him no mind as they giggled and gaggled their way down the sidewalk, rolls of toilet paper tucked under their arms. Looked like they planned to decorate someone's trees with the bathroom tissue.

A minute later he reached the house, took a quick look up and down the street, and darted into the yard. He knew which window was the bedroom. All it took was driving by late a couple of nights and discerning which light was still on at ten o'clock. *The second window down on the right side of the house.*

A thick fabric shade with a scalloped edge hung inside the window. While little light escaped around the sides of the shade, the space between the curves along the bottom let out the flickering light of a television. The flickering light that filtered *out* told him that those same curves would also let him peek *in.* What's more, the noise of the television would help to mask any noise he might inadvertently make.

So far, so good.

He crept forward, stepping onto the small lava rocks that served to retain water in the flower bed. The rocks were sharp and hard but, while they would help the bed preserve moisture, they wouldn't preserve a footprint.

As he crouched down, the rocks shifted, giving off a grating, gravelly sound. Luckily for him, it was faint enough that it drew no attention from the woman inside.

She was dressed only in a baby-blue knit nightie, so short that it rode up nearly to the top of her thighs as she sat on the edge of the bed and bent over to rub lotion on her legs. Her long, dark hair swung forward and he longed to reach out and grab it and bury his face in it, feel the silky strands on his bare skin.

Shifting to his knees on the pointy rocks, he grimaced against the pain. My God! The fucking rocks were like tiny arrowheads trying to pierce his clothing and skin. The bark chips at Kirstin Rumford's place had been much more forgiving. He wished he'd had the forethought to wear knee pads.

He pulled out his small video camera and readied it, aiming it at the woman through the window. When she bent her right leg and lifted it up to apply lotion to the back of her thigh, his groin sprang to life and he nearly buckled in two. He knew then, without a doubt, that all of the pain he felt was worth it.

She's not wearing panties under her nightie.

He pressed the button to begin recording. *Click.*

FORTY-FOUR
DEUS *EX* MACHINA

Megan

Jamie Gowan might have gotten away with slapping Korinna Papadakis, but he wasn't about to get away with assaulting a cop. After I'd informed Detective Bustamente about Korinna's abusive ex, he'd contacted Houston PD and requested an officer stop by Jamie's place to question him. It had taken until Tuesday evening to catch the guy at home, but officers finally managed to connect with him. Jamie had taken offense to the officer asking where he'd been the night someone had been outside Korinna's window. He'd gone from taking offense to taking a swing, and had promptly been arrested.

Whether he'd been the one at Korinna's window was still anyone's guess. He'd offered no rock-solid alibi, claiming he'd been home alone at his apartment all night, though after he'd been cuffed he told the police that his Netflix viewing history would show he'd binge-watched several seasons of *Breaking Bad* that night. It was possible that someone else had used his account to watch the movies, or that he'd streamed them on his laptop to cover his ass but not actually watched them.

I was back on the day shift this week. While my body and brain rejoiced to return to their natural biorhythms,

I feared for the women of Berkeley Place. I knew my fellow officers working the swing and night shifts would pay extra attention to the area, but it was a large neighborhood with lots of places where someone could hide from even the most dedicated eye. Having responded to the calls and interviewed the victims, I felt personally responsible for them and the other women in Berkeley Place.

Evidently, Bustamente realized how emotionally invested I was in this case. He phoned my cell at nine Wednesday night. "I just got a call from Jerry Jeff Gilbreath."

Gilbreath. The *Wheel* watcher who'd been convicted of two attempted sexual assaults. I wondered what he'd called about. "Wh-what did he say?"

"That some quote-unquote Terminator just came to his apartment with two other men and threatened him."

There was no doubt in my mind that the Terminator was Garrett Hawke. The other two men were likely members of the neighborhood watch, as well.

"What are you going to do?" I asked.

"I'm going to visit with Gilbreath," the detective said, "then I'm going to visit with Garrett Hawke. I was thinking maybe you would want to come with me."

Heck, yeah, I would! Never mind that my shift had ended four hours ago. I'd gladly put in some unpaid overtime. "Thanks, Detective."

We arranged to meet at Gilbreath's apartment. I pulled my hair up into a quick bun, put my uniform back on, and rounded up Brigit from the backyard, where she'd been lying in the grass, probably hoping a possum or raccoon would be dumb enough to venture into the yard and provide her with something to pursue. "We're back on, girl."

She was on her four feet in an instant. She took her job as seriously as I took mine.

We sped to the station to retrieve our cruiser and headed over to Gilbreath's apartment complex to find the detective already waiting in the lot, standing next to his unmarked car.

He issued a sigh. "So much for my warning to tread lightly."

My K-9 partner and I followed Bustamente to Gilbreath's door. "Any word on the broken plastic?" I asked. "Did it turn out to be part of a sprinkler head like Mr. Rabinowitz thought?"

"Nope. The finish on the broken piece was different than the finish on the sprinkler heads at the house. The thickness was different, too. The tech thinks it could have been part of some equipment used by the lawn-care service. Maybe part of a weed-whacker spool."

Or it could be something else entirely. When would we get a definitive clue in this case or locate Ralph Hurley? I was growing more frustrated by the minute and living in constant fear that a woman in W1 would end up assaulted or dead. While I knew my fellow officers were doing their best to keep residents safe, having been drawn more deeply into the investigation I couldn't help but feel that the safety and lives of the women in W1 were primarily in my hands and Brigit's paws. It was a heavy responsibility to bear.

When we reached the door, Bustamente knocked once with his meaty knuckles and said loudly, "Fort Worth Police."

Gilbreath opened the door. My Lord, I hadn't thought it possible but the man was even uglier in person than he'd been in his photo. Thinning pewter strands stuck to his greasy scalp, the brown hair he'd sported in his mug shot from a decade earlier now reflecting how much he'd aged in prison. His eyes sat in deep-set sockets under a thick, protruding brow that left them in constant shadow. He was dressed in dirty blue work pants and a yellowed undershirt, along with the filthiest socks I'd ever seen. A pair of mud-encrusted steel-toed boots had been kicked off and lay just inside the door on the stained carpet. The television set was tuned to the Game Show Network, an episode of *Deal or No Deal* playing. A lopsided recliner sat in front of the TV, a pizza box and a can of cheap beer on the table next to it. Both Gilbreath and his apartment smelled of sweat and beer and feet, with undertones of a corn chip aroma that probably had nothing to do with actual corn chips.

"So you gonna arrest the guy or what?" Gilbreath said without preamble, looking from Bustamente to me and back to the detective.

"We need to ask you some questions first," the detective said.

Gilbreath scowled at Brigit. "That dog ain't coming in my apartment."

"None of us are." Bustamente's thick lip curled in disgust as he looked past Gilbreath into the garbage heap the man called home.

A cockroach zipped past Gilbreath's filthy feet and fled the apartment. Even bugs were repulsed by the man and his habits.

"Tell us what happened," the detective said.

"I was just sitting here watching TV," Gilbreath said, "when all of a sudden someone's banging on my door. I answered it and there were three guys, like I told you on the phone. A big motherfucker with a gun on his hip and a medium-sized one and some shrimp."

The shrimp might have been Todd Conklin. The identity of the medium-sized one was anyone's guess at this point. Westmoreland maybe? Paludo?

"The big one said if he finds out that I've been peeking in on women in his neighborhood he'd make me sorry I was ever born."

"Sorry you were ever born," the detective repeated. "Those were his exact words?"

"Damn straight!"

"Did the men identify themselves?" Bustamente asked.

"Hell, no!" Gilbreath huffed. "The big one told me I better not call the cops on them, neither. Then they left."

Bustamente issued a grunt of acknowledgment. "Did the other two men say anything to you?"

"No. They just stood there like a couple of pussies."

"Did you see what kind of car they were driving?"

"Are you kidding me?" Gilbreath cried, his mouth gaping with incredulity. "The guy just threatened to kill me! I wasn't about to follow him out to his car and get myself shot!"

Bustamente's eyes narrowed. "You told me the man said he'd 'make you sorry you were born.' That's not a specific death threat."

"If it ain't," Gilbreath cried, "I don't know what is!"

After the way Gilbreath had terrorized his victims, it gave me no small sense of satisfaction to see the fear in his eyes. "Looks like karma caught up with you."

Gilbreath cast a look of utter contempt my way before returning his focus to Bustamente. "You going to let this girl talk to me like that?"

My hand went involuntarily to my baton. *Girl?* Did he not see my police uniform? My gun? My baton? My badge? Clearly this guy was some kind of misogynist. A misogynist who was two seconds away from meeting my nightstick.

While I was having a hard time keeping my cool, Bustamente didn't bat an eye. "I'm not only going to let this 'girl' speak her mind, I'm going to let her finish your interrogation."

Ha! If he wasn't married and I didn't fear a sexual harassment charge, I would've kissed Detective Bustamente about then.

My mind began working at warp speed, determining what questions I should ask Gilbreath. I decided to ask him some questions under the guise of identifying the men who'd come to his door, but with the real intent of determining whether he might be the Berkeley Place Peeper. "Any idea where these men might be from? What neighborhood the big man was referring to?"

Gilbreath frowned at me and hesitated, probably debating whether he should stoop so low as to answer questions from a "girl." But he seemed to realize that if he failed to respond, we'd do nothing to pursue the man who'd threatened him. "I don't know. Probably Berkeley Place."

He'd come up with the answer awfully quick. *Does that mean he's the guy we've been after?* "What makes you think they were from Berkeley Place?"

He rolled his eyes. "Because it's all over the goddamn news, that's why. That slutty reporter from Dallas keeps harping on it, like it's the story of the year. So a guy looked in some windows. So what? Who gives a shit?"

So what? So women felt fearful and violated, that's what. And as far as who gave a shit, *I* did. It was my job to make sure the residents of W1 felt safe and secure and protected. And when I had a job to do, I was going to do it to the best of my ability.

"Have you been in Berkeley Place recently?" I asked Gilbreath.

"No."

"You sure?"

He rolled his eyes again. "I got no reason to be over

there. It's nothing but a bunch of rich bitches and assholes looking down on people."

I decided to turn his words and stereotypes back on him. "So you're familiar with the area, then?"

He paused a moment, his eyes narrowing as he realized a mere girl had tricked him. "I didn't say that."

I gestured toward his Jeep Renegade. "Do you have a built-in GPS in your Jeep?" If he'd left the system on, maybe there'd be a way to check the history, see if he'd recently driven through Berkeley Place late at night.

"No. Nice try." He punctuated his words with a knowing smirk, as if he'd read my mind.

I asked whether there was anyone who could vouch for his whereabouts on the nights Kirstin Rumford, Alyssa Lowry, and Korinna Papadakis had been spied on.

"Like a family member?" he quipped. "Or a friend?"

"Sure."

"Why," he said, stretching a hand out to the inside doorjamb. "Here's one now!"

He closed his fist around something and, before I realized what he was doing, tossed an enormous cockroach into my face. The bug's hard shell hit the side of my nose and I felt its tiny legs grappling for purchase on my cheek. Instinctively, I cried out and stepped back, slapping it away. It fell to the ground and scurried off to join its friend.

Gilbreath emitted a nasty chuckle scented with sour beer. "Screaming, just like a girl. What did I tell you?" He cast a glance at Bustamente and shook his head.

When my hand went instinctively for my baton the detective grabbed my wrist to stop me. "We're done here." He released my arm, turned, and walked away.

I followed suit, leading Brigit along with me.

"You better do something!" Gilbreath hollered after

us. "If that guy comes back and shoots me I'll sue the police department for a million dollars!"

I was tempted to turn around and ask Gilbreath how he planned to file a lawsuit from hell, but decided instead to repeat a calming mantra, a technique I'd learned in the anger management class the police chief had ordered me to take after I'd Tasered Derek. With no mantra at the ready, I went for the first thing that popped into my head, the Fort Worth Police Department Honor Code.

> *I will respectfully serve the citizens of Fort Worth and the Fort Worth Police Department. I will dedicate myself to the protection of life, property, and our public trust. My integrity, character, and courage will be above reproach, and I will accept no less from other members of our department.*

Of course, I added my own new closing verse. *I will not beat that bastard into a pulp and let the cockroaches feast on his dead flesh, no matter how much he deserves it.*

The detective and I reached our cruisers, which sat side by side in the lot.

"Sorry," I said. "I lost my temper. But in my defense I would've only hit him once."

He chuckled and heaved a weary sigh. "Protecting a man with two convictions for attempted rape. Not exactly what I'd aspired to when I joined the force."

Me, neither. Still, we had to protect all of the people in W1, even those we deemed unworthy. We both knew it.

"Let's go find Hawke," the detective said resignedly.

I consulted my Berkeley Place roster, found Hawke's address, and gave it to the detective, following him as he drove over. We exited our cars and went to the door, where Bustamente pushed the doorbell button, holding it down for several seconds, probably a subconscious indicator of his frustration with this case. *Diiiiing-doooong.*

Standing at my side, Brigit perked her ears as she heard sounds from inside that were audible only to her superior ears. Her tail wagged, slapping against my leg. A moment later, we humans heard a soft, muffled sound from the other side of the door, probably someone looking through the peephole.

The door swung open to reveal Hawke's wife. She wore spandex exercise clothes and sneakers, her dark hair pulled back from her face into a braid that hung halfway down her back. Judging from the pink flush on her face, the damp tendrils that had pulled loose from the braid, and her body mass index—which I estimated to be a low 18.5—the detective and I had interrupted an intense workout. Next to her stood a small fawn-colored Pekingese, its long, thick hair reminiscent of Cousin Itt from the classic *Addams Family* television show. The small dog took a step forward and lifted its head to exchange sniffs with Brigit.

Worry flickered across Mrs. Hawke's face, her features tightening. "Is everything okay?"

Bustamente raised a hand. "No need for concern, ma'am. We're here to speak to your husband."

"He's out on patrol," she said, her face relaxing. "He won't be back until his shift ends at one o'clock."

It dawned on me then that, as protective as Garrett Hawke seemed to be, it was odd that he'd leave his wife at home to defend herself if the BP Peeper or Ralph Hurley happened to set his sights on her. The dog certainly couldn't provide any protection, and the fact that it hadn't even bothered to bark upon hearing the doorbell told me it was no good as a watchdog, either. As much as I tired of having to constantly feed, water, and clean up after

Brigit, at least she earned her keep. Then again, their house was well lit outside, and a glance into the home told me their windows were securely covered with thick drapes. A keypad for a security system was also visible on the wall behind Mrs. Hawke, a red indicator light blinking. Maybe Hawke thought these precautions were enough to keep his family safe.

"Would you like Garrett's cell number?" she offered.

"No need," I told her, remembering that the cell phone number for each member of the watch was listed next to their name on the schedule. "I've got it in my car."

FORTY-FIVE
KEPT K-9

Brigit

Brigit exchanged sniffs with the fluffy little creature, though she only did so to be polite. Heck, the little thing was more toy than dog. It hadn't made a peep when the doorbell rang. Barking at a doorbell was Canine 101. *Sheesh.* What an embarrassment to their species.

FORTY-SIX
BLACK AND WHITE

Tom

His heart leaped into his throat.

Shit!!!

Are they on to me?

He let out a relieved breath when the unmarked white cruiser drove past him and turned down a side street, followed by the black-and-white patrol car. Of course everything at night was black-and-white, or one of the many shades of gray that spanned the color spectrum between them.

Night is like an Ansel Adams photograph.

FORTY-SEVEN
GETTING THE PICTURE

Megan

From the glove compartment of my cruiser, I retrieved the Berkeley Place Neighborhood Watch schedule that Nora Conklin had given me. The schedule showed four men on duty at the moment. Garrett Hawke, of course. Nora's husband, Todd. A man named Rasheed Chutani. And Victor Paludo, who'd been on duty the night before Kirstin Rumford had discovered her broken azalea bushes, the night the Lowrys had summoned the police after hearing someone outside their window, and the night that someone had cut the screen on Korinna Papadakis's window.

Is he our man?

He certainly gave off a pervy vibe, staring at women's chests the way he did. But at his age he didn't move fast. I had a hard time believing he could have fled each crime scene quickly enough to avoid being caught. Still, it was possible. By the time people got over their initial fear and dared to take a look outside, he might have had enough time to scurry out of sight and get to his car.

As I rattled off Hawke's cell phone number, Detective Bustamente input the numbers in his phone and pushed the call button.

"Hello, Mr. Hawke," he said into his phone. "This is Hector Bustamente." He paused a moment to allow Hawke to respond. "I'm at your house. I'd like to talk to you." He paused again, silently shaking his head at whatever Hawke was saying on his end. "Yes, it's important. Come here right away."

A minute later, Hawke's Expedition pulled into the driveway. Hawke emerged, his tool belt not only stocked with a flashlight, pepper spray, and gun tonight, but also a walkie-talkie. He pulled the walkie-talkie from his belt and held it to his mouth, pushing the talk button. "I'm on a short break at home, men. I'll check in when I'm back on duty. Carry on."

I noticed he didn't tell the others the reason for his break. He seemed to know that we weren't here to discuss a development in the case, but rather to speak to him about threatening Gilbreath. Nonetheless, he feigned innocence.

"What's this about?" he asked. "Is there some breaking news?"

Bustamente grunted. "If you'd call your earlier visit to Jerry Jeff Gilbreath's place 'breaking news,' then I suppose so."

Hawke said nothing, merely staring at us as if waiting for me or the detective to say something else.

"You can't just go threaten someone," Bustamente said, "no matter how much of a lowlife he is."

Hawke's jaw flexed. "Is that what he told you? That I threatened him?"

"So you admit you went to his apartment?" the detective asked.

Hawke crossed his arms over his chest. "I did."

"And you threatened him?"

Hawke didn't admit it, but he didn't deny it, either. "All I'll say is that anything that lowlife got he deserved."

Hard to disagree with that.

Bustamente took a step back, not necessarily conceding but deciding to put an end to the exchange. I didn't blame him. Hawke wasn't the easiest man to reason with and, frankly, we had better things to do. "If you go to see Gilbreath again, you're going to force our hand. Don't do that, all right? Your neighborhood needs you."

Hawke chuckled. "No need to worry about me, Detective." He returned to his car, climbed in, and set back out on patrol.

Bustamente and I parted ways at the curb. "Go home," he told me. "Get some sleep."

I gave him a two-fingered salute and climbed back into my cruiser. Despite the salute, I had no intention of going back home, at least not for the moment. Ironically, I did some of my best thinking while cruising mindlessly around in my car, my subconscious taking over where active contemplation fell short.

I drove down Seminary to Hurley's sister's apartment. Her windows were dark. No sign of the stolen white pickup in the parking lot. Would we ever catch that man? Was he even in the Fort Worth area anymore, or had he realized his odds of evading arrest would be better in another part of the country where his mug shot hadn't appeared repeatedly on the evening news and in the papers? Fort Worth PD constantly received reports from other jurisdictions about suspects. Frankly, with so many criminals on the loose, we officers had little time to pay attention to bad guys more likely to be apprehended in Boise or Des Moines. No doubt other police departments would pay little mind to a report of an escapee from Texas.

I cruised past the Shoppes at Chisholm Trail, the shopping mall where a bomber had planted an explosive in the food court late last summer on one of the sales-tax-free shopping days that precede the start of the school year. The food court had been packed to the rafters. Thank God Brigit had alerted on the bomb in the trash can before it exploded or dozens of people, including women and children, could be dead or dismembered now, my partner and I included. I preferred my arms and legs and head to stay firmly attached to my body, thank you very much.

It was odd that Brigit had alerted on the bomb. After all, unlike Seth's dog Blast, Brigit had not been trained to sniff for explosives. Best I could figure is that she smelled some type of drug or drug residue in the trash can. Heck, maybe she'd simply been interested in a discarded pizza crust. Either way, that dog had saved my life. No human partner could have done that.

I eyed Brigit in the rearview mirror. "Have I told you lately how much I appreciate you?"

She eyed me back, her tail wagging.

I headed back out onto Seminary, working my way west this time. I drove through the Fairmount neighborhood, passing the home of two men who'd taken in a troubled teen. I'd met the three working an earlier case. I had no doubt that, with a couple of good role models now looking out for him, the boy would turn himself around.

I cruised through Mistletoe Heights and soon found myself back in Berkeley Place. A FOR SALE sign with the Conklin & Associates pastel blue door logo stood in the yard of a large two-story Colonial. No doubt that sale would earn Nora a nice commission.

My mind ventured back to the night I'd met Nora, when she'd handed me her business card. The card bore the same blue-door logo. It had also featured a thumbnail-sized photo of a smiling Nora, along with the copyright of the photography studio. It had been something a little corny. What was it again? Smiles, Inc.? No, that wasn't quite right. Was it Say Cheese!?

While my conscious mind said to disregard this errant, random thought, my subconscious told me to pull over. I rolled to a stop at a curb, turned on my squad car's interior light, and fished though my pockets until I found Nora's business card. I glanced at the copyright inscription next to her photo. Yep. Sure enough it read © *SAY CHEESE! INC.*

As I stared at the card, my mind began to cough up some of those factoids it had stockpiled. Lint-free, powder-free gloves were used by those who worked in evidence to prevent X-rays from being damaged. The crime scene tech had told me that. Presumably, the same type of gloves could be used to handle photograph negatives. Then again, old-fashioned camera film was pretty rare these days. Even professional photographers used digital equipment. But what about the final product? Some of the higher-end photography studios charged a pretty penny for their professional portraits. Surely special gloves would be needed to prevent leaving fingerprints when handling the photographs, right?

I might not know. But a photography supply store would.

I logged into my computer, clicked to get on the Internet, and ran a search for "photography gloves." While the search produced several types of gloves intended to facilitate outdoor, cold-weather photography, the results also included several links to lightweight white cotton gloves that were touted as both lint-free and disposable, intended for use in handling negatives and prints.

My entire body began to tingle. Was I on to something here? After all, it wasn't entirely clear the glove even belonged to the peeper. Still, it felt like I was heading in the right direction.

I sat back in my seat, thinking consciously now. My mind went back to the Saturn Vue sitting in the Forest Park lot, the one with the Say Cheese! mouse decal on the back window. Without the license plate number, it would take a while to figure out who owned the vehicle. It would be quicker to start with the business.

Pulling up the Texas Secretary of State's Web site, I clicked on the business filings tab and ran a search for Say Cheese! Inc. A few seconds later, the information popped up. The corporate officers were listed as Todd and Nora Conklin. Obviously, Nora was far more involved in her real estate business. Todd Conklin must be the one who ran the photography business.

But *Todd Conklin*? The guy seemed harmless. Even Gilbreath had thought so, calling Conklin a "shrimp" who'd just "stood there like a pussy" when Hawke had led his brigade to Gilbreath's apartment. He'd never given me a second's pause. But maybe I should pause and think about it for a moment.

Hmmmmm . . .

After mulling things over, I still wasn't convinced Todd Conklin could be the peeper. Even so, I hadn't entirely convinced myself he couldn't be. A good investigator keeps an open mind, right?

I ran a search of the motor vehicle records next. Sure enough, a Saturn Vue popped up in the name of Say Cheese! Inc. A second search told me that the Conklins owned the dark blue Mercedes I'd seen at the Rabinowitz house when Hawke and the watch team had gathered there after the incident with the au pair. I wondered briefly why Todd used Nora's Mercedes rather than his SUV, when he was out on patrol, but I quickly realized there could be any number of perfectly valid reasons. Maybe it was more comfortable, or got better gas mileage. Maybe he was trying not to put too many miles on it. Maybe it was loaded with valuable photography equipment and better kept locked up in his garage at night.

I closed my laptop and sat back again, angling my rearview mirror to check on Brigit. She lay quietly on her cushion, panting softly, her eyes beginning to droop. She'd alerted on Todd Conklin earlier even though he'd had no drugs on him. Though I had many ways of communicating with my partner—words, hand gestures, body language, even involuntarily through the scents I released—her passive alert stance was one of the few ways she could communicate information directly to me. Had she been trying to tell me something?

I turned around in my seat. "Were you trying to tell me something, girl?"

Her only response was to glance my way and open her mouth in a wide yawn.

I felt a yawn begin to bubble up inside me, too. "Great," I told her. "Now you've got me doing it."

My yawn completed, I contemplated my next step. My thoughts could be totally off base here, but nonetheless I felt inclined to share them with Detective Bustamente. If nothing else, it would impress him that I'd put some serious thought into the matter. Given that I'd need a good recommendation when it came time for me to apply for a detective position, it couldn't hurt to get his opinion on the matter. But first, I needed to do a little digging, see if Todd Conklin had a record. I logged into the criminal records database, typed in his name, and ran a search. Nothing popped up. Conklin had no convictions and no arrests.

I returned my laptop to its mount and dialed Bustamente's cell. "I've been driving around," I told him. "And—"

"Didn't I tell you to go home and get some sleep?"

"You did, sir. Evidently, I didn't listen."

"Yeah. I was able to put those clues together. Go ahead then."

"Okay," I continued. "So, I had a thought. It could be an epiphany or it could be a dead end, but do you think there's any way Todd Conklin could be the peeper?"

"The little fellow?" Bustamente asked. "What makes you suspect him?"

I told him what I'd found out about the gloves, that they were used by photographers, and that Conklin owned a photography business.

"Good work, Officer Luz. Even if it turns out to be nothing, it's the first reasonable lead we've got. Keep an eye on him."

"Will do. Good night, Detective."

"Good night."

I returned my phone to the cup holder and took one last look at Brigit in the mirror. Looked like she was drifting off. "Sweet dreams, girl."

FORTY-EIGHT
DOUBLE SHIFT

Brigit

Brigit wasn't sure why Megan kept patrolling the streets long into the night given that they'd worked a shift earlier in the day. The dog knew from experience that there was normally a much longer break between their work schedules. But, whatever. It didn't make much difference to Brigit. She simply lay down on her cushion inside her enclosure, rested her head on her paws, and let the soothing hum and vibrations of the cruiser's engine lull her to sleep.

Zzzzz . . .

FORTY-NINE
LOTION IN MOTION

Tom

He must've looked over the footage six dozen times since he'd taped it, but still he hadn't tired of watching the woman rub her hands up and down her leg, applying lotion to her bare skin, and lifting her leg to give him a full-on view of her goodies. He'd stored the video clip in a file he'd named PeeperT, following their standard naming system of using the full last name and first initial, which in this case stood for Tom Peeper. A little inside joke with himself. He had no worries that anyone else would find the file. He'd added password protection. This file was for his eyes only.

He slowed down the speed and watched the video in slow motion, the gorgeous woman plunking her ripe ass down on her bed and reaching down for her calf . . . her hand moving up her leg . . . then down . . . then up again . . . then down . . . she put her hands around her thigh, lifting her leg up . . .

up . . .

up . . .

up . . .

and there it was, in all its glory.

The thing that made women, well, *women.*

"Tacos?"

His skeleton virtually ejected from his skin. He'd been so engrossed in the video that he hadn't heard the approaching footsteps. He looked up at the man in his doorway. "Excuse me?" he squeaked.

The guy laughed. "Didn't mean to startle you. I'm going for lunch. You want me to pick you up a couple of tacos?"

"Make it three." He maneuvered his mouse and clicked on the *X* to close the file. "I've worked up quite an appetite this morning."

FIFTY
BACK BEHIND BARS

Megan

After cruising through Berkeley Place, making passes by the homes of Todd Conklin, Victor Paludo, and Garrett Hawke, I headed for Blake Looney's place on McCart. Given that the man never seemed to be home, I was beginning to wonder if he still lived in the house. Today I hit pay dirt. Looney was home.

He opened the door tentatively, making a gap barely wide enough for him to stick his white-blond head through. "Yes?" he said, his ice-blue gaze going from me down to Brigit. He gasped and closed the door a bit, virtually putting his own head in a vise.

If he thought he could stop Brigit by leaving only a small gap, he'd better think again. If I gave her the order, Brigit would find a way to squeeze herself through.

"Hello, Mr. Looney," I said. "Got a minute?"

"I guess so," he said, looking back up at me. "What's this about?"

"Have you heard about the prowler in Berkeley Place? The one spying on women through their windows?"

His head wobbled as his neck squirmed. This conversation appeared to be making him uncomfortable. No wonder, really. It was pretty clear where I was going with my questions.

"I think I saw something about it on the news," he said.

I decided to cut right to the chase. "I'm sure you can guess why I'm here," I told him.

"Because of what happened at Nordstrom." It wasn't a question. It was an open acknowledgment.

"That's right." I eyed him for a moment, assessing him. His face burned so bright it was a wonder his skin didn't burst into flame. Obviously, he was embarrassed by what he'd done. Or maybe just embarrassed he'd been caught doing it.

"If you think I had something to do with what's happened in Berkeley Place," he said, "you're wrong. I learned my lesson."

Had he? Could someone really learn not to be a pervert? Or could they simply learn to be more subtle about it, better cover their tracks, be satisfied with strip clubs and porn? Hell if I knew. Sexual deviance wasn't exactly my thing.

"Besides," he added, "I've been in Florida for the past month. My mother had hip replacement surgery. I went to stay with her while she recovered."

"You have anything to back that up?" I asked. "Maybe a plane ticket?"

"I used paperless ticketing."

He might be lying. But then again, he might be telling the truth. After all, we could call the airline and verify what he was telling us if needed. He'd be a fool to lie to the police. It would only make him look more guilty.

His face brightened. "I think I've got something else that will prove I was gone. I'll be right back."

He closed the door and I wondered whether he might

be running through the house, planning to exit out a back window. But a few seconds later he returned and thrust two rectangular slips of paper at me. "Here. These are the receipts for my baggage fees."

I looked down at the papers in my hand. The first, which was for his outgoing flight to Jacksonville, was dated approximately four weeks earlier. The second, for his return flight, bore yesterday's date. I looked back up at him. "Where did you stay in Florida?"

"At my mother's house."

"Does she live alone?"

"Normally, yes."

"So it was just you and her?"

"That's right."

A variety of possibilities went through my mind. The first was that he was telling the truth. After all, I had evidence in my hand that he'd flown out to Florida last month and hadn't returned until last night. The second possibility was that he could've come home during that month. Florida was only a fifteen-hour drive or bus ride away. The third possibility was that I was desperate to solve this case and grasping for straws. Who would make a fifteen-hour road trip to return to Texas to ogle women when there would be plenty of bikini-clad women to ogle on the beaches of Florida?

"Where are you working now?" I asked, wondering what kind of place would hire a man with a voyeurism conviction. Then again, it was only a misdemeanor. Did employers ask about misdemeanors on job applications? I wasn't sure. Probably not.

"I work in a warehouse," he said.

"You behaving?" I asked.

He lips pursed. "It's an all-male crew. I couldn't misbehave even if I wanted to."

Well, he *could*, but he wouldn't. Men clearly weren't

his cup of tea. I handed the baggage-fee receipts back to Looney. "Thanks for your time."

"We're done?"

"For now," I said. Might as well keep the door open, just in case. The figurative door, that is. His actual door was still open only enough for his skull not to be crushed. I left him with an ironic warning. "Watch yourself." *And don't watch anyone else.*

He closed the door behind me as I headed down the steps. Just in case his receipts had pervert cooties, I wiped my hands on my pants and made a mental note to wash them with antibacterial soap ASAP. When we reached the squad car, I opened the back door for my partner. "In you go, Briggie Boo."

She hopped into her space, seeming to have less trouble today. Perhaps her diet and her workouts with Frankie were paying off. I'd have to get her on the scale later and find out.

When I'd looked into Todd Conklin and Say Cheese!, I'd learned that his photography studio, like his residence, was located within the boundaries of W1. In fact, the studio was housed in a small strip center near the intersection of McCart and Park Hill, not far from Looney's place. I headed for the center, cruising slowly by, but saw only a glass-front space with the smiling mouse and cheese logo on it.

"What do you know, mouse?" I asked.

Alas, the mouse didn't answer.

We drove next to Nathan Wilmer's apartment. To my surprise, I found a U-Haul parked out front and the scrawny, ginger-haired Nathan Wilmer inside, wrestling with a metal bed frame. So far, the frame was winning. It came apart and one of the pieces swung forward to smack him in the forehead.

"Dammit!" He flung the frame back against the inside

wall of the truck. Big mistake. The metal bar bounced off the side and fell at him again, this time hitting him directly on top of the head as he ducked.

While Brigit sniffed along the ramp, I looked into the back of the truck. "Hello, Mr. Wilmer."

Startled, he snapped his head my way. A look of panic crossed his face. As well it should. Unless he'd provided the police department with the address where he was moving to, his sorry ass would soon be hauled off in handcuffs.

"I'm Officer Megan Luz." I raised Brigit's leash. "This is my partner, Brigit. Having a bad day?"

He swiped at a trickle of blood seeping from the gash in his forehead. "A bad *day*? Try a bad *week*. I've already been evicted and threatened. And I can't imagine you've got good news for me."

Evicted, I understood. But *threatened*? Had Garrett Hawke and his cronies paid Wilmer a visit, too? "Who threatened you?"

He opened his mouth as if to speak, then seemed to decide against it. "It was nothing. Never mind."

"Let me guess," I said. "It was a big man with a gun and two others."

"If you already know," he said snottily, "I guess I don't need to tell you, then."

An open cardboard box filled with a jumble of shoes sat near the back of the truck. I reached in, snagged a Da-Glo orange sneaker from the top, and lifted my own foot to compare soles. The brightly colored shoe was only slightly longer than mine, small for a man. When Brigit noticed I held a loose shoe, she sank her teeth into it and yanked it from my hand. Shoes were Brigit's kryptonite.

"Drop it, girl," I ordered.

She cut me an irritated look but dropped the slobber-covered shoe at my feet. I picked it up, chunked it back into the box, and returned my attention to Wilmer. "Moving out?"

He gestured down to the boxes, then around to indicate the truck. "Uh, *yeah*." His tone said what his words did not. *Of course I'm moving. No shit, Sherlock.*

When would people learn that sarcasm was no way to score points with a cop? "Did you notify the police chief's office of your new address at least seven days before your move like you are required by law to do?"

"I couldn't," he said, the sarcastic tone now more of an *uh-oh*. "I'm not sure where I'm going."

"Not sure?" I said. "How can you not know where you're going?"

"I got behind on my rent and my landlord evicted me. I haven't had a chance to find a new place yet."

"Tough break," I said. "Unfortunately, it doesn't relieve you of your obligation to notify the chief's office."

He tossed his hands in the air. "What the hell should I have done? Tell the chief to look for me out on the streets?"

If he was looking for sympathy, he'd get none from me. The guy had been convicted of drugging and having nonconsensual sex with at least two women. "Did you think of calling Bill Cosby? He might've let you use his guest room."

Okay, so it was a low blow. But this guy was low, so it was the right kind of blow.

"As a registered offender," I told him, "you're expected to plan ahead. You knew you were behind on your rent. This eviction couldn't have come as a surprise. Your parole officer could have helped you find a new place."

I took a step closer to the tailgate of the truck. There was no telling whether he might have a weapon in one of his pockets. I didn't want his hands getting anywhere near them. And I certainly didn't want to get into the cargo bay not knowing whether he might be armed. Close-quarters combat wasn't really my thing.

"Put your hands on the back of your head," I told him, "and turn to face the wall."

"You've gotta be fuckin' kidding me!" he shrieked, throwing his hands in the air again.

"Not at all." I pulled my baton from my belt and opened it with a flick of my wrist. *Snap!* "Now do what I told you to do or I'll deploy my dog."

Knowing those words were a precursor to action, Brigit's ears pricked and she watched me intently, her tail whipping back and forth in anticipation. What can I say? Brigit liked to kick ass.

Wilmer looked down at the anxiously prancing dog at my side and let out another wail, but finally turned away from me and put his hands on the back of his head. I walked up the ramp to get into the truck, but Brigit elected to simply hop up. I looked down at her. "Show-off."

Tucking my baton under my arm, I retrieved my handcuffs, pulled Wilmer's hands down behind him, and closed the cuffs around his wrists. *Click-click.*

"Anything sharp in your pockets?" I asked.

"There's a box cutter in the front pocket of my jeans," he said. "I was using it to cut the packing tape."

Carefully, I reached around his front and slid my hand into his right pocket. Nothing there. I slid my other hand into his left pocket. Nothing there, either.

He laughed. "I must've left it inside. But thanks for the hand job."

"Jackass." I patted the rest of him down, finding only a wallet in his back pocket. The pat-down complete, I ordered him to sit on the ramp of the truck while I radioed for transport. Once dispatch acknowledged my request, I reached back into the box for the sneaker and handed it to Brigit.

"Hey!" Wilmer cried. "You can't just give her my shoe!"

"It's evidence," I said.

"Of what?"

"Your bad taste in footwear."

He looked down at the floor and muttered the C-word.

I chose to ignore his insult and eyed him closely. "You the one who spied on those women in B-Berkeley Place?"

He sneered. "You'll never know."

A couple of minutes later, a cruiser whipped into the lot, tires squealing as it took the turn much too fast. The squeal turned to a screech as the officer at the wheel slammed on the brakes. One glance at the cruiser told me who was behind the wheel. Derek. His flaming red hair was nearly as bright as Nathan Wilmer's Da-Glo orange sneakers. Normally I wasn't happy to see Derek, but right now I couldn't have asked for a better officer to transport Wilmer.

The Big Dick unrolled his window and looked over at me and Brigit. "Well, well, well. If it isn't my two favorite bitches." He threw his door open. "Where's the pervert?"

"Here I am!" Wilmer called in a falsely chipper sing-song voice before resuming his sulking.

Derek sauntered over, strolling up one side of the ramp and then the other as he looked Wilmer over, his lip quirking in disgust. "No wonder you had to drug women to sleep with you." He grabbed Wilmer's arms and jerked him to a stand. "Let's go."

I walked over to Derek's cruiser and opened the back door. Derek shoved Wilmer inside, slammed the door, and climbed in the front. As he rolled up his front window, the unmistakable sound of Derek passing gas reached my ears. *Brrrratttt!* It was the Big Dick's personal brand, his own form of cruel and unusual punishment.

In the backseat, Wilmer ducked his head to his chest, his cheeks bulging as he tried to hold his breath against the fumes. I knew from experience that it was an exercise in futility. There was no escape from Derek's gas chamber.

As Derek floored the gas pedal and turned the wheel at the same time, his cruiser performed a half doughnut, causing Wilmer's body to lurch involuntarily to the side, his face slamming against the back window. *SMACK!* With that, the cruiser zipped out of the lot.

Given that we'd just arrested Wilmer, I had probable cause to enter his apartment. I phoned the crime scene department first to see if they wanted to secure the area. Since no fingerprints had been found at the scenes where the BP Peeper had struck, they weren't overly concerned with me contaminating his apartment with my prints. They also weren't concerned with coming to take a look themselves. I couldn't really blame them. They were busy folks and at this point all we had on Wilmer was that he'd failed to update his sex offender registry as required. There was nothing definitive linking him to the incidents in Berkeley Place.

Nonetheless, I figured I'd take a look around. Who knows? Maybe I'd find a bulletin board covered with pictures of the women who'd been spied on, or napkins on which their addresses had been jotted down. Unfortunately, I found neither of these things, nor anything else to indicate he'd been the one at the windows of Kirstin Rumford, Alyssa Lowry, or Korinna Papadakis. I did, however, find plenty of evidence of how much a creep the guy was. His dresser drawers contained an extensive hard-core porn DVD collection, while copies of *Hustler* lay on his nightstand, coffee table, and in his bathroom. *Ew. Ew. And Ew.* He also had multiple pairs of high-powered binoculars in all different sizes, some large enough to require their own cases, others small enough to fit into a shirt pocket. *Had he been using these to spy on women? Was he looking for his next victim?* There was no way to tell.

While I'd been searching the apartment, Brigit had lain on Wilmer's floor and happily torn his shoe to shreds. Even so, she wasn't ready to give up on it yet. When I rounded her up to go back outside, she picked up the ragged shoe and carried it with her.

We returned to the truck, where I performed a quick search of the few boxes he'd managed to load onto the truck before I arrived. When I found nothing incriminating, I plunked my butt down on the tailgate and pulled the box of shoes over, picking them out one at a time and sniffing the bottom of each for a telltale scent of fresh compost. Brigit wasn't the only one who could use her nose in her work.

A fiftyish man who'd passed by a half minute earlier on his way to get his mail came back by, caught me sniffing the shoes, and muttered, "Now I've seen everything."

When I finished sniffing for clues, I pulled the back door down, and secured it the best I could with a zip tie. If someone stole Wilmer's stuff, it would be *too bad, so sad.* I really didn't give a rat's ass. I also put in a quick call to the truck rental company to let them know where they could find their truck.

Back in my cruiser, I phoned Detective Bustamente. "I just arrested Nathan Wilmer. He was moving out of his apartment without giving advance notice of his address change. I looked through his things but didn't find anything incriminating."

"His arrest could help us," the detective said. "If the peeper strikes again while Wilmer's in jail, we'll know it's not him."

Good point.

"Let's keep this bit of info between you and me," the detective said. "If he's not the peeper, we don't want the real culprit to lie low until Wilmer gets out of jail to throw us off his scent."

Also a good point. "Consider my lips sealed."

FIFTY-ONE
SHOE-BE-DOO!

Brigit

What a great day! Megan had given her a shoe! And not just any old shoe, this one was wonderfully stinky and had laces she could pull on.

She plopped down on the platform in the back of the cruiser and set back to work on the sneaker.

Life doesn't get any better than this.

FIFTY-TWO
ABRACADABRA

Tom

Thanks to the neighborhood watch schedule, Tom knew Rasheed Chutani had volunteered for shifts last night and tonight, and wouldn't be at his home between the hours of 9 P.M. and 1 A.M. Less risk of Tom getting caught, with the husband out of the way. A wife was likely to merely scream, run, and call the police, but an angry husband might choose to pursue him. Best not to chance it.

Tonight's session was turning out to be a special coup. He'd known Wasima Chutani must have long, dark hair under her hijab, but up until now, only her husband, family, and female friends had seen it. But now, he was not only seeing it, he was recording her on tape, brushing out those long, lustrous locks, stroke after stroke after stroke . . .

The wooden blinds over the bedroom window were closed tight, but with his cheek flattened up against the exterior wall of the house he could see her through the tiny gap between the edge of the blind and the window frame.

Ironically, she wore a long-sleeved robe zipped up to her throat, revealing her face and hair but nothing else. Hell, he couldn't even see her feet! He supposed it was too much to ask for a repeat of the lotion application/crotch shot he'd got last time. After all, beggars can't be choosers. And peepers have to take what they get. In fact, part of the fun was not knowing just how far things might go . . .

Still, if he could will her robe to vanish, he would. If only he could conjure up a genie by rubbing a magic lamp.

I may not have a magic lamp, but I do have something else to rub . . .

He tugged off his right glove, tucked it into his pants pocket, and unzipped his fly to release himself. As sexually stoked as he was, it took virtually no time for him to reach his release.

Abracadabra and alakazam!

No sooner had he zipped his fly than a car appeared on the street, the beam of an oversized LED flashlight playing across the space between the adjacent house and the Chutanis'. The beam swept toward him like a Jedi light saber ready to make a deadly strike. He had to move. *Now!*

Tom turned and sprinted toward the back fence. He'd made it only five steps when *fwump!* His foot tangled in a garden hose coiled next to the house and tripped him, sending him skidding face-first across the grass.

This is it.

They have me.

It was over.

Or is it?

The beam sailed two feet above him, leaving him in shadow on the ground. The light continued on down the side of the house, over the window where he'd been spying only seconds before, and disappeared as the car continued on down the street.

He gasped for air and rolled onto his back, looking

up at the night sky. A bright star twinkled at him, as if it had seen what he'd been up to down here on earth and given him a conspiratorial wink.

That must be my lucky star, he thought. *I'd better thank it.*

FIFTY-THREE
TIME TO WASH THE WINDOW

Megan

I'd just set out on patrol for the morning when a call came in on my cell from Detective Bustamente.

"Good morning, Detective."

"We'll see about that," he said. "I've told dispatch to refer all nonemergency prowler calls in W1 to me. I'm heading out to one right now. You and your partner meet me there."

"Of course!"

He provided an address in Berkeley Place, and within minutes I was pulling to a stop in front of the house. A man in a business suit and a tall woman in jeans, a striped blouse, and a turquoise-blue hijab stood on their porch, speaking with the detective.

I climbed out of the cruiser and opened the back to let Brigit out, attaching her lead. We made our way to the porch.

Bustamente made quick introductions. "Mr. and Mrs. Chutani, this is one of our finest K-9 officers, Megan Luz. Officer Luz, this is Rasheed and Wasima Chutani."

I shook each of their hands in turn, and tilted my head to indicate my partner. "Her name is Brigit."

Though Mrs. Chutani smiled down at my four-legged partner, her expression was also wary. Typical. People were intrigued by police dogs, but were often a little apprehensive, too. They had nothing to fear where Brigit was concerned, unless they were a bad guy. When not pursuing a suspect, Brigit was a friendly, fluffy goofball.

Mr. Chutani gestured into the yard. "This way." He proceeded to lead the rest of us around the corner of his house. "I came out to put seed in the bird feeder this morning and found something very disturbing." He stopped before a window about halfway down the side and jabbed an angry finger in the direction of the glass. "There."

On the glass, about three feet up from the ground, a congealed streak began, running down to the bottom of the pane, where the substance sat in a glob, drying in the morning sun.

Ewwwwww.

A dry heave caused me to involuntarily *hork*. I put a hand over my mouth. "Excuse me."

Wasima looked my way, her face now a mix of fear and revulsion. "I had the exact same reaction."

I had no idea whether Todd Conklin might be responsible for leaving this sample, or Victor Paludo, or even Dalton Livingston. Heck, for all I knew this could be Garrett Hawke's *dishonorable discharge*. The only thing that was certain was that DNA evidence was *irrefutable* evidence. This blob could be our smoking gun.

The detective eyed Rasheed. "Were you home last night?"

"I was on patrol with the watch group from nine to

one," he said. "I don't know if this happened during that time or after, when I was back home."

"Neither of us heard anything," Wasima added.

Careful not to touch the evidence, Bustamente stepped up to the window. "The blinds were closed last night? Like they are now?"

"Yes," Wasima said. "I keep them closed all the time now."

The detective angled his head first one way, then the other, finally turning his head to the side and putting it up close to the wall. "I suppose it's possible a person could get a glimpse inside if he put his cheek against the wall here."

Rasheed fumed; fury radiated off him in such strong waves it was a wonder he didn't levitate. "I want whoever spied on my wife to pay!" He swung an index finger into the air over his head. "String him up!"

Bustamente took the man's words in stride. "I'd feel the same way if someone had been watching my wife. I'll get a crime scene tech out here to collect the sample. The lab will run it, see if the sample matches anyone in the system. If it does, we'll let you know."

"How long will that take?" Rasheed asked.

"Honestly?" Bustamente said. "At least a week or two. The lab is backed up and sexual assault cases take priority."

Rasheed's brown skin turned purple. "Two weeks?" he shrieked. "Are you kidding me?"

"Wish I were," Bustamente replied. "In the meantime, Officer Luz and her dog can see if they might be able to track the guy who did this."

I reached down to free Brigit from her leash. "We're on it."

I gave my partner the order to track. A fresh trail would have been easier for her, but Brigit's nose was up for the challenge. She snuffled around the window, sniffed the sample, and put her head to the ground, moving it left to right. A moment later, she set off toward the backyard.

I followed her for a few steps, stopping behind her when she halted to sniff at a garden hose. The hose lay in a tangle of coils on the ground.

Mr. Chutani stepped up beside us. "That hose was in a neat pile yesterday."

"The prowler must have tripped over it," I said. "Maybe he tried to escape in a hurry."

Brigit sniffed around the spot, making her way up and down in a line that spanned approximately six feet before turning around and trotting toward the street. The Chutanis, the detective, and I followed as she led the way, tracking a little slower than she did with a fresh trail, eventually coming to a stop three blocks down. She sat and looked up at me.

"Good girl!" I praised her, tossing her a liver treat. I was tired of holding out on her. Besides, Frankie had been taking Brigit with her as she skated around the neighborhood. Brigit's weight was on its way down.

"When we're done talking," Bustamente told the couple, "I'll come back here and talk to the residents, see if they saw a car out here last night. I'm not going to tell them why I'm asking, and I'd like you two to keep the information about the DNA sample quiet. If the peeper realizes we found the sample, he might flee the area or go into hiding." He cast a glance my way. "Same goes for you, Officer Luz. Don't tell anyone about the DNA."

I pretended to zip not only my lips, but Brigit's as well.

We returned to the Chutanis' house, stopping on their front walkway to wrap things up.

The detective gave the couple his business card. "I'll be back in touch as soon as I hear from the lab."

"Thanks," Wasima said.

Rasheed, though equally grateful, was still thirsty for vengeance. "I hope you nail the bastard."

"You and me, both," Bustamente replied.

The sound of a car engine caught our attention, and all five of us turned to see Garrett Hawke pulling to the curb in his Expedition. He unrolled his window. "What's going on here?" he called, his brow furrowed. "Did the peeper strike again?"

My mind briefly toyed with the old adage that wrong-doers always return to the scene of their crimes. *Is that what Hawke is doing here? Or is he simply on his way to work?*

The Chutanis, the detective, and I exchanged glances.

"Nothing to worry about," Bustamente said. "Mr. Chutani got a call from a collection agency about a bill that's not his. Looks like a run-of-the-mill identity-theft issue."

Hawke ran his eyes over the group as if trying to assess whether he was being told the truth. Our expressions must have been convincing because he raised a hand in farewell and said, "All right. Y'all have a good day."

Rasheed's gaze followed the Expedition as it pulled away from the curb. *Does he, too, think Hawke could be the peeper?*

He turned back to me and the detective. "That man seems to be everywhere."

Everywhere, huh? Had he been in the Chutanis' yard last night?

Having done all we could here, the detective, Brigit, and I returned to our vehicles.

As my partner and I set back out on patrol, my mind pondered these recent developments. The DNA sample could put a relatively quick end to the case by positively identifying the creep responsible. Of course nailing him via his sample depended on whether he had been arrested for a serious crime and his DNA was already in the system. If not, the sample wouldn't lead us to our man, though it could still help us convict him. If we had probable cause to arrest someone and could then obtain a DNA sample from the suspect, the new DNA could be compared to the sample from the Chutanis' window to determine if there was a match.

If Ralph Hurley, Nathan Wilmer, Blake Looney, or Jerry Jeff Gilbreath were the culprit, we'd be able to positively identify them since they had criminal records and their DNA was on file. Though Wilmer's MO in his earlier cases was different, it sure would make things easy if the DNA proved to be his. The guy was already in custody. All we'd have to do was slap more charges on him. If the DNA proved to be Looney's or Gilbreath's, we'd have to go out and make an arrest. While Looney had been nonthreatening and cooperative, I had no doubt that attempting to arrest Gilbreath would end up in a tussle. That jackass didn't seem like the type to go down easy. If I was involved in his arrest, I'd force-feed the guy a cockroach before taking him in. It'd serve him right.

I'd run criminal background searches on Garrett Hawke, Victor Paludo, and Todd Conklin. Other than Hawke's arrest for public intoxication, none had records. Their DNA would not be in the system. Still, if we later obtained probable cause to arrest one of them, we could check their DNA. If it matched the sample being collected this morning, bingo-bango, this case would be closed.

Though neither Bustamente nor I thought Leonard Drake was responsible for the peeping incidents, he hadn't been ruled out conclusively yet. Of course there was a very real, perhaps even likely, possibility that none of these men was the peeper. Perverts were everywhere, new ones cropping up all the time. The guilty party could be someone who wasn't even a blip on our radar. He was also someone who could very well get away with his crimes if he was smart enough to realize that the police could be honing in and that he should seek his jollies elsewhere before we could nab him.

Paludo's silver hair flashed through my mind. Though I'd heard that hair and eye color could be determined by DNA, I realized that while a person's DNA coding didn't change over the course of their life, hair color could nonetheless change due to a loss of pigmentation. My ponderings were probably pointless, though. The police lab didn't regularly check for hair and eye color of suspects. It would be too time-consuming and expensive to run a full battery of tests on every DNA sample. Such extensive analysis was reserved for the bigger, violent cases.

Still, while peeping might be a minor crime under the penal code, it sure could get a community riled up. The situation in Berkeley Place proved it. Not only had the watch beefed up patrols, they'd had signs printed for the residents to put in their yards. The signs read ONLY CREEPS PEEP! THE WATCH WILL GET YOU. Nearly every front lawn sported the sign on a stake. Many of the residents wore T-shirts bearing the neighborhood watch eyeball logo while they were out and about, working in their yards or walking their dogs or strolling with their babies. I briefly wondered whether someone who owned a sign-making business or a T-shirt shop had invented the peeper just to earn a few bucks.

I was just about to head over to Hurley's sister's apartment complex for the umpteenth time when I spotted Derek Mackey's cruiser pulled up alongside Hawke's Expedition in the road ahead, blocking the way. The two men were engaged in conversation through their open windows. What they were discussing was anyone's guess. Maybe Hawke was hitting Derek up for information, seeking verification that the Chutanis had, in fact, been victims of identity theft. Was he panicking? Wondering if his sample had been found on the window? Of course Derek didn't know about the DNA waiting to be collected. No doubt Bustamente would request that the crime scene tech come in an unmarked vehicle and keep a low profile so as not to alert anyone to the situation. Derek would be in the dark. I felt special and privileged to have the inside scoop.

Rather than wait for the two to get out of the way, I hooked a right down a side street. Might as well make a run by Hurley's sister's place. The guy hadn't struck in several days and could be long gone by now, but it couldn't hurt to make sure his big sis wasn't enabling his life of crime by giving him a place to crash.

Speaking of crashes, a small SUV had T-boned a city bus up ahead, motorists in need of an authority figure to sort things out. I flipped on my lights and rolled to a stop behind them. If Hurley was at his sister's this morning, he'd been granted a temporary reprieve.

I was cruising through Berkeley Place that afternoon when I came up on Nora Conklin using a rubber mallet to hammer one of her realty company's FOR SALE signs into the yard of a white brick saltbox-style house. When she spotted my squad car, she raised a hand to stop me.

I pulled my car to the curb and unrolled the passenger window. She tiptoed over in her heels, trying to avoid getting them dirty in the soft grass and soil. "Garrett Hawke's been telling everyone the news. We're all so relieved."

News? "What news?"

"That Officer Mackey arrested the peeper. He said it was some guy on the sex offender list who lives close to here."

Ugh. Telling people the peeper had been jailed was a bad move on Hawke's part. The peeper's MO was different than Wilmer's and there was no direct evidence linking Wilmer to the crimes. If Hawke gave the impression that the peeper had been apprehended when, in fact, he had not, the people of Berkeley Place might let down their guard and make it easier for the BP Peeper to strike again. Hawke could end up looking like a fool instead of a hero.

Admittedly I also felt frustrated by the fact that Derek had claimed accolades that should have been mine. *I* was the one who'd followed up on sex offenders in the area. *I* was the one who'd learned that Nathan Wilmer was at risk of eviction. *I* was the one who'd caught him trying to slip away without giving proper notification and *I* was the one who'd arrested and handcuffed him. All the Big Dick had done was provide taxi service for Wilmer. Even though I didn't do this job for the glory, it nonetheless rankled.

"Please tell everyone to remain vigilant," I told Nora, knowing she was well connected and could quickly spread the word. "Wilmer might not be the peeper. There's no direct evidence to prove it was him. The bad guy could still be out there."

Nora frowned. "Well, darn. I'd hoped this whole thing was over. It's really been putting a dent in my business. Nobody wants to buy a house in peeperland."

Sheesh.

"Have a good day," I called as Nora returned to the sign to give it a final whack with her mallet.

I rolled up the window and resumed my patrol, mulling over this latest development. Hawke seemed sure that

Wilmer had been the peeper and that his arrest would put an end to the reign of terror he'd caused to residents of Berkeley Place. It seemed very odd to me that Hawke would be so sure of himself. Was he merely taking advantage of the situation to build himself up again, to claim some type of hero status for having confronted Wilmer prior to his arrest? Doing so seemed risky. After all, the people he was trying to impress could very well turn on him if he were later proven wrong. Or did Hawke know, for sure, that Wilmer's arrest would put an end to the peeping? Of course, the only way he could be certain that the peeping would now stop was if he, himself, were the peeper.

Once again, I had too many suspects and too few concrete clues

FIFTY-FOUR
QUEEN OF THE JUNGLE

Brigit

Brigit loved going to any park, but she especially loved Forest Park since that's where the city zoo was located. Megan had brought her to the park for lunch today, and Brigit couldn't be happier. While Megan sat at a picnic table eating her lunch, Brigit roamed around the immediate area, putting her ears and nose in the air, the sounds and scents telling her everything that was going on across the parking lot inside the zoo's walls.

A tiger was eating his dinner of beef shank.

An elephant was taking a poop.

Two chimps chittered in their trees.

She pitied the poor creatures, trapped as they were in their enclosures. She, on the other hand, was free to roam as she pleased. Well, mostly as she pleased. When on duty she had to defer to Megan, but off duty Brigit had the entire house and backyard as her domain. To heck with lions. This shepherd mix wasn't just prom queen, she was the queen of the jungle, too.

FIFTY-FIVE
EVADING ARREST

Tom, aka Todd Conklin

When the group showed up for watch duty that night, Garrett Hawke gave them some unexpected news.

"I spoke with Officer Mackey earlier today," he told the three men gathered about him. "He arrested Nathan Wilmer yesterday. The guy was packing up a truck and preparing to flee."

"So . . . ?" Todd asked, raising a seemingly innocent palm in question. He thought he knew where the big lunk was going with this, but wanted to be absolutely certain they were on the same page.

"So?" Hawke scoffed in that condescending way of his that made Todd want to beat him to death with one of his wife's FOR SALE signs. "So Wilmer must be the peeper. Why else would he be trying to sneak off without providing a forwarding address to the sex offender registry?"

"It's about time he was caught," Paludo said.

Damn hypocrite. A woman couldn't get within a hundred feet of Victor Paludo without the old man staring at her boobs. He'd even ogled Nora's 32As on more than one occasion. The coot didn't have the sense or self-control to be subtle.

"I'm glad to hear this," Westmoreland said. "We needed some good news."

This news wasn't *good.* It was fucking fantastic! Wilmer would take the blame, the heat would be off, and Tom could peep to his heart's—*and a certain other organ's*—content.

"The troops are getting battle fatigue," Hawke continued. "I'm sure Wilmer's our man, but since he hasn't yet been charged for any of the peeping incidents it won't look good if we stop the extra patrols immediately. We'll cut back to three volunteers per shift for the next few days, and if things look good we'll drop that down to two in the next week or so. If there have been no further incidents a month from now, we'll go back to one patrol per shift."

Having issued his orders, Hawke dismissed his platoon.

"See you guys!" Todd raised a friendly hand in good-bye and headed to his car to set out on watch duty, laughing to himself because these stupid, stupid people had no idea he—*the BP Peeper*—had been right there under their noses for weeks. He'd been a late bloomer and had never managed to break five feet six no matter how many vitamin-fortified protein shakes he'd forced down. He hadn't liked being overlooked by the girls in high school. He'd had the same experience in college before meeting Nora, whom he suspected was attracted to him for that very quality, his virtual invisibility. She wanted to be the star of her one-woman show and would never have chosen a man who might draw attention from her. She'd needed a man only to escort her to events, take out the garbage, and satisfy her rare sexual urges. She tended to save her energy for her real estate business. Those big commissions seemed to please her more than anything Todd could do.

But while he'd been annoyed to be so easily overlooked before, it definitely worked to his benefit now. Nobody suspected the small, unassuming guy could do something so risky and reckless and brazen as peeping on women.

What a bunch of naïve dumb-asses.

FIFTY-SIX
HOSED

Megan

Seth and I saw a late movie Friday night, a light romantic comedy, the perfect thing to take my mind off the BP Peeper case and the icky sex offenders I'd had to deal with lately. When we arrived home I checked in with the dispatcher to see if there'd been any reports of peeping in Berkeley Place tonight. There'd been none.

"That's good, right?" Seth asked.

"Honestly," I said, "I don't know." I liked it much better when we knew without a doubt that we'd arrested the right persons for the right crimes. But in the dirty business of law enforcement, things were rarely so neat and tidy.

On Saturday night, Seth and I left the dogs at my house and went on a second double date with Frankie and Zach. Tonight, we opted for bowling.

After my third gutter ball in a row, Frankie said, "You really suck at this. I thought a cop would have better aim."

I didn't admit it out loud, but I wasn't that great with my gun, either, barely making the minimum score needed to be certified. I was much more adept at handling my baton.

"Don't give her a hard time," Seth said as he retrieved his ball. "She's really good at other things."

He sent a sexy, knowing smile my way before sending his ball rocketing down the lane at warp speed. *Kabam-bam-bam!* He'd earned yet another strike. Not surprising, given those strong shoulders and arm muscles of his.

Zach took a swig of his beer. "I saw on the news that the police caught that creepy peeper guy."

Frankie and I exchanged glances. As my roommate, she'd been forced to listen to me think out loud and speculate about the case, to lament the lack of progress, to worry that he'd strike again, maybe this time gaining access to a woman's bedroom and doing God knows what to her.

I clarified the situation for Zach. "A sex offender was arrested for failing to notify the department of his new address. That's all."

"You don't think he was the one who was spying on the women?" Zach asked.

"Maybe." I shrugged. "Maybe not. Time will tell."

Zach fished a fry out of the cardboard basket on the table in front of him. "You mean if nothing else happens, it was probably him?"

"Yeah."

Unfortunately, the lack of further crimes was sometimes the best evidence that a suspect under arrest was the guilty party. Such had been the case with Wayne Williams, suspected of committing the infamous Atlanta child murders in the late seventies and early eighties. The same went for the arrest of Albert DeSalvo, who claimed, amid widespread skepticism, to be the Boston Strangler.

Of course it was also possible that the guilty party realized that, with someone else on the hook for his crimes, he had an easy out and should maybe consider ending his crime spree or moving on. Still, I wasn't sure the peeper would be capable of that. Theoretically, someone who commits a robbery or burglary might, at some point, have fulfilled his need for cash. But a sexual predator's needs were never completely satisfied. They tended to be repeat offenders, with their crimes often escalating after they were released from jail. When their convictions were based largely on personal testimony, some learned not to leave subsequent victims alive to testify against them.

Frankie's turn was up. She stepped into place, performed a funky little hop-skip as she moved forward, and sent the ball down the center of the lane. *Ka-bam-bam!* Nine pins met their doom. Her second ball, however, missed the remaining pin.

"Now who sucks?" I said, arching a brow.

"Still you," she teased.

When we were done bowling, the four of us continued the party at home, joining the dogs and cat in the living room while we watched *Saturday Night Live*. When the show ended, the guys offered many not-so-subtle hints about staying the night. Frankie made it clear she had no intention of moving so fast. She'd been too accommodating with her last boyfriend and he'd taken her for granted. She wasn't going to make that mistake again.

She offered Zach a slight smile. "You want this?" She raised her hands and twirled in a circle, stopping when she was facing him again. "You're going to have to work for it."

A grin played about Zach's mouth as he tugged his wallet from his back pocket and removed a twenty-dollar bill. "Can I just pay for it?"

"Twenty bucks?" I said. "That won't even get you a mani-pedi."

I put a hand on his back and Seth's, ushering them to the door. Not that I wouldn't have loved a nice romp with Seth, but we'd wait until another time, when we had more privacy.

Brigit insisted on an early breakfast and potty break on Sunday, but when I returned to bed after feeding her she thankfully let me sleep in. After working late nights and overtime and worrying incessantly about both Ralph Hurley and the BP Peeper case, I was both physically and mentally exhausted.

When I woke at noon, I felt fresh and alert and clear-headed for the first time in days. The sun was shining through the window, as if calling me to come outside. Frankie must have heard the call, too, because I found her sunbathing in a bikini top and a pair of shorts in a sunny spot in the backyard.

She held up her cell phone and grinned. "Zach just texted me. He wants to take me to dinner tonight."

It would be their first date without me and Seth along as a safety net. I was glad the two had hit it off. Frankie deserved a nice guy in her life. The fact that Zach was good-looking, too, was the icing on the cake.

"I was thinking about washing my car," I said. It had been weeks since I'd run a hose over the thing and it was coated with dirt and leftover spring pollen. Frankie's Nissan Juke was in even worse shape, the bright red paint dull with grime. "Want me to wash yours while I'm at it?" It was the least I could do after she'd taken Brigit out for all that exercise and helped her lose her excess weight.

She stood from her lounge chair. "Let's do them together. It'll go faster that way."

I went back to my room, threw on my bathing suit and a pair of shorts, and slid my feet into a cheap pair of flip-flops. Even though it was only May, the Texas sun could turn concrete into a grill. The last thing I needed was blisters on the bottom of my feet.

"C'mon, girl," I called to Brigit, patting my leg. "Let's go outside."

Her ears perked and she hopped down from the couch to follow me.

Frankie was already out front with a hose and a sponge, squeezing the nozzle to spray down my car with a tinny *kshhhh.* Her phone was propped on the porch railing, playing some classic Pink.

As Brigit began to snuffle around in the ivy, I admonished her to "stay in the yard!" She cast me a look that told me she thought I was a total party pooper. It was her poop I was concerned about. No sense letting her wander into an adjacent yard and drop a load that might irritate the neighbors. Not everyone was a dog lover. Though how they could resist such sweet creatures was beyond me.

As I headed to the driveway, a cold, wet spray hit me right in the stomach, causing me to rise up on my toes, arch my back, and shriek in an involuntary response. "Hey! W-watch the hose! My cell phone's in my pocket!"

Frankie, who'd aimed the hose at me, cringed. "Oops. Sorry! Does it still work?"

I pulled the phone from my damp pocket and thumbed the button. The screen popped to life. "It's fine."

"Good. Take a pic of me for Zach." She dialed the nozzle to the mist setting and sprayed it into the air in front of her, striking a sexy, arched-back pose. "How's this?"

"It's perfect," I said, "if you're trying to look like Beyoncé or a Kardashian." Hey, what are roommates for if not to give each other a little crap now and then?

"As a matter of fact," she said, tossing her head, "Kardashian is exactly what I was going for."

"If you want to really pull off that look, you'll need butt implants."

She put her hands on her rear. "Ouch!"

As she struck three different poses, I snapped a quick series of photos.

After, she held out her hand. "Let me take some of you for Seth."

I rolled my eyes, but then figured, why not? I handed Frankie the phone and put my hands under my hair, pulling it up so that it draped sexily down over my arms. She took a couple of shots and returned the phone to me before picking the hose back up from the driveway. She cut a smile my way. "I'm thinking maybe I should get an even bigger hose."

"What do you mean?"

"I'm thinking of going to the fire academy."

"Seriously?"

"Seriously. Seth was right when he mentioned it at the VFW. It would be the perfect job for me."

With her height, strength, and pluck, Frankie would make a great firefighter. "That's a great idea, Frankie. I bet you'd enjoy it, too." After all, the woman loved a physical challenge. That's why she played roller derby.

She crinkled her nose. "You think I could do it?"

"I have no doubt."

She turned the hose back on to my car. "It's nice to finally feel like my life has some direction. Like I'm not just going in circles."

An ironic thing to come from the mouth of someone whose favorite pastime involved skating in endless circles. Still, I could relate. My job gave me a sense of purpose and meaning, goals to strive for. I was lucky that I'd found my calling early. Some people took much longer. Some never seemed to figure it out, no matter how old they got. But I couldn't imagine what it was like to be caught in life's eddies with no sense of destination. It had to be frustrating. A lack of goals and purpose is how many criminals ended up where they were.

Frankie handed me the sponge and I started at the top of my small Smart Car, wiping off the grime, which flowed down the sides in muddy rivulets. A few minutes later my car was clean and we moved on to Frankie's car.

I'd just begun to wipe down the windows when Brigit stepped to the front edge of the yard, her nose in the air, twitching, as she looked off down the street. All I could see were a couple of girls playing hopscotch in a driveway, a boy on a scooter zipping toward us, and several cars parked along the curb. Probably there was a squirrel or rat hiding somewhere in the vicinity.

I didn't want her taking off into the street if a rodent suddenly decided to make a run for it. "Come over here, girl!" I called.

FIFTY-SEVEN
WATER TORTURE

Brigit

Brigit ignored Megan's call. No way would she get anywhere near a water hose. She trusted Megan, but yet she couldn't overcome the memories of her first owner, a dip shit stoner, and how he thought it was funny to turn the hose on Brigit in the backyard, to follow her with the stream as she ran back and forth, desperately trying to escape the forceful spray. She should've torn his throat out while she had a chance.

Besides, Brigit was curious. Her nose detected a scent that was both familiar yet out of place. It was the scent of the man who'd been in the bushes at those houses they'd visited, the scent of the man whom she'd tracked from the windows to the spot where he'd climbed into his car, the man she'd also scented at Forest Park a few nights ago and alerted on when she and Megan had been on that porch with him.

She'd never smelled him near their home before.

What is he doing here?

FIFTY-EIGHT
SAY CHEESE!

Todd

Click. Click. Click-click.

He snapped shot after shot with his high-speed camera, capturing the cop as she washed her car in her driveway. My God, she'd made it so easy with the way she was playfully misting herself while the other woman snapped photos with her phone. It was as if she were posing for him, too.

He knew she worked at the W1 station, and all he had to do to find out where she lived was follow her home after a shift.

She should be more careful.

So here he was, sitting in his wife's car two blocks down on Travis Avenue, taking photos of the cop and fantasizing what it would be like to bury his face in her long, dark hair while he buried himself in her.

He zoomed in, the lens lengthening and extending while, lower down, his cock did the same thing. The thought of spying on a female law enforcement officer caused such a quick and extreme reaction in his groin he was surprised his pants didn't rip, Hulk-style.

Click.

The dog began to swivel its head, still scenting the air.

A moment later, the dog turned his way, her eyes locking on him with absolute certainty.

Nobody else knew he was the one who'd been peeping at the windows.

But that dog does.

Thank goodness she couldn't tell anyone. Still, he figured he'd better get out of there before the dog started barking and drew attention to his car.

He attached the lens cap, laid his camera on the passenger seat, and started his engine, quickly disappearing down a side street.

FIFTY-NINE
RAIN, RAIN, GO AWAY

Megan

Figures it would rain cats and dogs the day after I washed my car. To make matters worse, my car now smelled like wet dog, Brigit having been drenched as we dashed to my car this morning to drive to work. My partner didn't seem to understand the concept of an umbrella and had run ahead of me.

We transferred as quickly as possible from my personal vehicle to our cruiser, but still my uniform was damp by the time I settled in my seat. Normally, I didn't spring for expensive coffee, using my precious pennies to pay off my student loans and monthly bills. But today I drove through Starbucks and splurged on the largest vanilla soy latte they offered. Rainy days were always crazy-busy for first responders and I'd need the caffeine to get me through. Besides, soy was good protein. Really, the coffee was a health drink, right?

I texted Seth. *You're lucky you have the day off.* His coworkers would surely be running nonstop all day.

Hell yeah, was his reply, to which he added, *Stay safe.*

Aww. The sentiment warmed my cold, damp heart.

The only saving grace today was that this storm was a steady downpour without much lightning or wind, not the type that normally produced tornadoes or dangerous straight-line winds. Thank heaven for small favors.

As expected, I spent the first five hours of my shift dealing with car accidents, all fender benders where someone had hydroplaned or driven too fast around a corner and spun out. One had managed to hit a light post, which in turn fell and landed on top of another car parked in a driveway. At least I hadn't had to deal with the seven-car pileup on University. In multicar accidents, motorists tended to get very riled up and point fingers at each other, which was no fun to deal with, not to mention all of the paperwork.

A collision involving a Toyota and a Subaru, both Japanese carmakers, inspired me to write a haiku in my report.

As rain washes Earth,
Drivers fueled by destiny,
Meet on life's wet streets.

It might not be up to the standards of Emily Dickinson or Elizabeth Barrett Browning, but still, not bad, huh? I only hoped Captain Leone would overlook it. He might not appreciate my creative reports, but a street cop has to keep herself entertained somehow.

As usual, I kept an eye out for the white pickup Hurley had stolen and cruised by his sister's apartment several times to no avail. The lowlife was either keeping a low profile, or was seeking victims elsewhere.

I was cruising eastbound on Rosedale when I noticed traffic swerving to avoid a disabled car in the rightmost lane. I turned on my lights and pulled up behind the car. The hazard lights were flashing, which was surprising given that so many other things were wrong with the car. The vehicle had bald tires, no back bumper, and a trunk that was held closed by a twisted wire coat hanger. Where the back window should be was instead a sagging sheet of clear plastic held in place by duct tape that was beginning to give way. Rust had eaten away at the edges of the wheel wells. And this list was only things I could see through the windshield of my cruiser.

Sighing, I donned my bright yellow poncho, wondering why I had even bothered to take the thing off after the last accident. "I'll be back, girl," I told Brigit, who was standing in her enclosure, looking forward, tail wagging. "Sit tight."

I took a look back to make sure no cars were coming before stepping out of my cruiser into the torrential rain. I hurried to the driver's door, expecting to find a face at the window. To my surprise, I found neither face nor window. No one was in the car, though it was rapidly filling with rain. The seat was soaked and the floorboards bore at least a quarter inch of water. Looked like whoever owned this car didn't have Triple A or a cell phone.

I noticed the inspection was two months out of date. Ditto for the registration. Ironically, the dollar value of citations I could write for all of the vehicle violations would add up to nearly a grand. The car itself wasn't even worth that much.

I pushed the button on my shoulder mic to call dispatch. "I need a tow truck." I gave dispatch the location so they could have the vehicle removed. It was a safety hazard.

Tow trucks were in big demand today, and it was half an hour before one made it out. At least it gave me a chance to relax in my cruiser while I waited and listened to an author interview on NPR.

Once the towing service had hauled off the car—if the hunk of metal and plastic and rubber could even be called a car—I set out again, continuing down Rosedale. I reached the end of W1 and was just about to turn south when I noticed a woman walking along the side of the road ahead, rolling a large suitcase behind her. Despite the fact that she was slightly outside of my usual jurisdiction, I decided to see if I could offer her some help. Maybe she just needed a cell phone to call a friend or family member to give her a ride.

I turned on my lights and slowed as I approached her, noting that she was having a hard time managing the battered suitcase over the uneven terrain. She had no umbrella, but held a plastic grocery bag over her head in an ineffectual attempt to shield herself from the rain. As I pulled up next to her, she stopped and turned to look at me.

Odd.

I didn't think I'd ever met this woman before, but something about her seemed very familiar. She had dishwater-blond hair made stringy from the rain, green eyes, and a chin dimple, like Seth's. Her makeup was smeared and smudged from the rain. She looked to be in her early forties, and had the thin build that came not from working out at the gym but from working too hard. Her drenched jeans looked like they could slide off her at any moment, and the silky blouse she wore was stuck to her chest. Victor Paludo would have been in hog heaven to see it.

Life had not been kind to this woman. But as long as she cooperated, I would be. She looked like she was overdue for a break.

I unrolled my passenger window just enough to be able to speak with her. "Can I be of some assistance?"

Her face drooped with a world-weary expression as she pointed back in the direction from which I'd come. "My car ran out of gas back there. I'm trying to get home but I'm out of gas and I'm out of money. My cell phone's dead, so I'm out of luck, too, I guess. The only thing I have is a headache." Tears began to fill her eyes. "I just lost my job and I—"

She broke into sobs then, her shoulders shaking.

I rolled up the window lest my cruiser also fill with water and climbed out, glad I'd opted to leave the poncho on. I walked around the car to stand in front of her and held out my cell phone. "Would you like to use my phone to call someone?"

She shook her head, choking back her sobs. "I can walk. It's not far. I don't want to bother them."

I wondered who "them" was, why she was going to see these people if she thought they cared so little about her they'd be annoyed by her call. I also wondered if this woman might have mental health issues, or an alcohol or drug addiction. At the very least, she seemed to have serious financial and interpersonal problems.

"Can I see some ID?" I asked.

"Oh. Okay."

She stood the suitcase upright, slid one of her purse straps down her arm, and stuck her hand inside. Lest she pull out a gun or pepper spray, I watched her closely. We never knew who we might cross paths with on the streets. A cop could never be too careful.

A moment later she pulled out a wallet, using her chipped fingernail to finagle her license out from among several cards. She held it out to me.

I took it from her and looked down at it. The photo on the license told me that this was indeed the woman who stood before me, and that she was much more attractive when she hadn't just walked a mile in the pouring-down rain. It also told me her address was in Lubbock, a town in the southern part of the Texas panhandle, a four-and-a-half-hour drive west. Lubbock was known for being the hometown of both Texas Tech University and singer Buddy Holly.

I looked back up at her. "You said you were going home, but according to your license you live in Lubbock. Did you move here recently?"

If so, I'd simply remind her that she needed to update her address with DMV. I wasn't about to issue this woman a ticket when she was already so down on her luck.

"By 'home,' I meant my parents' house," she said, using her thin fingers to swipe at her tears. "Well, I guess it's just my father's house now. My mother passed away."

I looked back down at the license, this time focusing on her name. *Lisa Rene Rutledge.*

Rutledge?

Oh, my God.

No wonder she looked familiar. She was Seth's . . . *mother*? I looked at her birthdate and performed some quick math. If she was his mother, she'd given birth to him when she was only fifteen years old.

Whoa.

Seth hadn't told me that piece of information. Suddenly, the way she'd treated him, abandoning him with her parents and running off, sounded so much less malevolent. She'd probably been a frightened kid, not ready for motherhood. It didn't excuse what she'd done, of course, but it did explain it.

I handed the license back to her. "I'd be happy to give you a ride."

"You would?" Her face brightened. "Really?"

"Sure," I said. "Hop in the front. My dog's in the back."

"Dog?" She bent over to look in the window. "Oh! She's fluffy! Is she friendly?"

"When she's not eating your shoes."

Lisa issued a laugh that sounded as rusty as her car. She apparently hadn't had much to laugh about lately.

I grabbed the handle of her suitcase. "I'll put this in the trunk."

As Lisa climbed into the passenger side, I stashed her luggage in the trunk of my cruiser and circled around to slide into the driver's seat. Lisa reached back for the seat belt and snapped it into place. *Click.* Once I was buckled in, too, I pulled away from the curb and aimed for Seth's place, where he lived with his grandfather, Lisa's father. The house was also out of my jurisdiction, but I could count the time as my afternoon break.

Lisa turned to the side to look at Brigit. "Hi, girl," she said. "You're a pretty, pretty doggie."

Brigit wagged her tail as if in agreement and tried to sniff the woman through the metal mesh that separated us. As if scenting the woman's tears, she began licking at the screen. She'd licked my tears away on more than one occasion.

"What's she doing?" Lisa asked.

"She's trying to cheer you up," I said. "She doesn't like to see people sad."

My comment only caused the woman to tear up, sniffle, gulp, and break into fresh sobs.

I had no idea what to say to her, just as I'd been at a loss at times on how to deal with Seth and his attachment issues. I'd taken criminal psychology as part of my Criminal Justice studies at Sam Houston State University, but I'd never taken a regular psychology class.

I fished a napkin out of the console and handed it to her.

"Thanks." She dabbed at her eyes as she tried to get her crying under control. "I'm sorry I'm such a mess."

"No need to apologize to me," I said. *But maybe you*

should start with your son. "How'd you lose your job, if you d-don't mind me asking?"

She exhaled a breath as she tried to get her emotions under control enough to speak. "I was working doing maid service at a hotel. I'd even worked my way up to crew chief. Yesterday, one of the other ladies came in half dead. She'd been up all night with her sick baby. I told her she could nap in one of the rooms and I'd skip lunch and cover for her. When our boss found out"—she sniffled again—"he fired us both. Never mind that it was the first time we'd ever done anything like that."

"He sounds heartless."

"He is. Heartless and soulless."

As I turned into Seth's neighborhood, she cast a sudden glance my way. "Wait. I never gave you the address. How did you know where I was going?"

I looked her in the eye. "I'm dating your son."

Conflicting emotions flickered across her face, and I could guess at their source. The first was surprise. The next was alarm that Seth might have told me bad things about her. The third was happiness that her son had someone in his life who cared about him.

"How . . . how is he?" she asked tentatively.

I debated my answer, and decided to go with honesty. I'd never been one to sugar-coat things. I'd rather lay it out in the open and deal with it. "He's still getting over all the loss he's had in his life. We had a hard time at first because of it. But he's doing better."

"Is he . . . is he *happy*?"

The look of sincere and deep concern in her eyes, the guilt and regret, were heartbreaking. But those emotions told me she cared, and as long as she cared there was hope for them, wasn't there?

"Happy?" I gave her a soft smile. "I think so. For the

most part, anyway." He'd probably been happier if I'd let him sleep over last weekend, but that wasn't anything this woman needed to know.

She looked away, staring out the window. "I don't know if he even wants to see me."

Though she phrased it as a statement, it was clear from her inflection that she was asking me a question.

"Honestly?" I replied. "I don't know how he'll feel. He doesn't t-tell me a lot."

She looked down at her lap, her lips quivering. "I've really screwed things up."

"Maybe," I agreed. "But you can always try to un-screw them."

She issued a soft chuckle. "You're pretty and smart. It's clear what Seth sees in you."

Her words warmed me even more than the coffee had.

Seth's Nova was in the driveway, so I pulled up to the curb in front of the house, an old and ugly one-story model with orange brick, gray trim, and mismatched shingles on the roof. The garage had been converted into additional living space with a patchwork of building materials. Seth had yet to invite me over or introduce me to his grandfather. He seemed to consider his time with me to be an escape. While I understood that, at some point he'd have to let me know the whole him if we were going to advance our relationship.

Lisa merely stared at the house for a moment or two, as if unsure whether she truly wanted to go inside. But eventually she reached for the door handle. I hopped out and retrieved her suitcase from the trunk, setting it on the street behind the cruiser.

"Thanks so much," Lisa said as she rounded up her suitcase. "You've been so nice."

"Glad I could help."

As I returned to the cruiser, she turned and headed for

the driveway, making her way to the front door. I started the car and was about to put it in gear when dispatch came on the radio with a report of another wreck, this one on the eastern side of W1, not far from where I was now.

I grabbed my radio. "Officers Luz and Brigit responding."

By this time, Lisa had knocked on the front door. It swung open to reveal a barefoot Seth in a pair of knit shorts and a wrinkled tee, comfy off-duty clothes. Blast stood by his side, his tail wagging. When Seth saw his mother on the porch, his face lit up with what can only be described as boyish joy. For a brief moment, he was the young child thrilled to see his mother. But just as quickly a door seemed to slam shut and his face went impassive, his instinctive defense mechanisms kicking in. This woman had let him down too many times.

He looked past Lisa, his gaze meeting mine across the yard. He didn't wave, probably too shocked and trying to figure out why I was in my cruiser at the curb with his mother on the doorstep.

I raised a hand in good-bye and drove away. Given that their problems had been going on for decades, it was probably too much to hope for, but I nonetheless said a quick and silent prayer that Seth's family could somehow heal, could be a real family for each other.

As if to tell me that anything was possible, the rain abruptly stopped and the clouds broke, an intense beam of sunshine lighting up the world.

SIXTY
EVERYONE NEEDS A DOG

Brigit

Brigit looked back as Megan pulled their patrol car away from the curb, disappointed that her partner hadn't allowed her to say hello to Blast. But she was glad Blast was at the house. The lady that had been in the front seat was very sad and she could use a dog to cheer her up. After all, nobody could stay sad when a dog was licking their face.

SIXTY-ONE
SHOOT TO KILL

Todd

It had been over a week since Nathan Wilmer's arrest. He'd laid low since, trying to satisfy himself with his photos and videos.

But it's killing me.

He'd looked the pictures over and watched the videos so many times they no longer gave him any sort of thrill, not even a tiny tingle or tickle of titillation. He needed fresh fodder. A new fix.

"Chin up," he advised. "Now tilt your head a little to the left."

The woman seated on the velvet-covered Queen Anne chair in front of him complied.

"That's it," he said, snapping several photos. *Click. Click. Click.*

God, head shots were a bore. The only thing worse was taking shot after shot after shot at high school and college graduations, the pose and angle the same every time, the only thing changing being the goofy, beaming face of the graduate. But dull as they might be, head shots and graduation photos were his bread and butter, along with family Christmas portraits, parents and kids dressed in cheesy holiday sweaters, pretending to be the perfect, problem-free family. As if such a thing even existed.

At least this woman was hot. She had dark brown hair that hung in loose curls all the way down to her tits. It dawned on him then that maybe he didn't have to go looking for scantily clad or nude women to photograph.

Maybe I could convince the women to come to me . . .

He took a deep breath to steady his nerves. "I noticed you're wearing a wedding ring," he said, hoping the slight quaver in his voice was noticeable only to himself. "Been married long?"

"Almost three years," the woman said.

Three years. *Perfect.* That was the point in a marriage where the honeymoon phase had ended, and each spouse realized the other could be unattractive and annoying at times. A wife would think back on old boyfriends, maybe catch the eye of a good-looking man in the grocery store and wonder whether she'd made the right choice. Even more so, a wife would worry that her husband might be having the same thoughts.

"Almost three years?" he repeated. "Got an anniversary coming up soon?"

"June twenty-third."

"That's only three weeks away." He raised his camera again, hoping that covering his face would hide the gleam in his eye and make her more comfortable. "You know what would make a great anniversary gift for your husband?" he said, snapping another shot. *Click.* "Some boudoir photos."

The woman blushed lightly, looking simultaneously taken aback and thoughtful.

He snapped another shot. *Click.* "I don't advertise it," he said. "After all, I can't exactly hang those types of photos in my lobby or put them on my Web site. But you'd be surprised how many women have them done. Some wear lingerie, but others prefer nude shots."

It was an outright lie. The only naked subjects he'd ever photographed were babies, and at least three of those had peed on his sets. Another had puked pureed peas all over his fake bearskin rug. Why did everyone think it was cute to have a bare-butt photo of their infants? Didn't they realize their children would hate them for it when they grew up?

"Nude photos?" the woman said, her tone equal parts skepticism and intrigue. "Really?"

"Really," he replied, trying to sound as matter-of-fact as possible. "I can't name names, but you'd know some of them. It's all very discreet and classy and artistic. With soft focus and dim lighting, I can make a woman look very attractive, put those centerfolds to shame. Not that *you* would need any of that." He hoped he hadn't gone too far. He wanted to flatter and entice her, but not make her feel creeped out. He offered a nonchalant shrug. "A boudoir photo is a playful way to keep the spark alive. Men like sexy surprises."

The woman pondered the offer for a moment, her inner Girl Scout wrestling with her inner vixen. Luckily, the vixen emerged victorious, the Girl Scout thus denied her wrestling badge. "What the heck," she said. "Let's do it!"

Hot damn! He felt himself elongate and harden. Hell, if he unzipped his pants, he'd be a human tripod. *Why hadn't I thought of this before?*

SIXTY-TWO
YOU NEVER KNOW

Megan

It was now Saturday, May 30, more than a week since Nathan Wilmer's arrest. There hadn't been a single report of a prowler or suspicious person in Berkeley Place since, let alone a report of a peeper at someone's bedroom window. Still, I couldn't shake the feeling that Wilmer was not the BP Peeper. While he'd been suspected of spying on women with the binoculars and telescope found in his apartment at the time of his arrest, there'd been nothing to suggest he took a greater risk by peeking directly into windows. It was the next logical step, I supposed. But given the cowardly way he'd taken advantage of his innocent victims, by rendering them unconscious and incapable of defending themselves, I didn't think he had it in him. Of course, I could be totally wrong.

This uncertainty, the not knowing, was one of the most frustrating aspects of police work. Why couldn't actual police work be like it was on television and in the movies, where conclusive evidence tied a particular suspect to the crime, where guilty parties confessed all?

If only . . .

I was back on night shifts this week. According to the revised neighborhood watch schedule, Victor Paludo and Todd Conklin were scheduled to work the nine-to-one shift tonight. Given that Paludo was himself an ogler, that Conklin was a mousy little man who looked incapable of hurting a fly, and that both could potentially be the peeper themselves, the women of Berkeley Place weren't in very good hands tonight. Of course all the watch patrol was supposed to do was call the police, so maybe it didn't much matter that the men weren't prime specimens of virility. The only thing the patrol needed to be capable of was dialing 911.

Just after midnight, I drove by Ashley Pham's house, wondering if the girl had yet figured out who her secret admirer was, whether Dalton Livingston had ever summoned the courage to make his move, whether the kid was actually both the BP Peeper and an evil genius who'd snowed me. Lord, I hoped not. I'd look like an idiot.

As I turned north onto Rockridge Terrace, my eyes spotted a dark Mercedes parked at the curb between two houses. Nobody was inside.

That's Nora Conklin's car, isn't it?

It was, and tonight it bore the watch signs on the doors, telling me the vehicle was currently in use by Todd, not his wife.

I slowed, pulling to the curb just past the car, and glanced around. There was no sign of Todd. No sign of anyone, as a matter of fact. It was as still and quiet as the night before Christmas.

Having looked up the Conklins' home address when I'd first considered Todd a potential suspect, I knew his residence wasn't here on Rockridge Terrace. He and Nora lived over on Pembroke. So what was Todd Conklin doing out of his vehicle here?

Could he be peeping on someone at this very moment?

I unrolled the cruiser's windows and turned off my lights and engine. No sense wasting gas, polluting the environment, and exacerbating global climate change any more than necessary. Also no sense warning Conklin of my presence via the noise of my motor. For the millionth time since the glob had been collected at the Chutanis' house, I found myself wishing we had the results of the DNA test. If we did, we'd know whether the suspect was a previous offender or someone else. Without that information, the case was still up in the air.

I pulled out the Berkeley Place roster Nora Conklin had given me and searched for the address.

Hmm . . .

I checked the addresses on the houses on either side of Conklin's car, and found their listings on the neighborhood watch roster. The house to the left belonged to Fred and Betsy Meyer. No other residents were listed. A quick check of Fred and Betsy's driver's license records told me they were an older couple, both in their late seventies. While the porch light was on, all of the interior lights appeared to be turned off, the windows dark. Either the Meyers weren't home or they were already in bed. To the right lived Patrick and Shannon Cleary, along with their daughters Noelle and Kerry, good Irish names if ever I'd heard any. A car parked in the driveway bore a Paschal High parking sticker, telling me that Noelle or Kerry or both were teenagers.

Unlike the Meyers's house, the Clearys' house was well lit, despite the late hour. The two porch lights on either side of the door were on, as were the up-lights mounted at the base of the exterior walls, shining up on the house in a manner reminiscent of a person telling ghost stories around a campfire, holding a flashlight up to their chin to give their face an eerie glow. While two of the four upstairs windows showed light behind the curtains, lights seemed to be on in all of the downstairs rooms with front-facing windows. Looked like the Clearys were night owls. Not surprising given that they had two teenaged girls and teenagers, like bats, possums, and fireflies, tended to be nocturnal.

Could Conklin be visiting with the Clearys? That would explain why his car was parked here. With two daughters, the Clearys would likely be very concerned about the peeper. Perhaps Conklin had come to provide reassurance that the patrols were still being vigilant. Or perhaps the Clearys had called in some type of report and Conklin had come here to discuss the matter with them. Still, unless it was an emergency, it seemed odd that he'd visit them so late. And if an emergency had taken place, why hadn't the Clearys called 911 and have dispatch notify the officers on duty in W1?

There could be a valid reason why Todd Conklin had parked here. Then again, he could be somewhere nearby with his pants down.

As quietly as I could, I opened the door to my cruiser. *Time to find out what Todd Conklin is up to.*

SIXTY-THREE
SPLISH-SPLASH

Brigit

Brigit stood at her window, her nose twitching as it took in the night's scents. She smelled the acrid odor of a skunk rooting around a block over. She smelled the sweet scent of the rosebushes that stood in front of the house next door. She smelled the faint whiff of chlorine from somewhere farther down the street.

Her ears were at work, too. She heard a bird flitting about in a nearby tree. The buzz of a mosquito as it searched for prey. The moans and groans and grunts that accompanied human sexual intercourse. Oddly, those sounds were accompanied by a soft splish and splash, like the sounds Megan made in the bathtub.

SIXTY-FOUR
MAKING A SPLASH

Todd

He aimed the lens of his low-light video camera through the open knothole in the fence as the couple went at it in their hot tub. With the late hour and the houses around them dark, they'd probably assumed they had complete privacy.

They'd assumed wrong, hadn't they?

The woman's lower half was submerged in the swirling water, but her upper body rose from the water as if she were a sexy siren, singing a song only for him. She leveraged her hands against the edge of the tub as she allowed herself to be taken from behind. She rose with each forceful thrust, her breasts pointed skyward, her eyes closed in ecstasy, her mouth falling open as she panted for air, beads of water rolling down her body.

Damn, that woman seems to be enjoying herself.

He only wished *he* were the one giving her pleasure rather than that overblown gorilla, Garrett Hawke. What the hell did his wife see in him, anyway? He was nothing more than a poser, pretending to be a war hero when in reality he'd taken a bad landing during paratrooper training thanks to a hangover. The asshole had admitted as much once after a few too many shots of whiskey at a backyard barbecue. Of course he'd only admitted it to Tom, and had promptly sworn the guy to secrecy with an implied threat. *That stays between us. Got it?*

Tom got it, all right.

Tom might not like being overlooked, but at least he wasn't some pathetic attention seeker like Hawke.

He wished Hawke wouldn't be in the footage, but he knew he could edit the ape out later, zoom in on Hawke's wife and her gorgeous hair and body. Hawke was nothing more than a prop.

As he watched through the camera, the woman's face contorted and she threw her head back. With a gasp and a cry of "Oh, God!" she quivered and quaked, then slowly sank back into the water, like a mermaid who might have merely been an illusion.

SIXTY-FIVE
EARLY WITHDRAWAL PENALTY

Megan

As I opened the back door of my cruiser, Brigit stood up in her enclosure, her body rigid as she stared intently forward, looking out the windshield.

I looked down the dark street but saw nothing. "What is it, girl?"

A moment later, Todd Conklin emerged from the shadows ahead like an apparition. He stopped abruptly when he saw my car, his eyes popping wide, but a moment later he continued toward me, raising a hand to wave in greeting. When he drew close enough he called, "Hi, there!" in a stage whisper, as if not wanting to disturb the neighbors.

"Hello, Mr. Conklin," I said. "I saw your empty car here and thought there might be trouble."

"Nothing but a loose dog," he said, stopping in front of me. "I tried to chase it down but it got away."

That would explain why he seemed flushed and out of breath.

"What did it look like?" I asked.

"Dark," he said. "Medium-sized."

"What breed?"

"No idea," he replied. "I couldn't get close enough to it to tell. It just ran in front of my car and took off when I got out and tried to catch it."

Not surprising. Stray dogs were often fearful. But was he telling me the truth? I couldn't tell. "Brigit and I will keep an eye out."

"Great. Thanks." He stepped toward his car, turning to call back over his shoulder, "Have a good night!"

Before I could return the sentiment, an urgent call came through my shoulder-mounted radio. "Robbery reported in Mistletoe Heights. Suspect entered home and demanded victim's debit card and PIN at gunpoint."

Ralph Hurley has struck again.

Dispatch continued. "The night watchman at Wells Fargo reported a white pickup pulling into the lot."

Finally! A chance to catch the guy and end his reign of terror. But we had to move fast, before he could make the withdrawal and escape.

I squeezed the talk button on my mic. "Officer Luz—" I began.

Once again, Derek attempted to override me in claiming the call, interrupting my response with, "Officer Mack—"

"—and Brigit respond—"

"—ey respond—"

"—ing!"

"—ing!"

I was back in my car in half a heartbeat, glad that I'd worn my ballistic vest under my uniform. In rapid-fire motion, I switched on my lights and floored the gas pedal, shooting off down the street, sliding my seat belt into place as I went. The LOST DOG poster taped to the lamppost barely registered as we flew by.

I hooked a left on Colonial Parkway and zipped

through Forest Park so fast it was a wonder the car didn't go up on two wheels on the curves.

I turned right onto University and pressed my foot to the floor, the powerful engine roaring like the lions in the zoo we'd just passed. Whipping around the few cars on the street I arrived at the bank in record time.

Unfortunately, the Big Dick had arrived in less than record time, pulling into the lot two seconds before me. A white pickup was pulling out of the drive-thru ATM lane on the right side of the building. Derek's cruiser screeched to a stop at an angle in front of the pickup. As the truck's white reverse lights came on, I screeched to a stop at an angle behind it, blocking it in.

At least I'd thought so, anyway.

I'd been wrong.

The truck roared backward, the tailgate slamming into the driver's side fender of my car. *BAM!*

Brigit and I were thrown to the right, her claws scratching at the carpeted platform as she sought purchase behind me. While my seatback jerked me back into place, I ordered Brigit to lie down, figuring it would be the safest position for her.

Hurley's face turned and looked through the back window as he floored the gas pedal, doing his best to push my squad car farther out of his way. Though he managed to move my cruiser only a foot or two, it was enough to shift the angle of my car so that the driver's door was now exposed.

I grabbed my mic and placed an urgent call to dispatch. "Backup needed at the Wells Fargo!"

Hurley put his truck into drive and rammed the gas pedal, slamming now into Derek's car, the tires squealing and giving off the smell of burning rubber as they spun in place on the concrete. Hurley shifted into reverse again, coming straight for my door.

Holy shit!

There was no way I could get out of the driver's side without being run over or crushed between the tailgate of the pickup and the side of my cruiser. I reached for my seat-belt release, threw the strap back, and crawled into the passenger side of my car, grabbing at the door handle.

BAM! The truck hit my car, sending me headfirst into the inside of the passenger door. *Ow!* It was a wonder the impact didn't knock me out.

When Hurley shifted into drive again, I knew I had only a few seconds to make my escape. I climbed out of the passenger side and ripped Brigit's door open, ordering her out. She leaped to the ground next to me just as Hurley slammed into my cruiser again. *BAM!*

We rushed away from the truck, meeting up a few yards away with Derek, who'd likewise evacuated from his cruiser.

Derek yanked his gun from his holster and held it up, storming toward the truck. He motioned to me. "Cover his other side!"

I called for Brigit to follow me and circled behind my cruiser, yanking my baton from my belt and extending it with a *snap!* I scurried behind the ATM machine, peeking around the side at the truck, which sat only four or five feet from me now.

Derek stood a few feet back on the other side of the truck, his gun aimed at Hurley through the passenger window. "Hands up!" Derek hollered. "Now!"

Hurley dropped his hands from the steering wheel, but when he brought them back up again, a shotgun was in them. My cry of "Derek!" was drowned out by the blast of Hurley shooting at Mackey through the closed window. *Blam!*

My heart clenched in terror as Derek dropped to the

ground amid a shower of tinkling glass and the echo of the shot off nearby buildings.

Is he dead?

OH, MY GOD! IS DEREK DEAD?

I'd never much liked the guy, but I wouldn't wish something like this on anyone, least of all a fellow officer.

The wail of approaching sirens told me that backup was nearing and told Hurley he better get the hell out of there if he didn't want to find his ass back in jail for the rest of his lifetime. His shotgun clutched in his right hand, he threw his door open with his left, slamming the door into the ATM machine. *Bam!* The truck was too close to the machine for the door to open all the way. *But it was open enough for me to bring my baton down in the space between the edge of the door and the truck's frame.*

I stepped from behind the ATM machine and brought my nightstick down with every bit of force I could muster. *WHAP!*

Hurley's gaze met mine for a split second, his eyes still flaming with rage, before the flame fizzled out and his eyes rolled back in his head. As he melted to the ground like the Wicked Witch of the West, his fingers involuntarily contracted, pulling the trigger on the shotgun once more, sending a spray of shot down toward his feet. *Blam!* His foot exploded in a splatter of flesh and blood among the brake and gas pedals.

I pushed my shoulder mic again. "We need an ambulance!" I cried. "Officer down! Officer down!"

Brigit scurried after me as I ran around to the other side of the truck. Derek lay on the ground, rolling silently from side to side.

He's not dead! Thank God!

I needed to tend to Derek, but first I had to make sure Hurley was disabled and disarmed in case he regained consciousness. I yanked open the passenger door, grabbed his shotgun, and pulled it out, setting it out of reach in the bed of the truck. Reaching back in, I grabbed Hurley's limp right wrist, slapped a cuff on it, and attached the other cuff to the steering wheel. If he came to, he wouldn't be going anywhere. At least not without dragging the truck along with him.

Brigit pranced around between the truck and Derek, waiting for instruction. I ordered her to my side as I bent down to speak to my former partner. There was no blood on his head, thank goodness, and none on his torso that I could tell in the dim light. He'd no doubt have all kinds of bruises, but his ballistic vest had done its job, protecting his vital organs. There were dark wet spots on his arms, legs, and crotch, though, spots that must be blood. "Are you okay?"

"He shot me in the nuts!" Derek cried as he rolled away from me. "He shot me in the nuts!"

It was standard protocol to apply pressure to a bleeding wound. Touching Derek's nether regions ranked equal to eating a decomposing rat on my list of things I never wanted to do, but I couldn't let my personal feelings get in the way of doing my job. I hurried to my car, retrieved my first aid kit, and returned to his side. Just as I opened it and pulled a gauze pad from the box, two FWPD squad cars and an ambulance pulled into the lot.

Phew. The medical experts could handle this.

I rushed to my banged-up cruiser and pulled open the back door. "Get in, Brig!"

Brigit obeyed, leaping into her enclosure where she'd be out of the way and safe while the other first responders did their work.

My partner now secured, I turned and waved my arms, gesturing that it was safe for the other cops to come forward. "Hurley's cuffed!" I yelled as Summer and Officer Spalding exited their vehicles. "He's in the truck!"

Two EMTs leaped from the ambulance, one male, one female. "What do we have?" the female called as she rushed toward me with her kit.

I pointed down to Derek. "Gunshot wounds here." I gestured into the truck. "The suspect has a head wound and a leg wound."

The male EMT tended to Derek, while the female carefully looked in on Hurley. Summer and I stood behind her, shining our flashlights into the truck to augment the pickup's interior lighting.

"Uck," the woman said. "Looks like he shot his foot off."

Minutes later, Derek had been loaded into one ambulance, while Hurley, who had yet to regain consciousness, had been loaded into another.

"You sure do pack a wallop," Spalding told me as the ambulance containing Hurley pulled away. "Remind me never to piss you off."

Though I knew he was joking and probably meant the comment as flattery, the night's events had left me with a sick feeling. I didn't have much of a stomach for violence.

A car whipped into the lot, tires squealing. The car screeched to a stop and out hopped a local photojournalist I recognized from earlier cases. He must have been monitoring the police scanner. He pulled the black plastic lens cap from his camera and began snapping photos, careful to keep back a reasonable distance.

My cell phone vibrated in my pocket, the display indicating the call came from the W1 station.

It was Captain Leone. "As soon as you finish the paperwork," he said, "you're dismissed for the rest of the night. Go home and take a load off."

He wouldn't have to tell me twice. There might be several hours left in my shift, but my entire body was shaking and my head felt light. I'd be no good to anybody in this condition.

"You'll call once you have an update on Derek?"

"Sure," he said. "You need a ride?"

"I'll be okay. That's more than I can say for my cruiser, though."

He groaned. "You're killing me, Officer Luz."

The car had only recently been returned to me after being flipped by an EF-5 tornado. The damage had been extensive and the repairs must have cost a small fortune. Looked like the car would be heading back to the shop for some body work now. Fortunately, the engine still seemed to be running fine. I was able to drive it back to the station with no problems.

As I climbed out of my battered squad car, I glanced over at Derek's black pickup. He'd wiped off the lipstick smiley face I'd drawn on his truck nuts weeks ago, and they hung from his trailer hitch in their full rubber glory. Retrieving my first aid kit once again, I pulled out a Band-Aid, removed the wrapper, and took it over to Derek's truck, affixing it firmly to the pendulous rubber scrotum as a small symbol of my empathy.

There. That's better.

SIXTY-SIX
BEST FRIENDS FOREVER

Brigit

Megan lay next to her in their bed, her shaking causing the entire bed to vibrate. Brigit could smell the adrenaline on her partner, too, and she knew it meant Megan had been terrified.

She draped her head over Megan's belly and whimpered to let her partner know she was concerned and that she was there for her.

Megan reached down and stroked her head. "I'm glad you're here, girl."

Brigit was glad she was there, too.

SIXTY-SEVEN
DOGGONE IT

Todd

I'd nearly been caught with my pants down. Literally.

Thank goodness Hawke and his wife treated sex more like a sprint than a marathon. With all those kids they had, they'd probably had to learn to get things accomplished quickly. If they'd taken even another minute, that cop might have come looking for him and caught him in the act.

He'd been shocked when he'd seen her car parked in front of his, had frozen for a moment, his fight-or-flight instincts telling him to turn and run. But then he'd spotted that sign on the light post farther down the street, behind the cop, one of the many signs someone in the neighborhood had posted about their missing spaniel.

A loose dog.

That would explain why I'd been away from my car.

Previously, if he'd been spotted, he'd been ready to say he thought he'd seen the peeper creeping between houses. But with the peeper purportedly behind bars now—*thanks for taking the heat off me, Nathan Wilmer!*—he didn't want to use that excuse.

Despite the fact that he'd gotten away once again, he decided he'd better stop pushing his luck. Besides, he knew of no other women in the area with the long, dark hair he preferred. Hell, his wife didn't even have long, dark hair anymore. The first sign of gray and she'd gone blond, hoping it would mask her age.

It was too bad, really. Her hair had been the last thing he could stand about her. The personality that he'd once thought so cute and bubbly now got on his nerves. The woman just wouldn't shut up! He'd thought she'd been friendly and caring, always wanting to know what was going on in everyone's life, convincing them to confide in her. Now she constantly babbled on about which couples were having marital problems, whose kids were failing their classes, which neighbors were suffering financial setbacks. She didn't care about other people's problems. She only wanted to know about them so she could gossip and feel better about her own life.

He'd been disappointed at the time, but now he was glad that, after ten years of trying, they'd been unable to have children. The doctor said his swimmers were slow, but maybe they'd taken one look at his wife's eggs and thought, *Oh, hell no!*

He should probably stop the spying, but it had become an addiction by this point, a necessary thrill, the one thing he lived for. He realized others would consider him a creep, a pervert even, but he couldn't fight the compulsion. He needed these fixes the way a heroin addict needed to shoot up.

Besides, what was the big deal? He wasn't hurting anyone. It was harmless, more prank than crime. When he'd been thirteen at summer camp and a male counselor had caught him and another boy peeking through an air vent into the girls' showers, the counselor had merely laughed and told them to get back to their bunks.

Hell, even the Texas penal code was on his side. Like that fat detective had pointed out, voyeurism was a measly misdemeanor, a crime that a person could only be fined for, hardly even against the law. Even if he were caught, tried, and found guilty, he wouldn't spend a single night in jail. He doubted things would even go to trial if he were caught. Being part of the watch gave him the perfect alibi. He could always claim he'd heard a strange noise or thought he'd seen a prowler. He'd have plausible deniability. Of course Nora would still make them move to a different neighborhood if he were caught. Or maybe she'd divorce him. He really didn't care. At this point he was only staying with her because she provided him with a good cover as a purportedly happily married man with a willing sexual partner. No need for a man like that to look for cheap thrills elsewhere, right?

And speaking of elsewhere, that's where he needed to go. Beyond Berkeley Place. He knew exactly where he'd head next. To the home of that woman who'd come in for head shots a few days ago. He thought he'd had her convinced to do some boudoir photos. She'd even scheduled an appointment several days out, saying she wanted time to get a wax and have her hair done before the shoot. But then she'd got cold feet and canceled on him.

Frigid bitch.

One way or another, he was doing that photo shoot.

SIXTY-EIGHT
HUNCH

Megan

As exhausted as I'd been when I arrived home after the run-in with Ralph Hurley, I couldn't seem to get to sleep. Maybe it was the adrenaline. Maybe it was because I was worried about Derek and his bullet-riddled nards. Or maybe it was that niggle in my brain that told me Todd Conklin's dog story sounded just a little too convenient . . .

I texted Seth. He was off duty and probably asleep, but Frankie was working her usual overnight stocking shift at the grocery store and I really needed someone to talk to. *Any chance you're up?*

My phone rang a few seconds later, the readout indicating it was Seth.

"You okay?" he asked.

I told him what happened with Hurley, ending with, "There was blood all over the floorboard. His little piggies won't be going to market again."

"Megan, my God! He could've killed you!"

"Occupational hazard," I said. "Besides, you're one to talk. You run into burning buildings and defuse bombs for a living."

"Yeah, but I'm—"

"You better not say 'I'm a guy.' "

"What? And risk you whacking me like you did Hurley? Never. I was going to say 'at least I'm wearing protective gear and I know what I'm getting myself into when I go to work.' Every one of your shifts is a crapshoot."

It was true. That was part of what kept the job interesting.

"I'm coming over," Seth said. "You don't need to be alone at a time like this."

"I'm not alone," I said. "I've got Brigit."

On hearing her name, my furry partner lifted her snout from my stomach and cocked her head, her ears pricked.

"Yeah, but you need *me*," Seth said. "Otherwise you wouldn't have texted me."

He was right and, truth be told, it kind of scared me to need someone like this.

"Could you stop at the store on your way?" I asked.

"For wine or for chocolate?"

"For raspberry sorbet," I told him, "and a box of liver treats."

"Just when I thought I was starting to understand women . . ."

The following morning, Seth and I took Brigit and Blast to the dog park to let them romp with their furry friends. As they chased a Doberman about, I asked Seth about his mother. "How's everything at home?"

He cut a look my way and groaned. "You know I don't want to talk about it."

"I know," I replied. "Which is exactly why you *need* to talk about it."

He crossed his arms over his chest. But while his protective body language told me he wasn't comfortable with this conversation, he nonetheless managed to eke out a few words. "I don't know how things are, really. The three of us hardly talk to each other."

"That beats arguing," I said.

"Does it?"

He had a point. When people argued with each other, even if they were yelling and screaming, it meant they cared enough to get worked up. Silence could indicate apathy. But it could also indicate fear, or an inability to know how to start a very long overdue conversation.

I reached out and grabbed one of his hands, pulling it free from his chest and giving it a squeeze. "Maybe you three should try counseling."

"My grandfather would never go for that."

"I have a gun and handcuffs," I said. "I could force him."

"Now there's a thought."

My cell phone jiggled in my pocket. I pulled it out to see Detective Bustamente's name on the readout. "Good morning, Detective."

"Nice work nabbing Hurley," he said.

"Just doing my job."

"And doing it quite well. You should be proud of yourself."

I'd be more proud if I'd caught the peeper, too. Right now, I was only one for two. Still, I'd taken a violent felon out of commission. "Thanks."

"We got the DNA results."

"And?"

"There was no match."

I closed my eyes and put a hand to my brow. The lack of a DNA match ruled out Wilmer, Gilbreath, Looney, and Hurley. It also ruled out anyone else with a criminal record. Would this peeper case *ever* be solved?

Of course the failure of the DNA to match anyone in the system meant several suspects were still in play.

Victor Paludo.
Garrett Hawke.
And Todd Conklin.

"A journalist came to the bank after we nabbed Hurley last night," I told Bustamente. "He had a camera with him. It made me wonder if that piece of b-broken plastic that was found outside Korinna's window could be part of a lens cap. If it is, it could tie Todd Conklin to the crime." After all, the vast majority of people these days shot pics and videos with their phones rather than traditional cameras. But a man who ran a photography business could be expected to own and use higher quality equipment.

"Smart thinking, Luz," Bustamente said. "Problem is, we don't have probable cause to search Conklin's studio or home."

"Yet," I said.

He chuckled. "You're a hardworking woman, Officer Luz."

"Can you get me a raise?"

"I can get you a paper clip."

"Thanks. But I'll pass." I went on to tell him about my interaction with Todd Conklin the night before. "His wife's car was parked at a curb with the watch sign on it, but nobody was in the car. I thought that seemed a little odd, so I pulled over to see if something was going on. Next thing I know, he's coming down the street on foot. He looked surprised to see my cruiser."

"Not unusual," Bustamente said. "Even law-abiding folks are taken aback when they come upon a cop car."

"Yes, I know. But the look on his face wasn't just surprise. It looked a bit like *panic.*"

"Did he run? Try to evade you?"

"No, he came back to his car. When I asked him what he was doing out of his vehicle, he said he'd seen a loose dog and had left his car to try to catch it."

"That's plausible," the detective said. "Did he look like he'd been chasing a dog? Was he out of breath? Sweaty? Flushed?"

Yes, yes, and yes. "Well, yeah, but something still felt *off* to me."

The detective was quiet for a moment. Either he was mulling things over, or he was trying to find a polite way to tell me I was off my rocker. He came back with, "We don't have probable cause to force a search," he said. "But that doesn't mean we can't pay Conklin a visit."

I raised a fisted hand in excitement, garnering me a questioning look from Seth. "I can be ready in half an hour."

"Slow down, eager beaver. I'm tied up with church and family stuff today and booked solid tomorrow. Double-booked at a couple of points. This is what you have to look forward to when you make detective. What say we meet at Conklin's studio Tuesday at three-thirty?"

My first impulse was to scream in frustration. I wanted to follow up on my hunch *now.* But justice wasn't just blind, it was busy. Hard as it might be, I'd have to wait. "It's a date."

Sunday afternoon, shortly after Seth and I had returned from taking the dogs to the dog park, Captain Leone called my cell. "Figured you'd want an update on your former partner."

"I do, sir. I've been worried."

He told me that the doctors had been able to remove all of the shot from Derek's scrotum, and that it had caused no permanent damage. "God help us if that man decides to reproduce one day. At any rate, the shot in his arm has also been removed with no problems. He'll get a few paid days off to recover and will be back to being a pain in all of our asses by the end of the week."

"That's good to hear," I said. "What about Ralph Hurley?"

"Hurley suffered a severe concussion but came around early this morning. Of course the foot was a total loss. He's threatened to file excessive-force charges."

"Are you worried?"

"Pshaw. Not for a second."

"You don't think he's got a leg to stand on?"

"If that was a pun, you're fired."

I pled the fifth. "Thanks for the call, Captain."

Seth and I had a nice, relaxing day together. It was exactly what I needed. That night, though, my demons returned. I tossed and turned so much in the bed that Brigit finally cast me a dirty look, climbed down, and went to sleep on the futon in the living room. Finally, I gave up on sleep, rounded up my laptop, and decided to find out a little more about Todd Conklin. I typed his name into the search bar and hit enter. Several items popped up.

The first was his Web site for Say Cheese! The "About Us" page featured head shots of both Conklin and a full-time male assistant who worked for him.

The next item was a Web site set up by a bride and groom who'd hired Say Cheese! to take their wedding photos. They'd been kind enough to give a shout-out to the business.

The third entry was a photo of Conklin's home featured in the Berkeley Place homeowners' association newsletter. The front yard featured a cute display of pumpkins, along with Indian corn and a smiling scarecrow family, the two "parent" scarecrows standing while the two "children" scarecrows perched on hay bales. In the photo, Todd and Nora stood next to the adult scarecrows, which towered over their real counterparts. Apparently, this festive display earned the Conklins their homeowners association's yard-of-the-month award last October.

The other entries merely identified him as a member of the neighborhood watch or as the generous contributor of a free photo session at various charity silent auction events.

I sat back to ponder what new information I'd learned from this search. All I'd gleaned was that Todd Conklin was smaller than a scarecrow. Not exactly useful information, was it? But, with any luck, Detective Bustamente and I woud get more information out of him on Tuesday.

It took everything in me not to cruise constantly by Conklin's photography studio during my shift on Monday. *Is he the peeper? Or am I barking up the wrong tree?*

I eyed Brigit in my rearview mirror. "What do you think, Briggie?"

She gave me a look that said, *I think you should buy me a bacon double cheeseburger.*

When I arrived home from work, I changed out of my uniform, retrieved my twirling baton from my closet, and wandered into the living room, where I found Frankie packing up her things for roller derby practice.

I plunked down on the couch, clicked on the television, and tried to relax. Not easy, as excited and anxious as I was about questioning Conklin tomorrow. I twirled my baton in a flat spin but the *swish-swish-swish* failed to calm me today.

Frankie glanced my way. "Why are you so jittery?"

"Does it show?"

She gestured to my knee, which was bouncing up and down, then to my spinning baton. "Uh, yeah."

Given that Frankie was a civilian, I had to be careful not to give her too much information and risk blowing the case. "I think I might have identified the person responsible for a string of recent crimes."

"The BP Peeper," she said.

"I didn't say that."

She snorted. "You didn't have to. That case is all you've been talking about lately."

Looked like in my search for clues I'd been fairly clueless myself.

She lifted her bag to her shoulder. "Why don't you come with me to practice? Skating is a great way to relieve tension. Second only to sex in my book."

I hadn't strapped on a pair of skates since adolescence, but why not? It could be fun. And after sitting around all day in my cruiser I could use a workout. Unfortunately, I didn't own any skates. "I don't have roller skates."

Frankie eyed my feet. "What size are you?"

"Eight and a half."

"I'm a nine," she said. "Close enough. Put on thick socks. You can use one of my old pairs."

She scurried back to her bedroom and returned with a pair of well-worn skates, the leather soft and supple from use. With the skates broken in and then some, at least they wouldn't give me blisters.

I leashed up Brigit and the three of us headed out to Frankie's car. Twenty minutes later, we arrived at the rink. I walked Brigit over to the weeds at the edge of the lot so she could relieve herself, then followed Frankie into the building.

Several women had already arrived and were warming up, making slow laps around the rink. Others stood on the carpeted area flanking the rink, circling their arms and heads to warm up their muscles. Still others were on the ground, stretching their hamstrings and calves. A set of portable metal bleachers was folded up and pushed back against the wall where they wouldn't take up too much of the floor space now, but could easily be expanded for use by spectators during an actual bout.

I left Brigit tied to a bench along the wall where she could watch the activity but wouldn't be at risk of having her paw accidentally run over. After warming up ourselves, Frankie and I donned our skates. I had no trouble making my way across the carpeted floor, which provided resistance and friction, but once we rolled onto the hard surface of the rink it was an entirely different matter. My feet seemed to be moving faster than my body and before I knew it—*whomp!*—I'd landed flat on my butt on the rink.

"Owwww," I moaned, rubbing my lower back. "I think my tailbone is broken."

Frankie reached down a hand to help me up. "Don't be a wimp. It's probably just bruised. Besides, I've fractured mine three times. The doctors can't do anything about a broken tailbone anyway so you might as well suck it up."

I looked up at her as I took her hand. "The least you could do is show some sympathy."

"Oh, boo-hoo." She yanked me to my feet. "I'm in derby mode now. No mercy."

She gave me a few pointers and stayed with me as I took a couple of laps around the rink, managing, barely, to stay on my feet and off my ass. By the third go-round, I felt that I'd gotten the hang of things.

"I think I've got it now," I told her.

She gave me a thumbs-up sign. "I'm off." She bent low, swung her arm wide, and took off like a blue-haired bullet.

I skated slowly near the outer wall, doing my best to stay out of the way of the team members racing around the rink. Thank goodness they wore helmets. At the rate some of them were going they could suffer a massive head injury if their skull hit the floor or wall.

After ten minutes of warm-up, the team divided in two

for a practice bout. That was my cue to leave the floor. I skated off through the opening and returned to Brigit, who was sitting on top of the bench I'd tied her to, softly panting as her eyes followed the women barreling past.

I sat down next to my dog and bent over to unlace the skates, stowing them in Frankie's bag when I'd removed them. I put my tennis shoes back on, untied Brigit, and ventured over to the half-wall with my baton so I could watch the bout more closely. Brigit stood on her hind legs next to me, her front paws resting on the top of the wall as she watched the women roll by. When Frankie passed, Brigit gave her an *arf!* of encouragement to cheer her on. I, in turn, tossed my spinning baton into the air.

The bout ended with Frankie's team besting the other, but just barely. The women exchanged high fives and butt slaps as they took a few cool-down laps and exited the rink. Frankie rolled over to me. "What do you think? Want to join the team?"

As if they'd take on a lousy skater like me. Then again, maybe I'd fall and trip up their opponents. Was that a legal strategy? "The Whoop Ass would be better off if I just twirled my fire batons for them."

"You have fire batons?"

"Yeah. I can twirl three at a time."

"Kick ass!" Frankie turned and hollered to the team captain. "Can my roommate twirl her fire batons at our next bout?"

"Hell, yeah!"

Frankie packed up her things and we headed out to her car. She unrolled the windows so we could enjoy the fresh evening air, and so Brigit could stick her head out.

On the drive home, we stopped at a red light on Berry Street, just a few blocks from Say Cheese!

Impatience got the best of me. "Mind if we take a short detour?"

SIXTY-NINE
RUNAROUND

Brigit

Brigit had enjoyed watching the women skate round and round and round the rink, chasing each other. Dogs liked to do the same thing. She didn't understand many of the things humans did, bathing, for instance, or reading, but this type of play she could relate to. When Megan led her to the wall, she stood on her hind legs to get a closer look. When Frankie had zipped past, she barked to let their roommate know Brigit hoped she'd win the chase.

Woof! Woof-woof!

But now they were in Frankie's car, driving slowly past a shopping center. Brigit looked out the window. *Nope.* This wasn't the place where Megan bought her food and treats and chew toys. *Phooey.*

Brigit stuck her snout out the window, which Frankie had left cracked enough for Brigit to stick her head out, but not so much that the dog might fall out. She twitched her nostrils, scenting the air.

She smelled Italian food from a nearby restaurant.

The faint scent of jasmine.

Car exhaust.

And *him.*

SEVENTY
CAMERA SHY

Todd

At ten Monday night, he sat at his desk in his office at the studio, going through the files on his computer until he found hers.

ChastainG.

He remembered Gina Chastain mentioning that she lived in the Westcliff area southwest of Texas Christian University, but he needed her address. He needed it quick and he needed it *now.*

According to the information she'd provided, she lived on Hilltop Road. He typed her address into the GPS app on his cell phone, slipped his high-res low-light video camera into his camera bag, and headed out to his car, turning to activate the alarm and lock the door behind him. A person couldn't be too careful, especially with the types of expensive equipment he owned. After all, there were all kinds of lowlifes out there, just waiting for someone to let their guard down.

SEVENTY-ONE

TAILS

Megan

"Follow him."

"Whatever you say, boss." Frankie turned into the far end of the strip center parking lot, circling back to exit where Todd Conklin had pulled out in his Saturn SUV. She cast a glance my way as she turned onto the street. "Does this mean I'm officially deputized?"

"I'm not the sheriff," I said. "I can't deputize anyone."

"So I'm working undercover for Fort Worth PD for free?"

"You're doing your roommate a favor."

"So *now* you're just my roommate," she said. "What happened to 'a cop is never truly off duty'?"

I shrugged. "That line doesn't fit my current needs."

Conklin turned right onto Berry Street and, ten seconds later, Frankie turned right after him.

"Don't get too close," I warned. "We don't want him to know he's being followed."

"I know how this works," she said. "I've watched cop shows on TV."

She changed into the left lane so that she wouldn't be directly behind him. We followed along as the road curved south at the outer edge of the TCU campus, and again as Conklin exited onto Stadium Drive just before the football field. When he slowed to take a right on Hill-top, Frankie slowed even more to put additional space between her car and Conklin's.

He slowed to a crawl on the block between Alton and Road and Simondale. *Could he be scouting the house of his next victim? Has he decided to peep beyond Berke-ley Place? Has he been doing so all along? Are there more victims than we'd realized?*

We couldn't pass him or he might recognize me. Even if I ducked down, he might recognize Brigit. Not too many hundred-pound shepherd mixes out there.

I quickly checked my phone's GPS map for options. "Take a left here," I said as we reached Alton. "We can circle around on West Biddison."

Frankie made the block, pulling to the side and cut-ting her engine on Simondale as directed.

"Wait here," I told her. "I'm going to see what he's doing."

Given that I was off duty, I hadn't brought my tool belt. I had no gun, no pepper spray, and no flashlight. I felt exposed and vulnerable. Instinctively, I grabbed my twirling baton. I might not have any official weapons on me, but I wanted something, just in case. Even normally nonviolent people could react with force in the heat of the moment. And while I didn't have my other tools, I did have Brigit.

Of course, for all I knew, Conklin could be simply vis-iting a friend or family member. This trip could be to-tally innocent. Still, it was full dark, after ten P.M. Not exactly usual visiting hours.

I let Brigit out of the back of Frankie's car as quickly and quietly as possible. My heart banged in my chest, each pulse like a minor explosion. I took a deep breath in a vain attempt to calm myself. *You can't fight adrenaline.*

It took a moment for my eyes to adjust to the dark. Sticking to the shadows next to the fence, I crept along, my baton held straight down by my side, Brigit skulking along next to me. When we reached the front edge of the fence, I slunk up to the house, hoping the residents hadn't installed motion-activated lights down the dark sides of their home. Fortunately, no lights came on.

Crouching, I carefully peeked around the corner of the house. I could see Conklin's SUV parked a block and a half down. He'd turned it so that it faced the other direction, ready for him to make a quick getaway if needed. But there was no sign of the man himself.

Brigit's ears perked and her eyes locked on a house across the street, one door down. I squinted, trying to get a better view. I could see nothing, but I trusted Brigit. With her superior senses of hearing and smell, no doubt she knew exactly where Todd Conklin was.

Whispering the order for her to stay by my side, I crept forward, around the edge of the house and into the front yard, doing my best to stay in the shadow of an enormous magnolia tree. I stopped again, crouching under the tree.

And then I saw him.

Dressed in dark colors, Todd Conklin stood on tiptoe at a small window on the side of a house across the street. The size of the window told me it was likely a bathroom. Slices of light came through the blinds at the window, which were mostly, but not fully, closed.

Brigit and I headed across the street, making our way as quietly as possibly. Still, as on edge as my nerves were, our steps sounded like a stampede to my ears. Not to Todd Conklin, evidently. He continued to stare through the window, rapt. Whoever was inside that bathroom had his complete and undivided attention.

My partner and I stepped onto the lawn of the house next to the one where Conklin stood spying. Luckily, the thick grass muffled our footsteps as we approached the peeper.

When we reached the corner of the house, I glanced toward the backyard. Both this house and the one at which Conklin stood had privacy fences. It was doubtful he would try to escape by scaling them, or even by taking the time to try the gates. No, it was far more likely that he'd make a break for the street, attempt to get to his car and make a fast getaway.

No way would I let that happen.

I'd agonized over this case for much too long, worried myself sick about the women of Berkeley Place, that this bastard might do something vile and violent to them. I used a hand signal to communicate with Brigit. Her eyes told me my message was received. Slowly, softly, silently, we stepped toward Conklin.

When we were a mere three feet away from his back, I activated the flashlight feature on my cell phone, aimed the intense beam at him, and raised my baton in case he attacked. "Fort Worth Police!" I shouted. "Put your hands up!"

Conklin cried out and turned toward me. In his left hand was a camera, but in his right, lower down, was something else entirely and it was aimed at me. Before my mind could process that the thing in his hand, though long-barreled, was not actually a gun, my reflexes and instinct of self-preservation caused me to swing my twirling baton at it as hard as I could in an attempt to defend myself.

He ducked his head and attempted to turn away but wasn't quite quick enough. There was a loud *WHOP!* as the metal of my baton impacted the flesh of his thigh. While I was proud of the force I'd managed to muster, it was far more than necessary. As Conklin pivoted away from me, momentum carried my arm through the swing, taking my entire body with it. The next thing I knew—*fwomp!*—I was on my back in the grass, the wind knocked out of me, my hand still clutching my baton. Brigit loomed over me, waiting for further instruction.

My cell phone had fallen to the grass, screen-up, the flashlight now like a searchlight aimed up at the sky. Despite his battered thigh, Conklin managed to yank up his pants with his other arm and take off running, adrenaline both fueling his flight and masking what had to be incredible pain.

I tried to issue Brigit the order to chase him, but had yet to catch my breath. All that came out was a gasp. *Wuhh!*

Brigit put her face in mine, her head tilted, her brow furrowed as she tried to figure out what I was trying to say.

I gulped three rapid breaths of air—*UH-UH-UH*—and finally managed to catch my breath. Though I could have issued the order now, my eyes spotted headlights coming up the street. No way would I deploy Brigit if there was any chance she could be hit by a car.

I leveraged myself to my feet and ran to the curb, looking down the street for Conklin. The headlights of the passing car illuminated the street, making it easier for me to see. There he was, a block down, running like a bat out of hell, nearly to his SUV by now.

Kshh-kssh-kshh! There was a grating noise as Frankie sailed past on her skates, hunkered down in her derby skating position to reduce wind resistance. "I'll get him!" she hollered.

"Be careful!" I called after her. A ridiculous sentiment to offer to a woman like Frankie. "Careful" was not in her vocabulary. Besides, Todd did not appear to be armed. Without a weapon, Todd Conklin stood little chance of physically besting Frankie. There was a much greater chance Frankie would obliterate the man and tiny Todd would end up nothing more than a bloody, fleshy smear on Hilltop Road.

I issued Brigit the order to take down Conklin and she took off running after him, quickly catching up with Frankie, who was quickly catching up with Conklin. I, on the other hand, lagged three houses behind, despite running as fast as my legs could take me.

With a primal battle cry, Frankie slammed into Conklin, hitting him down low, sweeping his legs out from under him and sending him into the air like those bowling pins she'd so mercilessly slaughtered on our recent double date. Brigit pounced a half second later, hitting Conklin up high as she'd been taught. The force sent Conklin back in the other direction and he ended up slamming, face-first, into the asphalt. If all of his teeth were still in his mouth it would be a miracle.

Brigit grabbed the back of his collar and held tight, while Frankie skated circles around the guy in case he got any dumb ideas and tried again to make a break for it.

When I finally caught up to them, I had to stop for a moment and bend over, hands on my knees, to catch my breath. *Pant-pant.* "Great job"—*pant-pant*—"you two!"

Todd Conklin lay there, unmoving, his face smushed against the street.

When I could finally breathe at a relatively normal rate, I stood and nudged him with my toe. "Hey. Do I need to call an ambulance?"

Everyone in custody had a right to adequate medical care. Even disgusting perverts.

He rolled onto his back, a bloody, gravel-encrusted mass where his face used to be. "You tell me."

Frankie went up on her toes, skating to an immediate stop and looking down at the man. "I'd say it's a definite 'yes.' "

I called 911 on my cell phone, identified myself as a police officer, and requested both an ambulance and an officer to accompany Conklin to the hospital. After all, I was technically off duty tonight.

When I finished speaking with dispatch, I dialed Detective Bustamente. "Your Tuesday afternoon just freed up. I caught Conklin peeping at a window in Westcliff."

"I thought you had the night off."

"Justice *never* has the night off."

Frankie rolled her eyes and began skating in circles around us, this time facing backward.

I explained to Bustamente that after attending my roommate's derby practice, we'd taken a detour by Say Cheese! and found Conklin setting off to spy on another woman.

"Good job, Officer Luz. I knew you'd be a big help."

I looked down at my partner and ruffled her head. "Brigit deserves some of the credit."

"You two are quite a team."

A warm sense of satisfaction and pride flowed through my veins. "We are, aren't we?"

SEVENTY-TWO
MIDNIGHT SNACK

Brigit

Brigit wasn't entirely sure why Megan gave her sixteen liver treats when they arrived back home. After all, taking down that man had been easy work given that Frankie had already knocked his legs out from under him. But the dog wasn't about to question her partner's judgment. If Megan wanted to give her a hundred liver treats she'd gladly eat them.

SEVENTY-THREE
EXPOSED

Todd

The emergency room doctor took one look under Conklin's hospital gown and cringed. "That had to hurt."

Hurt? His entire thigh was bruised black and providing him with no end of agony. The ice pack the nurse had placed on his leg barely dulled the pain. As hard as Officer Luz had whacked him it was a wonder his leg was still attached to his body rather than lying on the Chastains' lawn.

He looked up at the doctor. "Can you give me something for the pain?" *Like a million CCs of morphine? Or a lobotomy?*

"Of course," the doctor said. "In fact, that's about all I can do for you. The only thing that heals an injury like this is time."

Time. That was something Todd would likely have a lot of in the days to come.

The doctor stuck his head out of the curtain and called instructions to a nurse.

As the doctor left, a female nurse arrived, yanking the curtain open and allowing it to remain that way, leaving him exposed to the dozen or so medical staff milling about the emergency room. Given the disgusted looks they cast his way, he realized they knew he was the Berkeley Place Peeper. Apparently word had gotten around the ER. To be expected, he supposed, given that a police officer was sitting just outside the curtain, making sure he didn't attempt an escape.

The nurse held a clear IV bag of morphine drip in one hand, a catheter in the other.

Grimacing against the pain the movement caused, he gestured to the curtain. "Could you close that, please?"

She cut him an incredulous look. "Suddenly you're interested in privacy?"

Ignoring his request, she set the catheter down on the gurney and attached the morphine bag to the IV stand. She did not, however, attach the IV to his arm.

Picking up the catheter, she circled around in front of him. "Lift your gown, please."

"Can't you give me the painkiller first?"

She looked him directly in the eye. "I could," she whispered. "But I *won't*."

He lifted his gown and the nurse proceeded to shove the catheter tube into his urethra, offering him a soft smile when he gasped in pain.

SEVENTY-FOUR
PICTURE PERFECT

Megan

When Frankie, Brigit, and I had returned to the house where I'd caught Conklin spying, I'd found a small, handheld video camera on the ground under the window.

Frankie shook her head. "Looks like he was taping some homespun porn."

After summoning a crime scene team, I'd gone to the door to let the residents know what was going on. It was no surprise when a thirtyish woman with long, dark hair answered. Her hair was damp, as if she'd just taken a shower. Her husband stood behind her.

"I'm Officer Megan Luz with the Fort Worth Police Department," I said. I raised Brigit's leash. "This is my partner, Brigit."

"Hi," said Frankie, greeting the couple with a wave of her hand. "I guess you could say I'm with citizen patrol."

The couple looked us up and down, their brows furrowed in skepticism.

"We're not in uniform because we're working undercover." It wasn't exactly the truth, but it was the quickest and easiest way to explain our appearance. I stepped back and pointed down the street, where EMTs were loading

Conklin into an ambulance under the watchful eye of two officers from the W3 division, which encompassed Westcliff and the nearby areas. "See? We've got officers down there arresting a suspect."

The two stepped forward, looked down the street, and exchanged nervous glances.

The man put a protective arm around his wife's shoulders. "Exactly what is going on here?"

"Does the name Todd Conklin mean anything to you?" I asked the woman.

Her eyes narrowed, worry lines forming between her brows. "That's the man who owns Say Cheese!, right? He did some head shots for me a week or so ago."

"I hate to tell you this," I said, "but I don't think those head shots were the only photographs he took of you."

The woman's hand flew reflexively to her chest. "What are you saying?"

I motioned for them to follow me. "Come take a look." I led them around the side of their house, admonishing them not to touch the camera that lay on the grass lest they contaminate the evidence. "I caught him with a camera to your window a few minutes ago."

The woman shrank back. "Oh, my God! I was taking a shower!"

Her husband swelled with rage and his hands clenched by his sides. "I'm going to beat the shit out of him!"

When he took a first step, I stopped him with a hand to the shoulder. "No need, sir. When I caught Conklin at your window, I gave him a good whack with my baton. He tried to make a break for it, but my partners tackled him on the asphalt."

"Good! I hope he's in a world of pain."

The woman went on to tell me that when she'd gone to him for the head shots, Conklin had tried to convince her to have boudoir photos taken at his studio. She looked up at her husband. "He said they'd made a good anniversary present for you." She shuddered. "I'm glad I chickened out!"

"Me, too," her husband said, though he seemed a little less convinced.

Conklin's arrest gave FWPD probable cause to search his photography studio and home. After leaving Frankie and Brigit at home and collecting my car, I met Detective Bustamente and the evidence collection team at Say Cheese! They seized a laptop and desktop computer from the photography studio, along with a multitude of cameras and their memory cards.

Conklin's brand of choice seemed to be Canon, and I noticed that the original lens covers on most of his equipment bore the Canon logo. However, the lens cover on the video camera he'd used at the Chastains' home tonight was a cheap, generic replacement. Looked like I was right about that broken piece of plastic found under Korinna's bedroom window. It had been part of a lens cap.

On a shelf in the storage room, we found a box of disposable darkroom gloves, the same type I'd found in the street near the Lowrys' house. According to the text on the box, the gloves were a special lint-free type used for handling photo negatives.

"Check this out," I told Bustamente, pointing to the box.

"Just as you'd thought," he said.

"Yep." *Damn, I'm good.*

When we finished at the studio, we drove to the Conklins' home.

Nora answered the door in a short satin robe. Her gaze volleyed between the detective and me. "What's going on?"

"Your husband was arrested in Westcliff an hour ago,"

Bustamente told her. "He was peeping in a window and videotaping a woman inside."

"What?" Nora's face contorted in confusion and shock. "What are you saying?"

"We're saying we believe your husband is the Berkeley Place Peeper."

Her shock and confusion turned to humiliation, her face turning as pink as bubble gum.

"We're going to have to search your home," Bustamente said, stepping past her into the foyer. The evidence collection team followed, with me on their heels.

"Todd can't be the one!" Nora cried as the techs rummaged through their dresser drawers. "I'd never marry a pervert!"

Not knowingly, anyway, I thought. "He took advantage of his watch assignments to peep," I explained. "Several of the incidents happened on nights when he was on patrol."

"But he was home with me on at least some of the nights," she insisted.

"*All* night?" I asked.

"Yes! I'm sure of it!"

A crime scene tech pulled a bottle of extra-strength liquid sleep aid from under a stack of underwear in the bottom drawer of Todd's dresser and held it up. "How sure?"

Nora eyed the bottle in surprise, clearly much less certain now.

Over the course of several days, the evidence continued to mount against Todd Conklin. It took one of the department's computer experts to work around the password protection on a file identified as "PeeperT," but once she'd managed to break through she found photographs and videos of several women, including a video of Garrett Hawke and his wife having sex in a hot tub in their backyard. Of course the men on the crime scene team insisted they had to watch the video several times in order to extract its full evidentiary value.

Yeah, right.

The tech who'd broken the encryption sent me an e-mail that read *these pics might be of special interest to you,* along with several attachments. I clicked on the first to open it, gasping when it revealed a photo of me in shorts and a bikini, bending over to sponge off the wet bumper of my car in my driveway. *Holy crap! Todd Conklin had even photographed me!*

I prayed that was as far as he'd got with me, that he hadn't somehow managed to capture me naked, coming out of the shower. Surely Brigit would have alerted me if someone were outside our house, right?

I clicked on the other attachments, opening each of them in rapid-fire succession, breathing a huge sigh of relief to see that the most titillating shot was a close-up of my ass as I stood on my toes, sponge in hand, to wash the top of Frankie's Juke.

I knew the violation I felt was only a fraction of that experienced by his other victims, who'd been photographed and videoed nude or only partially dressed. Luckily, despite their humiliation and horror, each one of them was willing to testify against Conklin. While voyeurism alone might be only a misdemeanor, under Texas Penal Code Section 21.15 it was a state jail felony to photograph or record a person without their consent with the purpose of sexual gratification. Such felonies carried a minimum punishment of six months in jail, with a range of penalties up to two years in jail for each violation, plus a fine of up to ten grand. Conklin would be getting a little more than a slap on the wrist for slapping his salami to these women's images.

It took Nora Conklin only three days to file a petition

for divorce and to put a FOR SALE sign in her yard. She was moving on, in more ways than one. Who could blame her? If I were in her position I'd want a fresh start, too. I'd also want to peel off my skin. It had to be beyond repulsive to know she'd slept with a pervert.

It felt good to know I'd ended Conklin's reign of terror. And in other good news, Hurley's victim in San Antonio had turned the corner. She'd need months of physical therapy, but things were looking good for her. Not for Hurley, though. He was looking at a life sentence for his crimes. So long, *amigo.*

A week later, Seth and I took an overnight trip to a campground along the Brazos River west of Fort Worth. While the dogs romped around the site, we'd pitched an old army tent, rolled out sleeping bags inside, and set up housekeeping at a picnic table nearby.

"How's Frankie doing at the fire academy?" I asked as I spread a checkered tablecloth. Once she'd made the decision to become a firefighter, she'd wasted no time, snagging a seat in a class that started immediately.

"She's putting everyone else to shame," Seth said. "She's faster than most of the men and just as strong."

"Good for her."

With her newfound sense of purpose and direction, she seemed happier, too. I knew how much my job meant to me, and I was glad my roomie had finally found a profession that could bring her the same sense of achievement and satisfaction.

Our temporary home complete, Seth dragged the scratched and dented aluminum canoe we'd rented down to the water's edge. The dogs trotted after him, bounding in and out of the water, sending up a shower of river water as they shook themselves dry.

He held out an oar. "Ready to explore the river?"

I took the paddle from him. "Aye-aye, captain!"

We spent the day canoeing, drifting in the currents, rowing in to explore hidden coves. I'd sat in the back so I could get away with paddling as little as possible. Also so I could ogle Seth. But unlike Todd Conklin, I'd chosen a willing victim. Seth had taken off his T-shirt, giving me a nice view of his broad back and strong shoulders as he rowed, the dogs sitting happily between us. The wings of the army eagle tattooed across Seth's shoulder blades moved with each stroke, as if the bird were flying.

The sun warmed our skin as we floated, a gentle breeze keeping the temperature pleasant. Occasionally one of the dogs would stick their head over the side of the boat and lap water directly from the river. At one point, they both jumped into the water to chase a couple of ducks. Brigit cocked her head and barked, unsure what to make of a turtle that floated by.

When we'd tired of canoeing, Seth and I strung the wide hammock he'd bought me for Valentine's Day between two trees and lay side by side in it. The hammock made a fantastic reading spot, and it was great for cuddling, too, the perfect place to retreat from the world.

Seth intertwined his fingers with mine and raised my hand to his mouth, giving my knuckles a soft kiss. "You're some kind of woman, Megan Luz."

Lying on the grass next to us, Brigit issued an insistent *arf!*

Seth chuckled. "You're some kind of dog, too, Brigit."

I had to agree. I reached down to ruffle her ears.

As the hammock swayed in the breeze, Seth turned his head to face me. "You two caught a peeper and took a killer off the streets. What's next for the dynamic duo?"

I groaned. Though I loved my job, the last thing I wanted to think about with the sun shining, and the birds chirping, and Seth lying next to me was work. "What's next?" I said. "How about this."

With that I leaned over and pressed my lips to his.

Look for the other titles in
Diane Kelly's K-9 mystery series!

LAYING DOWN THE PAW

UPHOLDING THE PAW
(an e-original novella)

PAW ENFORCEMENT

PAW AND ORDER

From St. Martin's Paperbacks

Don't miss these Tara Holloway novels from Diane Kelly

Death, Taxes, and a French Manicure

Death, Taxes, and a Skinny No-Whip Latte

Death, Taxes, And Extra-Hold Hairspray

Death, Taxes, and a Sequined Clutch
(an e-original novella)

Death, Taxes, and Peach Sangria

Death, Taxes, and Hot-Pink Leg Warmers

Death, Taxes, and Green Tea Ice Cream

Death, Taxes, and Mistletoe Mayhem
(an e-original novella)

Death, Taxes, and Silver Spurs

Death, Taxes, and Cheap Sunglasses

Death, Taxes, and a Chocolate Cannoli

Death, Taxes, and a Satin Garter
(coming in August)

From St. Martin's Paperbacks